"Oh God!" said Rick in horror.

"What's the matter?" asked Con, her voice filled with concern.

Rick whirled around, then froze when he spotted the image of the slowly tumbling rock. "Those symbols on your wall . . . on those charts . . . on that screen . . ." Rick said in a shocked, quiet voice. "They *are* clocks. They're counting backward."

"Backward? To what?"

"The K-T event." Rick's agitation exploded into frantic activity . . . "Don't you know what this island's for?" asked Rick incredulously. "Don't you know where we are? This place was built to observe the K-T event."

Con grabbed Rick's arm. "You're scaring me," she said.

Joe turned to Con. "Do you know what he's talking about?"

"Sixty-five million years ago, a nine-mile-wide meteor hit the Earth," said Rick. "It's called the K-T event. It wiped out the dinosaurs. It wiped out damn near everything. Only for us, it isn't 65 million years ago. For us, it will happen today."

CRETACEOUS SEA

WILL HUBBELL

ACE BOOKS, NEW YORK

CRETACEOUS SEA

An Ace Book / published by arrangement with
the author

PRINTING HISTORY
Ace mass-market edition / November 2002

Copyright © 2002 by Will Hubbell.
Cover art by Les Edwards.
Cover design by Judith Murello.
Text design by Julie Rogers.

Visit our website at
www.penguinputnam.com
Check out the ACE Science Fiction & Fantasy newsletter!

ISBN: 0-441-00989-1

ACE®
Ace Books are published by The Berkley Publishing Group,
a division of Penguin Putnam Inc.,
375 Hudson Street, New York, New York 10014.
ACE and the "A" design
are trademarks belonging to Penguin Putnam Inc.

PRINTED IN THE UNITED STATES OF AMERICA

10 9 8 7 6 5 4 3 2 1

Dedicated to Richard Clements Hubbell

1949–1971

Vivere in cordibus quae ament est non mori.

1

CON'S COMSET SILENTLY VIBRATED. SHE SURREPTI-
tiously removed it from her pocket and glanced at its screen
when her calculus teacher turned his back. The message from
Mother was short and cryptic—"Your father called. Has surprise. Limo to meet you after school." Con wondered what
the surprise could be. She doubted Mother knew. Most likely,
it was another of her father's sporadic and extravagant ges-
tures, like the horse she received a month after he forgot her
sixteenth birthday. The limo was a dead giveaway.

Limousines were common at Con's school, so no one betrayed any interest when she departed in a big hydrogen-
electric Mercedes. It took her to an office building in a
fashionable district of the city. When the driver opened the
car door, Con's father was waiting outside. Con groaned in-
wardly when she saw that he had his new fiancée with him.
Con recognized her from the tabloids, but she was even more
striking in person. Curvaceous, with intense green eyes and
dramatic black hair, she seemed too perfect to be real. Con
suspected little of her was.

"Hi, Daddy," she said.

"Hi, honey. I'd like you to meet Sara."

"Hi," said Con. "I've seen you on the news."

"Don't believe everything they say," said Sara, smiling
and extending her hand. "I've been looking forward to meeting you. John's told me so much about you."

Con shook Sara's hand. "Don't believe everything Daddy
says about me."

"He says only the nicest things."

"That's what I mean."

"We're expected," said John Greighton impatiently, ush-
ering his daughter and his fiancée inside. An elevator took
them to an expensively decorated office on one of the upper

floors. As soon as they entered, a receptionist rose to greet them. "Mr. Greighton," she said, "welcome to Montana Isle. Ms. Smythe is expecting you."

Con watched the aforementioned Ms. Smythe advance toward them. She was elegantly dressed, and her smiling face had been redone in the currently fashionable angular look. Con recognized the designer. The surgery was almost certainly a knockoff, but it was well-done. None of the exaggerated planes of Ms. Smythe's face seemed overly unnatural.

"Mr. Greighton, I'm so pleased you've come. I'm Ann Smythe. I can answer your questions about our unique offering."

John Greighton shook her offered hand. "This is my fiancée, Sara Boyton, and my daughter, Constance."

Con spoke up and corrected him, "It's 'Con.' "

"Will Constance accompany you and Sara, Mr. Greighton?" asked Ann.

"*If* we go . . . yes. You weren't very clear about the nature of your resort. What you told me was intriguing, but vague . . . damned vague."

"We've been secretive," admitted Ann, "I think soon you'll understand why. This is something extraordinary, and we're not catering to the general public. Our clientele appreciates privacy." Ann, a consummate salesperson, paused for effect before proceeding. "If you're expecting a sales pitch, don't worry. This isn't just a resort. Words can't possibly describe Montana Isle. It's almost beyond belief, nothing is remotely like it. Fortunately, we have this . . ."

A pair of doors glided open to reveal two seats floating in a short hallway that led to a large, empty room. The chamber beyond was spherical, and the hallway formed an opening halfway up its sides. The room's shimmering silver walls revealed it was a holotheater. Over thirty feet in diameter, it was the largest Con had ever seen. Ann appeared pleased with the effect such a huge expenditure made on her prospective customers; even John Greighton seemed impressed.

"Only a holovision could possibly convey what we're offering. You'll be the first people outside our organization to see it." Ann gestured toward the two waiting seats. Mr.

Greighton, why don't you and Sara get comfortable while I get another seat for your daughter."

Con watched Ann and the receptionist struggle to lug a heavy seat to the hallway from a nearby supply closet. Once it was in place, Ann went to a console outside the hall and activated some controls. The seat levitated upward to the proper height. Con walked over to the floating seat and sat down. Once Ann saw that everyone was buckled in, she returned to the console, pressed a button, and the outer doors of the holotheater closed.

Con's seat bobbed slightly as it levitated to the center of the holotheater. Once she was in position, the chamber's silver walls darkened until she could barely see her father and his fiancée floating close by. The holovision began subtly. First, the darkness above was pricked by stars. The soft sounds of water became perceptible. Con looked down and saw the starlight reflected on the gentle waves of a sea. For a short while, all she could see was water and the night sky.

The waves continued to move in a natural manner, but the sky changed at a pace accelerated for dramatic effect. It lightened, and soon dawn painted the heavens with increasingly bold colors, which the waves reflected back. On the horizon, snowcapped mountains glowed orange pink in the day's first light. The sun rose higher, and its rays touched the sea, seeming to set it on fire. It rose higher still, and the water, which had blazed rosy gold just moments before, became clear. Con peered into its crystal depths. A school of fish swam beneath, the sunrise sparkling pink and gold on their silver scales.

A huge, dark green creature swam into the school, flapping its front flippers like wings. The animal's long and snakelike neck thrust its head among the fleeing fish, grabbing one. Next, the creature swam upward until its head and neck burst through the waves. It seemed so close that Con could stare into its golden eyes. A large fish flapped crosswise in its jaws. As Con stared in wonder at the plesiosaur, she heard Sara squeal like she was at an amusement park. The creature, being only an illusion, ignored them both. It flipped the fish into the air and caught it to swallow headfirst. Then, arching its neck downward, the animal submerged and swam off into the depths.

The view began to change again. Soon Con felt that she was flying rapidly over the surface of the sea. Only the lack of wind in her face made the illusion incomplete. The sense of motion was accompanied by music, then words. "Come to the springtime of the world . . . a time when the Earth was new . . . unspoiled . . . and filled with wonders. A startling scientific breakthrough allows Temporal Transport to offer the ultimate travel experience." The music began to swell as an island became visible in the distance, the early-morning sun glowing on its rocky sides. ". . . Montana Isle, set in the pristine beauty of America's ancient Montana Sea. The most exclusive destination in history . . . enjoy absolute privacy amidst the untouched splendor of nature." Con's seat seemed to fly over the island, then circle back. The island was small and mostly rocky. In its center, a mesa of dark rock rose from a grove of trees. For an instant, Con thought she spotted some structures clustered at the base of the spire, but her perspective changed before she could be sure. Her seat dipped toward low rocky cliffs above sandy beaches. Now the gently rolling waves appeared inches beneath her feet. Instinctively, she lifted her legs. A haze, tinted gold by the morning light, gave the view a dreamlike quality. "Montana Isle . . . as close as your back door and millions of years from everything." The music swelled to a crescendo as Con's seat seemed to soar higher and higher above the island until it was a tiny fleck of gold in a sapphire blue sea. The mainland was now visible, covered with greenery and cut by rivers flowing from the nearby mountains. The unpolluted air was so clear she could see for miles. It was a sight of breathtaking beauty.

The vision faded, and they were once again looking at the silver walls of the holotheater. Con's father grinned like a kid discovering an exotic new toy. Sara glanced at him, then formed her expression into a demure imitation of his. Con's reaction was more complicated. She was enchanted, even dazzled, yet dubious that the holovision was genuine. While part of her hoped it was, she also found that prospect unsettling.

As the seats floated back to their starting places, the doors parted to reveal Ann Smythe waiting for them. Next to her was a small table with champagne in a silver ice bucket and four glasses. "You're the first to see it," she said, popping the cork. "I thought we'd celebrate. Dom Perignon, vintage 2047."

By the time they were out of their seats, Ann had filled three glasses. She hesitated and looked to John Greighton before filling the fourth. "I know your daughter's not quite eighteen, but perhaps you'd . . ."

"I don't drink," said Con before her father could answer.

Ann gave John and Sara their glasses. They were made from hand-cut crystal. "A toast!" she said. "To the ultimate travel experience . . . time travel!"

2

ANN SMYTHE WENT TO HER OFFICE AND SHUT THE DOOR before entering Peter Green's code in her computer. When the link was established, she submitted to a retinal scan and entered her password before Green's face appeared on the viewscreen. His features had been redone by a well-known designer, but his handsome face had a harsh cast. Ann was convinced that his somewhat sinister appearance was intentional. The cold, pale eyes, however, were beyond artifice. They bore into her. "Well?" Green said.

"I sold him," said Ann. *Tell him the good news first*, she thought.

"He didn't balk at the price?"

"He didn't blink. Convincing him the offer was genuine was the hard part, even with the holovision. Once he believed he would actually go back in time, the privacy won him over. He's been hounded ever since he got engaged again. I told him that only he and Sara would ever know if they packed their swimsuits."

Green smirked. "You're good."

"The best," agreed Ann. "Three million Euros in one afternoon."

"*Three* million?"

"He's taking his daughter, too."

"I didn't know he had a daughter," said Green.

"I thoroughly research my prospects. That's why I'm worth my commission," replied Ann. "She's from his first marriage. Doesn't live with him. When he brought her to the showing, I knew she was the key to the sale. They're not close, and that's why he wants her on this vacation."

"What for?" asked Green. "Having a kid hanging around would be the last thing I'd want."

"I believe he wants to resurrect his family," said Ann.

"Only with a younger wife," said Green cynically.

"Yes," agreed Ann, "that's his pattern." She saw her opportunity to break the bad news and took it. "But you're right about him. He doesn't really want the kid hanging around. That's why I told him our staff naturalist would keep her busy."

"You told him *what*?" said Green angrily. "I don't want anyone else in on this! Too many know already. Who the hell do you think you are?"

"I'm a salesperson, the best. I trust my instincts, and I felt it was necessary to close the sale. If you disagree with my judgment, I'll call Greighton up and tell him I was mistaken about the naturalist. But I guarantee he'll cancel."

"I don't want a scientist snooping around. You know that!"

"He'll be a naturalist, for heaven's sake. I said he'd be young, too. How much trouble could he cause?"

"You didn't listen to me," said Green coldly.

"Look, I think Greighton's more to you than a customer. If you need a big investor, he's as rich as they come. I delivered him. I'd think you'd be grateful."

"You think too much," replied Green. He glared from the screen while he thought. "Okay," he said finally, "*you* find the naturalist. Research him like you would a prospect. Someone to keep the girl out of Greighton's hair and someone who'll keep his nose out of my business. I'm holding

you responsible. Don't screw up!" The screen went blank as
Green broke the connection.

Ann Smythe found her hands were shaking as she sat at
her computer to begin her research. As a freelance marketer,
she was used to demanding clients, even abusive ones. It
came with the territory. Yet, Green unnerved her. She relied
on her instincts, and she trusted them. They told her to be
cautious; there was something going on.

THREE DAYS LATER, Ann Smythe was picking her way
through the cluttered basement of Horner Hall on the
campus of the University of Montana. She was annoyed
with Rick Clements already, and they hadn't even met.
They were supposed to have met an hour ago, but he
hadn't shown up. She had been forced to track him down.
A series of inquiries had led her first to the paleontology
department, then to the preparation lab in the basement.
She was not pleased to be there. Disorder irritated her,
and the ubiquitous rock dust had soiled her expensive
suit. There, amid cartons of specimens and scattered
tools, she located a muscular, sandy-haired young man
staring intently through a stereo macroscope. Despite his
youth, he had a weathered look, as if he spent a lot of
time in the sun. He was using a needlelike tool to delicately remove the rocky matrix from a fossil, grain by
grain.

"Rick Clements?"

"Yeah?" said Rick, not removing his eyes from the macroscope.

"I'm Ann Smythe, we had an appointment."

Rick suddenly started back from the macroscope,
glanced down at his watch, then looked up at Ann. "I'm
sorry. I lost track of the time." He rose and wiped his
dusty hand on his pants before extending it to Ann. He
had a disarming, guileless smile that made her decide to
forgive him. "It's a *Multituberculate* from the Upper Cretaceous," he said by way of explanation.

"What?"

"The fossil, it's . . ."

"Never mind," said Ann. "I've come a long way to talk, but not here."

"Sure. Is the commons okay? Look, I'm really sorry about . . ."

"It must be someplace where we won't be overheard."

"There's my room, but it's a mess."

"Your room sounds fine."

Rick's dorm room resembled a more compressed version of the paleontology department's basement. Rick cleared some books and rocks off a chair, then offered Ann the seat. She decided to stand.

"Professor Harrington said you had some kind of job offer," said Rick, "but he didn't say much more than that."

"I didn't tell him more than that," said Ann. "The people I represent are starting a new venture and they're not ready to make it public yet. It's an opportunity for you to get in on the ground floor."

"New venture . . . ground floor . . . are you sure you're talking to the right person? I study fossils. This doesn't sound like my line of work. Besides, I've already lined up some fieldwork this summer."

Ann ignored his question. "You should be a senior this semester," she said, "except you haven't fulfilled the core requirements. Just biology, geology, comparative anatomy, and paleontology courses, some of them on the graduate level. You won't get a degree that way."

Rick sighed. "I've heard this before. Did my brother put you up to this?"

"No, I brought it up to make a point. Single-minded people like you generally have a hard time in this world. If you ever want academic work, you'll have to study literature and history also."

"Now I *know* my brother set you up."

"No, quite the contrary, I'm here to offer you a way out. To do what you love without the compromises." She pulled a small viewer from her pocket and inserted a disk. "This is raw input, straight from the datacam. Take a look."

Rick peered at the screen and saw an aerial view of an

open landscape dotted with clumps of trees. The ground was covered with low vegetation upon which a herd of large animals grazed. The view zoomed in closer on the herd, and soon Rick recognized them. "They're ceratopsids. *Triceratops . . . Torosaurus . . .* I don't know that one . . ." He watched for a while with fascination. "This is very realistic, who programmed this?"

"I *said* it was raw input. It's not computer-generated. It's realistic because it's real."

"You mean a theme park?"

"No. Real. Actual living animals."

"Genetically engineered?"

"No," replied Ann, "these are wild animals in their natural habitat."

"Cut the bull," said Rick good-naturedly. "That's not possible. You're talking time travel."

"Yes."

Rick's only response was a derisive snort.

"Time travel's not only possible," responded Ann, "but you can experience it yourself. That's what I'm here to talk about."

"This has got be a hoax."

"My client requires strict secrecy, hardly what you'd expect in a hoax . . . don't you agree?"

"How can this be real?"

"I don't expect to convince you," said Ann. "You can see it for yourself. I'm just here to make that possible. If you agree to go, I'm authorized to transfer a five-thousand-Euro advance to your account, plus provide you with airfare." Rick whistled at the sum. "That's real money," continued Ann, "maybe not proof, but a start."

Rick stared silently at Ann with an expression of disbelief. She read his thoughts, and said, "You're not the only candidate. If you're not willing to listen, then I'm wasting my time." She shut off the viewer, put it away, and started walking for the door.

Rick watched her with a perplexed expression on his face. As she reached for the knob, he called out, "Wait. Wait!"

"Why? You obviously think I'm a charlatan."

"Look, you appear out of the blue and tell me my wildest fantasy has come true. Of course I'm skeptical. Who wouldn't be? If you were in my place, would you believe it?"

"Maybe not," admitted Ann, "but I'd keep an open mind."

Rick looked at her with indecision, as hope battled with skepticism. When he spoke again, it was as if he were pleading on behalf of hope. "All I think about is fossils. Searching for them . . . imagining the animals that made them. Can I really visit their world?"

"Yes," said Ann.

"Why are you offering this?"

"We need a naturalist on our project."

"A naturalist?"

"That's what we're calling the position. Someone who is knowledgeable about the animals and plants of the area."

"The Upper Cretaceous, judging from what you showed me."

"Correct."

"Why me? Surely there are more qualified people."

"This is a commercial venture, not a scientific one. I think you meet our requirements perfectly. To be frank, we're looking for a tour guide, not a researcher. Someone with personality. Professor Harrington assures me you have one . . . when your nose isn't in a rock."

Rick smiled at her remark. "Assuming that I don't wake up and find I've been dreaming, what kind of tours are you talking about? Aren't you afraid of having your clients eaten?"

"Of course, that's why we have a special aircraft for sight-seeing and our base is on an island. You'll be pointing out the sights from a safe distance."

"Can I see that disk again?"

I've got him, thought Ann. "On one condition," she said, knowing she had gained the upper hand. "My client insists on strict confidentiality."

"Sure," said Rick, reaching for the disk.

"I'll need that agreement in writing. You must keep

our discussion strictly confidential, regardless of whether you accept our offer or not." Ann produced some legal documents from her suit pocket.

"Where do I sign?" asked Rick.

"Read them first," insisted Ann. "There are severe sanctions for violating its provisions. This is a serious document."

Rick took the document and quickly skimmed through text specifying the damages should he ever mention someplace called Montana Isle, its physical or temporal location, or the means of traveling there without the explicit permission of . . . Rick stopped reading and quickly scrawled his signature on the page. There was a faraway, eager look in his eyes as he said, "Okay, show me the dinosaurs again."

PETER GREEN HAD listened to Ann's report about her meeting with Rick Clements and grudgingly conceded that he would do. Afterward, he had abruptly terminated the call. He did not wish Ann to feel comfortable about the situation. He certainly was not. He was already upset about that girl, Greighton's daughter. Now this naturalist, Clements, added another factor to his plans. Still another person he would have to include in his calculations.

Green paced about with an anxious restlessness. Then, for the third time that day, he left his office and entered the fenced area behind the building to check the time machine. It stood there looking almost exactly like the twentieth-century conception of a flying saucer. Just as in the old movies, the saucer stood on three legs with an open panel on its underside, which functioned both as door and staircase. Only the black solar panels on the saucer's upper surface marred its resemblance to the fictional spacecraft.

It was these panels that were Green's concern. The short, overcast winter days and the high fence cut down on their input. He climbed the stairs into the machine and went to the controls to check the charge. Little had changed; the machine would not be fully powered for another week. *Damn!* he cursed to himself, *another week of exposure. If Greighton comes in on this, that's the first thing I want to change.*

At least, Green thought, *as soon as the machine's ready, we can go.* Part of the sales pitch for the resort was that, from the perspective of the present, a trip there would seem almost instantaneous. "Just think," ran the sales script, "you'll leave for a two-week vacation and return, rested and relaxed, only a few seconds after you departed." Such a getaway was easy to fit into anyone's busy schedule. It was a great selling point, and Ann had used it very effectively, all the more so, because she didn't know it was a lie. Green believed in telling the truth only when it was useful. By the time it was necessary to tell Greighton the truth, Green hoped that Greighton would be on his side. As for the others, he would find new lies for them.

The idea of an instantaneous vacation had another benefit—no one would feel the need to explain where they were going. Everyone involved with the trip had agreed not to talk about it and probably wouldn't—for a while. It was the long term that bothered Green. He had little faith in nondisclosure agreements. It was his experience that people talked; a piece of paper wouldn't stop that. In the end, there was only one way to assure silence.

3

CON FULFILLED THE NONDISCLOSURE AGREEMENT UNTIL it came time to pack. There were strict weight limitations on what she could bring, and her frequent trips to the bathroom scales caught her mother's attention. She looked into Con's room and saw small piles of clothing spread over her bed next to a duffel bag.

"Con, what's going on?"

"Nothing, Mom." Con put the stack of underwear she was about to weigh down on the bed.

"It looks like you're going somewhere."

"I'm just sorting through my things."

"I don't believe you. You're up to something."

"Daddy said that I couldn't tell anyone. I had to promise in writing that I wouldn't."

The suspicion on her mother's face changed to alarm. "Not even me? What are you two up to?"

"It's just a trip, a little vacation."

"To where? For how long? Why the secrecy?"

Con sighed. "It's nothing to worry about, Mom. I'll be gone less than a day. If you hadn't caught me, you'd have never missed me."

Con's mother looked dubious. "That's a lot more than one day's worth of clothes." She picked up a sleeveless top from off the bed. "It looks like you're going someplace warm."

"It's some new hush-hush technology. We all had to promise to keep it secret, even Daddy. It's like an instant vacation. I'll be gone only seconds, literally. I wasn't even supposed to tell you this much."

"That's nonsense. Don't lie to me."

"I'm not," said Con. "I know it sounds crazy. I have a hard time believing it myself. Look, if it's going to be a hassle, I'll just stay here. This was all Daddy's idea."

"Then you should go," said Mother.

"But I thought . . ."

"It's important to maintain good relations with your father. You're his only child. You should be his heir."

"Don't start, Mom."

"He owes you that! Besides, I only want what's best for you."

"I don't care about being an heiress, I just want to be myself," said Con.

"And you will be. But to the world, you'll always be John Greighton's daughter. You can't escape that, so you might as well benefit from it. It won't compromise you to accept your due."

"I don't need anything."

"Not even a new face?"

"Mom! We've been through this before. My face is fine."

"It's not very fashionable. Why seem common? All your friends . . ."

"All my friends look the same now!"

"Stylish," retorted Con's mother, "that's what they look. I told your father when he named you 'Constance' it would make you old-fashioned."

"You used to tell me it'd make me rich, like my ancestor that discovered all that gold."

"Oh yes," said Mother, "the family legend. Well, you don't have to look like a nineteenth-century woman, just because you're named after one."

"Mom, could we stop this. If you want me to go, I need to weigh these so I can finish packing."

Mother held up a swimsuit, saying, "*This* certainly isn't going to put you over your limit."

"We're going to an island, there'll only be the three of us."

"The three of you?"

"He's taking Sara," said Con.

"The new one? What's *she* like?"

"We didn't talk much. She seems fairly young. She looks a lot like Daddy's last wife."

"The next one will probably be younger than you," said Mother.

"Maybe there won't be a next one," said Con.

Her mother's face colored at that remark. "There's always another one. But I gave him his only child," she said with fierce satisfaction. "Take that trip and have a good time. I'll leave you to finish packing."

"Don't let Daddy know I told you about it."

"Small chance of that," said Mother as she left the room.

Con sighed and looked at the pile of clothes on the bed. Ten kilograms was not a lot of clothes, especially since Daddy insisted she bring two dinner dresses. She put a light sweater in the duffel bag along with the underwear and made one more trip to the scales. When she took off her shoes and put them on the bag, she was still over. She rummaged through the bag and removed her makeup case. *There,* she thought as the scale registered ten kilograms, *no one will really care how I look anyway. If Daddy wants me made up for dinner, I'll borrow Sara's. I bet she didn't have a weight limit.*

When Con put the makeup case back on her bureau, she saw herself in the mirror. Her short, brown hair framed large hazel eyes, a petite nose and full lips. She would have been considered pretty in earlier times, but the softness of her features ran contrary to current tastes. *It isn't a fashionable face,* she thought. Con assessed herself critically. *My nose is wrong, my mouth's too big and my chest—forget it*! Then she stopped herself. It was a stupid game, and she hated when she gave in to it. *If I don't like the way I look, Daddy will be glad to pay to change me,* Con reminded herself. *Then I'd end up looking like Sara.*

TOM CLEMENTS STRUGGLED to hide the disappointment in his eyes as he looked at his younger brother. He failed miserably. "Not going on the dig?" he said incredulously.

"It's not definite," said Rick, "but something's come up. I may not be available this summer."

Ever since their parents had died, Tom, who was twelve years older, had been both brother and father to Rick. The summers they spent excavating fossils together were special times for them both. When they had begun, Tom was a first-year graduate student at the university. Now he was an assistant professor of paleontology.

"What's come up?"

"I can't tell."

Tom's face colored. "You haven't signed on with a commercial collector?"

"God, no!" said Rick. He hesitated a moment, weighing the hurt in his brother's eyes against all the lawyers' threats. Then, five days after he signed the nondisclosure agreement, he broke it. "I'll be in trouble if this gets out. I've promised in writing I wouldn't discuss it."

"Discuss what?"

Rick looked around the faculty dining room nervously and lowered his voice. "Time travel," he whispered.

"Time travel!" said Tom so loudly it made Rick wince.

"Keep it down," whispered Rick.

"This has got to be a joke," said Tom more quietly.

"No, it's serious," replied Rick, "I've been hired as a guide for a trip to the Upper Cretaceous. I've already received airfare and a five-thousand-Euro advance on my salary. If it were some joke, would they pay me an advance?"

Tom appeared dumbfounded. After a long silence he said, "We need to talk about this seriously, but I've got a class in a few minutes. Why don't you drop by my apartment this evening? I'll cook dinner."

"You've got to keep this secret."

"Don't worry," said Tom, "I've a reputation for sanity. I want to protect it."

"Okay, I'll see you at dinner." Rick got up to leave.

"One thing, before you go," said Tom.

"What's that?"

"Who invented this . . ." Tom lowered his voice to a dramatic whisper. ". . . time machine?"

"Someone named Peter Green. But, Tom, please don't talk . . ."

"Don't worry, bro, mum's the word."

TOM'S APARTMENT LOOKED like a stage designer's idea of a bachelor professor's habitat. It was crammed with clutter reflecting his fascination for the past. Books, papers, and maps mingled with geologists' tools, camping gear, fossils, and an extensive collection of toy dinosaurs. When Rick entered the door, he smelled the pungent spices of Southwestern cooking combined with the scent of rock dust. Tom called from the kitchen, "Want a beer?"

Rick walked to the kitchen and grabbed one from the fridge. "Thanks."

Tom threw some chilies in oil. "You're going to miss

my cooking this summer. Is that when you're going?"

"Tomorrow, actually. At least, that's the first trip."

"At the beginning of the semester?"

"I'll be gone from the present time frame for less than a minute."

"Oh . . . I forgot. This is *time travel*."

"You still don't believe me," said Rick.

Tom added some chopped onions to the oil and gently stirred them as he talked. "I made some inquiries this afternoon," he said. When he saw the alarm on Rick's face he quickly added, "Don't worry, I've been very discreet. I called up David Ross over in the physics department—said I needed information on time travel for a lecture—and he did a literature search. Rick, there's been almost no research in the area, except Eckmair's work in the thirties. He claimed to have demonstrated it on the subatomic level, but his findings are still in dispute. The rest of the papers were strictly speculative. Most physicists believe time only goes in one direction. Those that don't think it might reverse inside a black hole or some other exotic place in the universe, but certainly not inside a man-made machine."

"What if they're wrong?" replied Rick. "I've got some evidence, five grand and airfare."

"That's hardly evidence," answered Tom. "This doesn't make sense. A discovery like that doesn't appear out of nowhere. There should be research papers leading up to it. Green would get the Nobel Prize for something like that."

"There could be some reason why he hasn't published. Maybe he doesn't want the government involved. Maybe the government *is* involved."

"There's another thing," said Tom. "Who's this Peter Green? There are only two scientists by that name—one's a botanist and the other's a retired chemical engineer."

"Dammit, Tom!" said Rick irritably. "If your snooping spoils this for me, I'll never forgive you. You forget, I saw the pictures. I believe they're real. I'll risk being fooled over missing out. This is a dream come true."

"I'm sorry," said Tom. "It's just seems so improbable."

He browned some cubed beef among the onions and chilies, then began adding spices.

Rick silently watched his brother cook, the smells bringing back memories of so many meals together. After a while, he broke his silence. "What's the point in fooling me?" he said. "If this were a hoax, why trick a college student? No one would believe me. You don't. What would they gain?"

"I have no idea," admitted Tom. "It just bothers me. Are you sure you'll be all right?"

"Of course."

"All the same, could you leave me your flight information and destination? I'd feel better."

Rick decided not to tell Tom he didn't know his final destination. "Sure," he said, "I'll leave it in my room. If there's an emergency, you have the key."

Tom cut open a plastic pouch of tomatoes and another of beans, then added them to the meat. After some more stirring, he turned the heat down and covered the pot. "This can simmer for a while," he said, taking a beer from the fridge and heading out of the small kitchen toward the living room. He sat down on the couch, and Rick sat down in an armchair close by. "Okay," said Tom, "I'll stop being a party poop. Tell me about this trip."

Rick's eyes lit up with excitement. "The woman I talked to didn't seem to know a lot about the place we're going to, but she showed me two datacam disks, and I learned a lot from them. The images of the dinosaurs were definitely Upper Cretaceous—*Triceratops* and the like."

"Are we talking K-T boundary here?" teased Tom.

"Come on, they have more sense than that. With millions of years' worth of sites to choose from, do you think they would open their resort at the time of the impact?"

"A *resort*?" exclaimed Tom incredulously. "Someone builds a time machine and the best thing he can do with it is open a *resort*?"

"If you saw the island, it wouldn't seem so far-fetched. It's beautiful. There hasn't been anyplace like it since the seas rose. Everything's pristine, unspoiled. They're getting a million Euros for a reservation."

Tom whistled. "That's more than my department's budget. This Green sounds pretty mercenary."

Rick shrugged. "He probably has a lot of expenses."

"Do you have any idea where this island's located?" asked Tom.

"They say it's in the Montana Sea."

"Never heard of it. Sounds more like advertising copy."

"Yeah," agreed Rick. "It's obviously the Interior Seaway. The island's somewhere on the western side of the seaway, not too far from the coast. There's some mountains nearby."

"The seaway didn't extend as far north as Montana by the Upper Cretaceous," said Tom. "My guess is their 'Montana Isle' is in New Mexico or Colorado. Those mountains must be part of the Sevier Orogeny."

"They were big," said Rick. "The peaks had snow on them."

"Not much left of them now," mused Tom.

Talking about the ancient land drew Tom's imagination toward it. As a paleontologist, he sometimes felt like he had spent his life trying to imagine a grand party by picking through its garbage. Now, Rick had an invitation to that party. Tom started to envy him, as his doubt paled before such a wondrous vision. "The weather should be nice," he said almost dreamily. "Not too hot. There'll be flowers, too . . . and birds . . ." Tom laughed. ". . . and poison ivy."

"And a sea full of plesiosaurs and a continent full of dinosaurs," continued Rick.

"With my baby brother acting as tour guide. Maybe I could come along to fluff the pillows."

They both laughed at that idea. Tom picked up a large fossil shell from off a table and, as he turned it in his hands, he grew pensive. "Remember when you found this?"

"That's my first ammonite," replied Rick. "I must have been eleven."

"It was the first time I saw you happy after Mom and Dad's accident," said Tom, handing Rick the fossil.

The rock brought back a flood of memories with its touch. "I slept with this fossil for years."

"Your stone teddy bear," mused Tom. "Grandma feared you'd grow up strange."

"I did," said Rick.

Tom chuckled, then grew serious. "When you gave it to me as a graduation present, I was really touched," he said. "It's hard to believe you'll soon be picking them up off the beach, brand-new. I wonder what colors they'll be."

Rick tapped into his brother's reflective mood. "All those summers, looking for fossils . . ."

"I remember a few winter trips, too," said Tom. "We nearly froze our butts off."

"Yeah, but we found some great stuff," said Rick. "Those were good times, Tom, all of them. Good times."

While the chili simmered, the talk turned to past trips and past eras. As they spoke, the past wove in and out of their conversation, and the ancient sea flowed through it. They spoke of their visits to its dry, ossified shores and imagined the bones of its creatures clothed again in flesh. They ate dinner and remembered the camps in the desert, where the smoky taste in the food did not come from a bottle of seasoning. The evening wore on, and eventually it was time for Rick to go. Tom left the room momentarily and returned with something in his hand. He held it out to Rick. "You've had your eye on this ever since you were a kid. I think it's time you had it."

Rick looked down at the precious hunting knife in its weathered leather sheath, the thing he coveted most as a child, and a lump formed in his throat. "Tom . . . I . . . I . . ."

"Can't send my baby brother to the Cretaceous unarmed, can I?" said Tom with a false heartiness to mask his feelings. "I want you to have it."

"I don't know what to say."

"Say thanks. Then say good-bye, you've got a plane to catch tomorrow morning."

Rick hugged his brother. "Thanks."

"Bring me back an ammonite," called out Tom, as Rick headed down the hall.

Rick turned. "I'll try," he said. Then, with one last wave, he walked out of Tom's life forever.

4

RICK GREW INCREASINGLY ANXIOUS DURING HIS TRIP TO the rendezvous point. The closer he got to his destination, the more Tom's arguments on the improbability of time travel weighed on his mind. By the time his flight landed, Rick almost expected disappointment. Still, he could not figure out what anyone had to gain by fooling him. Only that slim rationale sustained his hope that the trip was not pointless.

The man who met Rick when he disembarked did not identify himself. He drove Rick in silence to the outskirts of Chicago. "Here's your stop," the stranger finally said. As the car drove away, Rick found himself outside a small, one-story brick building in an industrial zone. The building and the surrounding area looked run-down and late-twentieth-century. A small sign taped to the inside of the glass door to the building read P.G. ENTERPRISES. It seemed an unlikely site for the greatest scientific breakthrough of the twenty-first century.

The door was locked, and Rick had to pound on it loudly before anyone came to open it. Eventually, a burly, dark-haired man appeared. He looked Rick over thoroughly before entering a code on a keypad next to the door. The bolts snapped open.

"You Clements?" the man asked.

"Yes," replied Rick.

"I'm Nick," said the man without offering his hand, "I work for Mr. Green. Come on." He turned and walked down a corridor. As Rick followed him, he heard the bolts in the door automatically snap shut. Nick led him to a door and opened it. "In here." Rick passed through the doorway; then Nick, who had remained in the corridor, closed the door. Rick stood and glanced at the three other occupants of the room.

A dark, tall black man in his late thirties smiled sympathetically at Rick's confusion. "I see you've met the ever-charming Nick Zhukovsky," he said. "I'm Joe Burns, the pilot for this little junket."

Rick shook his hand. "I'm Rick Clements."

"Our naturalist," said Joe. "So you're the guy I'll fly around when we get downwhen."

"Downwind?"

Joe laughed. "That's down*when*, short for 'back in the past.' I fly in all four dimensions."

"You've done it before?" asked Rick. "What's it like?"

"Ever fall down? Like from a ladder or something?"

"I walked off a twelve-foot ledge one night."

"Well, remember the instant you started to fall? Stretch that feeling out over an eternity and you have time travel."

"It doesn't sound pleasant," said Rick.

"It isn't," said Joe with a grin, "but I guess the trip's worth it."

"To see living dinosaurs? I'll say!" said Rick.

"An enthusiast," said Joe wryly. "Let me introduce the others." Joe turned to a man in his sixties whose leathery, sun-darkened face contrasted with his blue eyes and white hair. "James Neville, meet Rick Clements."

"Pleased to meet you," said James with an exotic accent that blended British with African. "As the camp guide, you'll be working for me."

"James ran a safari camp in the Serengeti Park. He goes back to when the animals were still real," said Joe.

"No bloody poachers where we're going," said James with satisfaction. He turned to a short, slightly plump dark-eyed man in his twenties, and said, "This is Pandit Jahan. Hasn't been downwhen, but he was with me in Uganda. Damned good chef, in or out of the bush." Pandit smiled modestly at James's praise and shook Rick's hand. James continued, "We'll run this just like a safari camp. Hear you've done your share of camping."

"Entire summers," replied Rick, "some winter trips, too."

"Good. Main difference between your camping and a safari is we have guests. They don't rough it. For them, it's a fine hotel, only alfresco. You'll be the camp guide, but you'll pitch in on the other work, too—washing dishes, tending the guests, whatever's required. We're shorthanded. In Uganda, I'd have a staff of twelve for four guests."

As James detailed Rick's duties, Rick was chagrined to discover how much Ann Smythe had left out. He began to feel he had been conned into becoming a glorified busboy. Yet, already, he sensed it was useless to protest. James did not give the impression of flexibility. Rick considered approaching Peter Green on the matter.

As if on cue, Green entered the room. James instantly fell silent. One look at Green and Rick abandoned all ideas of complaining. Green's expensively sculpted face bore an intimidating look. His cold eyes fixed on Pandit and Rick, sizing them up. "I'm Peter Green, CEO of Temporal Transport. Welcome aboard."

With those minimal pleasantries aside, Green addressed the group. "This evening, we will leave on our first paying excursion downwhen. All of you need to know how important this trip is. It's much more than a maiden voyage. The future of time travel and the future of mankind are at stake. This is no exaggeration.

"If this trip seems shrouded in secrecy and hurried, it is because of our situation. Consider for a moment how truly dangerous time travel is. I'm not referring to any danger to the traveler—that's negligible. But think of the effects such travel could have on history itself. It does not take much imagination to conceive how even a minor alteration of the past could cause unpredictable changes to the present. If those alterations were motivated by greed or a political agenda, catastrophe could result. I feel so strongly about this, I would halt all development in this technology if it were in my power. Unfortunately, it is not. Others, without my scruples, are also working on time travel.

"One of the paradoxes of this technology is that, even though I am far ahead of my competitors, being first means nothing. If they ever succeed in discovering its secrets, they can go back in time, destroy my research, and gain sole control over the technology. With additional capital and research, I believe that I can prevent that. I am working on a system for Temporal Field Stabilization. To put it simply, it will prevent anyone from altering the time continuum. The future will unfold without interference.

"At the present, this field is not in place. This is the reason why your nondisclosure agreements are so important. Upwhen, people are researching history to pinpoint our precise location in time. Talk to your grandchildren years from now about this trip, and these people may find out. With that information, they might travel downwhen to kill your mother."

Green paused to let the implications sink in. Already, Rick regretted his talk with Tom. *Have I already said something that might be traced in the future?* he wondered. *Was that the real cause of Mom and Dad's auto accident? I was in that car. Was someone trying to get me?* This convoluted chain of causation was as confusing as it was ominous. It meant that there would have been an unaltered past where the accident did not occur. Yet somehow, Rick would have spoken to his brother in that time line also. *But why?* puzzled Rick. *My life would have been completely different.*

Rick became aware that Peter Green was staring at him. He hoped he did not look guilty and was relieved when Green continued his talk. "The real purpose of this trip is to gain money to fund my research into temporal stabilization. I chose our destination, aside from its obvious appeal, because it's far enough downwhen to prevent us from affecting the present. Our first client will be the billionaire John Greighton, along with his fiancée and daughter. I hope to demonstrate the potential of time travel to him, both for good and ill, and obtain his backing for my research."

"Your jobs are to make this trip as enjoyable as possible for Greighton and his party. That's *all* you need to do, nothing more and nothing less. Everything I just said stays in this room. Remember, they're on vacation. I'll broach the funding matters with Greighton myself. That's *my* job. Just do your parts and it will be easier."

As Green finished talking, Nick entered the room pushing a cart laden with food and a huge bottle of champagne. "That's enough of business," said Green as his expression softened. He popped a cork and started filling glasses. "We have something to celebrate." He handed out glasses to everyone, then raised his own in a toast. "To Montana Isle!"

The power of Peter Green's personality was such that everyone in the room soon mirrored his festive mood. Rick dismissed his guilty fears about his parents' accident and began to feel excited again about the trip. By his second glass of champagne, he was even ready to chat with Green himself. When Rick caught Green's eye, he said, "Now I understand why we're going so far downwhen."

"I'm glad," said Green.

"Just before the K-T event, it's perfect."

Green got a confused expression on his face, as if he didn't understand what Rick had just said. Rick clarified himself. "I mean, the asteroid impact will wipe everything clean. It'll be as if we were never there."

"Oh yes," said Green, "of course. Well, we can't be too careful, can we? By the way, I need to discuss your job. I'll need your help if I'm going to get to Greighton. I can't do that with his daughter hanging around. I want you to keep her away from camp as much as possible. That's the main reason you're on board, to arrange trips for her."

"Won't Mr. Greighton and his fiancée be interested in the sights also?"

"Maybe one trip, if that. We've researched them pretty well. They're more interested in the birds and the bees than wildlife," said Green with a knowing look. "Greighton's only other interest is business. When he talks business, his fiancée gets bored. She'll go off sunbathing or swimming."

"I don't think swimming would be a good idea," said Rick. "The Interior Seaway had some pretty dangerous creatures in it—mosasaurs, crocodiles, and not all the plesiosaurs ate fish."

"Don't worry, we have a protected beach. But it's good you're on your toes. We'll need that expertise." Green abruptly turned toward James and Pandit and began to discuss provisions. Rick felt that he had been dismissed and wandered over to the food cart.

Joe was there, making himself a sandwich. "Trying to schmooze with the boss?" he asked in a joking tone.

"Was it that obvious? Then I guess I'm not very good at it."

"Mr. Green has a lot on his mind," said Joe. "Your best course is just to do your job," Joe lowered his voice to scarcely above a whisper, "*and stay out of his way.*"

5

A LIMOUSINE PICKED UP CON OUTSIDE OF HER APARTMENT building. A burly, dark-haired man got out, took her bag, and opened a door for her. Her father and Sara were seated inside, drinking champagne. Sara had kicked off her shoes and snuggled close to Con's father. "Constance!" she said gaily, holding up her glass. "We're on vacation!"

Con was already regretting her decision to go, but she forced a smile onto her face. "Hi, Daddy. Hi, Sara."

"What did you tell your mother about tonight?" asked John Greighton.

"I told her we were going out to dinner, just the two of us," lied Con. "I said I'd be back before eleven."

"I wonder how you'll explain your two weeks' worth of tan," said John, cracking a smile. "This time travel thing's a great idea; I won't miss a single meeting tomorrow."

Sara ran her fingers through John's hair. "And we'll have two weeks together."

Con recognized Sara's gesture—she was staking her claim.

"You sure you want me along, Daddy? I'll just be a wet blanket."

"Nonsense, you and Sara need to get acquainted. You're not a child anymore, it's time you took your proper place."

"Where would that be?"

"Why . . . by my side, along with Sara. Maybe as a kid you resented how busy I was, but now you're old enough to understand. This is the perfect opportunity for us to spend time together. For you to get to know me better."

"And you won't miss a single meeting," said Con.

"That's not the point!" said John irritably. "I spent a million Euros so you could come. That proves something."

"Just kidding, Daddy. If you spent more time with me, you'd know."

"Come on, Constance," said Sara, "it was very nice of your dad to invite you."

Nick Zhukovsky spoke over the intercom from the driver's seat, which was partitioned from the passenger compartment by a glass panel. "Mr. Greighton, for security reasons, I'll be blacking out the windows." The windows and the glass partition darkened until they were opaque.

Con stared at her reflection in the black glass. "Well, *this* is cozy."

"Try a glass of champagne," said her father. "It'll relax you."

"Maybe I will."

"Good. Sara, pour Constance a glass."

Con took a little sip of the wine and tried to decide if she liked it. The bubbles were nice, but she expected it to be sweet and it was not. Still, she continued to sip as she contemplated the man she called Daddy. His face was not the one she remembered as a child, though the eyes were the same. His chin was a little like the old one, but the rest of his features had been redone. They looked like they had come out of a fashion magazine, which was undoubtedly the case. It was the face of a stranger.

She mused that, as a younger girl, she would have given anything to be with her father. Then, she loved him with the desperate yearning of the ignored. Now, she wasn't sure how she felt. So many disappointments lay between them, perhaps

it was too late for closeness. Yet the old longings rose up
from deep where she had banished them. They caught her
off guard, and she found herself thinking, *Maybe this time
will be different*.

The three of them sat in awkward silence, watching the
bubbles rise in their glasses. Finally, John said, "Giving any
thought to college?"

"I'm going to Harvard this fall."

"Oh, of course," replied Con's father. "I remember. Do
you know what you're going to study?"

"I'm thinking about art history."

"Then this trip should be just the thing, seascapes and all."

"Too bad I can't tell anyone about them."

"What *I* want to see," said Sara, "is a real beach, like in
those old movies."

"How about our trip to Miami?" reminded John.

"That beach was fake, part of the sea wall. We couldn't
see the sunset from our hotel balcony because of that stupid
wall."

"The sun sets in the west," countered John.

"So? All we saw was concrete. And the *crowds* . . ."

"It was packed," agreed John, "considering it was a 'private beach.' Well, we won't have that problem where we're
going. We'll have the whole beach—the whole world—to
ourselves."

"That's good," said Sara with a coy smile, "because I
didn't pack a suit."

Con flushed at that remark. "You can always borrow
mine," she said with mock solicitude.

"I don't think I'd fit into the top."

John Greighton let out an exasperated sigh that terminated
the exchange.

"Daddy, what are you looking forward to on this trip?"

"I just want to relax with the two women in my life. I
only hope they'll get along."

"We will, John," said Sara.

"We'll be just like sisters," said Con, holding out her glass.
"Big sister, would you pour me some more champagne?"

Sara looked at John for permission. "What the hell," he
said, "she's on vacation."

AS EVENING BEGAN, Rick finished up helping Pandit load provisions into the time machine. Most of the items consisted of cookware, foodstuffs, wine, and liquor in addition to a large tent and a set of folding cots. Joe kept a running tally of the weight of everything that went into the machine. He also was very particular where the items were loaded in order to distribute the weight evenly.

Each time Rick entered the machine, he took an opportunity to examine it. His first impression was how finely constructed the machine looked. It lacked the makeshift appearance of a prototype. Only the partitions around the control center looked to be last-minute additions. The rest had the level of finish superior to any car or plane he had ever ridden in.

The stairway into the saucer-shaped machine led to a single room. Except where the control center was walled off, the room was a perfect hemisphere. The outer walls of the room featured various-sized hatches to the storage bays and what appeared to be several evenly spaced windows. These puzzled Rick at first because no windows were evident from the outside of the machine. Upon closer examination, Rick realized that they were actually viewscreens of incredibly high resolution. Set back from the wall was a circle of seats, all facing the center of the room. This was dominated by a thick, transparent column containing a cylinder that seemed disturbingly immaterial. Rick found it hard to look at, and tried squinting to focus his vision. The squinting did little good, for he could neither identify the cylinder's shifting colors nor determine its precise diameter. Trying only gave him a headache.

When Joe and Pandit were finishing up outside the saucer, Rick cracked the door to the control center and sneaked a quick peek. A single chair faced a viewscreen in the outer wall. Below the viewscreen was a large control console. The console had a bewildering array of switches, gauges, and knobs, and a bank of monitors showing puzzlingly complex displays. Plastic tape labels affixed beneath the switches and the monitors reminded him that this machine was, indeed, a prototype. Although this area was strictly off-limits, Rick was tempted to examine it more closely, but he heard footsteps on the stairway. He quickly shut the door and tried to appear busy. Joe looked at him suspiciously when he ascended the stairs, but he all said was, "Loading's done. We're to go to the meeting room and wait for the guests to arrive."

Rick followed Joe back to the meeting room. Peter Green and James Neville were engaged in a conversation concerning the guests. Joe commenced to pace about in a preoccupied manner. Pandit sat calmly by himself. Rick sat next to him.

"We're the only two that haven't been downwhen yet," said Rick. "You excited?"

"I am most pleased to be working with Mr. Neville again," replied Pandit. "Otherwise, for me, it will be like any other safari camp."

"But it's a whole different world downwhen, so much to discover."

"You are the guide, so that is true. I am the chef. Cooking doesn't change."

"Isn't there something that stirs your sense of adventure?"

"Did they show you the datavision of the island? The one with the creature that swam? You know, the one with the long neck?"

"Yes," replied Rick, "that was a plesiosaur."

"Well, I would like to cook a fish like the one that creature caught. I have never seen such a fish."

Rick looked at Pandit in disbelief. "What?"

"You asked me about my sense of adventure."

"Maybe I should fetch a dinosaur to roast."

"Yes," said Pandit, "but a small one."

Rick laughed. "It'd probably taste like chicken."

"Perhaps," admitted Pandit. "There is only one way to find out."

"Are you serious?"

"Why not? Mr. Neville said, long ago, safari cooks

always served game. Back then, catching dinner was part of the guide's job."

"I guess the robotic animals they have nowadays don't make for much of a stew."

Pandit sighed. "In Uganda, we just pretended we were on safari. That's why Mr. Neville quit, you know. He could remember when it was still real. But this will be real," said Pandit with dawning enthusiasm. "You know, I never considered the possibilities. There are all sorts of things downwhen people have never tasted."

"Or tasted people," added Rick.

"True," said Pandit. "But, as the chef, what people eat is my concern. What eats people is yours."

"I'll try to remember that," said Rick.

"I'm sure Mr. Green will be most gratified."

AS SALVATORE RUSSO parked his car, he was filled with hope that his luck was about to change. So far, his persistence had gone unrewarded, for images of Greighton and his fiancée were old news. The other paparazzi had gone off to chase more lucrative celebrities, but Sal had kept up his pursuit. Tonight, it looked like it might pay off.

What inspired Sal's hope was that Greighton's daughter had joined him and his fiancée in the limo. That alone was something; there were no shots of the fiancée and the kid together. Maybe tonight he could bag that special image that would bring in the big bucks. A full-blown argument would be worth a small fortune, but any conflict, even hostile looks, would sell. He trailed them hoping to catch them at the restaurant or wherever they were going. All he needed was to get in close. Even if nothing was happening, he was confident he could provoke a reaction that any good caption writer could make interesting. Surprise was on his side. Best of all, he was alone. With no competition, he needn't be rushed.

His quarry led him to a strange destination, a building in a run-down industrial part of town. Sal stayed in his car and spied on Greighton and the two women through the telephoto lens of his datacam. He shot a few images, but doubted they'd bring much. He watched the chauffeur unlock a door to the building and escort his passengers inside before returning and removing luggage from the trunk. *What's that for?* wondered Sal. *A secret wedding? A honeymoon?* He fantasized what images of that would be worth.

Sal forced himself to wait a few minutes before he left his car. He had turned off his headlights for the past few miles, but he still wanted to be sure he hadn't been observed. Just when he was reasonably sure he was not expected, all the streetlights went out. *This* is *my lucky night*, he thought. *No one will see me now.* He slipped out of his car into the darkness.

Sal did not even try the door to the building—he had seen the chauffeur lock it. The high fence in the rear looked more promising. He knew most people placed a naive faith in fences, assuming they brought privacy. Yet climbing was an essential skill in Sal's business, and he approached the obstacle as a seasoned professional. A quick walk around the perimeter revealed a spot with promising handholds and footholds. He slung his datacam around his neck and began to climb.

The sight beyond the top of the fence was totally unexpected. The screened-in area was almost entirely filled by a strange craft. Although Sal had never seen anything like it, the words "flying saucer" immediately came to mind. Using one hand to grip the top of the fence, Sal used the other to aim his datacam. He adjusted the zoom lens to wide-angle and framed an image of the saucer. Now he wished the streetlights were on so he'd have more light for the shot. As he recorded the image, questions popped into his mind. *What the hell is this thing? What does it have to do with Greighton? Why did he bring his daughter and his fiancée here?* Sal was convinced the answers to those questions could only be found on the other side of the fence. He lowered the datacam to let it dangle from its neck strap and, grabbing the top of the fence with both hands, prepared to pull himself over.

There was a muffled popping sound, instantly followed by an intense burning sensation in his right shoulder. Sal lost his grip and fell backwards off the fence, slamming into the ground. He lay on his back in a haze of pain. Staring at the fence, he dully realized that the dark stain near the top was his own blood. The next thing he saw was a burly man standing over him. He had a dispassionate look. Sal thought that he might be the chauffeur, although he wasn't sure. It was dark, and Sal's eyes were having trouble focusing. The man leaned over. There was something in his hand. Sal tried to make out what it was. When it was inches from his head, Sal saw it was a gun. Tonight was not lucky after all.

NICK ZHUKOVSKY REENTERED the meeting room and stood out of the way, waiting to catch Peter Green's eye. His boss was talking up the clients. "It'll be a vacation for me, too," Green said. "After years of research, I need a break." He looked over and spotted Nick. Nick glanced around to ensure no one was watching; then he moved his finger across his throat in a slicing motion. Green subtly nodded, acknowledging the message.

"I've put together the most experienced staff possible," continued Green, without the slightest hint of what had transpired. "James Neville's family ran safari camps in the Serengeti for three generations. His hospitality and exacting standards are renowned throughout Africa. Now he is bringing his expertise to our new frontier. We couldn't be in better hands."

James smiled modestly at the compliment. "Mr. Green has kindly provided me with a new challenge. I will do my utmost to meet it.

"Our chef, Pandit Jahan, was handpicked by James himself," said Green. "He assures me there is none better." Pandit bowed his head toward the guests. "Joe Burns is our pilot. He'll operate both the time machine and our sight-seeing aircraft."

"You won't be operating the time machine yourself?" asked John Greighton.

"As I said, I'm on vacation. I believe in getting the best people available, then giving them responsibility. Joe's already better at it than I."

Joe grinned. "Thank you, Mr. Green. That's *quite* a compliment."

"Last, but not least, is the newest member of our team, Rick Clements, our naturalist and guide. Don't let his youth fool you, he's had ten years' worth of field experience and . . ."

"In the *Cretaceous*?" interrupted Con incredulously.

"The Cretaceous fossil beds," replied Rick.

"Have you ever seen these animals alive?" asked Con.

"Not yet."

"Rick has studied paleontology at the graduate level," said Green.

Con muttered, "Some guide!" just loud enough to be heard.

Rick flushed at the remark, then noticed Green was glaring at him as if this were his fault. *Great,* Rick thought, *this is the girl Green wants me to baby-sit.* Up to then, his first impression of her had been a good one. She did not have that rich person's face like her father and his fiancée or, for that matter, Peter Green. Her features appeared natural, not altered to fit the current fashion. Rick took that as a good sign. She had the trim body of an active person, and her hazel eyes had an intelligent look. After her snide comment, he feared all those things were simply superficial, and she was a rich, spoiled brat after all.

6

CON WAS NOT USED TO CHAMPAGNE AND SHE CLIMBED
the stairs to the time machine with a little difficulty. She
hoped no one noticed. Aware that she was not in full control,
she regretted that third glass. She had already insulted the
guide. Hopefully, she would not fall on her face also.

She was led to a high-backed seat that appeared more comfortable than it really was. It seemed to have been designed
for a much larger person. Certainly, its molded contours did
not match her body. After she sat for a moment, the seat's
sides moved and gripped her waist snugly. Con let out a
surprised squeak. Her father grinned. "Didn't you listen to
Peter's warning?" She didn't answer. She was fighting to
subdue her growing unease. The idea of time travel had suddenly been transformed from an abstraction to imminent reality.

The stairway silently rose as the opening in the floor
closed up. To Con, it seemed that the edges of the opening
simply grew together like a rapidly healing wound. Soon
there was no evidence that there had ever been an entrance
to the cabin. Joe announced they would depart in a few
minutes, then disappeared into the control room. Con avoided
looking at the column in the center of the cabin. The thing
inside it made her dizzy, and she was already feeling dizzy
enough. Instead, she stared at the viewscreens on the opposite
wall.

The image on the viewscreens shifted, and instead of displaying the fence, they showed the ground of the courtyard.
There was a sense of motion, and the viewscreens revealed
that the time machine was rising rapidly. The building below
was lost in an irregular patch of darkness set in a grid of

lighted streets. The machine entered a cloud, and the view momentarily dissolved into dark gray. The image of the city reappeared on the screen, though this time it was delineated by radar or some similar means. The pattern of streets and buildings receded rapidly. The view changed again, and Con gazed at the tops of moonlit clouds.

"How high up are we going?" asked John.

"About twelve miles," answered Green. "Then we'll commence time travel."

A few minutes later, the saucer slowed to a stop. Con nervously waited for something to happen. At first, she noticed no change at all. The cabin was eerily silent, and there was no sense of motion. Con was watching a viewscreen when something passed in front of her eyes. She couldn't make out what it was, but it emanated from the strange cylinder inside the transparent column. The cylinder was transforming, enlarging. Incorporeal tendrils shot out beyond the clear column into the cabin. They seemed to move about as if blown by imperceptible winds. The tendrils thickened into arching branches and became more numerous, yet retained the disturbing quality of seeming simultaneously real and illusory. *It's as if nothingness has taken on a form*, thought Con. What was even more disturbing was that the groping entities altered everything they touched. The column and the floor and ceiling surrounding it no longer existed. They had been transformed into writhing nothingness.

The nothingness grew and, to Con's horror, advanced towards her. She shrank back into her seat. If it had not tightly gripped her, she would have fled and cowered against the wall. *I'm drunk,* she told herself, but she knew that wasn't the cause of the frightening vision before her. An arch of dazzling fog enveloped Con's foot. She felt like it had been painlessly amputated. Another streamer flowed through her thigh, and it, too, was removed from her consciousness. Only when the nothingness washed over her like a wave did she regain a sense of her body. Now she felt like she was falling, that the solidity of everything around her had only been an illusion. There was nothing to hold on to. Nothing had substance, not even herself.

The sensation lasted for 65 million years or, perhaps, only

a nanosecond. Duration was irrelevant. Time, in any mean-
ingful sense, did not exist. Then it returned abruptly. Solidity
surrounded Con. Her body had reality again. The memory of
her surreal journey slipped from her mind almost instantly,
as if it were beyond her power to conceive of it. What remained was a faded disquiet, the echo of a forgotten nightmare. She wiggled a toe and felt it move. The ordeal had
left her unscathed. Then, to her surprise, she realized that it
had also left her sober.

Con gazed about the cabin. The transparent column
seemed virtually empty, the cylinder inside reduced to an
insubstantial, flickering thread. The viewscreens peered down
on cloud-flecked, blue-and-turquoise sea. The clouds glowed
gold in the late-afternoon light. Con peered at the faces of
her traveling companions. They looked relieved as the terror
of the journey faded.

The saucer began to descend, and Con could make out
more details of the sea below them. The water was so clear
that the drowned landscape beneath its surface was plainly
visible, like a topographic map drawn in shades of green and
blue. As they approached, she caught fleeting glimpses of
creatures that swam in the sea or flew above it. The images
on the viewscreens shifted toward the horizon. The island
she had seen in the holovision was visible in the distance,
standing out against a backdrop of shadowed mountains.

"There she is," said Peter Green, "Montana Isle."

"God, it's beautiful," exclaimed Sara.

"Sure is," agreed John.

The flight to the island took only a few minutes, but to
Con it seemed longer. She was anxious to leave the time
machine and its vague, yet disquieting, associations with falling. Also, their destination looked beautiful and peaceful. She
would be glad to feel it solidly beneath her feet and experience it with all her senses. Eventually, the time machine
halted a few hundred feet over the island, then gently descended. Only the viewscreens indicated that they had arrived—the landing was so soft that it had been imperceptible.
An opening formed in the cabin floor revealing stairs leading
down to sand-strewn rock. Warm, strangely scented air

flowed in. Con's chair relaxed its grip. The new world awaited.

PETER GREEN HAD slipped from the role of host to that of a guest. It was James Neville who gave the orders now. He rose from his seat and addressed Rick and Pandit. "I'll show our guests to their accommodations. You follow me with their luggage, then get started on dinner."

James led the guests down the stairway while Rick and Pandit scurried for their luggage. Pandit was obviously used to the drill, but the delay in seeing the island was torment for Rick. He grabbed a pair of bags and hurried after James.

The time machine stood in a flat depression among the rocks. It was evident that depression was partly artificial. Tops of some of the boulders had been neatly sheared off to level the landing surface. The path away from the landing site was also, in places, carved through rock. Rick was amazed that such effort would be expended on a mere trail. The path led to the interior of the island, dominated by a towering upthrust of dark gray rock. Rick surmised that the island was the remnant of the core of an ancient volcano, weathered until it was denuded of its mountain. Now it defiantly jutted out of the sea while wind, rain, and the weight of years slowly subdued it.

The island was small, not much more than a quarter of a mile at its widest point, and supported only sparse vegetation. Most was in the interior, where there was a small grove of trees. The path crossed through it into a clearing at the base of the outcropping. In the center of the clearing was an open-sided pavilion. It was a simple, rustic structure constructed of small trees and branches with a palm-thatched roof and a flagstone floor. It was furnished with a single large table, dining chairs, and a sideboard. The remaining three structures provided a startling contrast to the pavilion, for they were carved out of solid rock. Each featured a colonnade, which served as its outer wall.

"Mr. Green's quarters are on the left," said James. "Mr.

Greighton and Ms. Boyton will have the central unit, Miss Greighton will be on the right." As Rick carried John's and Sara's luggage to their quarters, he examined the structure more closely. The carving featured no embellishment, but was executed with great precision. Everything was square or rectangular in form. The planes cut into the stone showed no tool marks and were perfectly smooth, but unpolished. The colonnade gave the large room behind it an open, airy feel. Farther back into the rock were two additional rooms, a bathroom and a simple storeroom. Rick caught only a glimpse of the bathroom. All its fixtures were carved from rock and either coated with a sealer or highly polished. He placed the bags in the storeroom. In contrast to the bathroom, it was crudely finished. Its interior wall was covered with plaster, which supported several rows of wooden pegs. There was a simple wooden chest of drawers beneath the pegs.

James poked his head in the colonnade. "Don't look for light switches," he called out. "They work by command. Lights on." The ceiling, which previously had seemed featureless, began to glow. "You can tell them to get brighter or dimmer, too."

"What do you have to say?" asked Sara.

"Long as you don't get too poetic, they'll understand," replied James. "The water fixtures in the bathroom work the same way."

"I'm impressed," said John Greighton.

"I'm glad you're pleased," returned James. Then he turned to Rick. "Get Joe to help you with the linens, I want Pandit to start on dinner."

Rick headed back to the time machine feeling frustrated. *Here I am back in the Cretaceous, and, instead of exploring, I'm running around like a damn servant,* he thought irritably. He found Joe sitting in the time machine control booth relaxing and having a drink. "James says you and I are to make the beds."

"To hell with that," snapped Joe. "I'm a pilot, not a damn maid."

"Look, I'm only repeating what he said. No one told me about this extra crap either."

"Who does he think he is," said Joe angrily.

"Take it up with Green," Rick suggested. "You know him better than I do."

That remark effected an immediate change in Joe's attitude. "Hell," he said with resignation, "Green knows about this. Probably his idea. I guess I *am* a damned maid."

Joe helped Rick with the beds. Next, they hung mosquito netting in the dining pavilion and set up the table for dinner. The latter task was done under the watchful eye of James, since neither Joe nor Rick understood the proper way to do it. Before he sent them off to help in the kitchen, he gave them a quick lesson in the formalities of serving.

One of the aftereffects of time travel was a ravenous appetite. Fortunately, Pandit had prepared cold entrées in advance, so it did not take long to serve dinner. The meal provided Rick's first introduction to safari camp life. Used to the easy camaraderie of camps at fossil digs, he found the atmosphere at dinner appalling. He disliked the stuffy formality of the tablecloth, the elaborately folded napkins, and the fancy table setting, complete with china and crystal. He hated the class distinctions far more. On a safari, there were the guests and below them, in every way, was the staff.

JAMES NEVILLE PRESIDED over the meal like a ship's captain, the junction of the separate universes of staff and guests. He had dressed for the occasion. Indeed, everyone at the table was dressed as if they were at an elegant restaurant. Con had worn a dress at the insistence of her father, who dined in a white dinner jacket. To Con, it felt silly and pretentious. *Am I the only one who thinks we look ridiculous?* thought Con. *No, the guide does, too. I can see it in his face.*

Although Con had acquiesced to her father about the dress, she went barefoot in quiet defiance. He hadn't noticed. Indeed, John Greighton scarcely noticed his daughter at all. He spent most of the dinner discussing vintage wines and investments with Peter Green, who seemed very knowledgeable in both areas. Con thought they were strange expertises for a research scientist. She turned to Sara for conversation, but soon tired of her monologue about the upcoming wedding. Nothing else seemed to interest Sara, neither their journey nor the island. All the other diners, with the exception of Mr. Neville, seemed completely blasé about their surroundings. They behaved as if nothing wondrous had happened, as if they had voyaged 65 million years merely for exotic decor.

Con finished dinner in silence. By then, she had begun to sense the return of a familiar pattern. Her father, having purchased a symbol of parental affection, had assumed it would substitute for the genuine article. His claim to Constance renewed, he had turned his attention to other matters. Con was not surprised it had happened; she had been through it before. What surprised her was that it still hurt.

ONLY WHEN THE after-dinner cognac was served, did Rick, Joe, and Pandit sit down on rocks to wolf down leftovers. Then there was the cleanup, followed by setting up the staff compound. The compound was put up out of sight from the guests and consisted of three tents—a kitchen tent, a sleeping tent, and a latrine tent. In contrast with the carved stone guest quarters with voice-activated lights, the staff compound was basic, even primitive. It was like the camps in the desert that Rick was accustomed to. There was no electricity and no bathing facilities beyond a plastic tub. The sole convenience was a water hose.

Throughout the work of setting up camp, James pushed himself harder than anyone. He was an exacting taskmaster, but he obviously knew his trade. Under his direction, the process of setting up camp went quickly and smoothly. The resentment Rick felt toward James abated. *Joe's probably right*, he thought. *My extra duties were Green's idea. James is just doing his job.*

Once camp was set up, James allowed everyone, except himself, the rest of the evening off. "I'll tend to any of our guests' requests," he said. "Just get a good night's rest, tomorrow will be busy."

Rick discovered that an additional aftereffect of time travel was exhaustion. The work had not been that strenuous—he was used to much harder—but it had left him bone tired. It was dusk, and the thought of sleep was almost irresistible. Almost. The lure of this unexplored world was even stronger than his fatigue. He wandered toward the shore.

A path led him to a cove. Its rocky walls enclosed a sandy beach. The water glowed silver against the dark rocks, and its waves painted the sand with the colors of the evening sky.

"Pretty sight. Especially this time of day."

Rick turned to see Joe sitting on a rock, watching the water. "I'm finishing that drink you so rudely interrupted," said Joe with a friendly tone. "Care to join me?"

"Thanks, but I only drink beer."

"Beer weighs too much when you're counting every gram of cargo. Though, I figure if Greighton was a beer drinker, we'd have packed a dozen cases."

"Somehow," said Rick, "he doesn't seem the type."

"Good thing, or you and I would get to bring only one change of underwear."

"I believe you," said Rick. "I waited on those people at dinner. Fancy china . . . champagne . . ."

"Green has a thing about champagne."

"The daughter was wearing a dress, for God's sake. A dress, out here. Who was she trying to impress?"

"The rich, if you haven't noticed, are different from you and me," said Joe. "Hell, they even look different now."

"I thought the girl might have been okay. I mean, she wasn't redone."

"Bet she's souped, though."

"Genetically enhanced?"

"Sure," said Joe. "All rich kids are. You served tonight, bet she ate like a pig."

"Five helpings."

"Yep," said Joe. "Probably has the metabolism of a hummingbird. That's how she keeps that nice slim figure."

"Then she's probably smart, too," said Rick.

"*And* sassy." Joe chuckled. "Just you remember what 'rich' rhymes with. It begins with a 'B.' "

"I'm afraid you're right."

Joe and Rick silently watched the waves, each caught up in his own thoughts.

"I don't get this setup," said Rick after a while. "Some of it's the height of technology and the rest is downright primitive. Why don't we have a power hookup? The guests' quarters have voice-controlled lighting while our kitchen has only a small propane-powered refrigerator. We're washing dishes in cold water. A lot of the basic stuff is missing. It doesn't make sense."

Joe looked down and shook his head. "Green was worried about you. I can see why."

"What do you mean?"

"Look, I don't speak for the man. Don't want to. But I know him, and I know he doesn't like questions. That's why you're our naturalist. He wanted a college kid rather than some scientist."

"You don't need a degree to be a scientist, just curiosity."

"Curiosity's exactly what Green wants to avoid. He wants this place kept secret."

"Then why build a resort?"

"He has his reasons," said Joe, "and you don't want to know them."

"Why even pretend you can keep this place secret? Those guest quarters must have involved a massive construction crew. Surely, some of those people have talked by now. It's pointless to be so hush-hush."

"There was no construction crew."

"Are you telling me Green built this place without help? That's absurd."

"Green didn't build this place," replied Joe, "he found it." He looked at the stunned, puzzled expression on Rick's face. "There, now you know too much already."

"But . . ."

"I told you so you'd keep your mouth shut. I'm not going to tell you more, and, if you have any sense, you won't ask any more questions. Focus your curiosity on this place"—Joe swept his hand over the sea and the land beyond—"not on Green's business. Trust me, it's safer."

Rick sensed that Joe's warning was earnest, and he tried to suppress the questions that bubbled inside his head. He watched the waves roll into the cove, hoping they would calm him and wash his mind clear. As it grew darker, he spotted something strange about the water. "Joe, are my eyes playing tricks, or is that stretch of water glowing?"

"It's some kind of field that protects the beach. Don't ask me what it is, it was already here when we came."

Rick could now make out a dimly glowing band of shifting colors that stretched through the water at the entrance to the cove. As he watched, a portion of the band glowed briefly brighter. It silhouetted a huge eel-shaped creature under the water. It turned sharply, flaring out its flippers and twisting into a "C" shape when it contacted the band. Then, with a powerful thrust of its tail, it sped off into deeper water.

"What the hell was *that*?" asked Joe in astonishment. "It looked thirty feet long!"

"A mosasaur," replied Rick, "From its size, I'd say a *Tylosaurus*."

"A what?"

"A marine reptile, related to the monitor lizards. A carnivore."

"Damn!" said Joe. "I don't care if this beach's protected, I'm not going in the water."

"Heck, there was—or I guess I should say—there *is* a crocodile around here called *Deinosuchus* that's fifty feet long."

"Double damn! That thing out there was big enough!"

Rick stared into the darkening sea, hoping to catch another glimpse of the mosasaur, but it did not return.

7

CON WOKE TO THE TOUCH OF A COOL BREEZE FLOWING
over her bare legs and feet. She remained still, enjoying the
sensation. She had drawn aside the curtains strung across the
colonnade of her room the previous evening so she could
view the grove beyond. It made her feel like she was outdoors. Brought up in a high-rise amid a sprawling city, it was
the first time she had ever been close to nature. The experience was well worth any loss of privacy. Besides, privacy
wasn't much of a concern on a world that contained only
eight people.

Despite the impression that the colonnade was completely
open, there was some sort of imperceptible barrier that kept
insects and even dust from passing between the columns.
Con had discovered it yesterday by noting its trace on the
floor. Inside the barrier, the floor was immaculate, while beyond it, dirt and dead mosquitoes clearly marked its boundary. Fortunately, the invisible protection did not shut out the
breeze.

Now, as predawn twilight slowly illuminated the world,
Con listened to the rustling of leaves and savored the air that
moved them. Its richness made her realize that she had lived
her entire life smelling millions of chemicals and pollutants.
Here, they were gone, and the very experience of breathing
was altered. The pristine air had cleansed the taints of civilization from her nose while she slept, revitalizing her sense
of smell. She became aware of the rich mixture of fragrances
that wafted in with the breeze. There was the tang of the sea,
the herbal scents of spring and hundreds of other smells her
mind could not wrap in words, but only experience on a
deeper, more primal, level.

There was one puzzling scent that was both new and vaguely familiar. Con breathed in deeply, seeking it out. Eventually she recognized it. It was her own body. *How strange I don't know my own smell,* she thought. On further reflection, she decided it wasn't strange after all. Mingled with her own scent were the obscuring perfumes of shampoo, soap, and deodorant. Con breathed deeply searching for her essence. She liked the concept of her uniqueness borne on the wind. *No more perfumes,* she resolved. *I'll wash in pure water and smell like myself.*

The trees, which had been but shadowy shapes earlier, assumed form and detail as the light grew. For the most part, they looked ordinary. They were predominantly conifers mixed with a few small broadleaf trees. Except for the absence of grasses and the profusion of cycads, plants that resembled crosses between giant pineapples and palm trees, the woods outside could have been an unkempt city arboretum.

Flying among the branches were pale creatures which Con at first assumed were birds. Only when one flew close did she recognize it was a small pterosaur. It veered away with a flap of its sickle-shaped wings and landed outside the dining pavilion. As it alighted, the pterosaur leaned forward so the paws in the middle of its wings rested on the ground. The tips of its folded wings were held upwards, out of the way. It entered the pavilion through a gap in the netting and began searching the floor for scraps. Soon it was joined by several of its fellows. They scampered about on all fours, wingtips waving comically.

Con got out of bed, pulled on a pair of shorts, and walked very slowly toward the pavilion for a closer look. The pterosaurs ignored her. Utterly alien to them, she represented neither a threat nor an opportunity. Just when she was near enough to see that the animals were covered with fur, one of them found something edible. A second pterosaur tried to steal the morsel away, and the group soon erupted in a cacophony of cries that sounded somewhat like a cross between a squeal and a hiss. After a brief tussle, the victor flew off with its prize, pursued by the others. Con wandered away from the deserted pavilion.

RICK AWOKE WHEN the first rays of sunlight hit the wall of his tent. Rising with the sun was a habit he had acquired from hunting fossils in the desert. It took a groggy moment before he remembered that he wasn't in the desert and that the quarry he would seek still had meat on its bones. Once he realized where he was, his thoughts returned to the mystery that troubled him as he had drifted off to sleep—who, or what, had built the stone rooms in the cliff?

Rick reviewed all his possible answers to that question. Each seemed improbable. Perhaps some unknown civilization had risen in the Mesozoic. He recalled the speculative drawings of intelligent dinosaurs, bulbous-headed and looking remarkably like humans. Yet these hypothetical images envisioned a world where the dinosaurs had never become extinct and had, instead, evolved to fill mankind's role on the planet. So far, the fossil record showed that the cleverest animal in the Cretaceous was as smart as an ostrich.

Alternatively, the rooms might have been constructed by extraterrestrials. Yet, if they were made by aliens or intelligent dinosaurs, why did the rooms respond to English commands? *Maybe they respond to thoughts, not words*, Rick speculated. He wished he remembered enough Spanish to test that theory out. *Perhaps,* he reasoned, *they were built by other time travelers*. Yet considering the nearly infinite possible locations for the structures in space and time, it seemed an extraordinary coincidence that Green would have stumbled upon them. *Perhaps*, thought Rick, *a future Peter Green constructed the rooms to help his earlier self*. Rick wondered if it was possible to go back into the past to alter one's own life. The paradoxes associated with that idea set his brain spinning.

Rick did not have the temperament to lie in his bunk for long. He had always preferred fieldwork to theorizing. Problems and puzzles made him restless, eager to search for hard evidence. Besides, direct investigation seemed the most promising approach. Certainly, asking questions was out. Joe was not going to provide any answers. Rick was unsure why it was risky to speak to Green about the matter, yet that seemed to be the case, if Joe were to be believed. *Can I believe him?* wondered Rick. *But if he's lying about Green, he might be lying about the rooms also.*

Rick was up when he heard a noise outside the tent. There was the soft clanking of pots, then the sound of running water. He looked about and noticed that James's bunk was empty. Rick dressed and left the tent. He found James heating some water on the stove.

"Good morning, Rick. Care for some coffee?"

"You've read my mind."

James tossed a handful of grounds into the water and waited for it to boil. "It's camp coffee, I'm afraid. Pandit finds it appalling."

"Camp coffee's fine with me," replied Rick. "I grew up on it."

"So did I," said James. "We'll make a more civilized brew for our guests."

"Are they up yet?" asked Rick.

"Why don't you check," said James. "Mr. Green will want his breakfast in bed. The coffee should be ready when you get back."

RICK RETURNED TO the aroma of coffee. It seemed especially intense and made him think of camping with Tom.

"Should I wake Pandit?" asked James.

"Everyone's asleep, except the girl," answered Rick. "Her room's empty."

"She's not here," said James. "That means she's wandered off."

"She'll be all right," said Rick.

"You don't know that. As the guide, you're responsible if she stubs her bloody toe. Maybe you should skip coffee and find her," said James in a tone that made it clear it wasn't a suggestion.

Rick sighed as he rose.

James understood the cause for the sigh, and said, "That's the price we pay."

"What price?"

"Being nursemaids. Serving high tea to rich twits. Putting up. It lets us live in the bush. Maybe it's a devil's bargain, but . . ." James looked about. "I think it's worth it."

"That's why you're here?" asked Rick.

"I grew up on the Serengeti when it was still wild," replied James. "It was fading even then, but the animals were real." James paused, caught up in the memory. "Lions. Elephants. Antelope. They were something to see. There's nothing as magnificent as a wild animal. God's creatures, they are. I stayed until they were completely gone . . . had to . . . but even at its height, the Serengeti was nothing compared to this! This is Eden before the Fall! Perfect. Unspoiled."

"I suppose you're right," said Rick. "It's just no one told me about the . . . the price, as you put it."

"It won't always be like this. We're just starting. Eventually, we'll staff up. You'll be a proper guide by then."

"I hope so."

"First lesson—a proper guide protects his clients from themselves. Find that young lady and make sure she's safe."

Rick gave one longing look at the steaming coffee, then wordlessly walked toward the guest quarters.

CON STOOD ATOP the low cliff above the beach, watching the rising sun paint the sea with opalescent fire. Coming from an era where the rising oceans were barricaded behind massive seawalls, it was Con's first experience of a seashore's elemental pleasures. Everything was imbued with the thrill of discovery. Con closed her eyes and felt the sun's warmth on her face. She breathed deeply, relishing the scents of the seashore. The air was full and rich, moist with salt spray and laden with the essence of countless living things. Her eyes still closed, Con listened. The ever-present din of civilization was gone, leaving pure, unpolluted sound. She concentrated on the gentle rhythm of the waves until she imagined she could make out the sound of each drop, of each pebble and shell as it was rolled about. Con opened her eyes again and climbed down to the dancing water. As she walked across the cool, soft sand, the sea seemed to rush up to greet her.

This world was so completely different from her gray, artificial home that she could not contain her astonishment and joy. She trembled before its awe-inspiring beauty. *How long has it been since anyone experienced this?* she wondered. *Centuries?* She gazed at this newly found world, trying to absorb every detail. "I claim all this!" she called out. "I claim it for Con Greighton." She smiled at her conceit. *I can't claim this world. It's claimed me.*

RICK WENT TO Con's quarters to make sure she hadn't returned. They appeared empty. "Miss Greighton?" he called out softly. "Constance?" No answer.

Rick scanned the area with eyes sharpened by years of hunting fossils. One set of footprints diverged from the rest. Rick walked over to examine them more closely. He felt certain they were the girl's. She was barefoot and walked where the ground was soft, making a clear trail. It led toward the shore, but away from the protected beach.

THE MOSASAUR ROSE slowly to the surface of the sea. The thirty-foot-long reptile resembled a massive eel with a huge, pointed head. Breaking surface, it gulped air, then angled its exposed back to catch the first rays of the sun. It held its four flippers motionless and swam by sculling its powerful tail. The mosasaur's blood warmed and, as the night's sluggishness fell away, its hunger returned.

The creature knew through age-old instinct that the sea turtles were returning to the island to lay their eggs. Each

morning, female turtles could be found near the shore.
Exhausted from their nocturnal labors, they were easy
prey. The mosasaur's massive jaws and three-inch teeth
could easily crush a turtle's shell, exposing the soft meat
inside. Egg season was a time of plenty. With a deft
movement of its flippers, the mosasaur changed direction
and headed for the island to feed.

FROM THE CLIFF, the beach had appeared to be littered
with cobblestones, but when Con had reached the sand
she discovered the "stones" were actually shells. They
were like none she had ever seen. Many were large—the
sizes of apples and grapefruit, and some were bigger than
dinner plates. There were neat symmetrical coils and
wildly twisted tubes. Some were smooth, while others
were ruffled like petticoats. Con vaguely remembered a
name from her biology book. *Ammo-something.* She recalled they were somewhat like squids. The fossilized
shells pictured in the text were dull gray, but these were
vividly colored and patterned.

Con gathered up shells as she walked until there were
too many to carry. She deposited her collection on the
sand and went off to get more. There was such an abundance of choices, it was difficult to make selections.
Within a short time, she had gathered a sizable pile of
shells. She sat down to examine them. The sand about
her was marked by the tracks of sea turtles, but, intent
on her treasures, she didn't notice them.

The shells' hues ranged from warm earth tones to stark
white and black to iridescent shades of pink and blue.
Many of the shells were banded with elaborate, contrast-
ing designs. Even worn and broken ones were beautiful,
revealing an intricate pattern of inner partitions. Con had
decided that the three-inch pink shells were her favorites
when she spotted the same shade in the middle of a small
wave. She rose for a closer look and saw a small flotilla
of pink shells suspended in the clear water. They moved
together in a coordinated manner, like a school of fish.

Con waded out for a closer look. The first thing she

noticed was the animals' large eyes, which resembled those of cats. In front of the eyes was a mass of short tentacles. Occasionally, a pair of longer tentacles would flash out from this mass to seize some swimming prey. Just as quickly, the long tentacles would contract back to the shorter ones, which would writhe briefly as the animal fed. The ammonites did not scatter at Con's approach, but maintained their distance. Con waded deeper until a wave splashed her shorts and shirt. She looked at her dripping clothes—another civilized convention, like perfumed soap—then at the empty beach. "This is ridiculous," she said out loud, returning to shore. Impulsively, she shed her wet clothes, then reentered the water.

Con had never been skinny-dipping, and, as she waded toward the shellfish, she felt daring and free. The wind and water caressed her bare body. It was a mildly erotic sensation, yet one that seemed completely appropriate. The last barrier between her and nature was gone. The ammonites retreated toward deeper water in pace with her advance. When the water reached her breasts, Con gently pushed off the sandy bottom and drifted. She floated where the waves pushed her, lifting her head only to gulp air. She watched the ammonites, blurred by her underwater vision into pink planets. They seemed to accept her and swam closer.

I'm being reborn, thought Con. Botticelli's painting, *The Birth of Venus,* came to mind. Con pictured herself rising, newly made, from the ocean—nude and borne upon a seashell. It was an absurd but compelling idea. Con surrendered to its imagery and let the current carry her farther from shore.

RICK TRIED TO stifle his irritation as he rehearsed in his mind what he would say to Greighton's daughter when he found her. "Excuse me, miss, but I was concerned for your safety." *Too stuffy*. "Hey, Constance, what's up?" *Too lame*. "Mr. Neville ordered me to check on you." *Too blunt, but true.*

This job was not turning out as he had envisioned. Rick

saw a guide as part explorer and part teacher. He wished to share his interest in the Cretaceous, more as an enthusiast than as an authority. Apparently, Green and James conceived of his position far differently. Green had touted him as an expert. It was a claim that Rick would never have made. As a scientist, he was aware of how little he, or anyone, really knew about this period. At least, James recognized that Rick would have to learn on the job. Yet James, as well as Green, seemed to expect him to be a nursemaid, entertainer, and servant to the guests. Rick felt uncomfortable and ill suited for such a role. He had little idea how to fill it.

The path grew stonier, and the footprints became harder to spot. Rick thought less about his job and more on tracking the girl. *Surely, she's safe somewhere, watching the sunrise,* he thought. *The sooner I find her, the sooner I'll get my coffee.*

Despite his immediate task, Rick had to resist being distracted by his surroundings. After all, this was the Cretaceous. Everything, from the smallest insects and plants, constituted a new discovery. Objectively, he recognized that he came from a time where human development, introduced species, and global warming had impoverished the biosphere. The landscapes Rick was familiar with were depleted and weedy. In comparison, even this tiny island seemed overflowing with abundance. He wondered if a twentieth-century visitor, someone from a world that still contained wild tigers and rain forests, would find this island equally astonishing.

The tracks approached a low cliff overlooking the sea, then ended. Rick walked to the edge and looked down on the beach for signs of the girl. About thirty yards to his left, he spotted her footprints in the sand. They disappeared at the edge of the surf, then reappeared sporadically farther down the beach. They led to a pile of shells and a wad of clothing before vanishing into the sea.

Rick's speculations about biology were instantly forgotten. He wildly scrambled down the cliff. As soon as he reached the beach, he began to run.

CON DRIFTED, ALMOST in a trance. The sea rocked her
and washed her thoughts clean. Last night was forgotten.
Daddy and Sara were forgotten. Only calm remained.
Then, as she raised her head to breathe, a jarring sound
shattered her tranquillity.

"Constance!"

Con turned and saw the guide running down the beach.
Embarrassment surged through her. *Does he know I'm
naked?* A worse thought came. *He's been watching me!*
She was about to flee to deeper water when she heard
him shout again.

"Get out of the water!"

There was something in his tone that stopped her
cold—a note of fear, even panic. She saw that he was not
looking at her, but farther out to sea.

Con was gripped by Rick's fear and began to swim as
fast as she could toward the shore. When she reached the
shallows, she rose to her feet and began to run. The water
slowed her movements like in a nightmare where everything is slow motion. Rick dashed into the waves, extending an arm. Where the water was as high as Con's
knees, they met. Rick grabbed Con's arm and wrenched
her toward him. She almost fell. As she staggered to regain her balance, something caught the corner of her
eye—a huge dark shape moving in the water.

The mosasaur snapped its jaws on the empty water
where, just an instant before, Con's legs had been. The
momentum of its final burst of speed carried it toward
the beach. Its underside scraped against sand and, as the
wave receded, the reptile was momentarily exposed. It
peered around in confusion and saw its prey standing out
of reach on the shore, staring back.

Con gazed in horror at the cold green eye that watched
her. There was no question that she was staring at death
itself. Beneath the eye was over two feet of triangular
teeth. The reptile was an ambush hunter that expended
its energy in a single savage burst. Foiled, it displayed
no more emotion than a sprung trap. A wave washed over
the three-foot head. The water churned as the creature

bent like a serpent and twisted back into deeper water. A final thrust of the mosasaur's powerful tail splashed both Con and Rick as it disappeared.

Con swung around and glared wildly at Rick. Terror, shock, and embarrassment transformed into hysterical rage.

"Don't look at me!" she screamed.

Rick stood transfixed, his expression unreadable.

Con struck him, scraping his face with her nails. "Go away!" she cried, as she hit him again. "Leave me alone!"

Rick passively submitted to her blows. Frozen by awkward confusion, he had no idea how to react.

As suddenly as it arose, Con's anger dissolved. She ran sobbing to her wet, sandy clothes and quickly dressed.

When she dared to look at Rick, he stood a short way down the beach, touching a cut on his face.

"Just go," yelled Con. "I'll be all right."

Rick seemed struggling to say something, but remained speechless.

"Go!" screamed Con.

Hesitantly, Rick turned and walked away.

8

CON SAT ON THE BEACH AND WEPT. CONTRADICTORY emotions swept through her, waves of an inner storm that batted her one way, then another. She trembled as she imagined those cruel teeth tearing her apart, staining the water red as she dissolved into nothingness. There was no emotion in the nightmare eye that burned in her memory. It said, "You are merely food. Your existence, your pain mean nothing beside my hunger." Yet the eye was gone . . . foiled. She had

survived unscathed. Relief swept over her and grew into
giddy jubilation. She was so happy, if she could only stop
crying, she'd shout. Shout to the world how good it was to
be alive. Beautiful. The world was beautiful. As lovely as a
tapestry. Yet, the tapestry hid monsters. Now she could smell
their breath—the stench of death. The lovely vision that had
enthralled her that morning was shattered. A feeling of profound loss overwhelmed her. Con, racked by sobs, mourned
her innocent paradise. The bliss of floating with the ammonites had been defiled. She had not risen from the sea like
Venus, she had been chased naked to . . . *the guide! What
must he think?* Humiliation gripped her. *So stupid! I've done
everything wrong. How can I ever face him?*

Con replayed everything over and over until she was emotionally drained. Nothing was resolved. Then she recalled
stories of her namesake, the pioneer woman. *That Constance
faced worse than this,* she thought. It was small comfort. *She
was made of sterner stuff.* Still, thoughts of her ancestor's
trials—tales of panning gold while nine months pregnant—
made Con cease crying. She peered about and saw she was
alone. The sun had risen higher in the sky and had lost its
rosy color. Its hot light revealed a different landscape, harder
and stripped of fancy. With one last convulsive sigh, Con
rose. With wariness and with trepidation, she walked to the
water and attempted to wash the redness from her eyes. She
doubted she had succeeded. Then she walked back to camp.

JOE LOOKED AT Rick's battered face with wry amusement as they walked to the aircraft. "You *sure* have a
way with the ladies. Most guys would get smothered with
kisses when they saved a girl's life, but not you."

Rick remained silent.

"So what happened?" asked Joe. "You say something
wrong?"

"I didn't say anything," replied Rick.

"Nothing?"

"Not a word."

"You're kidding!"

"It was an awkward moment. She was . . ." Rick hesitated.

"She was *what?*" queried Joe.

"She was unclothed."

"So? You must have seen a woman naked before." Joe looked at Rick and read his expression. "No! Don't tell me . . . you've gone through college with your nose in a book."

"More like a rock."

"No girls at all?"

"I'm not gay, if that's what you're asking."

"Just shy," said Joe.

"I've had girlfriends. But they were friends. Friends and colleagues."

Joe snorted. "That Greighton girl's sure no 'colleague.' Not likely she'll be your friend, either. So what'd you do, just walk away?"

"She told me to."

"Oh man, that's ignorant! She was probably hysterical," said Joe. "She needed comfort. Someone to talk to, no matter what she said."

"What makes you an expert?" countered Rick.

"I'm no expert, but I know a thing or two. You have to listen with more than your ears. Women don't always say what they mean."

Rick sighed. "I feel like a dope."

"Good . . . then our little chat taught you something." Joe looked at Rick's downcast face. "Don't worry," he said more gently, "it's curable."

AS CON APPROACHED the compound, she smelled the aroma of cooking bacon. It was a comforting smell, and it made her aware of how hungry she was. She went straight to the dining pavilion and found her father seated with Sara and James. There was a silver coffeepot on the table along with platters of omelets, muffins, bacon, and a large bowl of fruit. Sara was taking grapes from the bowl and feeding them to John, one at a time. Engrossed

in one another, they didn't notice Con until she reached
the table.

"What have you been doing?" Sara asked, staring at
Con's disheveled hair and damp, sandy clothes. "You're
a mess."

John Greighton glanced at his daughter. "Go change
before you eat."

"Daddy, something happened. I . . ."

"Tell me when you're properly dressed."

"But . . ."

"Now!" he commanded.

Con tried to remain composed, but felt sobs welling up
inside her. She quickly turned and retreated toward her
quarters before she burst into tears.

"Well, *she* has an attitude," said Sara. "You've spoiled
her, John."

"My ex did that," he replied. He leaned back in his
chair with his hands clasped behind his head "Now why
don't you spoil me? I'd like some of those strawberries."

Sara smiled and, placing a berry between her teeth,
leaned over, and fed it to John.

James sat and silently sipped his coffee, his face as
bland as the brew in his cup. He was playing "the host,"
genial and discreet. He understood that to people like
John and Sara he was only "the help," a species of human
wallpaper. The family drama had unfolded before him
without his comment. He knew none was expected or
desired.

WHEN CON RETURNED, rinsed off and in fresh clothes,
she found James seated alone at the pavilion. "Your father and Miss Boyton have finished breakfast and left for
the beach. The protected one," he said pointedly. "If
you've forgotten where it is . . ."

"I remember," said Con in a small voice.

"Good. Would you care to eat something, Miss Greighton? I fear the omelets and bacon are cold. I can have
Pandit make some fresh."

"You needn't bother, this is fine. I'm famished."

"Nothing like a little adventure to whet the appetite," said James. He watched Con flush red.

"He told you?" said Con, with a flash of anger.

"I had some questions when I saw his face," replied James evenly. "I'd like to hear your version. I need to know if he acted properly."

"What did he tell you?"

"Only that you had a near miss with some sea creature, and you might be upset. Is there more I should know?"

Con blushed under James's intense gaze. "No," she muttered.

"I'm relieved to hear that," said James.

"Does . . . Does my father know?"

"I thought you might want to tell him yourself."

"Why bother?" said Con bitterly. "He has other things on his mind."

"Indeed," said James dryly.

"The guide . . . uh . . . Rick . . . where's he?"

"I sent him with Joe on a reconnaissance. I think they just left. I don't expect him back until this afternoon. His face should look better by then."

"Would you . . . Would you thank him for me? I . . . uh . . . forgot."

"Certainly." James rose. "If you don't mind, I have to go over today's menu with Pandit. If you want anything, just ring this bell." James placed a small silver bell in front of Con and departed. She finished breakfast alone. Afterward, she returned to her quarters, pulled the curtains and flopped down on her bed.

9

THE PATH JOE AND RICK FOLLOWED WAS LIKE THE ONE
leading from the time machine's landing site. It, too, was
carved in places from solid stone and ended at a circular
depression. Placed in the center of the circle was an object
that Rick first thought was a sculpture. It appeared made from
crystal and onyx. "That's our plane," said Joe.

Rick realized that the graceful object before him was not
an artist's expression of flight, but an engineer's means to
achieve it. The "crystal" portion of the plane consisted of a
clear bullet-shaped tube. Within the tube floated three pairs
of seats, with a seventh single seat in the front. There was a
sloping panel, no thicker than a pane of glass, in front of that
seat. From the panel protruded switches leading Rick to assume it was the pilot's controls. Behind the transparent portion of the fuselage was the "onyx" portion of the plane. It
was less the color black than the absolute absence of light,
without highlights or shadows. This part of the plane in-
cluded a stubby set of wings, tipped in silver, and a graceful
V-shaped tail. Under the wings were swellings that Rick
guessed were the plane's engines although it was hard to see
them against the fuselage. The aircraft rested on a tripod of
delicate-looking legs, which ended in broad, flat disks.

"Ain't she a beauty," said Joe.

"It looks like it's already flying," said Rick. "I've never
seen anything like it."

"She's one of a kind," replied Joe.

"Why is it so black?" asked Rick.

"Touch it," answered Joe.

Rick walked over to the wing and placed his hand on it.
"It's cold," he said in astonishment.

"Its surface is a kind of solar panel, a damn efficient one. It absorbs more than the visible spectrum. That's why it's cold"

"Do you mean this plane's solar-powered? What if we fly into clouds?"

"It runs on stored energy," answered Joe. "The panels just keep it charged."

"This is amazing technology!" said Rick. "Why doesn't Mr. Green . . ."

"Do you want to fly or ask questions?" asked Joe sharply.

"Fly," said Rick meekly.

"Right answer." Joe walked over to the black part of the fuselage. An opening appeared, and a broad silver ribbon emerged. When the ribbon touched the ground, it changed shape and became a set of steps. Rick watched this in astonishment, but said nothing. Joe turned, and said, "She recognizes me. Before we leave, I'll set her to recognize you, too." Joe partly climbed the steps and reached in the plane to retrieve two objects. He handed one to Rick. "Ever use a rifle?"

"No," replied Rick. "Couldn't afford a permit."

"No matter," said Joe. "These almost shoot themselves."

Rick examined the weapon in his hand. It felt light and only vaguely resembled a rifle. It was in the shape of a cylinder two inches in diameter and about thirty inches long. There was no muzzle, but one end of the cylinder was open. There were two pistol grips on the cylinder, one at the end opposite the opening and another in the middle. No triggers were visible. A second, shorter and thinner cylinder was mounted atop the rear of the larger one. Rick assumed this was a kind of scope. The grips and the scope were made from a dark gray plasticlike material, as were portions of the main cylinder. The rest of the weapon was same shadowy black as the rear of the plane.

"This button turns on the gauges and the targeting mechanism," said Joe, demonstrating. Three rows of different-colored lights appeared on the side of the weapon and a silver-colored trigger and trigger guard formed in front of the first grip. "You try it."

Rick pressed the button, and the trigger and the lights appeared.

"The line of red lights indicates your charge," continued Joe. "The yellow lights show the power setting, I'll explain that latter. The blue lights show your ammunition level. The fewer the lights, the lower the reading. Now look in the scope. See that yellow circle and a red dot in the center?"

Rick looked and nodded.

"Fix that dot on something," said Joe, "and pull the trigger."

Rick located the dot on a tree trunk and pulled the trigger. The dot started blinking and the gun immediately felt different in his hands. Rick looked up from the scope to see if Joe had gripped the gun's barrel. He hadn't.

"Try to move the gun," said Joe.

Rick complied. Some force kept the weapon pointed at the tree.

"Didn't I say it almost shoots itself?" said Joe, grinning at Rick's startled look. "Pull the trigger again."

Rick did so and the force gripping his weapon relaxed instantly. "What does this thing shoot?" he asked. "Laser beams?"

Joe pulled a lever on his gun. The rear cover of the cylinder popped open and a clear tube slid partly out. He removed the tube and handed it to Rick. It felt very heavy for its size. Rick examined it and saw it was filled with what appeared to be loose, metallic-colored sand.

"It shoots that silvery stuff," said Joe.

"Just sand?" said Rick incredulously.

"Just sand? You watch." Joe took the tube, inserted it into his gun, then flicked another lever. A trigger formed in front of the rear grip. "That was the safety," he explained. He sighted through the scope and aimed at a small pine tree. After pulling the trigger on the forward grip, he stopped aiming. The weapon remained pointed at a tree. Joe squeezed the rear trigger. The gun did not recoil, and the loud "crack" Rick heard seemed to come not from the barrel opening, but from several feet in front of it. The upper portion of the tree disintegrated into a powdery mist. The gun stopped pointing at its vaporized target.

"Damn!" exclaimed Rick.

"That's just one of its tricks," said Joe. He made some

adjustments on the gun, then aimed at a boulder. This time, Joe kept his eye on the scope and moved the gun slightly as he pulled the rear trigger. There was a sharp hiss, and a thin, glowing line appeared near the top of the boulder. Rick approached for a closer look.

"Don't touch it!" said Joe. "It's hot." He picked up a rock and used it as a hot pad to push the boulder. Its top slid back. The rock had been neatly sliced through. Rick immediately understood how the pathway had been carved.

"I'll show you the rest of the controls, then you can practice a little before we head out," said Joe. "The hardest part is getting down which trigger's which. You don't want to confuse them in a tight spot."

"Been in any tight spots?"

Joe smiled ruefully. "Plenty." Then he added, "But none here."

Joe demonstrated how to adjust the force and the width of the blast, how to fire single shots, controlled bursts, or continuously, and how to use the targeting system. Rick was amazed to learn that the gun could also track a moving target. Joe answered all of Rick's questions except those about the weapon's technology. Those he tersely rebuffed by saying, "proprietary information."

The instruction and following practice lasted much longer than Rick wished. He was impatient to be off. Eventually, Joe was satisfied with Rick's marksmanship and took his gun. Joe entered the plane, followed by Rick. Joe set the guns in their charging stations before taking his seat behind the control panel. Rick looked at the panel. The controls, like those in the time machine, were labeled with plastic tape. *Another prototype,* Rick thought.

"Grab any seat," said Joe.

Rick sat behind Joe so they could talk easily. Except for floating in air, the seat was identical to the ones in the time machine. Joe flicked a switch, and the control panel lit up. Simultaneously, Rick's seat grasped him. "Here we go," said Joe.

There was no sound of engines revving, just a noise like wind. Dust and bits of gravel flew up from the landing platform as if blasted by jets. Rick noticed that any debris that landed on the plane flowed off like water on greased metal. The sound of the wind increased, and the plane began to rise straight up.

The clear fuselage offered a perfect view of the beach and the sea beyond. As they gained altitude, the view expanded. Rick could see the drowned landscape of the sea's depths and shallows. Its larger denizens were visible also. A plesiosaur gracefully glided through a submerged ravine. Three immense ammonites, probably several feet in diameter, hung suspended in the clear water.

They rose just below the top of the island's mesa; then, Joe touched the controls, and the plane halted its ascent. For a moment, it remained still while the silver tips at the end of the plane's stubby wings expanded outwards until they formed the long, graceful wings of a glider. With another touch of Joe's hand on the panel, the plane soared forward. The floating seats compensated for the plane's every movement.

This technological marvel was lost on Rick. His thoughts were elsewhere. He was in a state of absolute bliss, barely able to contain his excitement. He was about to live his wildest fantasy. He was going to explore the past.

Joe had to shake him to get his attention. "Where to, Mr. Guide?"

CON LAY ON her bed, paralyzed by the tumult within. She wished the drawn curtains could black out everything, obliterate even the sounds and smells from outside. She had just experienced the most traumatic event in her life, and she felt sure no one here would really care. *Why bother telling Daddy? He'll barely listen before giving me a lecture.* This trip was her father's idea, and Con knew he wouldn't accept responsibility if something went wrong. That wasn't his style. *It would be all my fault.*

Or maybe he'll blame the guide, thought Con. *That would serve him right! The Peeping Tom!* Yet, even in her dark mood, Con realized that wasn't completely fair. He *had* saved her life. Still, she didn't have to like him. It was more than his spying that bothered her. *He's like so many people.* People who judged her without knowing her. People who assumed, because she was Constance Greighton, she was spoiled and snobbish. *They're the real snobs!* Even though the guide hadn't said anything, he had given her that look at dinnertime. Con was all too familiar with it.

Forget the guide . . . forget Daddy . . . and then there's Sara. Con wrinkled her nose at the very idea of confiding in her. *Sara's already acting like she's my stepmother.* Con suspected the closeness in their ages drove Sara to treat her like a kid. In her relations with Con, Sara would take her cues from Con's father. There would be no sympathy from her.

The rest of the people were strangers. James, Pandit, and Joe, like the guide, were merely help. They would be polite and guarded in their responses, that's all. *As for Peter Green . . .* The very idea of talking to him made Con uneasy. He reminded her of too many of her father's friends—polished on the outside, but cold and calculating.

That was everybody. *How strange,* thought Con. *Only seven other people in the world.* She felt very lonely. She missed her friends, people she could talk to. Con was desperate to talk and express her fears . . . her relief . . . her embarrassment . . . to someone who would listen and care. That would be impossible for two weeks.

Con remained in her quarters, melancholy and lethargic, until lunchtime. The smell of food lured her out. Regardless of her mood, Con always kept her appetite. Sometimes, it seemed like she was constantly hungry.

The fresh air bore the tantalizing aroma of Indian spices. As Con arrived at the dining pavilion, Pandit opened a covered dish to reveal several kinds of warm pastries. Her father and Sara helped themselves. Sara looked up at Con. "Done moping?" she asked in a perky voice.

Con flashed Sara a saccharine smile, grabbed a pastry, and wolfed it down.

THE AIRPLANE FLEW slowly, following the river. Rick
stared at the riverbank with rapt attention. Despite their
low speed and altitude, it was difficult to spot animals.
The trees grew right to the bank, hiding the creatures
almost as soon as they were sighted. They had mostly
seen crocodiles. Some of those had been immense, well
over thirty feet long. The high point, so far, had been a
small group of hadrosaurs, duckbill dinosaurs, drinking
at the river's edge. By the time they had circled back to
see the animals again, they were gone.

"If we're going to see much, we'll have to find some
open ground," said Rick. "Were you flying when they
recorded the ceratopids?"

"The what?"

"That herd of horned dinosaurs, you know, like *Triceratops*."

"Oh sure," replied Joe. "We're headed there now. Farther upriver, the trees thin out."

Joe guided the plane higher and increased its speed.
Gradually the trees below became sparser. They flew until they spied a herd of gray dinosaurs approaching the
river. Joe descended to just above tree top level as they
neared the herd.

The view was breathtaking. Over a hundred animals
moved together in a loosely defined group. They were
massively built quadrupeds with medium-sized tails held
above the ground and the bizarre heads of the ceratopids.
The largest individuals were twice the height of a man,
with heads that measured, from the tips of their beaks to
the edges of their frills, over eight feet long. Two long,
wicked-looking horns rose behind their eyes, and behind
the horns extended a broad, long frill, like a rigid cape
covering almost half the animals' backs. A third, stubby
horn grew behind their nostrils.

"What are those?" asked Joe. "Triceratops?"

"No," answered Rick, "although they're related. Judging from the size of the frill, I'd say they were a species
of *Torosaurus*."

"Is that frill some kind of shield?"

"Maybe," answered Rick. "It's not solid bone, though.

More like skin stretched over a bone framework. Until now, we could only guess its purpose."

They circled back for a second look. Rick discerned a pattern in the herd's formation. Most of the larger animals walked at the perimeter of the group, encircling its smaller members. "Look," he said to Joe, "they protect their young."

Even flying at its lowest speed, the plane quickly passed over the herd. Rick sighed in frustration. "Joe, this is driving me nuts! I've got to see them from the ground."

"You mean land? Are you crazy?"

"Don't worry, I'll be invisible."

"You don't look invisible to me," retorted Joe.

"These creatures have never seen anything like human beings. We won't register as friends or foes."

"How about as food?"

"Same thing. We'll be ignored."

"When did you make up this theory?"

"It's a documented fact," replied Rick. "Whenever humans entered a new environment, the animals paid no attention to them. Darwin wrote that he could lift birds off their perches on the Galapagos Islands."

"Those were birds," retorted Joe.

"The first Native Americans were able to wipe out the mammoth, the mastodon, the giant ground sloth . . . dozens of large mammals and the big predators too—sabertooth cats, dire wolves, lions . . . and they did it with stone tools."

"These are dinosaurs, man. Don't you go to the movies?"

"They're animals. They'll behave like other animals. Please, Joe, this may be my only chance."

"Your chance to become dinosaur shit."

"I've got that gun . . ."

Joe remained silent for a while, then suddenly banked the plane "Oh, what the hell," he said. "Just make sure your gun's settings are at kick-ass levels."

Joe landed in a spot about one hundred yards downstream from the herd. The ground was open, except for an occasional tree, and covered with a combination of ferns and other low plants. The herd's lead animals had reached the riverbank and halted. Those behind them continued to march, grazing as they walked. Eager for a closer look, Rick was up as soon as his seat released him. He grabbed a gun, turned it on, and adjusted the settings. "I promise I won't be long."

"There's no way you're going by yourself," said Joe. "Even an invisible man can use some back-up."

"You don't need to, Joe. I'll be okay."

"Then so will I."

"Thanks."

"My pleasure," said Joe in an ironic tone.

Despite what he had told Joe, Rick was nervous as they approached the dinosaurs. Viewed from the ground, the animals' huge size made a much stronger impression. The largest ones were twenty-five feet long and massively built. Rick could have walked underneath one and scarcely ducked his head. Rick and Joe continued their advance without any reaction from the herd. Finally, they were so close they could smell the herd's musky scent, hear them snort and pant, see the faint pattern of greenish brown stripes on their thick gray skins, and feel their footsteps shake the earth.

The herd was beginning to bunch up at the shore. "What are they doing?" asked Joe.

"My guess is that this herd is migrating. They're probably about to cross the river."

"Then why don't they do it?"

"River crossings are tricky. See how they're milling about? I suspect none of them is anxious to be the first one in the water. Up in Alberta, there's a fossil bed with hundreds of horned dinosaurs drowned or trampled crossing a river."

Rick was totally absorbed in watching the herd. It was Joe who first spotted the carnivores. He jerked up his gun and whispered loudly, "Look at those!"

Rick turned to spot a group of five, mottled green, bipedal dinosaurs following the herd. They appeared to be about ten feet long and five feet high. They held their torsos and stiff tails nearly horizontal. Folded against their torsos, like the wings of birds, were long arms that ended in three-fingered hands, tipped with large curved, claws. Their long, flexible necks were held upright. Their quick head movements reminded Rick of birds. The heads were terrible to behold, with large mouths filled with curved, pointed teeth and fierce yellow eyes peering above deep, rounded snouts.

"Dromaeosauruses," whispered Rick, "relatives of the *Velociraptor.*"

"Are they as mean as they look?"

"Meaner. You can't see their toe claw. It's extra big and shaped like a curved sickle."

"Let's get out of here."

"We don't look like their prey; we shouldn't act like it either. Better to stay still."

"That's not so damn easy," Joe whispered back.

"Just remember—to them, we're invisible."

"I don't feel invisible. Besides, what are they doing here? They can't take on one of those big, horned monsters."

"One theory is they're pack hunters. They might be following the herd looking for an opportunity, an animal that's vulnerable in some way."

The herd appeared to be aware of the carnivores, but not panicked by their presence. The Torosauruses occasionally lowered their horns to warn the pack of Dromaeosauruses to keep their distance. Each group followed its part in the dance of life and death that had been performed for millennia. Rick and Joe warily watched the Dromaeosaurus pack until it moved to the other side of the herd and was out of sight.

The pressure of the herd finally forced the lead animals down the bank and into the river. The water was brown and swollen by spring rains, but not deep. Near the shore, it only reached the ceratopsids' calves. Once the first animals entered the river, the herd followed. A peninsula of flesh extended into the river disrupting its flow. A sound resembling rapids arose as the current broke against the trunklike legs of the dinosaurs. Toward the farther shore of the river, the channel was deeper, and only the dinosaurs' broad backs and huge heads were above the water. The crossing at that point became more chaotic as the animals struggled against the current. One of the smaller individuals was swept downstream. The herd ignored its bellows and continued to cross.

The dinosaur was carried by the current about fifty yards to a stretch of water closer to the near shore. There it regained its footing. It stood motionless for a minute, catching its breath before wading to shallower water close to Rick and Joe. Only when the animal was almost at the riverbank did it head upstream to rejoin the herd. It moved slowly, limping with its right front leg.

Rick and Joe did not notice that the Dromaeosauruses had entered the river until they approached the stranded animal. Three cut off its path to the herd while the other two approached from the rear. The Torosaurus lowered its head so its horns pointed at the three predators blocking its way. It made a short, feinting charge, and they backed off. The Torosaurus was still shaking its head at its three foes when one of the other two Dromaeosauruses rushed and dug its claws into the Torosaurus's flank. The Torosaurus bellowed and whirled about. Its attacker released its grip and retreated.

Another Dromaeosaurus charged. It dug its claws into its victim's flank, straightened its arms, and jumped. As it rose, it slashed out with its large toe claw. The claw raked through skin and muscle. The Torosaurus, bellowing in pain, swung around, but its tormentor leapt beyond its reach. The drawing of first blood seemed to encourage the predators, for they moved in closer. Still, they attacked warily, quickly darting in and, just as quickly, retreating. Although the beleaguered Torosaurus was still able to fend off most attacks, the number of its wounds steadily increased. With each long, bloody gash, its ability to defend itself diminished. Eventually, it stood still, seeming unable or unwilling to move.

A Dromaeosaurus dug its claws into its prey's ribs and kicked repeatedly at its belly, tearing it open. Intestines tumbled out. The Torosaurus's hoarse, high-pitched wail seemed almost mournful to Rick. Spurred by pain, it sud-

denly twisted around and impaled its assailant with one
of its horns. The skewered Dromaeosaurus thrashed about
as the Torosaurus lifted and shook its head. After a minute, its attacker hung limp. The great horned head
drooped, and the carnivore slid off into the river. It
slowly tumbled in the current, its blood mingling with its
victim's. That was the Torosaurus's last act of defiance.
Its head remained drooped, yet it stood on unsteady legs.
Rick could hear its labored breathing. One of the Dromaeosauruses bit the intestines trailing in the river and
began to tug at them.

"How can you watch this?" said Joe, raising his gun
to fire.

Rick stopped him by putting his hand on the barrel.
"It's nature's way. You eat meat, don't you?"

"Not like that!"

"It's all the same in the end."

The four remaining predators swarmed over their helpless prey in a final frenzy of kicking and slashing. The
Torosaurus fell over on its side and lay still in the red-
stained water. The frenzy subsided. The Dromaeosauruses began to feed. After the violence of the kill, the
scene seemed almost peaceful.

As Rick and Joe watched the carnivores feast, they saw
the Torosaurus move one last time. A huge crocodile had
seized its tail. The Dromaeosauruses watched helplessly
as their meal was dragged off into deep water and disappeared.

"Why this is just a vacation paradise!" said Joe. "Let's
go."

Rick was reluctant to leave, but acquiesced. He turned
for one last look and saw the four remaining Dromaeosauruses crossing the river to follow the herd.

10

"THAT LITTLE DRAMA PUT ME OFF MY FEED," SAID JOE once they were airborne. "I suggest we find more suitable viewing for our guests."

Rick realized Joe was right; the raw struggle between life and death was not tourist fare. They needed to find more picturesque locales.

They roamed through the sky and found many places worthy of a return visit. On a plain between two foothills, they discovered a small lake that served as a watering hole. Its shores were visited by all kinds of dinosaurs, some of which were new to Rick. A larger lake had a low island that was a nesting site for a colony of *Anatosauruses*, duckbilled dinosaurs over forty feet long. The entire colony was engaged in constructing bowl-shaped nests from mud. They located a herd of sauropods using their long necks to browse in the treetops. Although these animals were not nearly as large as the giants of earlier periods, they still made an impressive sight. Farther north, Rick and Joe discovered a herd of ceratopsids that stretched over several miles. Rick counted at least seven different species of horned dinosaurs among the teeming thousands. This herd, like the one that crossed the river, seemed to be migrating. In its wake, the land looked trampled and bare. Following the devastation were packs of Dromaeosauruses. Later, they spotted a pair of Tyrannosaurs feasting on a carcass. There was too little left to identify the species of their meal. Above the feeding carnosaurs circled a pterosaur, waiting to scavenge their leftovers. It was the size of a small airplane. Returning over the inland sea, they located an island that was a rookery for tens of thousands of pterosaurs. Later, they spied a sandbar where dozens of plesiosaurs basked in the afternoon sun. Each time they located a memorable sight, Joe entered its position on a holographic map. By the time they returned to the island, Rick felt confident they had locations for several excursions.

Rick was in a buoyant mood as he and Joe walked back to camp. The island looked lovely in the low, clear light of late afternoon. A clean-smelling breeze blew in from the sea. Rick was excited and uplifted by what he had seen and felt fully recompensed for the morning that had begun so badly.

Peter Green was walking up the path as they neared camp. Rick flashed him a broad grin. Green did not return the smile as he stopped on the path. The grin quickly faded from Rick's face as he saw his employer's irate expression.

"Joe, go check in with James," said Green. "I need to talk to Rick."

As Joe left, Green riveted his eyes on Rick. Their coldness contrasted with his flushed complexion. "Where have you been?"

"I've been working."

"The hell you were. That girl was a pain in the ass all day."

"But James said to . . ."

"*I* hired you!" yelled Green. "You do what *I* say!"

"I can't guide if I don't explore first."

"*Nobody* gives me excuses. Especially not some goddamn kid. You get that?"

"How . . ."

"Shut up! I don't want to hear it. Get that girl out of the way. That's what you're here for, and that's what I expect. You pull your weight. Understand?"

"Yes," replied Rick, taken aback by Green's unexpected rage.

"Don't screw up again. I mean it!"

Peter Green turned on his heels and strode rapidly toward camp. He paused only once to call over his shoulder, "Go help with dinner."

Rick remained still, stunned by the outburst and unwilling to accompany Green on the path. When he recovered from his surprise, he became angry. *Green has no right to treat me like that!* In any other situation, Rick would have marched down and resigned on the spot. His general philosophy was "life is too short to put up with jerks." Yet this was not like any other situation. He felt stuck, but not because Green had the only ride home. On the contrary, it was being sent home that Rick feared most. Today he had seen his personal version of paradise, a place where he would do anything in his power to remain. If that meant abasing himself to a jerk, that was the price he must pay. As Rick walked back to camp, he swallowed his anger and pondered how best to make his boss happy.

WHEN RICK ENTERED the kitchen tent, Pandit was whistling merrily as he expertly chopped vegetables. The sides of the tent had been rolled up, leaving only the insect screens to serve as walls. Pandit was obviously in a good mood.

"Hello, Rick. Did you bring me a dinosaur to cook?"

"Not today."

"When you get into trouble, you should have something to show for it."

"News travels fast, I see," said Rick. "Heck, I thought I was doing my job. What happened here?"

"Miss Greighton was moody today."

"That's all? Green nearly snapped my head off."

"Miss Greighton's mood irritates her father, and Mr. Green is most displeased by this."

" 'Displeased' is an understatement," said Rick. "But you seem jolly enough."

"One finds moments for bliss." Pandit looked up the path leading to the kitchen tent, and said in a whisper, "Here comes one now."

Rick heard footsteps on the path and turned to see Sara part the screening of the tent. She was carrying an empty bowl. Her attire immediately caught Rick's attention. She wore a white pleated dress that reminded him of the clinging dresses in ancient Egyptian frescoes. It was gathered at the waist by a simple gold belt that matched her delicate gold sandals. These were but accessories; the principal adornment of the dress was Sara herself. Her

finely sculpted body was clearly visible through the translucent fabric. Pandit froze where he stood, unable to
glance away. Sara smiled slightly and, looking him in the
eye, acknowledged his adoration.

"We'd like more fruit," she said, handing him the
bowl. Without removing his gaze from Sara, Pandit filled
the bowl with strawberries, grapes, and cherries. She took
it, leaned forward and, in a breathy voice that smelled of
wine, murmured, "Thanks." Then she turned and strolled
down the path as if she were modeling on a runway.

"That woman requires prodigious quantities of fruit,"
said Pandit. "I wonder what she does with it."

"Whatever it is," replied Rick, "it hasn't spoiled her
figure."

Pandit nodded appreciatively. "Oh, to be rich!" he
cried. "That woman is a goddess! She is supernatural!"

"I believe the word is 'artificial,' " replied Rick dryly.

"Is not the point of existence to strive for perfection?"

"I'd hardly call her perfect."

"Of course," said Pandit. "As a naturalist, you prefer
Miss Greighton. A natural beauty."

Rick grimaced at the idea. "She's hardly my type."

"Then you are a hard man to please."

"I'm more concerned with pleasing Mr. Green. He told
me to help you with dinner."

"Do you know how to reduce a sauce?"

"No," replied Rick. "My specialty is warming up
pouches."

"I thought as much. You can cut up the tomatoes for
the ragout."

"Where are they?"

"Right in front of you," replied Pandit, pointing to
some large globes surrounded by papery green husks.
"These are wild tomatoes. I picked them this morning."

Rick picked up one of the tomatoes and examined it.
It resembled the tiny tomatilloes Tom used to make salsa
verde. This fruit was much larger than those; it was big
even for a tomato. He peeled back the husk to reveal a
deep red skin. "Pandit, tomatoes are cultivated plants,
they don't grow wild."

"They do here," said Pandit. "There are several tomato trees growing on the other side of the island. They produce the finest tomatoes I have ever tasted. There are fruits and berries also. Mr. Neville is correct, this place is truly Eden."

Rick peeled away the husk from the tomato and bit into it. Pandit was right—the flavor was exquisite. Then he examined the tomato as a scientist. Although the fruit seemed perfectly ripe, the seeds were immature—in fact—they appeared vestigial. *This is no wild plant.* He suspected it was genetically engineered. *Another artifact from the builders of the stone rooms?*

Rick made himself as useful as he could, while Pandit cooked with efficient artistry. Before long, the first course was ready to serve. Pandit sent Rick to inform James. Once Rick accomplished that task, he returned to the kitchen tent to help serve the meal.

The dinner guests arrived and seated themselves. Green and Greighton were formally attired, as was James. To Pandit's disappointment, Sara wore a modest evening dress. The girl showed up barefoot in a tee shirt and shorts. That caused the first scene of the evening. Her father seemed provoked by her outfit, for he angrily ordered her to change. Wordlessly, but with a slouch that spoke volumes, she left the pavilion. John Greighton stabbed his salmon spring roll in gingered balsamic vinegar sauce as if he were trying to kill it. "Some vacation!" he muttered. Upon hearing this remark, Green glared at Rick.

The spring rolls were cold, and John Greighton had consumed most of a bottle of Sauvignon Blanc before his daughter returned to the table. She was wearing a dress, but was still barefoot. "Better?" she asked with a sarcastic edge. Her father ignored her question and her lack of shoes.

The meal proceeded with an undercurrent of tension. Both James and Green tried to lighten the mood with cheerful conversation, but to little effect. After a while, they, too, lapsed into silence. The girl had succeeded in setting the tone for the evening. She sat sullen and quiet as she wolfed down her food.

Rick observed this with discomfort increased by the knowledge that he was expected to placate this girl. His continued employment clearly depended on his success. He had no idea how he would manage.

CON LAY ON her bed in her darkening room, still wearing the dress her father had forced her to wear. *I should go swimming in this damn thing,* she thought, *then wear it to dinner.* Yet the idea of swimming brought up memories of the cold, deadly eye. Despite the warmth of the evening air, she shivered. *Thirteen more days of this place! How will I ever make it?*

The guide's voice came from outside the drawn curtain. "Constance?"

"Go away."

"I can't."

"I'm not dressed, so don't come in."

"I'll wait here."

"I'm not coming out."

"I'll still wait."

Con lay on her bed and waited to hear retreating footsteps. She heard the wind in the leaves and the distant surf, but nothing else. Minutes passed without a sound from him.

"Are you still there?"

"Yes."

"What do you want?"

"Just to talk."

"There's nothing to talk about. Now go away."

"I can't."

"You're a real pest, do you know that?"

"I'm sorry, I don't mean to be."

"Well, I'm not coming out. You can stay there all night."

"That's okay, I brought a blanket."

Con could hear the soft sounds of a blanket being unrolled. *He's bluffing,* she thought. She found herself straining to hear him. His silence made her all the more aware of his presence. Ten, maybe twenty minutes passed, it was hard to tell.

"What are you doing out there?"

"Watching the stars come out. Even in the desert, they were never as clear as this. I can't make out any constellations, though. The sky's all different."

Con didn't answer, resolved to ignore him. She found that she couldn't. It both irritated her that he was there and piqued her curiosity. After another ten minutes of silence, she changed into her tee shirt and shorts and drew aside the curtain. The guide was lying on a blanket, gazing at the stars.

"How can the sky be different?" asked Con testily.

Rick sat up and flashed her a smile. "I'm glad you asked."

Con looked up at the stars. "There are so many!" she exclaimed, amazed despite herself. Then she hardened her tone. "Why are you bothering me?"

"I just need to talk."

"About what?"

Rick sighed. "I shouldn't have walked away this morning. I feel like a jerk."

"I forgive you. Now will you go away?"

"I was almost killed as a kid. It shakes you up bad. The world becomes a different, a scarier place."

"It does," agreed Con in a small voice.

"I had to talk to someone about it before it got better. I pulled you from the sea this morning, I'd like to help you the rest of the way."

Con slumped down on the stone step of her quarters. Rick moved to sit on the step a few feet away. "I can't talk about it," she mumbled. "It's too . . . too . . ." Con sniffled.

"It's all right," said Rick gently. "You can cry. It was a terrible experience."

Con seemed about to melt into tears when she abruptly stiffened and glared at Rick accusingly. "You were watching me!"

"No . . . *honest!*" said Rick. "James sent me to check on you. You were already in the water when I spotted you."

"God! I'm so embarrassed."

"Don't be. I've seen lots of women undressed," lied Rick. "I mean . . . everyone bathes in the river on fossil digs. You get used to it."

Con found herself wanting to believe him. "You must think I'm a real pain."

"Not at all. You were just enjoying yourself. I feel I let you down."

"You saved me! I should have thanked you instead of . . . of . . ."

"Don't worry about it. You were in shock. I only hope this place isn't ruined for you."

"I'm afraid it is. I just want to go home."

"Could you give it . . . give *me* . . . another chance?" pleaded Rick. "There's something I want to show you."

"What?"

"It's on the beach. This time, I promise it'll be safe."

Con sensed Rick's desire to make things good after the morning's disaster. He seemed so disarmingly earnest and humble, she couldn't remain mad at him.

"Please, Constance."

"All right," she said. "If you're sure it's safe."

"Guaranteed," Rick said buoyantly.

"Call me 'Con.' That's what my friends do."

Rick led Con along a path to the beach. A nearly full moon was rising, and the way was easy to see. When they reached the cliff over the beach, the moon had cleared the horizon. Con gazed at the moonlight sparkling on the sea and felt the return of the wonder she had experienced at the beginning of the day.

"The moon's so big," she said.

"It's closer to the Earth than it is in our time."

"Is that what you wanted to show me?"

"No, there's something else. We'll need to climb down to the beach."

They climbed down and sat on the sand away from the

surf. The sand was still warm, and the air was mild. Everything was peaceful.

"Nobody has experienced the world like this for thousands of years," said Rick in a hushed voice. They watched the waves for a while; then, Rick pointed to the surf. "Here they come."

Con started as she saw something moving in the water. Rick gently touched her shoulder, and in a calm voice said, "It's okay. The mother sea turtles are coming to lay their eggs."

As if by some secret signal, the surf became filled with dark, flat domes, moving like living stones through the foam. Soon pale, dark-eyed heads and long, curved front flippers became visible. Con watched in fascination as the turtles struggled up onto the beach. Their shells were about two feet long and leathery-appearing. Despite their ungainly motion on the land, the creatures' streamlined forms gave them a certain grace.

"Will we scare them away if we move?" asked Con.

"They'll ignore us," assured Rick.

Con got up and approached a turtle. The animal kept up her relentless struggle against the sand even when Con touched her. She found something noble in the creature's dedication to bring its young into the world. Soon, she was surrounded by turtles. "This is so incredible!" she exclaimed. "Nothing seems to stop them."

"Sea turtles survived into the beginning of our century," said Rick with a touch of melancholy. "There might even be a few left, ancient ones still searching for vanished beaches."

Con picked her way among the moving turtles back to Rick. "How did you know they'd be here?" she asked.

"I saw their trails this-morning. I've seen fossilized tracks just like them."

Con felt Rick's infectious excitement. "This place is really special to you," she said.

"Let me show it to you! Joe can fly us all over. We'll keep you safe. Just don't let this opportunity pass by."

"What about the others?"

Rick made a face. "They act as if this place is just a hotel. They don't seem to give a damn."

"So, you noticed," said Con.

"But you're different."

A turtle stopped just inches from Con's foot and started digging a hole in the sand with her rear flippers. It was slow work. "Can we stay here until she lays her eggs?"

Rick smiled to himself. "I wouldn't miss it for the world."

IT WAS LATE when Con returned to her quarters. While the turtles had labored, she and Rick had talked. Gradually Con had let her guard down as Rick provided the sympathetic ear she so desperately needed. Now, she felt unburdened and pleasantly sleepy. Tomorrow beckoned with a promise of adventure and escape. *Daddy and Sara can rot, I'll be soaring over a new world!*

Con had pulled open the curtains, so she left the lights off and entered the small storeroom to change. In the darkness, a thin yellow light caught her eye. There seemed to be something glowing beneath a crack in the plaster. Con's curiosity got the better of her sleepiness. She climbed onto the wooden dresser and dug her nails into the crack. A small slab of plaster flaked off to reveal what appeared to be a portion of a symbol. It glowed brightly on a glassy black surface.

Con got off the dresser, found her nail file, and climbed back up. She slipped the point of the file between the plaster and the smooth surface beneath. The plaster fell away easily. Con pried away the plaster to expose a glassy black rectangle inset into a stone wall. Within it, a strange design glowed in the dark:

$$\oplus\Phi : \oplus\Phi\triangle : \boxminus : \triangledown\triangle : \boxtimes\triangledown$$

Con climbed down and looked at it. Some of the elements in the design changed. The rightmost pair changed rapidly, while the third from the right changed more slowly, and the remaining ones did not change at all. The purpose of the design eluded Con. She was too tired to dwell on the puzzle for long. She went to bed and soon was peacefully asleep.

11

RICK WOKE UP FEELING VERY PLEASED WITH HIMSELF. HE had managed to pull it off and win Con over. He was still a little amazed by his feat. Apparently, he possessed hidden charms he wasn't aware of. Now Green would get off his case. He could remain on Montana Isle and explore the world around it.

The previous night had improved his opinion of Con. She might be a little screwed up, but he figured that was to be expected. John Greighton didn't seem like much of a father. Rick didn't understand why she gave a damn about what he thought; yet in a perverse way, she did. *That's her problem*, he thought. *At least she's not a snob like him.* It wouldn't be too hard to put up with her, especially since she was his passport to the Cretaceous. Rick figured that as long as he kept Con busy, Green would let him do anything he wanted. He planned to keep her very busy.

The aroma of James's camp coffee wafted through the mesh of the sleeping tent's window. Rick rose and quickly dressed. James was pouring himself a cup when Rick emerged from the tent.

"You seem chipper for keeping such late hours," remarked James.

"Con's going on a tour. I need to set up lunch. I plan to have her out most of the day."

James's lips formed a slight smile. "So Miss Greighton is 'Con' now?"

"We worked things out last night."

"I suspected you had the makings of a guide. It seems that I was right."

Rick beamed and poured himself a mug of coffee. He took a sip and was glad it was strong.

"I trust 'Con' will not be wandering off this morning?"

"I'm sure she'll sleep in. We were up late watching sea turtles lay their eggs."

"Turtle eggs? You should inform Pandit. I'm sure he would welcome the challenge."

Rick shook his head. "Everything's a potential meal to him."

"The man's an artist," replied James. "He's not going to be happy until you bring him a dinosaur to cook."

"I suspect you're right."

"I am," said James with assurance.

Rick finished his coffee and stood up. "I thought I'd carry that bottled water Con drinks up to the plane."

"I'll rouse Pandit and get him started on your lunch," said James. "Then you can leave whenever Miss Greighton desires."

"That would be great," said Rick. "Please be sure he makes a lot. She's a big eater." Rick grabbed a small cooler and walked over to the camp's refrigerator. He removed two bottles of water. As he did, he couldn't help think what a waste of energy and cargo space these bottles of lemon-flavored water represented. He shut the top of the cooler and headed up the path to the plane.

That was easy, Rick thought. He expected James to question his errand, since the bottles could have just as easily accompanied the lunch. *Probably he's so relieved we're going, he doesn't care.* When he reached the plane, a door formed in its side for him, just as Joe had set it to do. Rick deposited the cooler inside the plane, then turned to the real purpose of his visit.

Fishing out a hand lens from his pocket, Rick walked over to the boulder Joe had sliced with the gun the day before. He carefully examined the newly cut surface through the magnifier. It bore scoring that precisely matched that on the walls of the stone rooms. Rick was certain the technology employed in the guns had also been used to make the rooms in the cliff. Yet, by solving this mystery, Rick had uncovered a far greater one.

Joe's statement that Green had found, not built, the stone rooms made even less sense now. *Why would he say that?* wondered Rick. *Green clearly had the means to construct them.* There was only one logical answer—it had not occurred to Joe that guns had carved the stone rooms. *Yet how could that be, if Green had invented the guns?* Rick pondered the implications of that question. All the technology on Montana Isle was interconnected. The guns were charged by the same black solar panels on the plane, the same panels on the time machine. *Green must have invented the guns, otherwise*—a disconcerting thought came to Rick—*He hadn't invented anything!*

Rick was taken aback by where his logic was leading. *It's just a hypothesis,* he reminded himself. *The cut boulder is no proof.* Perhaps, once Green invented the guns, other people developed the technology for different uses. Such people could have made the rooms for Green to find. With time travel, chronology was flexible; the future could affect the past.

Rick was beginning to take comfort in this new line of thinking when he looked into the clear portion of the plane. The bits of plastic tape on the control panel caught his eye. Instantly, he realized that the tape labels might provide a clue to the plane's origin. He entered the plane and, with a growing sense of apprehension, approached the control panel. The makeshift labels seemed particularly incongruous on its finished surface. With a trembling finger, Rick lifted up a corner of a label. As he feared, there was something underneath, integral to the panel's surface. It was probably a word, although Rick recognized neither the language nor the alphabet.

How could I be so dumb? Rick asked himself. *None of this is twenty-first-century technology!* It seemed so plain to him now, he was dismayed that he had ever been fooled. *No wonder Tom found no mention of Peter Green.* On further introspection, Rick saw why he had been so easily deceived. His only concern had been whether time travel was real. He hadn't truly cared where the technology came from. *Should I care now?* That was, indeed, the question. Regardless of how he had gotten there, he was in the Cretaceous. He had seen living dinosaurs. He would see more. *Isn't that enough?*

Rick carefully pushed the corner of the label back down on the panel. *I should return to camp and see if Con is up.* There were still details to check to ensure her first trip ran smoothly. *Stick to my job,* he told himself. Rick walked back to camp trying to focus his thoughts on the day's explorations. Again and again, he reminded himself that the time machine was Green's business, not his. By the time he reached camp, he was almost convinced that it was true.

JOE LOOKED UP from his coffee and flashed Rick a broad smile. "I hear you've arranged for a passenger. Good job!"

"Do you know if she's up?" asked Rick.

"Ask Pandit. I avoid that pavilion like the plague."

"Miss Greighton has indeed risen," said Pandit, "with a full appetite and a pleasant disposition. For that, we are all grateful."

"You're our man," said Joe.

Rick tried to smile at Joe's praise, while he sorted out his feelings about the man. It was hard not to like him. Still, Rick now knew that beneath that seemingly open friendliness was much that was hidden. Surely, Joe knew about the alien words beneath the labels on the controls. He had discouraged all Rick's questions. *Yet he told me about the rooms. Why had he done that? Was it a slipup? A warning? A threat? One thing's certain, whatever Green's up to, Joe's in on it.*

"You look distracted," said Joe.

"It was a late night."

"Have a cup of James's mud. It'd wake a stone."

BREAKFAST WAS ENDING at the pavilion when Rick arrived. The mood of the diners, in contrast to the previous evening, seemed relaxed. John Greighton sipped cham-

pagne, looking totally content. "Hey, Rick," he called in
a friendly voice, "I hear you're taking Constance sight-
seeing."

Con looked up from her second omelet at the mention
of her name. She flashed Rick an excited smile.

"We're going to explore the inland sea," replied Rick.
"Would you and Sara like to come along?"

"Maybe some other time," replied John. "We're just
fine here." He reached out and playfully squeezed Sara's
breast. She let out a surprised screech that transformed
into a giggle.

Con flushed and abruptly stood up. "I'm ready," she
told Rick.

"Then we'll head out," he said. "Everything is all set."

As they walked down the path, they heard Sara call
out, "Have a good time!" Then she screeched again.

Con's expression betrayed her irritation, and Rick
feared the return of her moodiness of the previous day.
They walked in silence until they reached the plane,
where Joe was waiting for them. There, to Rick's relief,
Con immediately brightened as she was taken by the aircraft's appearance. "It's like a Brancusi!" she exclaimed.

"A what?" asked Joe.

"Constantin Brancusi," replied Con, "a twentieth-
century sculptor. You know, *Bird in Space*."

"I'll take your word for it," said Joe. "But I agree, it
is a work of art."

"You must tell me all about it!" said Con.

"I'd like to, but dozens of patents are still pending on
this baby. Mr. Green's very security conscious. A touch
paranoid, if you ask me."

"That's Joe's polite way of saying 'Shut up and enjoy
the view.' You'll get more answers from a clam," said
Rick. "At least," he added for Joe's benefit, "more *direct*
answers."

"You wound me," replied Joe in mock sorrow.

The three of them entered the airplane and took their
seats. "Joe, I'd like to show Con the beaches around the
island. Could you slowly circle it a few times as we
climb?"

"Sure thing. You're the guide."

Con peered intently into the clear water as they rose, looking for sea turtles and also the mosasaur that still lurked darkly in her thoughts. She spotted neither. Rick's attention was elsewhere. While trying not to appear too obvious, he scrutinized the island for signs of the time machine's creators. From the air, Pandit's "wild tomatoes" were clearly part of a cultivated plot. That and the two landing sites, a few paths, the protected beach, and the three stone structures carved into the cliff seemed to be the only alterations to the island. Joe kept the plane's altitude below the top of the mesa, and Rick felt he could not ask him to fly higher without arousing suspicion. They were over a mile beyond the island before Joe took the aircraft into a climb. When Rick looked back at the island for the last time, a flash of light momentarily caught his eye. It seemed as if the sun had reflected off something atop the mesa. He strained to see what it might be, but they were too far away for him to see anything.

The sea was unusually calm, and its flat surface made a perfect window to the world beneath. They were over the shallower western portion of the sea, filled with the eroded runoff of mountains and carved by drowned rivers. The seafloor was usually visible, in shades varying from pale turquoise to deep blue, according to the water's depth. Its inhabitants appeared to fly through the crystal medium rather than swim.

Con was particularly charmed by the graceful swimming of the plesiosaurs. They found several kinds. The long-necked *Elasmosaurs* swam slowly while their heads snatched fish with the quickness of a snake's strike. A short-necked plesiosaur with a long head cruised swiftly through the depths searching for prey. They saw it chase down a small mosasaur and sever it in two with a single bite.

They spotted a huge mosasaur swimming leisurely near the surface. Because it was close to forty feet long, Rick thought it was probably a *Tylosaurus*. Con insisted that they follow it. The creature terrified and fascinated her, in the way a traffic accident does. Viewed from above, it

looked somewhat like a smooth-skinned crocodile, with
flippers instead of feet and a flattened tail topped with a
ridge-like fin. *In a way, it's a beautiful creature,* she
thought. Wavy, dark blue stripes contrasted with its light
olive skin. They were too high for her to see its frightening green eye.

Rick conscientiously watched Con for signs of lagging
interest, but could detect none. She was animated by all
she saw and filled with questions about everything. Eventually, it was he who suggested that they do something
different. Con agreed, and Rick told Joe to head for the
sand bar where they had seen the basking plesiosaurs. It
took them almost an hour to reach it.

The tide was low, and a portion of the sand bar was
above water, forming a thirty-yard-long white comma in
the turquoise sea. Over a dozen Elasmosaurs of varying
sizes basked in the shallows, resting on the sandy bottom
while exposing their backs to the air and sun. Rick turned
to Con. "Would you like to picnic here?"

Con's eyes lit up. "Could we?"

"Joe, can you set her down?"

"Piece of cake."

The airplane slowed as it neared the sand bar until it
hovered above it. The craft's long silver wings shrank
until they were mere slivers at the ends of the stubby
black ones. Then Joe guided the plane down in a gentle
vertical descent. Once they were resting on dry sand, the
seats released their passengers, and the door opened in
the rear compartment. Con kicked off her shoes and was
the first one out the door. The Elasmosaurs were bunched
together near the opposite end of the sand bar. All their
necks were raised, and they watched her as she emerged
from the plane. They were already losing interest by the
time Rick and Joe climbed out. The animals' necks gradually went limp until they floated on the warm shallow
water or draped over their neighbors' backs.

"They certainly look relaxed," commented Joe.

Con walked down the sand toward the basking animals
with Rick close behind. She slowed down as they got
near. "Will they bite?" she asked Rick.

"They're fish eaters, but that's all I know. They might bite."

One of the closest reptiles lifted its neck above the water and rapidly swung it in their direction. Both Con and Rick jumped back. The animal's head halted ten feet way. Sharp conical teeth projected up and down from its closed lips, making it look both fierce and comical. It cocked its head and studied them with its golden eye. The creature's stare gave no indication of what thoughts, if any, it had of the strange invaders. After a minute, the neck swung away.

"Is anybody hungry?" Joe called out.

"I'm starving," Con called back.

Joe went into the plane and brought out a large cooler covered with a beach blanket. They spread the blanket on the sand and sat down to eat. It was a perfect setting for a picnic. A slight breeze had picked up, cooling them as it created a soothing rhythm of gentle waves breaking on the sand. The basking plesiosaurs provided a languid note of interest in their tranquil surroundings. Pandit's lunch was delicious and ample. Soon Rick sat back, feeling full and perfectly content.

"Are you going to finish your sandwich?" asked Con, who had just eaten her second one.

"Have it. I'm stuffed," said Rick. "How can such a slender person eat so much?"

Con bristled slightly. "Are you asking if I'm souped?"

"No . . . no . . . not at all," said Rick quickly, already regretting his comment.

"I'm not responsible for what happened before I was born."

"Look, I . . ."

"I don't know why people make such a big deal over it."

"Parents always want what's best for their kids," said Rick, trying to mollify her

"So you approve?" challenged Con.

"Sure. It's just . . . well . . . sometimes what's best changes."

"Now you've stepped in it!" said Joe jocularly, while

flashing Rick a look that made him feel even dumber.

"And what do you mean by that?" asked Con.

"Just that genes that make you fat in times of plenty, help you survive in times of famine. It wouldn't do for everyone to get souped."

Joe laughed. "Small chance of *that*."

"For an individual, it's great," said Rick. "You'll probably reach a hundred and look great doing it."

Con looked somewhat placated. "Some people give me a hard time about it. I guess I'm a little touchy."

"Sorry," said Rick. "I wasn't being critical."

Con rose and began to wander along the edge of the sandbar. The tide was still going out, and the basking plesiosaurs had moved farther out with it. Rick noticed that she avoided the water. Suddenly, she yelled to them, "You've got to see this!"

Joe and Rick walked over and looked where she was pointing. Half-buried in the sand, about fifteen feet from the shore, was an ammonite shell. It was easily three feet in diameter. Between waves, a portion of its smooth surface projected above the water. The shell's exterior was golden brown with veins of yellow, orange, and mahogany, all overlaid with a pattern of irregular spots. The interior was deep purple shading into pink.

"Isn't it beautiful," said Con.

Rick removed his sandals and waded out for a closer look.

"Don't!" cried out Con.

Rick scanned the clear water around the sandbar. "I don't see anything to worry about." He grabbed the edge of the shell and gave a tug. It moved slightly. "It's stuck in the sand." While Con watched nervously, he bent over and began scooping sand from around the shell with his hands. A passing wave thoroughly drenched his shirt-front. He kept digging, revealing more of the shell. It seemed to be in perfect condition. Rising again, he once more tugged at the shell. It budged a little. "Joe, could you give me a hand?"

Joe waded out and assisted Rick. Straining together,

they were able to drag the shell a few inches. "Damn, this is heavy!" said Joe.

"Probably all the chambers are filled with water," said Rick.

Con, after some nervous hesitation, waded out, saying, "I'll push while you two pull."

Rick was surprised she entered the water and more surprised by her strength. Together, the three muscled the shell onto the dry sand. By then, they were completely drenched.

"Too bad I don't have a bathing suit," said Con. She turned to stare sharply at Rick. "I will *not*!" she said in a shocked tone.

"Not what?" asked Rick.

"Don't you know souped girls are telepathic?" Con said. She watched Rick flush red before she nearly fell over laughing. "For someone who claims to be a scientist, you sure are gullible." Rick blushed even more. Con grinned broadly at his embarrassment and pushed her point. "Apparently, you're not as used to it as you claim."

"Am I missing something here?" asked Joe.

"Just a private joke," muttered Rick.

By maneuvering the shell about, they were able to drain much of the water from its inner chambers. Eventually, it was light enough for them to lift and carry into the plane. They walked about to let the sun and wind dry their wet clothes before taking off to resume their travels.

They flew next to a spire of rock jutting two hundred feet above the sea. From a distance, Con thought the island was wreathed in swirling streamers of cloud, but as they came nearer, the "clouds" proved to be masses of white pterosaurs. Taking advantage of the winds, they soared gracefully through the air like living kites, flapping their long, sickle-shaped wings only occasionally. The animals appeared to consist of large-beaked and crested heads, longish necks, and small, tailless bodies, supported by large, narrow wings. These wings resembled neither those of birds nor bats. They were comprised of a stiffened membrane stretched between the animal's arm and a single, greatly elongated, finger and the ani-

mal's thigh. The smaller fliers had wingspans of nine
feet, while others had wingspans of twenty-three and
thirty feet. Rick pointed out the different kinds and
named them, *"Nyctosaurus ... Pteranodon ingens ...
Pteranodon sternbergi."*

"What do they eat?" ask Con.

"Watch," said Rick. "See them skimming just above
the water? Watch what they do. See that? One just caught
a fish."

"That's so neat!" said Con with excitement. "It
scooped it up without missing a wingbeat."

There was no place to land, so Joe simply circled the
island slowly. Occasionally they were able to follow a
pterosaur as it flew, sometimes approaching within a few
yards of the animal.

"They look like giant hairy birds or something out of
a medieval bestiary," said Con.

They soared among the pterosaurs for almost an hour
before Con asked if they could see how far the sea extended. Joe flew away from the pterosaurs, then put the
plane into a steep climb. As their altitude increased, their
view of the world became more expansive. The mountains of the western coast and the narrow, river-cut
coastal plain could be seen clearly. "Shall I just follow
the coastline?" asked Joe.

"It's up to you, Con," said Rick.

"That sounds good."

The view from such a high altitude, while impressive,
soon became monotonous. Con found her mind wandering. "I found something strange in my room last night."

"What was that?" asked Rick.

"Some luminous symbols on the wall. They had been
covered over with plaster."

Joe turned quickly around, paused for a moment, then
said casually, "Oh that's just one of Eduardo's things."

"Who?" said Con.

"He was the decorator, before he got canned. Wanted
everything to look high-tech. You know, sort of a 'time
travel motif.' It looked god-awful."

"You mean that thing is just a decoration?" asked Con.

"Yep. An expensive one, too. Mr. Green had me plaster it over when he went for the rustic look."

"Oh," said Con.

A few minutes later, Joe brought up the subject again. "I'd appreciate it if you didn't mention my lousy plastering job. Especially to Mr. Green."

"Sure," said Con. "In fact, I'll cover it with a leaf from one of those short, fat palm trees. I like the rustic look, too."

"Thanks," said Joe.

Rick sensed Con's waning interest in sight-seeing and suggested that they head back. "Tomorrow, if you like, we can see some dinosaurs."

"That would be great."

The trip back was uneventful. The late hours of the previous night before caught up with Con, and she dozed off. Rick was feeling tired, too, but nagging questions kept him awake. Something was going on. It bothered him he didn't know what it was.

12

WHEN THEY LANDED BACK ON THE ISLAND, CON WANTED to take the ammonite shell back to camp. Joe said he could make a litter to carry it more easily. He grabbed a gun and adjusted the settings, saying, "I'll cut some poles and rig up the litter while you two go back to camp to recruit some litter bearers."

Rick and Con headed back to camp. Once they were out of Joe's hearing, Rick said, "I'd like to see that decoration you found."

"It's no decoration," replied Con matter-of-factly.

"Why do you say that?"

"There was the same pattern on the control panel of the plane."

"So you think Joe was lying?" said Rick, attempting to sound disinterested.

"Of course. I just played dumb," replied Con. "Just like you are."

Rick turned to face Con. She looked him squarely in the eye and said, "You knew he was lying, too."

Rick glanced away and remained silent as he tried to think of how to respond. Finally, he said weakly, "How'd you know?"

"I could see it on your face. Back then, and just now," she said.

"I'm not in on some conspiracy, if that's what you're thinking."

"So, what are you hiding?"

Rick hesitated again, then sighed. "Will you keep this to yourself?"

"Why should I?"

"I have a feeling that if it got out, there'd be trouble. I won't tell you anything unless you swear not to talk."

"Okay, I promise."

"I've stumbled onto some stuff. This place is more than a resort, but I'm not sure what."

Con looked disappointed. "Is that all?"

"No. One more thing—one big thing—Green didn't build this resort or invent the time machine."

Con had stopped walking. "Wow! Then who did?"

"Joe probably knows, but besides Green, I think he's the only one. He's not talking. He seems afraid of Green."

"That's creepy."

"Glad you asked now?"

"I wasn't expecting *that*! What are you going to do?"

"I don't know," said Rick. "Nothing, I guess. That's probably the safest thing."

"Safest?"

"If Joe's afraid of Green, he must have a reason. I think we should simply enjoy our stay and leave Green alone."

Con gave Rick a dubious look, but said, "Maybe you're right."

"Come on, let's get to camp and find some litter bearers."

BY THE TIME Con and Rick returned to the plane with Pandit and James, Joe had constructed a litter for the shell. The poles were as deftly cut and trimmed as if he had used a fine-toothed saw. The crosspieces of the litter were precisely notched and held in place by pegs.

"You should have been a carpenter, Joe," said Rick.

"Once an engineer, always an engineer," he replied.

"How'd you get the pegs in?"

"Just drilled a hole with the gun and popped in a piece of a branch. If you fool with the settings, these guns are precision instruments."

"Joe did most of the work on the pavilion," said James. "He's very handy."

Rick was annoyed when Con took charge of the ammonite shell, automatically assuming it was hers. She had the men carry the shell back to camp and hide it near the pavilion. "Don't tell anyone about it," she told them. "I want it to be a surprise."

When he finished helping with the ammonite, Rick headed to the kitchen tent to help Pandit. James caught up with him. "Capital job, Rick," he said. "I'm very pleased, and so, I'm sure, will be Mr. Green."

"Thanks."

"Why don't you relax until it's time to serve dinner?" Rick was happy for the break and pleased with his apparent rise in status. He bathed standing in the small plastic tub in the sleeping tent and changed into fresh clothes. Afterward, he wandered off to the shore. He had fallen in love with the sea. He found its beauty and its vitality irresistible. For the first time, he truly understood why old people missed the beaches so. Watching the light on the moving water, it seemed strange and sad that one day this would become the Great Plains and the Dust Bowl.

A silver bell announced dinner, and Rick hastened to the pavilion to help serve. Con appeared wearing a dress and shoes.

"You look nice this evening," said her father.

Con smiled. "I brought you a present, Daddy."

"What?"

"A seashell"

"Oh," he said, sounding somewhat annoyed.

Con rang the silver bell and Joe and Pandit bore the ammonite from its hiding place. By the time they set it down in front of the pavilion, John Greighton was on his feet, staring in amazement.

"Your daughter's bagged you quite a trophy," said James.

"How sweet," said Sara.

John walked over to his present and appreciatively ran his hand over its glossy, smooth surface. "This will look great in my office."

"It'll be unique . . . priceless," said Peter Green.

Rick envisioned the publicity photographs—John Greighton with a hammy smile, showing off his latest possession. *So much for secrecy,* he thought. Strangely, Green seemed unperturbed, even pleased, with Greighton's plans for the ammonite. *A rich man's trophy—what a waste!* Rick thought of Tom and how he might use such a gift. *I'm merely the help,* he reflected with an edge of bitterness. *That shell was never mine to give.*

Pandit brought out a tray of filled champagne flutes. "A toast!" cried out James, lifting a glass high. Con's father took a glass, handed it to Con, then took one for himself.

"To the conquering huntress!" said James.

"To Constance!" said John Greighton. Beaming, he clinked Con's glass. "Thank you, honey."

John Greighton's excitement set an upbeat tone for the meal. Only Sara seemed unaffected by his mood. She appeared miffed by the praise he lavished on Con, but held her tongue. Con basked in her father's attention, her eyes shining. Both Green and James bore the satisfied look of hosts whose party was going well. Once, Green lifted his glass in Rick's direction and gave him a silent nod.

After Rick had his dinner with the staff, he walked out

to the protected beach. He found Con there, still in her dinner dress. The wine had obviously gone to her head. She had thrown off her shoes and was whirling about the sand in a tipsy dance.

"Rick," she cried. "Isn't it wonderful?"

"Sure," he replied, uncertain what she was referring to.

"I finally did it! I got 'em something he couldn't buy."

"You sure did."

"Sara Big-Tits-Boyton can't match that. All she gives him is . . . well, you know what she gives him."

"Yes," said Rick dryly.

"I could get tits like Sara's. Think I should?"

"Con."

"All I want is a scientific opinion. After all, you've seen mine. I *know* you've seen hers. Everyone has."

"My scientific opinion is you've had too much to drink. Maybe you should lie down."

"Yeah," said Con, collapsing on the sand.

"Not here!" said Rick. "In your quarters. Here, take my hand. You can show me that thing on your wall."

"Eduardo's mysterious decoration. Yeah. We could do that. Did you see my shoes?"

Rick helped Con up, then found her shoes. He offered Con his arm to steady her, but she refused it. As they walked, she seemed to stumble less as her sped-up metabolism broke down the alcohol. When they reached her quarters, Con groaned. "My head hurts."

"How much did you drink?"

"I don't know. Four . . . maybe five glasses. Daddy was toasting me. Toasting *me!*" she said with fierce satisfaction.

"He should have. That was quite a gift."

"Yeah," said Con proudly.

"So let's see this thing."

Con lead Rick into the storeroom and moved the large cycad frond she had placed on her dresser and propped against the wall. The yellow design gleamed in the dim room:

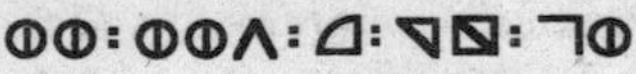

"Whaddaya think?" asked Con.

"I don't know yet, but it seems to be a line of symbols of some sort." Rick silently studied the symbols for a couple of minutes. "There's a pattern here. The symbols always change in the same order. They've got to be numbers."

"Numbers?"

"Yes. Some of them even look like our numbers—the zero, the one, the seven, and the eight. The upside-down 'V' is two; the equilateral triangle is three . . ."

"Three sides," said Con. "Bet the square's four."

"Pretty sharp for a drunk."

"I'm not drunk. Just a little tipsy. The square with the line, that's gotta be five." Con emphasized her certainty by sticking out her tongue.

"Okay, then—what's six?"

"The pointy down triangle?"

"That's nine," said Rick. "Six is the pie-shaped one."

"I was gonna say that. So . . . what is it?"

"Beats me," said Rick. "It's counting something."

"Daddy's credit limit."

Rick laughed. "The zeroes are in the wrong places." He studied the numbers some more. "The numbers to the left don't seem to change."

"Yeah," said Con. "No, wait. Maybe the number before all the zeroes was different yesterday. I'm not sure. I can't remember."

"Maybe it's a clock."

"It doesn't look like a clock."

"The numbers at the right could be counting seconds."

Con looked at the numbers. "No, silly. There aren't eighty-seven seconds in a minute."

"Different numbers, maybe it's a different system. A metric clock."

"No . . . no . . ." said Con sleepily. "It's all wrong. The numbers are counting down, not up." She yawned. "I gotta go to bed."

Con walked out of the storeroom and flopped down on

her bed without waiting for Rick to leave. Rick carefully
placed the cycad frond over the numbers. Con was snoring as he left.

13

WHEN RICK AWOKE, HE TRIED NOT TO THINK ABOUT THE
strange numbers or the other mysteries surrounding Montana
Isle. *The advice I gave Con was good,* he thought. *I should
follow it myself and simply enjoy my stay.* It was not hard
for him to do, when he had a day of exploration ahead. He
decided a leisurely air tour of the less wooded part of the
coastal plain would be perfect. They could visit the water
hole and the nesting site, then locate the huge migrating herd
of ceratopsids. That was just the planned itinerary, they were
bound to encounter a few interesting surprises along the way.

Rick imagined future trips of a more ambitious nature. An
aircraft that did not require fuel made all sorts of destinations
possible. There was the eastern continent, where the young
Appalachian Mountains rivaled the Alps. Up north lay the
former bed of the Pierre Seaway, high and dry and yet untouched by the coming ice ages. Perhaps they could even
visit the mysterious forests of the North Pole. That would be
a trip! Nothing remotely like that environment had existed
since the Cretaceous. It promised the possibility of all sorts
of strange plants and animals.

On this third day, camp life was beginning to establish a
routine. James rose, made his camp coffee, and shared a cup
with Rick before checking on the guests. He returned to wake
Pandit, who started cooking immediately. First, he made a
simple meal for Rick, James, and himself. Then he cooked
those items of the guests' lavish breakfast that could be pre-

pared in advance. Once that was done, Pandit prepared lunch
for Rick's excursion. Joe, whose breakfast consisted only of
coffee, rose last among the staff. He was usually loading the
plane before Rick had finished eating. Pandit served breakfast
to the guests, so Rick's workday began with helping Joe load.
Then he went through the formality of lining up his tour.

Passing the ammonite shell, Rick entered the pavilion
where John, Sara, and Con were eating crêpes, which Pandit
cooked at the tableside.

"Good morning, Rick," called out John jovially. "Where
are you taking my young adventuress today?"

"I thought we might go inland to see some dinosaurs."

"That would be great! Won't it, Constance?"

Constance looked up from her sixth crêpe. She seemed a
little subdued. "Sure," she said. "That sounds exciting."

"Would you and Miss Boyton like to come?"

"Oh, dinosaurs are more a kid's taste," said John. "I'll find
all the adventure I need on our private beach."

"Well, Con," said Rick, "whenever you want to go, we
can leave."

"On second thought, I'll spend the day watching the wildlife here on our private beach." She laughed at her father's
annoyed expression. "Just kidding. You're lucky, Daddy, I
have more juvenile tastes."

Rick did his best not to react to the exchange. "I'll wait
by your quarters."

CON SHOWED UP about ten minutes later, put on some
shoes, then headed to the plane with Rick. As they
walked up the path, Rick said, "I see last night's spell is
already broken."

"What do you mean?"

"Between you and your father. You're already pushing
his buttons."

"How's that your business?"

"For some reason, Green holds me responsible when
your dad gets upset."

"So you're my baby-sitter? Look, I don't have to go
anywhere with you."

"Con . . ."

"Did it ever occur to you that he pushes *my* buttons? That is, when he bothers to pay attention to me at all!" Con halted on the path, her eyes beginning to well with tears.

"I don't blame you," said Rick gently. "I've seen how he behaves toward you. It's just that Green's business involves your father in some way. He wants your dad to be in a good mood."

"So? I thought you said to ignore Green."

"I want him to ignore us also."

"You mean ignore *you*."

"Yeah," said Rick, "I suppose you're right. I was sort of hoping you'd help me out. Green can be a real jerk."

"And I'm supposed to just bite my tongue."

"I think it would help."

Con mulled over Rick's request. "Green's like a lot of Daddy's friends. I didn't trust him even before you told me that stuff."

"So, will you help me?"

Con made a face. "You don't ask much!" She paused, then sighed. "I'll try. I really will."

"Thanks, Con. I know it's not a little thing. Now, let's fly away and forget Green and your dad."

"Sounds good to me."

ONCE THEY WERE in the air, Con's and Rick's moods lifted as the spirit of adventure took hold of them. Joe, also, seemed to be happy to be away from camp. Soon he was regaling Con with a humorous telling of his and Rick's first trip. "Invisible?" he said, imitating his terror at seeing the Dromaeosauruses. "I'm looking at my shaking hand and thinking, this *sure* doesn't look invisible to me! Some fine guide! First day out, and I'm dinosaur shit." Con was laughing so hard she had to catch her breath. "Yessir, if that thing took one more step in my direction, I'd be needing a diaper!"

"You look unchewed," said Rick.

"Unchewed, but unnerved. I'm a broken man!" wailed Joe in mock anguish. "A *broken* man!"

"So that's Green's plan," said Con, still laughing. "To have Rick feed me to the dinosaurs."

"Mr. Green doesn't have a plan," said Joe abruptly. Then he cracked a smile, and said breezily, "Except for you to have a good time."

Soon they were flying above the cypress swamps of the low-lying coasts, and Con and Rick were intently peering at the scenery. Once they spotted a fifty-foot crocodile, a *Deinosuchus,* walking along the riverbank. They circled back around four times to view it before it disappeared into the river. As they headed upland, and the land became firmer, they saw their first dinosaurs of the day. A small group of *hypsilophodontids* were grazing on water plants in a shallow pond. The bipeds were shorter than a man, since a third of their nine-foot length was tail. Con said their short snouts made them look "cute."

As they crossed over the uplands, they encountered a herd of two dozen sauropod dinosaurs grazing the tree tops. They were heavily built animals, thirty-five feet in length, with shoulders higher than their hips. Their necks were relatively short and thick for sauropods, making their heads look ridiculously small.

"Somehow," said Con, "I expected them to be bigger."

"These are *Alamosaurs,*" said Rick. "The real giants, like the *Ultrasaurus* and the *Diplodocus,* went extinct tens of millions of years ago."

"They don't look too shabby to me," said Joe. "One of those babies would make quite a barbecue."

"For God's sake, don't tell that to Pandit!" said Rick.

"Speaking of food," said Con, "where are we going to picnic?"

"I thought the mountains might be nice," said Rick.

"Sounds great to me," said Joe. "I don't like unexpected guests."

They flew to the watering hole and the nesting site before Joe headed for the mountains to search for a landing site. He found a bare mountain peak not more than thirty feet wide, then impressed Rick and Con by neatly parking on it. On all sides, cliffs dropped precipitously, affording breathtaking views. On one side, a mountain range towered into the sky, while on the other, the land spread out to the gleaming sea. Below them, but still high above the foothills, huge pterosaurs wheeled gracefully on the updrafts. As far as the eye could see, the world stretched out like a green-and-blue tapestry, unmarred by the hand of man.

They lingered on the mountaintop long after they had finished eating and left it reluctantly. Joe guided their aircraft between the foothills and the coastal plain until they encountered the huge ceratopsid herd. Con let out a squeal of excitement as the plane slowly glided only yards above the animals' backs.

"We've got to land!" she said.

"No way!" said Joe firmly.

"You two did it. Like Rick said, we'll be invisible."

"Look, if I came back short a guide, that would be one thing. You're different. If you get hurt, there'd be hell to pay."

"If you two treat me like a baby, I'll just stay on the island. What will your Mr. Green say about *that*?"

"Joe . . ." said Rick with quiet urgency.

"Has everyone forgotten her first morning here?"

"That was different," said Rick.

"How was it different?" retorted Joe. "A meat eater's a meat eater."

"Mosasaurs probably learned to prey on wading animals."

"So? We'll be wading through the bushes."

"It's different with land predators," said Rick. "Look, do you bite everything you see to find out if it's edible? Hunting takes effort and involves risks. Predators stick to recognized prey."

"You're putting too much faith in a theory," said Joe. "Nothing doing."

"You act as if I have no say in this matter," said Con. "I meant it about staying on the island. I'll sit on the beach with Daddy and Sara and be the perfect wet blanket. Imagine dinner after a few days of that!"

"She'll do it, Joe," said Rick.

"Why do you want to risk your life?" asked Joe.

"Did you ever ride a horse?" asked Con.

"Not likely," said Joe.

"Well, if you get thrown, it's important to ride again soon. You've got to conquer your fear."

"That's what this is about? Proving something?"

"No . . . No. This place is really special. I don't want to miss out because I'm afraid."

Joe turned to Rick. "Have you been coaching her?"

"Hardly."

"Well," said Joe resignedly, "I guess we're setting down. Rick, no looking at the scenery. We've got to keep her covered at all times."

Without further discussion, Joe guided the plane to a landing spot about a quarter of a mile from the head of the herd. The gently rolling ground was covered with a low growth of plants interspersed with occasional clumps of bushes or solitary, broad-crowned trees. The herd was clearly visible. Once they exited the plane, Con headed toward the dinosaurs.

"Isn't this close enough?" said Joe, hastening to catch up.

"You got a lot closer," replied Con as she continued to walk.

"I wish I'd never told you that story," said Joe.

Rick followed to the rear, anxiously scanning the landscape with his gun. Previously, when only Joe and he had landed, he had not been nearly so nervous. Then, Rick had felt he was risking only his life. Being responsible for Con's safety made this experience very different. Con's exuberance did not make matters easier. She walked rapidly and noisily through the knee-high plants toward the dinosaurs in the near distance. Rick began to repent what he had put Joe through earlier.

As they approached, the tumultuous parade was nearly overwhelming. Noisy, odorous, always changing, the herd was life on a grand, almost exaggerated, scale. The animals numbered in the thousands. They ranged from youngsters the size of large dogs to massive individuals over twice the height of a man. The herd varied in more than size. The grotesque heads displayed different configurations of horns and frills. There were several species of the short-frilled *Triceratops*. These differed in coloration and the size and angles of their long eye horns. The huge, long-frilled *Torosauruses* stood out as the largest animals in the herd. The square-frilled *Chasmosauruses* were smaller, but still several feet taller than humans. Pointed bones, like small horns, lined the outer edges of their frills so they resembled giant saws. The various species tended to group together, so that the stream of animals seemed to change continually.

Rick watched Con as she halted, enthralled, not more than twenty yards from the moving herd. The beasts passed by, paying her no more attention than they would a stump. Rick's chief concern became that some animal might casually trample her on its path to a bit of greenery. For a moment, his fears seemed about to be realized when a Triceratops separated from the herd and headed in her direction. Con stepped out of its path. Then, as Rick watched in horror, she advanced and touched the creature's tail. She turned her gaze back at Rick with a look of triumph in her eyes.

The herd thinned out, and Rick was beginning to relax a bit when he spotted a pair of *Tyrannosaurs* in the distance. He pointed his gun in their direction, and called softly to Joe. "You see them?"

"Yeah, I sure do," asked Joe softly. "Right out of some movie."

"You lock on the left one. I'll take the right. Don't shoot unless we have to."

Rick aimed his gun and pulled the targeting trigger. The weapon came alive in his hand and tracked the huge carnivore as it advanced. He called to Con, who was still watching the herd. "Con, stay perfectly still."

"Why?" she called back. Then she froze in terror.

Even at a hundred yards away, the Tyrannosaurs seemed nightmarishly large. Rising eighteen feet above the ground, they moved with a powerful grace that

seemed impossible for such massive animals. Their heads
scanned about in an alert, watchful manner as they
walked, keeping pace with the herd. Their path headed
directly toward Con.

Rick called to Con as softly as he could and still be
heard over the herd's noise. "Come this way, but slowly."
A Tyrannosaur cocked its head in his direction.

Con walked toward Rick and Joe, her eyes never leaving the advancing monsters. The huge pair came closer.
Rick found himself staring at their legs, a combination
of birdlike form with an elephant's mass and power. The
three sharp, curved toe claws caught his eye at each step.

The pair came closer still. Rick had to bend his neck
to see their enormous heads. Their partly open jaws revealed six-inch teeth surrounding maws so large a child
could hide inside. Beneath horny ridges, yellow-green
eyes scanned the landscape, seeing it from a treetop perspective. Rick tried to imagine the view from those eyes.
What do we seem like to them? He wondered if they
might slay the way a bored child idly squashes an ant,
without interest or malice.

Still following the terrifying heads for some clue to
their intention, Rick arched his neck backward. The near-
est of the pair passed within five yards of him. Rick could
hear its breathing, smell the sweet odor of rancid meat,
feel the warmth of his urine as it trickled down his leg.

Then the Tyrannosaurs were retreating, still following
the herd. Rick had to duck a swaying tail as they departed. He took a deep breath, turned off his gun's targeting, and looked around him. Joe's hands were shaking
violently. Con's eyes were wide with excitement and terror. Even as he watched, the terror faded and the excitement grew. "Wow!" she said in wonder. "Wow!"

Rick, Con, and Joe stood immobile and silent for several minutes, watching the departing herd. Finally, Joe
said, "Maybe we should go back." No one said a word.
They just started walking toward the plane. About halfway there, Rick saw a flash of movement in a clump of
bushes about thirty yards to the left. "Hold up, Joe."

"What did you see?" Joe asked.

"A chance to bag Pandit a dinosaur. See that clump of bushes over there?" said Rick, pointing.

"Yeah."

"Set your gun at the lowest power and at a wide dispersal, then shoot the bushes to give them a good shake. I'll try to get whatever's scared out."

"Got ya," said Joe. "Tell me when you're ready."

Rick adjusted his gun to fire rapid bursts, then said, "Now!"

Joe fired, scattering leaves into the air. Three brown forms sped away. Rick followed them with his gun, raking the ground with shots.

"Did you get anything?" asked Joe.

"I think I hear something thrashing about." Rick ran to the site of the shaking foliage to fire one more shot.

As Rick looked down at the animal at his feet, a wave of regret briefly passed over him. Even in death, the lithe creature appeared graceful and dynamic. Rick consoled himself in the knowledge that, in less than a million years, all its kind would be extinct. At least now, people would hear of them.

Joe and Con walked over to see what he had hit. Joe laughed, "You got a bird."

"I did not," replied Rick. "Some dinosaurs had feathers."

Joe examined the dead creature and noted its clawed hands and long tail. "I guess you're right."

"What is it?" asked Con.

"Some kind of *Saurornithoidid*," said Rick, "a small carnivore. '*Saurornithoides*' means 'birdlike reptile,' so Joe wasn't that far off." Rick lifted the animal and slung it over his shoulder. It was about five feet long, but most of that was a long neck and an even longer tail.

"Is the cook really going to serve that?" asked Con, taken aback.

"I thought you'd eat anything," said Joe.

Con flashed him a dirty look.

"Pandit won't get it until after I dissect it," said Rick.

"Oh gross!" said Con. "I'll eat lots of rolls instead."

"I AM MOST gratified by your addition to our menu," said Pandit, eyeing Rick's catch with appreciation. "Two trips, and each time you return in triumph."

"Just doin' my job," replied Rick, grinning broadly.

"And now I must do mine," said Pandit as he surveyed the dinosaur. He took up his carving knife. "This will be most challenging."

"Hold it," said Rick. "I want to study this before you start slicing and dicing."

"I hope you are a quick study, dinner is in two hours."

Rick looked at his specimen, feeling chagrined by its ignoble fate. *Oh well, it wouldn't keep for two weeks without refrigeration.* He made mental notes as he did a quick field examination. The oily feathers were either light or medium brown, giving the animal a mottled appearance. They were like the short breast feathers of a duck, designed for warmth, not flight. Rick estimated the dinosaur's weight to be around forty pounds. The animal looked built for speed, slim with long legs. The feet had three forward-facing toes and a fourth vestigial one in the rear. All the toes were clawed, but the inner claw was enlarged and curved. It was a slashing claw, which was held above the ground when the animal walked or ran. The forearms looked designed for catching prey. They were long and ended in hands with three long fingers tipped with long sharp claws.

Rick turned his attention to the head. Mounted on a long, supple neck, it, too, seemed designed for catching prey. The skull was slender, with a long snout. The braincase was large for a dinosaur; *Saurornithoidids* were the intellectuals of the Cretaceous. Rick counted thirty-eight pointed teeth in the upper jaw, forty in the lower. These were sharp and curved, with serrations on the back. The most prominent features of the head were the very large yellow-brown eyes, the eyes of a creature of the night. Their position allowed binocular vision.

Rick saw a predator adapted to hunt active small prey, probably the nocturnal mammals of the period. It looked quick and agile. The feathers indicated that it was warm-blooded.

Conscious that Pandit was impatiently watching, he opened the chest cavity. The two items that interested him most were the heart and the stomach contents. The heart, as he suspected, had four chambers. It was another indication the animal was warm-blooded. Rick slit open the stomach next. It contained several partly digested hairy bodies.

"Must you do this in my kitchen?" protested Pandit. "Those little vermin are most unsanitary."

"Have some respect for your ancestors."

"Those cannot be my ancestors," said Pandit. "My ancestors got away."

Rick placed the remaining viscera in a bucket for later study. "You sure know how to spoil a guy's fun, Pandit. I trust you don't want the head, hands, and feet."

"Please take them and let me cook."

Rick cut off his specimens, then turned the severed head in his hand. "I think I'll name this *Noctecorreptus greightonae.*"

"How modest," said Pandit, "You should name it after yourself."

"That's not allowed."

"Why not?"

"It's against the rules of taxonomy."

"So you honor Mr. Greighton instead."

"*Miss* Greighton," corrected Rick.

"I see," said Pandit with a hint of a smile, "but what does the 'Noctecorreptus' part mean?"

"Nightstalker."

NOCTECORREPTUS GREIGHTONAE MADE its appearance at the dining pavilion in the form of heavily spiced cubes, stir-fried with vegetables and served over rice. All of Pandit's skill could not disguise the meat's strong, gamy

taste. The dish was pronounced "interesting" by the guest
of honor, who, like Sara and Peter Green, took only a
bite before turning to other fare. Even Con left most of
the meat untouched. Only James, aware that this entrée
would end up featured on the staff's menu of leftovers,
finished his serving.

The dinosaur's main contribution to the meal was a
topic of conversation. Here it was more successful. There
was a lot of lighthearted banter about Con's adventures,
and everyone was in a good mood. Peter Green was obviously pleased. By the time Rick cleared the dessert
dishes, he sensed that his place on Montana Isle was secure. He went back to the staff area feeling content. *So
what if I dine on leftovers,* he thought. He was the pos-
sessor of a complete, unfossilized dinosaur skull and a
set of limbs, also—the first, he was certain, of many extraordinary specimens. Everything else paled in signifi-
cance.

The festive mood of the dining pavilion was reflected
at the staff dinner. Green's good disposition had affected
his subordinates. James was particularly happy with the
way things were going. He produced a bottle of champagne, declaring, "All of you deserve a toast." He poured
the wine into plastic cups and passed them around. Then
he stood and raised his cup high. "To a fine beginning!"

When everyone sipped the champagne, James offered
a second toast. "To Rick and his taming of a difficult
client."

Joe emptied his cup, then said with a grin, "I'd say the
Greighton girl's tamed him."

"What do you mean?" asked Pandit.

"On today's trip back to the island," said Joe, "I
thought I detected infatuation."

James looked at Rick's crimson face, and said, "We
don't need a romance complicating things."

"There's no romance," said Rick quickly. "I admire
her . . . her daring."

"There," said Joe, "you heard him say it—he's her ad-
mirer."

"I'm her guide," said Rick, speaking more to James

than to Joe. "She's interested in going on tours. The only client who is, I might add. That's all there is to it."

Joe turned to James. "I was just ragging him. Rick's more interested in wildlife than women."

"I'm glad to hear it," said James.

As dinner commenced, it quickly became apparent why there was so much leftover dinosaur. While his staff picked at their food, James refilled their cups and resumed his cheerful tone. "If things continue to run smoothly," he said, "we'll have a proper safari operation in no time. More staff, proper equipment . . ."

"Proper food?" asked Joe. "Rick, can't you shoot something that tastes more like chicken?"

"That dish was a severe test," admitted Pandit.

"To bad you got an 'F' on it," quipped Joe.

"I think a herbivore might be more palatable," said Rick. "Perhaps a *Hypsilophodontid*."

"I prefer food I can pronounce," said Joe.

"I brought some fishing gear," James said. "Just hand lines, because of the weight limitations. Perhaps we could try some seafood."

"An excellent idea," said Pandit.

"Here," said Joe, pushing his plate forward. "You can use this for bait."

James, who had already eaten, went to check on the guests. When he returned, he said to Pandit, "Please get out the best cognac and two snifters and take them to Mr. Green's quarters." Pandit left his dinner to get a crystal decanter and two large bulbous glasses.

"I'm done eating," said Rick. "I can run it over."

He found Peter Green and John Greighton sitting in wicker chairs, finishing off their wine.

"Here we are, John," said Green, "one of the rarest and the finest."

Rick set down the decanter and the two snifters. Though he disliked playing the servant, he asked, "Do you need anything else?"

"Pull the curtain," said Green.

Rick pulled the curtain as he left. He was about to

return to the staff tent when two small pterosaurs alighted not ten feet from where he stood. They were behaving oddly, and Rick stopped to watch them. One of the pterosaurs assumed the usual quadrupedal stance, but the other reared up to balance awkwardly on its hind feet. While it was upright, the pterosaur puffed out a pouch in its neck like a small balloon. It pranced about for a few seconds in this posture, then dropped to a normal stance, rested, and repeated the display. Rick thought he might be witnessing courtship behavior. He assumed the pterosaur with the pouch was the male and wondered how the female might respond. He remained still to find out. The two pterosaurs performed their ritual in silence; the only sound was Peter Green's and John Greighton's conversation from the other side of the curtain.

". . . 2047, that was a good year, and not just for champagne . . ."

Snob talk, thought Rick absentmindedly. He focused on the pterosaurs ignoring the drone of talk until a derisive laugh caught his attention. "Twenty-nine?" said Greighton's voice in a condescending tone. "Where's your taste? All that stuff was crap."

"Not 2029," responded Green's voice, "I mean 1929."

"Expensive vinegar," sniffed Greighton, "if it even exists."

"Oh it exists, all right," said Green. "In the year 1929. That's when I'd stock up—at bargain-basement prices."

"You'd use your time machine to buy wine?" Greighton's voice sounded incredulous.

Rick forgot the pterosaurs and focused on the voices behind the curtain.

"I was just using wine as an example. Buying stock would be more worthwhile. Eastman Kodak in the 1890s . . . Microsoft in the 1980s . . . Biofab in the 2020s . . ."

"Have you done this?" asked Greighton, sounding intrigued.

"If I had, you wouldn't be sitting here. I'd own everything worth having in your portfolio. I'd be the billionaire and you . . . you couldn't even afford the fare to this place."

"Why are you telling me this?" asked Greighton in a cold voice. "Are you threatening me?"

"No, no, not at all. On the contrary, I have an offer for you."

Rick quietly moved to a less conspicuous position.

"I've proven that I have a working time machine," continued Green. "With such a machine, history is a treasure map. There are no gambles, only sure bets."

"Go on," said Greighton, sounding interested.

"But there are some difficulties. With your help, they'll be easily overcome."

"What kind of difficulties?"

"I'm going to trust you with a secret," said Green in a conspiratorial tone. "I didn't invent the time machine. I acquired it."

"From whom?"

"A party from the future."

"Are you telling me that they simply gave you a time machine?"

"The acquisition was more in the nature of a hostile takeover."

"I see," said Greighton.

"I'm not a man to miss an opportunity," replied Green. "I suspect you're not either. Am I right?"

"What kind of help are you looking for?"

"Scientific expertise, the kind a big corporate research division has. The best brains working in absolute secrecy."

"And why do you need that? You've already got the machine."

"The 'source' of this machine kept secrets from me about its operation. There are gaps in my knowledge that need to be filled before we can put our plans into operation."

"So it's 'our plans' now," said Greighton in a cynical tone. "Maybe you should tell me what 'our plans' are."

"Simply put—to change history in our favor."

"And the people from the future—they'll stand by while we do this?" Greighton asked skeptically.

"They'll want to stop us," admitted Green. "But they have problems we don't. First, they have to find us. Then they have an even bigger problem. They can't just kick in doors, guns blazing. If they did so, they'd alter their own past. Altering their past means changing their present. They are in a very delicate position. If we act quickly and secretly . . ."

"Wait, wait," interrupted Greighton. "You're proposing to alter our own past! We're in the same boat they are. I happen to know where my great-great-great grandmother found gold, but if I go back to the nineteenth century and jump her claim, I'll return to my century to find the family fortune gone!"

"*If* you came back, that might be true. But if you stayed in her century, your future would unfold from that point. You could kill the bitch if you wanted. You wouldn't suddenly disappear. Her present would be your present."

"You're talking about a one-way trip to the past. Why would I want to do that?"

"Two reasons. First, it would be a preemptive strike against the future. The people trying to recover the time machine would no longer exist. That brings me to the second reason—the real reason. They wouldn't exist because we'll have completely changed the world. We'll have conquered it!"

"Conquer the world?" said Greighton in an almost mocking tone. "Come on, that sounds crazy!"

"You can object to my wording, but listen to my plan. We arrive in colonial America in a fleet of time machines. We have modern medicine, weaponry, and communications, we have a complete library of technology, we know where every undiscovered natural resource is located, and, best of all, we own a map of history. The people speak English, they're literate, and they're used to rule by kings. They will flock to us!"

"What if they don't? There was an American Revolution after all."

"Smallpox . . . cholera . . . Ebola virus. We'll be vaccinated, they won't. Who needs armies with that?"

"It'd look like the hand of God," said Greighton.

"It would *be* the hand of God! We'll found a state that will overwhelm the world!"

"And what would I get for my help?"

"The vineyards of France . . . the treasures of Italy . . .

whatever you want. I'm not a greedy man. My gratitude would be generously shown."

"And if I refuse?" said Greighton.

"I'll find someone else. He help me rewrite history. Then, one day, you and your world will cease to exist."

"You don't seem to offer me a choice."

"Only opportunities, John. Only opportunities."

Rick had heard enough. Whether Greighton accepted Green's offer was ultimately irrelevant, and to listen further increased his risk of getting caught. He had an idea of how dangerous that might be. Quickly, but cautiously, he sneaked away.

John Greighton left Green's quarters about a half an hour later. The sunset had painted the sky a brilliant orange, but he was oblivious to it. In his hand was the bottle of cognac, a parting gift. He removed its cut crystal stopper. With an unsteady hand, he held the bottle to his lips and drank deeply.

Peter Green remained in his quarters. He already regretted the gift of the cognac. He would have enjoyed a celebratory drink at the moment. Reaching into a pocket of his dinner jacket, he extracted a small pistol. It had not been necessary. He placed the pistol under his pillow and prepared for bed.

14

RICK HEADED FOR THE SEA, HIS MIND IN TURMOIL. ON ONE hand, Green's scheme seemed unreal and absurd—a single man proposing to alter the destiny of humanity to satisfy his greed. It was hard to comprehend such a pathological ambition, much less see how it could come to pass. Still, the idea of standing on the shores of the Interior Seaway had seemed equally absurd and unreal only a week ago. Rick was no student of history, but he knew that all evil needed to flourish was acquiescence. Green had a time machine, and with it, he could wreak havoc. It was a fact Rick could not dare to ignore.

The sea glowed like molten metal against the darkening sky, but it did not calm Rick. Its unceasing motion dredged up disturbing echoes of the journey through time. An unquiet feeling that nothing was stable or permanent seized Rick's imagination. His very existence seemed tenuous. He might dissolve in an instant, along with everyone and everything dear to him.

I must calmly decide what to do, Rick told himself. It was not easy advice to follow. There seemed little chance of resolving matters peacefully. As Rick walked along the shore, he played out scenarios of confrontation, sabotage, and mutiny in his mind. Each ended in violence, and each increased his agitation. He was stabbing the air with Tom's knife, when Joe called out his name. Joe was sitting on a rock, flask in hand, watching the waves. Rick hadn't even noticed him.

"Hope you didn't mind my joking at dinner," Joe said good-naturedly. "I gotta admit it, that girl's one spunky kid!"

"Yeah, sure." said Rick tersely.

"Something buggin' you? You're looking at me weird. Like I crawled from under this rock."

"I'm just tired, that's all."

"You don't look tired. You look jumpy. Those Tyrannosaurs get to you?"

"Them?"

"Yeah. You were a little damp after our encounter. Not that I blame you, if it was up to me, I'd have blown them away."

"I'm sure you would," said Rick angrily. "That's where we're different. Blowing stuff away doesn't bother you."

Joe stared out to sea, saying nothing. Rick strode away, following the shore.

RICK LAY ON his cot, listening to the easy breathing of James, Pandit and Joe. He looked at his watch. No one had stirred for half an hour. Assured everyone was asleep, he pulled off his covers and rose from his bunk, fully dressed except for his shoes. These he grabbed to put on outside the tent. Rick walked quietly to the door flap and slipped into the night.

The full moon made the path easy to see. It took Rick only a few minutes to reach the plane. The doorway opened as he approached. Rick reached inside and grabbed a gun. He pressed a button and the rows of lights appeared on the barrel. He adjusted the power level to its highest setting and then set the firing spread to maximum. These were "kick-ass levels," as Joe would put it— messy, but effective. Rick turned off the safety and the firing trigger appeared.

Rick's hands trembled as he held the deadly instrument. He stood immobile in the moonlight, reluctant to start his trek to Peter Green's quarters. *This isn't murder*, he told himself. *I'll be saving lives. Murder is something different.* Rick wondered if anyone would believe that. He doubted that he believed it himself.

Shadows of trees lay across the path so Rick walked alternately in moonlight and in darkness. His thoughts, however, were always on the darkness. He would have to turn on the lights for a clear shot. *What if Green wakes up?* Rick was convinced he would. *Should I say something to him? Do I owe him an explanation? What if he pleads with me?* The idea of killing a man begging for his life was profoundly depressing. Rick wished he could be angry, but the only passion he could muster was sorrow.

"Going hunting?" asked Joe as he stepped out of the shadows to block Rick's path.

Rick gave a start, then quickly raised his gun and aimed it at Joe's chest. Joe stood still, his hands clasped in front of his waist. "It seems," he said calmly, "I'm not the only one who doesn't mind blowing stuff away."

"I know what Green's up to. He's got to be stopped."

"And you're the one to do it?"

"Yes," said Rick. "Now out of my way."

Joe sighed deeply. "You're not a killer, Rick."

Rick watched Joe through the targeting scope. "I'll do what I have to. Move!"

"You'll have to kill me first. If you're going to take on Green, you're gonna need practice."

Rick tried to pull the trigger, but couldn't bring himself to do it. He lowered the gun. "Damn you, Joe! Damn you!"

"Green would've killed me in a nanosecond," said Joe. "He's the real thing. If you go down there, you're gonna die."

"Is that a threat?" asked Rick, raising the gun again.

"No," said Joe, "more a statement of fact. He's always armed, and he doesn't flinch. Besides, it's not necessary to kill him."

"I'm confused," said Rick. "Whose side are you on?"

"Not Green's, if that's what you think. My own, I guess. I'm just trying to survive."

"How can you stand by and let Green pull it off?"

"I don't know what 'it' is," replied Joe. "Green doesn't confide in the help."

"You know Green's a fake. Don't pretend you don't."

"I won't," said Joe. "I also know that this 'resort' is only a means to get to Greighton."

"But you claim you don't know Green's plans?"

"Nope, though I have no doubt they're illegal and immoral."

"He wants Greighton to build him a fleet of time machines to invade the past. He calls it a 'preemptive strike' against the future. He actually plans to take over the world."

Joe chuckled mirthlessly. "That ruthless son of a bitch!"

"There's nothing funny about this! He's planning germ warfare. And our present—it'll cease to exist!"

"None of that's going to happen," said Joe.

"How can you be so sure?"

"I'm an engineer, or at least I was one. I've spent a lot more time with Green's new toy than he has. Those knobs and switches on the control panel look ordinary because they're made for human fingers, and people's fingers haven't changed. What's beneath them, the control panel itself, is a whole different story. It's engineered on the atomic level. It doesn't even use electricity, at least not the way we understand it. And that's just the control panel. Everything about that machine is completely over our heads. Who knows how many generations it took to discover its technology. No one's going to copy it."

"He still has this machine," Rick countered.

"Yeah, but it only goes to two destinations—this place and our own time."

"That doesn't make sense."

"I know you love this godforsaken place," said Joe, "but do you really think Green would take Greighton here if he had a choice?"

"You've lost me," said Rick

"Look," said Joe, "why don't you turn off that gun, and I'll explain the whole thing."

Joe reached into his pocket and Rick quickly pointed the gun at him. Joe very slowly pulled out his flask. "Another night like this, and I'll run out before we leave." He unscrewed the top and held out the flask to Rick. "Want some?"

"No."

Joe took a sip from the flask, then put it away. "Come on, the gun belongs in the plane. We can talk there."

Rick hesitated before he turned off the gun. When he finally did, a great feeling of relief came over him. Wordlessly, he began to walk to the plane. Soon, he and Joe were sitting inside it, watching the night sky through its crystal fuselage.

Joe broke the silence. "Green is a man with connections. Some are legitimate, most aren't. He gets his hooks into people, and then he uses them. He got me several years ago." Joe sighed. "It's a long, sad story. Anyway, he got connected with Sam somehow. That's what we called the guy with the time machine. I don't know his real name, probably something unpronounceable. He was an arrogant asshole and weird-looking, too—tall, baby-faced. Dressed like some guy from India. Wore an old-fashioned turban and had one of those dots on his forehead. He may have looked like a foreigner, but he spoke perfect English.

"Sam sought Green out, at least that's my impression. He had some scheme going, and he needed a native to carry it out. I never found out what the deal was about. Whatever it was, it was definitely illegal in the future. Sam was nervous as hell about getting caught in the twenty-first century. That's how I got involved. Sam wanted to do all the planning here."

"Why?" asked Rick.

"Because it was safe."

"Safe?"

"Manned time travel is banned in Sam's era, he wanted to go to someplace private."

"Then why go somewhere built by people from the future?"

"I don't think he had a lot of choices. From the little I know about it, navigating through time is mind-bogglingly complicated. I suspect this was one of the few places he knew how to reach."

"I still don't understand why it would be safe."

"Sam never told me why. I can only speculate. Maybe it's off-limits. Maybe it no longer exists in the future. That seems more likely."

"Now you've really lost me."

"Time travel becomes illegal when people figure out that traveling downwhen can alter their own present. After that discovery, time exploration is only done covertly by unmanned probes. Sam knew visiting our time would change history, and I suspect that was the point. It's likely he also altered events to erase knowledge of this place in the future."

"If he did that," said Rick, "how could he know it still exists?"

"If Sam initiated the change, he'd be unaffected by it. What you do in the past only affects the future. He wouldn't be in the future when the change occurred."

"That's what Green told Greighton," said Rick. "That they could change the future with impunity. If that's true, what did Sam have to worry about? He could wipe his pursuers out of existence."

"I imagine a change of that magnitude would not be easy to pull off. Also, he'd have to worry about betraying his presence. Cause and effect gets very tricky in time travel. As soon as Sam appeared in our time, his presence made changes that could be detected in the future. All the clues of a person's whereabouts—hotel records, communications logs, all kinds of stuff—would instantly appear upwhen."

"It would be like looking for a specific grain of sand on a beach," scoffed Rick.

"These people discovered time travel, Rick. Who knows what they're capable of? Sam did, and he was seriously worried about it. I imagine Greighton's unexplained two-week absence will be a red flag to them."

"Two-week absence!" said Rick. "I was told this trip would take up only a few seconds in our own time."

"It's easy to see why Green wanted you to believe that, but it's not true. Something Sam called 'temporal linkage' prevents that."

"Temporal linkage? What's that?"

"It's really pretty simple," said Joe. "Imagine a target range inside a moving airplane where I've locked my gun on the bull's-eye so I can hit it every time. I can do this because the gun and the target are moving together, linked by the aisle of the airplane. A temporal linkage works the same way, except the target and the gun are moving through time, not space. Sam set up the link to simplify navigating the time machine. Our own time and this time seem like fixed coordinates only because there's an inflexible connection between them. In practical terms, it means that if I spend three days in the past and want to return to my own time, I can only return to a time three days after I left. It works the same in reverse."

"Crap! I'll miss two exams!"

"Too bad. The two weeks we spend here will also pass in the twenty-first century. They're gone. Once a link's established, it determines which destinations are accessible."

"We're getting side tracked," said Rick. "How do you know all this? What's your involvement?"

"That's easy to explain," said Joe. "Green and Sam didn't trust each other. Green refused to come here unless he had his own pilot. I got mixed up in this because I was the guy Sam trained."

"So he trusted you."

"Hardly. I pieced together most of what I know from things he let slip. If he hadn't thought I was as dumb as a dog, he might have been more guarded. As far as trusting me—he taught me as little as possible. I only learned how to shuttle between Montana Isle and our time. Those are the only coordinates I have."

"Green spoke about 'gaps' in his knowledge'," said Rick. "That's what he must have meant."

"Fat chance of filling them," said Joe. "Ignorance sees easy solutions for all problems. Sam thought he could control Green by keeping him in the dark. In doing so, he underestimated Green's capacity for self-delusion. A fatal error, I suspect."

"You mean . . ."

"Green decided Sam was unnecessary. One day Sam was gone and the time machine was still there," said Joe. "You do the math."

"And you work for him," said Rick with disgust.

"Yeah, I do," said Joe with resignation. "But not for long. Soon, I'll be free of him. Sam's people will see to that."

"I thought their hands were tied, that's what Green said."

"That's his ignorance talking. They'll get him, all right. They know they have to. That's why Sam was so anxious to hide out here. Our own time is much more accessible to them. Even as we speak, they're scanning history for clues . . . sending probes . . . employing technologies we can't even imagine . . . and on top of all that, they have time. They can take centuries to track down Green, then show up the instant he returns to our time."

The moonlight reflected off Joe's eyes as they bored into Rick's. "You don't have to stop Green," he said. "Others will do that. All you have to do is bide your time." Joe continued studying Rick's face. "You'd like to believe me," he said, "but you're not sure you can."

"I believe you," said Rick.

"Ever play poker?"

"No."

"Good thing. You'd be lousy. I can read your face like a book."

Rick looked away. "You're not the first to say that."

"Soon as I saw you on the beach, I knew something was up. After that, it was only a matter of waiting for you to make your move."

"Why did you interfere?"

"If I thought you could have pulled it off, I probably wouldn't have stopped you."

"So, it was to save my life?" asked Rick dubiously.

"Not just yours. Once Green took care of you, he would have tidied up. Other people could get hurt."

"Including you."

"Me?" said Joe cynically. "I'm the only one that's safe. Green needs me. I'm his pilot."

Rick was seized by a sudden sense of failure, that he had been called to face evil and had not measured up.

Joe read his downcast expression. "Don't be hard on yourself. Be proud you're not a killer," said Joe. "Things will work out as long as Green doesn't get suspicious."

"How can I prevent that?"

"Stay out of his way and don't nose around. Stick close to Greighton's kid, too. Keep her happy, and you'll remain useful to him. Green's still courting Greighton. He won't want to rock the boat."

"It all sounds so . . . so cowardly," said Rick.

"Green's as good as caught the moment we get up-when. Be smart, and let Sam's people take care of him. You don't need to stick your neck out."

"Is that all?" asked Rick.

"Now you know everything," said Joe. "I wish you

didn't. The less you knew, the safer you were. Don't do anything to tip off Green."

"I'll be careful."

Joe watched his words sink in. *Green's right*, he thought. *This kid's too damned curious.*

15

THE CHIRPING OF BIRDS HERALDED THE ONSET OF CON'S favorite time of the day. She awoke to savor the landscape beyond the colonnade as it slowly came awake. The early-morning air was heavy with the smell of the sea and magnolias. It bathed her in fragrance as she lay on her bed, watching the soft blue light of dawn gradually brighten. Soon, pterosaurs added their less melodic cries to those of the birds. Before long, the first rays of the rising sun would strike the treetops.

Con enjoyed the calmness of morning. None of the on-coming day's irritants or problems need yet be faced. Daddy and Sara did not provoke her. The mysterious Peter Green remained forgotten. Rick's unsettling revelations were ignored. Con shut them all away while she recaptured the feeling of innocent delight she had experienced the first morning on the island.

Rick spoiled it by quietly emerging from the trees. He stopped outside her room, and whispered, "Con."

Con closed her eyes and pretended to be asleep.

"Con, are you awake?" whispered Rick more loudly.

Con remained still and waited for him to leave. Instead, she heard him enter the room. His hand softly shook her foot. "Con."

"What do you want?" she said, not bothering to hide her

annoyance. She opened her eyes to see that Rick had re-treated a few steps.

"Con, would you do me a favor?"

"Did you have to come here to ask? Couldn't it have waited?"

"Sorry," said Rick. "I had to ask before the others got up."

Con caught an anxious tone in Rick's voice. His face, also, had a disquietingly worried look to it. "What's going on?" she asked.

"I can't talk now. Just say you want to stay on the island today. Tell James you'd like me to take you fishing. Will you do that?"

"Why?"

Rick looked around nervously. "Please. I'll explain later."

"All right," said Con, somewhat grudgingly.

"Thanks," whispered Rick as he began a quick retreat from the room.

Con remained in her bed. The dawn proceeded, but it no longer seemed tranquil.

RICK WAS GLAD he had used an indirect return route to the staff compound when he encountered James making coffee. "You're up early," said James.

"I wanted to see the sunrise," said Rick.

"Thought you'd take a fancy to this place," replied James. "It reminds me of my boyhood. God, I loved dawn on the Serengeti."

"No seashore there," said Rick.

"No, but the feel's the same, a glimpse of the world before we ruined it." James poured himself a mug and sipped it as he contemplated. Rick helped himself and drank quietly, glad that James was not in a talkative mood.

James put his cup down and rose. "Guess I should see if our guests are stirring. What have you planned for to-day?"

"I thought we might follow the coast to the south."

"I'd like to go on one of your trips," said James, "after things settle down a bit."

"I'd love to have you," replied Rick. "The plains to the north should remind you a bit of Africa. No grass, though."

"None?"

"It hasn't evolved yet."

James shook his head as he strolled toward the guests' quarters. "Fancy that, no grass."

A few minutes later, James returned to wake Pandit, and the routine of camp began in earnest. Rick tried to seem surprised when James returned from dining with the guests to tell him, "Miss Greighton desires to be taken fishing."

"There's a likely spot for hand lines at the far end of the island," said Rick. "The bottom drops off right beyond the cliff."

"Good," said James. "Just make sure you throw her line out, I don't want her hooking herself." He turned to Joe. "It looks like you're on holiday today."

"I can live with that," said Joe with a smile.

"Just stay clear of the protected beach," warned James. "Mr. Greighton and Miss Boyton enjoy their privacy."

When James left to get the fishing gear, Joe turned to Rick. "I *bet* they enjoy their privacy," he said with a grin. Then in a lower voice, he asked, "Are you okay after last night?"

"Yeah," replied Rick. "Don't worry about me."

"Things will work out," assured Joe.

"Sure," replied Rick.

RICK WALKED ALONG the shore carrying a large picnic hamper in one hand and a cooler in the other. Con accompanied him, carrying a small bag of fishing gear and bait.

"Why are we going fishing?" asked Con.

"I thought you might enjoy it," replied Rick.

"Don't give me that!" said Con testily. "That's not why you sneaked into my room this morning. Don't treat me like a child."

"I just need to get away from Joe."

"I thought you two were friends."

"We were . . . maybe we still are. I just need to sort things out."

"Why drag me along?"

"You know why," said Rick.

"Baby-sitting," said Con angrily, and she sat down on a rock.

"Con . . ."

"Tell me what's up."

"I don't think I should."

"You promised! Besides, you don't have a choice. I won't play along if you keep things from me."

Rick hesitated, then sighed as if he were setting down a burden. "Last evening I overheard Green and your father talking. Green said he stole the time machine, and then he tried to get your father's help in some mad scheme to change history. It was like something out of science fiction, he actually said they'd conquer the world."

Con's face lit up, "That's wild!"

"This is serious. He's planning to wipe out our existence in the process. He figures if he does that, the people who want the time machine back will be wiped out also."

"What did Daddy say?"

"I don't know what his answer was or even if he gave one. Green offered to share the riches of Europe."

Con pondered Rick's story. Absurd as it sounded, it was easier to picture Green as an unscrupulous schemer than as a scientist. "He'll probably say no," she said without conviction. "I wish I could say for sure. But what does Joe have to do with this?"

"Last night, I was going to stop Green . . ."

"Stop him?"

"Kill him," said Rick.

Con gave him an astonished look, which grew as she saw he was serious.

"Joe intervened," continued Rick, "and said it wasn't necessary to do anything, that people from the future will stop Green."

"I'm glad he stopped you. I can't imagine you killing anyone."

"Neither could he," said Rick. "He said Green would have killed me first."

"This is too weird," said Con.

"That's my problem, too," said Rick. "Everything's so unbelievable. Should I buy Joe's story? I can see all sorts of alternatives."

"Well, he didn't tell Green."

"True," said Rick. "He could have easily shot me, too. I had no idea he was following me."

"I think he's telling the truth," said Con. "There's nothing to worry about."

"You're probably right," said Rick.

Con looked at him and knew he did not believe her. She picked up the fishing gear and started walking. "Then let's go fishing. This is supposed to be my vacation!"

They walked in silence, while Con tried to think of something to distract Rick from his brooding. "I'll have a birthday in four days," she said. "When we return to our time three seconds after we left, will I be eighteen or not?"

"Eighteen," said Rick. "That instant vacation stuff was bull."

"What do you mean?"

"It was a lie. We'll arrive two weeks after we left. Joe told me last night."

"Daddy will be pissed."

"He probably doesn't know yet."

"I was planning to give him two chances to remember my birthday—one here and one when we got back. He usually forgets."

"Here, he has an excuse," said Rick. "How can you have a birthday when you won't be born for 65 million years?"

"Maybe I should stay here and remain young forever."

"You almost had your chance," said Rick. "Last night, I considered sabotaging the time machine."

"Oh God!" exclaimed Con. "Marooned with Sara and Daddy! What a thought!"

"Maybe she'd see him differently when he wasn't a billionaire."

Con laughed wickedly. "I'm sure she'd stop feeding him fruit. She might stop giving him other things as well."

"Maybe Pandit would have his chance," said Rick. "I know he's smitten. He's more her age, *and* he can cook."

"Perhaps she'd prefer a jungle guide," teased Con.

"No way!"

"I might claim you for myself. Are you a good provider?"

"I could keep even you fed."

"Really?" answered Con. "Could you satisfy all my appetites?" She was amused when he blushed.

"We'll return to our time," said Rick, trying to change the conversation. "If Joe's right, we'll never see this place again."

"That bothers you, doesn't it?"

"Yeah," said Rick with a note of dejection. "What a waste. Only you and James appreciate what's here."

"Maybe the people who built the time machine will let you come back."

"I doubt it. Joe says they might not even know this place is here."

"How's that possible?" asked Con.

"It has something to do with history being altered."

"That's so mysterious!" said Con. "Don't you find it exciting? I wonder what this place is for."

"I have no idea," admitted Rick.

"Aren't you the least bit curious? Maybe there's more to this island than we've seen. Like the symbols on my wall."

"I did see something . . . a reflection on the top of the mesa."

"Let's go there and investigate!" said Con excitedly. "We can fish later."

"I don't know . . ."

"Where's your sense of adventure? You're supposed to be a guide. Guide me!"

"I'm supposed to keep you safe."

"Come on! I'm going, whether you do or not!"

Rick put down the cooler and the picnic hamper. "Are you always this headstrong?" he asked.

"Always."

Although the walls of the mesa rose precipitously where the stone rooms were located, on this end of the island they sloped, albeit steeply. The way was difficult, and much of the rock was loose. Con, who was wearing flimsy rubber beach thongs, had a difficult time.

"Maybe we should turn around," suggested Rick. "James would kill me if he knew I was taking you up here."

"Stop worrying about James," retorted Con. "How are we going to get up that cliff?"

Above the rocky slope, the last forty feet of the mesa rose as a vertical wall. As they approached the cliff, Rick looked for a route to the top. When they reached its base, it still appeared unclimbable. "Why don't you rest here," said Rick, "while I look for a way up." Con said nothing, but sat down on a rock. Rick scrambled along the base of the cliff, examining it with the eyes of a seasoned climber. He found a number of routes to the top he might attempt if he were properly equipped with climbing shoes, a rope, carabiners, and pitons, but nothing he felt secure freeclimbing in street shoes. Finally, about fifty yards from where Con sat, he discovered a fissure in the cliff. He stepped inside it. Its parallel sides were about three feet apart and rose straight up, forming what climbers call a "chimney."

When he exited the fissure, he saw Con walking toward him. "Any luck?" she called out.

"I think I can climb this crack," Rick called back.

When Con reached him, she looked up the fissure. Its rough walls appeared devoid of holds. "How could you possibly climb that?" she asked.

"There's a technique called 'stemming' that works for cracks. I've practiced it for years."

Rick entered the fissure and leaned his back against one of its walls. He then raised his left foot and placed it on the opposite wall at hip height. He pressed his left foot against the rock wall to wedge his body in place as he swung his right foot so that it touched the rock beneath his buttocks. Rick was wedged in the crack a few feet above the floor.

"I thought you were going to climb up," teased Con.

Rick didn't answer, but placed his palms as high as he could on the rock behind his back. He suddenly pressed his body away from the wall as he pushed up with both legs. His torso rose, and he quickly swung his right leg upward to the opposite wall at hip height. Both legs pressed his lower back against the wall, wedging him in place a foot higher than he had been before. Then he swung his left foot so it pressed the wall beneath his buttock, assuming his original position, only with his legs reversed.

Rick did the maneuver so quickly it looked like he was walking up the fissure. Con had to watch several repetitions before she understood exactly what he did. When he was about eight feet above the floor of the crack, he left both feet against the opposite wall and locked his knees. Wedged in place, he rested. "It's been a while since I've done this," he said. "When I get to the top, I'll you tell what's up there."

"I'm coming, too," said Con.

"I was roped in when I learned to do this," said Rick. "I fell several times before I caught on. Without a rope, you might . . ."

"I get your point," said Con.

She stood and watched as Rick raised himself in increments until he was a small figure five stories above her. Then, with a quick motion, he disappeared. A moment later, his head peered over the edge of the crack.

"There's something up here all right," he called down with excitement. "It looks like some kind of aircraft or a . . ." Rick's head disappeared.

"Rick, what is it?" No answer. "Rick!" His head did not reappear over the edge. "Rick, damn you, what did you find?"

Con waited impatiently for an answer. When she could

bear it no longer, she kicked off her rubber thongs and entered the fissure.

RICK STOOD AT the top of the mesa and stared in amazement at the craft twenty yards in front of him. It rested in a large circular depression cut in the rock of the mesa. It looked like a flying saucer twenty feet in diameter, with a fuselage made entirely of crystal. Its transparent shell was crammed with strange machinery and devices. He had been calling down to Con when he spotted the column in the center of the craft. Within the column was a strangely immaterial cylinder. He recognized it immediately. The craft was a time machine.

Rick forgot all about Con as the implications of his discovery hit him. Apparently, Green had more than one time machine already, and its existence contradicted Joe's version of their situation. Joe's calming assurances—that Green's scheme was impossible and he was as good as caught—were most likely fabrications to keep Rick in line while the plot proceeded. He found it hard to see it any other way. *Joe lied to me!* thought Rick angrily and, for a moment, he wished he had pulled the trigger when Joe had confronted him on the path. Once again, Rick felt that the world had been pulled out from under him like a rug, leaving him spinning.

Rick approached the time machine to examine it more closely. The sloping sides of the depression where it stood were covered with the same black panels found on the plane and on the other time machine. They were immaculately clean, as was the transparent craft they surrounded. Everything appeared brand-new, as if they had been placed there only moments before.

The interior of the time machine was filled with exotic machinery and what appeared to be instruments. Rick recognized a large telescope and numerous instruments with lenses. These, he assumed, were cameras. One followed his every movement. It gave him the uncomfortable feeling that he was being watched. *Perhaps by the time we reach camp, Green will know I was here,* he thought. *If that's the case, I might as well finish investigating.*

As he walked down the sloping sides of the landing site, an opening formed in the machine's fuselage. Behind it was a tiny chamber empty of instruments. It contained a small control panel and a simple transparent bench that served as the only seat. Rick was leery of entering the machine, so he examined the chamber from outside. It was so small only two, or possibly three, people could fit inside. The control panel lacked the tape labels of the other machine and seemed less complex. Rick noted that the glowing yellow symbols Con found on her wall were also on the panel.

Rick had turned his attention to the more mysterious-looking mechanisms, when he heard Con call out his name. She was standing barefoot at the edge of the cliff with an exultant expression on her face. It reminded him of the look she had after they encountered the Tyrannosaurs.

"Wow!" she said. "What's that?"

"Con!" yelled Rick. He did not know whether he felt more startled, annoyed, worried, or impressed, and his voice reflected his uncertainty. "What are you doing here?"

Con walked over to the rim of the circular depression. "Never keep a woman waiting," she said by way of explanation. Then she turned her attention back to the machine. "This is really incredible!"

"Your foot's bleeding," said Rick with as much authority as he could muster.

"Just a scrape. Stop being my nursemaid."

"You could have been killed!"

"But I wasn't," said Con with a note of finality. "Now . . . What do you think this is?"

Rick started to say something, but stopped. After a moment's silence he said, "It's a time machine. I'm sure of it. See the cylinder in the column?"

Con stepped on the black-paneled slope to walk down to the machine. She quickly pulled back her foot. "It's cold!" she said with surprise. As she watched, her dusty footprint blurred, then flowed off the black surface like water, leaving it perfectly clean.

"The black stuff is some form of energy collector, like a solar panel," said Rick. "It won't hurt you."

Con walked quickly down to the machine. "Look at my footprints," she told Rick. "This place cleans itself."

Rick watched the prints disappear. "Everything only looks new. This machine could have been here for years."

Con circled the saucer, peering inside with excited fascination. A lensed device swiveled as she passed. Con made a short hop backward. "It's watching me!"

"Yeah. Let's hope Joe isn't also."

"You still worrying about him?"

"How can't I?" asked Rick. "He said there was only one time machine. What else did he lie about? Everything?"

Con looked concerned. "You're not planning something crazy?"

"What do you mean by 'crazy'?"

"You know perfectly well," replied Con. "You were talking about killing and sabotage earlier. Don't do anything drastic. Promise you won't."

"What if my suspicions are true?"

"If they are, I'll help you stop them. I will. Just don't be hasty. We have time to figure things out."

"I won't do anything rash," said Rick.

Con appeared satisfied by Rick's promise, for she turned her attention back to the time machine. She walked around it slowly, minutely examining each part. After several minutes of silence, she pronounced, "I think it's an observatory, but not just for the stars. It seems to observe everything."

"Maybe it's one of those probes Joe told me about," said Rick.

"See?" said Con triumphantly. "He wasn't lying. You were worried about nothing."

She turned and began making faces at a lens, while Rick watched in amusement. In a mechanical voice he said, "This probe reports it found no intelligent life." Con stuck out her tongue at him.

The time machine did not yield any further information, and Rick wandered off to explore the rest of the mesa top. Con joined him. The view from the cliff top was spectacular, but Rick scarcely noticed it. He had a more pressing concern—he hoped to find a different route down. Descending a chimney was considerably more difficult than ascending one, and he was concerned that Con would not be up to it. He said nothing about this to her. It was too late for that. Besides, he wanted her to remain confident; panicked climbers make mistakes.

Rick's search for an easier route off the mesa proved fruitless. Con, enchanted by the scenery, did not seem to be aware of the true purpose of his inspection. As they walked about the cliff edge she was in a happy, playful mood. "We simply *must* picnic here. Guide," she said imperiously, "go fetch the hamper and the cooler."

"Yes, miss," answered Rick in mock subservience. "Soon as I evolve two more arms."

"Shall it take long?"

"A thousand generations or so. I pray you're not hungry."

"I'm always hungry," said Con. "If you're going to be pokey, I'll climb down myself."

"You ready to leave?" asked Rick, hoping he sounded casual.

"I guess so," replied Con reluctantly.

"I'll go first so you can watch."

"Can't we climb down together?"

"It's safer if only one person is in the crack at a time," replied Rick. He hoped that he wouldn't have to explain how a person falling from above would take out the climber below. Con didn't press him for a reason, but a shadow of fear passed over her expression. "You'll do fine," said Rick, hoping he sounded convincing. "The trick is not to rush things. Move down in small increments. Lock your knees to rest whenever you need to."

That was all the instruction he could give. He walked over to the fissure and sat down on one side of the crack. Then he placed his feet on the side of the crack opposite

him and, gripping the edge with his hands, pushed his
torso out over the void and lowered it about sixteen
inches. Pushing with his legs, he wedged his body between the walls of the fissure. The rocks below were
inches closer.

Con studied Rick's descent. In purely mechanical
terms, it was simply the reverse of ascending, but psy-
chologically, it was utterly different. Ascending focuses
the mind above, to the goal that gets ever closer. When
the danger is the greatest, safety is closest at hand. Descending is cousin to falling. The focus is downward, and
every descent starts at the point of greatest peril.

Watching Rick's climb downward, Con became op-
pressed by the emptiness below—the five-story drop. She
waited for her turn as Rick gradually got smaller and
smaller. It seemed to take forever for him to reach the
ground. By the time he called to her to start down, Con
was gripped by a fear that approached terror.

As Con sat on the edge of the fissure and placed her
feet on the opposite wall, she tried to force herself to
remain calm, to subdue the trembling in her legs. *There's
no other way down, I have to do this*, she told herself.
She became aware of her fatigue from the climb up. She
began to worry that her muscles would betray her. She
imagined a horrible moment when gravity snatched
her . . . the rush of wind . . . the snap of cracking bones.

"Con, are you okay?" Rick's voice sounded far away.

"I think so," she called back.

"It's okay to be scared. Take some slow breaths.
There's no hurry."

Con exhaled and breathed in slowly. *I can do this.* She
pushed her torso away from the ledge and out over the
yawning emptiness. A second later, she was wedged in
the crack. Her instinct to survive took over, washing her
mind clean of everything not necessary to continue living. Her attention was focused by fear upon balance, fric-
tion, and gravity until existence consisted only of these
things, as—inch by inch—she made her way downward.

After an eternity, it was over. Rick lifted her from the
wall before she could touch the floor of the fissure. He

set her feet on the ground, but continued to hold her for a moment, as if to convince himself she was truly safe. When Rick released her, Con thought he was trying to hide the depths of his concern.

"That was some climb," he said.

"You didn't think I could make it," replied Con, as she slipped her thongs on her sore feet.

Rick looked away and said nothing for a while. Eventually he asked, "You getting hungry?"

"Starved."

As they walked down the slope, both felt the exhilaration that follows a perilous climb. It heightened their senses so they more keenly appreciated the rugged beauty about them. The rocky landscape, brilliant beneath the cloudless sky, contrasted with the deep blues and soft turquoises of the surrounding sea. A gentle breeze dissipated the heat. The prospect of food seemed very inviting. Rick carried the hamper and the cooler down to a rocky part of the shore. There, they ate their lunch while Con cooled her feet in the water.

Rick fell under the spell of their idyllic setting and Con's exuberant mood, which had redoubled following the climb. He found her gaiety disarming and contagious. It was impossible to brood around her, and his forebodings about Green and Joe faded as they talked and joked. *I was wrong about her*, he decided. *She isn't spoiled, just self-assured*. Even Con's quick tongue, which Rick had found so sharp earlier, began to seem spunky and forthright to him.

Afterward, they went fishing. Not since the Europeans discovered the New World had anyone caught fish so easily. Con squealed with excitement as she pulled one fish after another from the generous waters. All of them had an unfamiliar, exotic look. One two-foot-long fish, which Rick identified as a *Bananogamius*, had a huge sail-like fin along its back. Another long fish with thin, pointed fins had a toothy protruding lower jaw that ended with a short sword. Once, a thirteen-foot fish swallowed another that was already hooked. It nearly pulled Con off the rocks before it snapped the line. Before long, the cooler overflowed with fish. Still, they were reluctant to return to camp.

It was late afternoon before they presented their catch to a delighted Pandit. Rick was not surprised to discover that it would be his job to clean it. It was a chore Con was happy to leave to him.

"When a woman will clean your fish," said Pandit, as Con walked away, "that is when you know she loves you."

"How about when she feeds you strawberries using her teeth, like Sara does?"

"That may be a sign," admitted Pandit, "but cleaning fish is the true test." He got a twinkle in his eye. "I see you are cleaning Miss Greighton's fish."

"I'm cleaning everyone's fish," said Rick.

16

THE EVENING MEAL IN THE PAVILION WAS THE PART OF THE day Con liked least. She felt diminished in the presence of her father and Sara, transformed back into a little girl. Despite that, she dutifully bathed and dressed for the occasion. She rationalized that she was helping Rick, not caving in to her father's dictates. It made her feel better to think so.

During this dinner, Con felt particularly neglected. Her one consolation was that Sara seemed to be feeling the same way. Peter Green and her father were deep into a conversation about, of all things, history. Con was surprised that Green seemed quite knowledgeable about eighteenth-century European politics. He did most of the talking. She was even more surprised that her father displayed any interest in what Green said. It was completely out of character. Business was his only passion, outside wine and women.

"They've been yakking all day," Sara said to Con, with obvious annoyance. When Con seemed more amused than sympathetic, Sara redirected her irritation. "Don't you wash your hair?"

"I do," replied Con, "but I've stopped using shampoo."

"It certainly shows. Why would you do something like that?"

"I want to smell like myself."

"I would think you'd rather smell clean."

Before Con could reply, James Neville injected himself into the conversation. "Constance, I'm dying to hear about your fishing. You're the first person ever to try these waters." Of all the diners, only James ever showed more than the most superficial interest in her activities. This evening, Con's account of her day was greatly abbreviated. The most exciting part, the discovery on the mesa top, was her and Rick's secret.

As Con finished her story, Rick and Joe arrived with the main courses. The evening's fare was better received than the stir-fried dinosaur. Pandit had prepared seven fish dishes; spiced baked fish, grilled fish on skewers, fish stir-fried with vegetables, fish curry, fish steamed in leaves, crispy fried fish Hunan style, and a fish soup. Conversation dwindled as the diners savored their first fish from completely unpolluted waters. Con ate silently and voraciously. She had healthy portions of everything and seconds of the grilled fish, the curry, and the crispy fried fish. As good as the food was, she would have enjoyed it more if Rick had not been required to wait on her. She would have preferred him to join her at the table or, better still, to eat with her on the beach—just the two of them, like they had that afternoon. *We had a good time*, she reflected.

Eventually, dinner was over. Rick cleared the dishes, then left to eat with the rest of the staff. Sara wandered off to her quarters, carrying a bottle of wine. Peter Green continued to expound on the wealth of the British and French aristocracies while Con's father paid rapt attention. James excused himself and went to join the staff at their dinner. Con thought that he looked relieved to be going. She gladly left also.

Con went back to her quarters to change. As she entered the room with the dresser, the cycad leaf caught her eye. She pulled it aside to reveal the symbols hidden beneath. She was intrigued to discover that they were now red, not yellow as before. She couldn't remember what the numbers had been the last time she looked at them, but she was sure they had changed. There seemed to be a longer row of zeroes. Con studied the numbers. They read:

$$\text{⊕⊕} : \text{⊕⊕⊕} : \text{⊓} : \text{⊕⊠} : \text{⊟|}$$

They still made no sense. Now there were two mysteries about the place, the strange symbols and the time machine on top of the mesa. Con remembered her harrowing descent from the mesa with a sudden chill. It was her second brush with death on the island. *It was a stupid thing to do*, she told herself. Yet it had been thrilling also, especially when it was over. Even better, Rick treated her differently afterward. She felt he no longer saw her as a girl to baby-sit, but as a young woman who was his equal. She liked the change.

Con's thoughts returned to the people who had left the time machine on the mesa. On the machine's control panel were symbols like those on the wall before her. The two were linked. *If these were the time travelers' rooms*, she reasoned, *they must have had a way to reach the mesa top*. Con recalled how the openings appeared in the seemingly solid fuselage of the airplane and the floor of the other time machine. *Was there a door hidden in the black sides of the landing site? Could we have been standing next to stairs or an elevator the whole time?* It seemed possible, even logical, but there was one problem—there was no trace of stairs or an elevator in the rooms.

Con immediately became suspicious of the plaster wall before her. *It covered up the symbols, what else does it hide?* She began tapping the plaster with her fist. It sounded solid until she tapped behind the dresser. There, the wall sounded hollow. Con thought she could probably smash a hole in the plaster with a large rock, but that would make too much noise. Cutting her way in quietly would allow her to keep any discovery secret. She decided a thin, pointed rock could serve as a tool and set out to find one.

She soon discovered that it was easier to envision the perfect rock than to locate one. All the stones along the shore were worn smooth. It wasn't until she reached the slope Rick and she had climbed earlier, that she found something suitable. Stone tool in hand, she returned to camp. Con briefly considered enlisting Rick's help before deciding it would be less obtrusive if she worked alone. Also, she liked the idea of surprising him with her discovery—if there was any discovery to be made.

Drawing the curtains across the colonnade of her room, Con pulled the dresser from the plaster wall and set to work. She planned to make an opening near the floor, something big enough to crawl through, yet small enough to hide behind the dresser. The plaster was relatively soft, but when she scored it, she encountered wood beneath. The plaster was attached to a framework of lath made from tree branches. The work reminded her of the litter Joe constructed. It took a considerable amount of scraping to expose enough of a branch to get a firm grip on it. Bracing her feet against the wall, Con tugged. The branch broke with a loud snap. Plaster went flying, and a large slab fell off the wooden framework. Con froze and listened for the sound of someone's approach. After a minute or two, she concluded that no one had noticed the noise.

Con peered into the hole she had made, but could not see anything. Only one thing was certain—there was an empty cavity behind the plaster. Now that the lath was exposed, Con was able to enlarge the hole without making too much noise. As soon as the opening was large enough, Con crawled through it. She found she was able to stand. It occurred to her that, since this space was connected to her room, there might be lights that worked by voice command. "Lights on," she said. The ceiling immediately glowed to reveal a long corridor cut out of the stone. Behind her was the makeshift framework that supported the plaster that hid the doorway. There was a thick, continuous metallic band running around the walls, floor, and ceiling about a foot from the opening. Other than that, and the overhead light panels, the corridor was featureless.

The passageway curved, so Con could not see its end. She walked a short way down it and soon came to a junction between corridors that led from the three guest rooms and a single passageway that led deeper into the cliff. She followed the latter for about fifty feet before she encountered a series of openings on either side. These led to rooms that appeared abandoned. Most contained a few bits of trash and perhaps a few simple chairs and tables, but were otherwise empty. One was filled with machinery from which a soft humming sound emanated. Con examined the unfamiliar machinery and, though she could not determine its precise function, she assumed it provided utilities for the complex.

The corridor ended at a large chamber that sprang to life the moment Con entered it. Con's eye was immediately drawn to the dozens of glowing viewscreens that had turned on to display a bewildering and fascinating collection of images. Many appeared to be complex graphs and charts. The writing on the charts was completely alien, although Con recognized the numerals from the symbols on her wall. Many of the charts were geological maps, and there were three charts of the solar system in differing degrees of detail. All appeared holographic, although their realism and detail exceeded any hologram Con had ever seen. There were several screens displaying images of a rocky landscape. It took a moment for Con to realize that they were views of the mesa top. *Oh no*! she thought. *We could have been watched!*

Con hastily walked back to the junction of the corridors. Only when she examined each sealed doorway to the outer rooms did her panic subside. She made her way back to the chamber with the viewscreens to continue her exploration. Her attention focused on the several screens that displayed views of Earth as seen from the vantage point of satellites. These were particularly interesting because the shapes and positions of the continents were different from what Con was used to. She studied them for quite a while. *Rick will love this!* she thought excitedly. There was also a puzzling screen that showed a gray rock slowly tumbling against a background of stars. Finally, there was a screen that displayed the same cryptic arrangement of numbers Con had found on her wall:

$$\Phi\Phi : \Phi\Phi\Phi : \varDelta : \Box\Phi : \Phi|$$

Distracted by the viewscreens, it was a while before Con remembered that she was looking for a means to reach the mesa top. This room, like all the others, had no stairway or elevator. "I want to go up!" she said aloud in frustration. Immediately, an opening appeared in the wall where none had been before. It revealed a small room with metallic walls. *An elevator!* Con entered it and the opening closed behind her.

Half a minute later, she was standing next to the crystal time machine. The light of sunset gave it the appearance of a jewel. Con walked to the edge of the mesa to watch the sun disappear behind the mountains. They appeared completely black against the glowing sky. Long shadows trailed from them, caressing the coastal plains like loving fingers. When the sun winked out behind the peaks, Con's eyes adjusted, and the mountains were no longer black. Instead, they were delicate shades of blue-gray. They reminded her of the mountains of Chinese landscapes painted on rice paper so every stroke blurs into softness. Never had she seen a vision so peaceful or beautiful. She only wished that Rick were there to see it too. *Tomorrow,* she thought, *we'll watch it together.*

Con lingered on the mesa top, watching the colors of the land and sea change as the sky darkened. She was torn between her desire to savor the moment and her urge to share the discovery with Rick. When the land was obscured by shadow, and the dark blues of sea and the sky merged, the latter urge took over. Con entered the elevator compartment, which projected out of the sloping side of the landing site like a small shack. "Take me down," she commanded. The opening closed, and she descended.

Con exited from the hole in the plaster a few minutes later. She shoved the dresser back in place and hastily pushed the chunks of plaster and lath beneath. She planned to do a neater job later, but, at the moment, she was anxious to find Rick. She was hurrying toward the staff tent when her father called from the dark dining pavilion. "Constance! Come here, honey."

"What is it Daddy?"

"I want your advice."

Con walked over to the pavilion. John Greighton was seated with Peter Green. They were drinking champagne. Judging from her father's voice, he had consumed quite a bit.

"She studies all that artsy stuff," he said to Green. "She'll know." He turned toward Con. "Honey, what should I do with my big shell? Pete thinks I should stick it in a vault."

"I'm just saying . . ." injected Green.

"I know. I know," interrupted Con's father. "I'll keep it hush-hush till you-know-when."

"John, I don't think you should be discussing . . ."

"She's my daughter for Christ's sake! It's only a god damned shell! Now, honey, whaddaya think?"

"About what, Daddy?"

"My shell! I was talking about my shell. I want to show it off. How should I do it?"

"I'd treat it like a sculpture and put it on a pedestal."

"Yeah, a fancy marble column," said her father.

"Actually," said Con, "a simple stone rectangle would show it better. Something rough to contrast with the shell's smoothness. Perhaps, stone with fossils in it."

"Damn, you're clever!" said Con's father, pouring her a glass of champagne. "Isn't she clever, Pete? She's gonna study art history."

"Then she's fortunate to have a wealthy father," said Green sardonically.

"Oh it'll be useful, Pete. Very useful when I make my acquisitions. I don't want any crap. Only the best stuff."

"What acquisitions, Daddy?"

Green shot Greighton a hard, cautionary glance. "Oh, you'll find out later, honey." He turned his attention back to Green. "I named her 'Constance' to keep the money rolling in. There's a family legend. Constance Cle . . ."

"Oh, don't start on Great-great-great-grandmother," said Con, eager to leave. "You'll bore him to tears."

John Greighton gave his daughter an irritated look, but he stopped his story. Refilling his glass, he held it up. "A toast! To generations of good fortune and to my future in the past."

Con simply looked at her glass. "Daddy, I don't . . ."

"Drink!" bellowed her father. "And stop calling me 'Daddy,' it sounds babyish. You'll be eighteen in a month."

Con made a point of gulping down the champagne. Setting her empty glass on the table, she said in a controlled voice, "Then what should I call you?"

"I think 'sir' would be good," said Greighton, as he refilled his daughter's glass. Con drained it also.

" ' Sir?' That's more than a little old-fashioned," replied Con.

"Eighteenth century to be exact," said her father, who seemed to think he was being witty. "You'll find out why soon enough."

"Can't you tell me now, *sir*?"

Greighton didn't seem to notice the sarcasm in Con's voice. "No, no, that wouldn't do. Would it, Pete?"

Con looked at Peter Green. He did not seem intoxicated at all. His cold pale eyes stared back, studying her and making her uneasy. As Con felt the first effects of the wine, she regretted drinking it. She sensed it was important to remain in control of herself.

"You looked like you were going somewhere," Green said evenly, as he refilled her glass.

"No," she replied quickly. "I was just out for some air."

"You had a very purposeful stride."

"I did? I hadn't noticed."

"I notice things like that," replied Green. "I'm very observant." The glass trembled in Con's hand. When she set it down untouched, he said, "You mustn't waste that wine, it's the 2047 vintage."

Con took a dutiful sip.

"Finish it," said Green in a quiet, but commanding, voice. He had a faint smile as Con drank the wine.

"Sit down," he said. "Relax. We're not keeping you from something?"

"No," said Con, as she took a seat.

For a while, they were silent. "So, what do you think of our guide?" Green finally asked. "Should I keep him on?"

"Oh, Rick? He's okay."

"He keeping you safe? There are things around here that are dangerous to see."

"You mean dinosaurs?"

"What else could I mean?"

"I wouldn't know," said Con quietly.

"You're John's daughter, I wouldn't want anything to happen to you."

"Rick will keep me safe."

"I certainly hope so."

17

AFTER WASHING THE DINNER DISHES AND SCRUBBING THE pans, Rick strolled to the seashore. He hoped to encounter Con, but he watched the sunset alone. He was still walking the beach when he ran into Joe, sitting on a rock.

"How you doing, Rick?" asked Joe.

"Okay," said Rick. They had barely spoken since the morning. "Enjoy your day off?" he asked for small talk.

"There's not much to do here," replied Joe. "I mostly stayed out of people's way. I hope you have something planned for tomorrow."

"I was thinking about heading south. South America was, I mean is, sauropod country. How far can that plane go?"

"She can cruise forever, as far as I know," replied Joe. "But she's not built for speed. A trip like that would take several days."

"Maybe we could camp."

"Camp? Aren't you getting carried away? You don't need to disappear altogether. Anyway, we don't have camping gear. This is supposed to be a resort."

"It was just a thought," said Rick. "We'll follow the coast south, but keep it to a day trip."

"Sounds good to me."

Rick looked at the darkening sea and sighed. "I'm going to miss this place."

"Speak for yourself," replied Joe.

Joe wandered back to camp, leaving Rick on the beach. He lingered there to watch the moon rise. Con never appeared.

CON ATE HER breakfast, eagerly awaiting Rick. Her father had yet to make an appearance. *Probably hungover,* she thought. Naturally, Sara was absent, too. Only James was at the table.

"You don't have to hang around for my sake," she told him. "I don't think Daddy will be up for a while."

"I do have some things to take care of," said James. "If you truly don't mind . . ."

"Not at all," said Con. "If you see Rick, tell him I'd like to speak to him. About today's trip, that is."

"Certainly."

When Rick appeared a few minutes later, Con grinned and said in an excited whisper, "Come to my room, I've got something to show you! I wanted to show you last night, but I got waylaid by Daddy and Green. Daddy's definitely in with Green. He wants me to help him pick his plunder."

"Slow down, slow down," whispered Rick. "They let you in on their plan?"

"Of course not," said Con. "But Daddy was drunk, and he let stuff out. God, Green's a creep. Scary too. But that's not my news. You've *got* to come to my room!"

Rick looked around, but spotted no one. "Okay," he whispered.

They walked rapidly to Con's chambers. Con pulled the curtains across the colonnade. "That will give us privacy," she said.

"Doesn't this look suspicious?" asked Rick. "I mean, both of us gone and the curtains pulled?"

"Then they *definitely* won't peek inside," replied Con with a giggle. While Rick tried to recover his composure, Con walked into the back room. She pulled the dresser from the wall to reveal the hole in the plaster. "Ta da!" she said. "A secret passageway."

"Where does it go?"

"It's so neat!" said Con excitedly. "You're going to love it!" Without further ado, she got on her hands and knees and disappeared into the hole.

Rick followed and found her standing in the lighted corridor. "Will you *please* tell me what's this about?"

"I found an elevator to the top of the mesa," she said, already walking down the passageway. "And there's a room . . . wait till you see it!"

Rick followed Con until they arrived at the room with the viewscreens. "You're right, Con. This is fantastic! A paleogeologist's dream!"

Con beamed. "I knew you'd like it. It must be some kind of observatory."

Rick walked over to one of the images of Earth. "This is so clear!" He pointed to an area where a huge bay entered the interior of the continent. "We're located here, near the northern coast. This is where I thought we'd go today," he said, tracing their journey south.

"It doesn't look much like America."

"Well, a lot of it's underwater in this time. That peninsula there will someday be Mexico." Rick's attention turned to a chart next to the satellite image. "This is cool," he said. "Here's the same view shown as a geological map. It shows the sea depth and . . ." He paused, looking perplexed. "That's strange."

"What's strange."

Rick pointed to red lines on the chart that formed a series of concentric circles similar to those of a target. "That's the location of the Chicxulub Crater."

"The what?"

"Something that hasn't . . ." Rick's face grew grave. He stared at the top of the chart where there were numbers arranged like those on Con's wall. They glowed red and pulsated:

$$\mathbf{\Phi\Phi} : \mathbf{\Phi\Phi\Phi} : | : \mathbf{\Phi\Lambda} : \mathbf{\Phi\Phi}$$

"Oh God!" said Rick in horror.

"Rick?"

Rick ran over to one of the holographic displays of the solar system. He looked at it, searching for something. "Shit!" he exclaimed.

"What's the matter?" asked Con, her voice filled with concern. "Did we set off an alarm? Is it Green?"

Rick whirled around, then froze when he spotted the image of the slowly tumbling rock. He stared at it with a dumbfounded expression. Con looked at it, too, and noticed that the rock had craters like a small planet. "Those symbols on your wall . . . on these charts . . . on that screen . . ." Rick said in a shocked, quiet voice. "They *are* clocks. They're counting backward."

"Backward? To what?"

"The K-T event." Rick's agitation exploded into frantic activity. He dashed from the room, calling as he ran. "Come on, we've got to find Joe! There isn't much time!"

"Rick, what's the . . ."

Rick was already in the passageway. His voice echoed from it. "Hurry, Con! Follow me."

Puzzled and frightened, Con rushed after him. She saw him smash through the plaster-and-wood barrier to her quarters. Rick ran over the debris without pausing and, jerking the curtain aside, dashed out into the morning. Con, who was barefoot, had to pick her way over the splintered barrier before chasing after Rick. She spotted him at the dining pavilion. James had returned, and Rick was questioning him in a loud, anxious voice while Con's father and Sara looked on with bleary expressions. She heard Rick say, "It's a matter of life and death."

James said something Con couldn't hear. Rick turned toward her and yelled, "Come on, Con!" before dashing toward the path to the plane. Con ran after him, ignoring her father's calls. When the path got stony, she found it was too hard on her feet to run and slowed down to a brisk walk. When she saw Rick again, he was talking to Joe, who was holding the picnic hamper.

"We can leave as soon as the plane's loaded," said Joe. "There's only the cooler left."

"No, no," said Rick. "Leave this *time*, not this place. We all have to go now."

"That's impossible," replied Joe.

"Don't you know what this island's for?" asked Rick incredulously. "Don't you know where you are?"

"All I know is we're at this godforsaken place, because Sam said it was safe," answered Joe.

"Safe?" exclaimed Rick. "Safe? Maybe it was safe when you came here with Sam, but how long ago was that?"

"Over three months."

"Well, I have news for you," said Rick. "This place was built to observe the K-T event. That's why it's deserted. Sam didn't need to change history—only fools would stay here."

Con grabbed Rick's arm. "You're scaring me," she said.

Joe turned to Con. "Do you know what he's talking about?"

"Sixty-five million years ago, a nine-mile-wide meteor

hit the Earth," said Rick. "It's called the K-T event. It wiped out the dinosaurs. It wiped out damned near everything. Only for us, it isn't 65 million years ago. For us, it will happen today. In a few hours. Now do you see why we have to leave?"

"Can't do it," said Joe.

"Weren't you listening? This is the greatest catastrophe on record. Fire . . . earthquakes . . . darkness . . . tsunamis . . ."

"What's a 'tsunami'?" asked Con.

"Tidal wave," said Joe.

"This one will be hundreds of feet high," said Rick.

"Do you have proof for any for this?" asked Joe.

"You sealed off the proof yourself, Joe," said Rick. "It's all there in that room with the screens. You can see the meteor . . . plot its trajectory . . . see where it will hit. There's a running countdown! You should have looked at what you were covering up before you hid the doors."

"You found them, I see."

"Con did, no thanks to you."

"Green's not going to like this," said Joe.

"Screw Green! None of that stuff matters now. If we don't go, we'll die!"

"Rick, the time machine takes two weeks to store enough energy for the trip back. We don't have enough power to reach our time."

"We don't need to reach our time," said Rick. "Just move us a few months downwhen."

"It's not that simple," said Joe. "I need coordinates."

"I'm only talking about a few months, figure them out."

"Look, Rick, the Earth spins, it rotates around the sun, the sun rotates around the galaxy, the galaxy's moving . . . hell . . . the whole damned universe is expanding. This particular spot is in outer space five seconds downwhen."

"Then how did you plan to find your way back to our time?"

"I already explained that," said Joe. "Those coordinates are fixed because of temporal linkage. We can't go downwhen, it'd be suicide."

"There's another time machine," said Con. "We found it on top of the mesa."

"That's a probe," replied Joe. "It's not made for people. We're stuck here."

"Okay, okay, we can't leave this time. I'll take your word for it," said Rick. "But that doesn't mean we can't leave this spot. This meteor doesn't destroy the world. Some life survived, or we wouldn't be here. It's just we're standing on one of the worst spots—out at sea only twelve hundred miles from ground zero." A frenzied look of hope came to Rick's face as he paced and talked. "We'll leave this place in the plane. Make our way to the southern hemisphere—southern Africa or someplace. Things will be tough, but we'll be resourceful. We can make it! Joe, you provision the plane. Con, come with me. We've got to tell the others." Without waiting for their agreement, Rick started back toward camp.

Joe looked at Con. "He's flipped out!"

Con looked back with anguished eyes. "Joe, we've got to help him." She turned and hurried after Rick, leaving Joe alone in thought. When she reached the dining pavilion, James, Pandit, her father, and Sara were there, staring at Rick with puzzled expressions while he paced back and forth as he talked.

". . . only the necessities and all your clothing," Rick was saying. "It's going to get cold. Hurry, there's not a lot of time."

No one moved. "John," said Sara, "what's going on?"

"Look here," said John Greighton. "We're supposed to abandon everything on your say-so? All because of some theory?"

"It's not a theory!" said Rick hotly. "The meteor strike is a fact. We've known about it for nearly a century."

"Then why doesn't Pete know about it?" asked Greighton. "Why should I listen to you?"

"You know, as well as I do, that Green's a fraud," said Rick. "He has no idea where he is."

Green emerged from his quarters, a look of rage on his face. "I've heard enough," he said in a cold, hard voice. "Who the hell do you think you are to frighten my guests?"

"Your game's up," replied Rick. "You're not going to conquer anything. In a few hours, this island and the time machine will be destroyed. Too bad you didn't ask Sam where you were going before you bumped him off."

Green pulled out a pistol from his pocket and aimed it at Rick. "You goddamn nosy sneak!" he said, his voice dripping with venom. "You'll learn what it means to cross me!"

Green was taking aim at Rick's stomach when Con darted in front of Rick to shield him. "You'll have to shoot me, too," she said.

"Move out of the way," ordered Green.

"No," said Con firmly.

Green did not lower his pistol as Con expected. Instead, he raised it until it pointed directly at her face. She looked at the eyes behind the gun barrel. She could find no reluctance in them. *He's weighing if it's worth it*, she realized. *If he believes it's truly over, he'll shoot.* Green's cold eyes confirmed her fears. Still, Con held her ground. She looked away to gaze upon the trees that glowed with morning sunlight. *This is the last moment of my life*, she thought.

"Peter, let's not be hasty," said Joe, as he approached the group. "I think you and I and John should leave in the probe. The kid's on to something. He may be right. Probably is."

"I have business to finish first," replied Green.

"You don't want to shoot your partner's daughter. Leave her here."

"I only want him."

Con flung her arms back, grasping Rick around the waist.

"For God's sake, Pete," said Greighton. "Put the gun away."

Green slowly lowered his gun. "He's lucky I'm a forgiving man. John, as a precaution, I think we should go."

Sara clutched Greighton. "Don't leave me, John!"

"He won't be gone long," assured Joe. "Remember, this is time travel. He'll return only seconds after he leaves."

Greighton took his cue from Joe. "I'd never abandon you, Sara. I promise."

"That's bull!" said Rick hotly.

"You don't know shit!" said Joe. "Don't scare the lady. You've made enough trouble already. Come on, Peter. Come on, John. There's no point in drawing this out."

John kissed Sara, then pushed himself away from her arms. "Good-bye, Sara. I'll be back soon. Good-bye, Constance."

"Good-bye, Daddy."

Joe led the two men into the storage room in Green's quarters. Pulling the dresser aside, he kicked in the plaster wall to reveal a passageway. All three men disappeared into it.

"Would you please tell me what's happening?" said James in an exasperated voice.

"A giant meteor will hit the Earth this morning," said Rick. "If you believe Joe, we'll be long gone when it happens. I believe we're going to die."

"Rick's right," said Con flatly.

"How can you doubt your father?" said Sara angrily. "He promised to come back."

"He abandoned my mother. He abandoned me. What makes you different?"

"You've never appreciated him! Never understood him!"

"I understand him, all right! He's leaving you to die!"

"He is not!" screamed Sara. She strode up to Con and slapped her across the face. "You spoiled, ungrateful brat!"

Con burst into angry tears as James separated Sara from her. "Ladies, ladies," he said, "you must remain calm."

Sara turned her back to Con and stared expectantly at the door. Con pointedly ignored her. Assured there would be no more fighting, James turned to Rick. "Okay, Rick," he said, "I'll assume you're right and we're here when this thing happens. What can we expect?"

"The meteor will hit the ocean about twelve hundred miles to the south. At the impact site, the temperature will be hundreds of thousands degrees. Everything will be vaporized and rise in a plume miles above the earth. That's what we'll see first. Debris will fall back and burn as it hits the atmosphere to form an expanding ring of fire. To the south, everything will burst into flame. Up here, huge fires will burn too. The Earth's crust will ripple like the surface of a pond. If we survive that, a tsunami will arrive in a couple of hours. It will tower over the island."

"There's nothing to be done?"

"Can you fly the plane?"

"No," said James, "only Joe can."

"Then we're stuck."

"How much time do we have left?"

"There's a clock counting down the minutes in Con's quarters. It works on a decimal system, but I can figure it out."

Rick walked over to the pulsating red symbols on Con's wall. James and Con followed. The row of zeroes had advanced:

$$\text{❶❶} : \text{❶❶❶} : \text{❶} : \triangledown| : \text{❶❶}$$

"If there are ten hours in their day," said Rick, "and a hundred minutes in their hour, then, they have a thousand minutes in their day instead of our 1440. One of their minutes is approximately 1.4 of ours. Ninety-one times 1.4 equals 127. About two hours."

"Two hours and seven minutes," said Con.

"Not much time," said James.

Rick turned to Con. "The world's going to change forever this morning."

"Then let's not stay in here," she said. "I want to see it one last time."

As they walked back outdoors, they saw the time probe sparkle in the sunlight as it rose into the sky.

18

CON FELT ALMOST NUMB AS SHE WALKED, AS IF THE things around her were happening to someone else. That person was going to die, not she. She dispassionately observed Sara glaring at her. She noticed Pandit speaking to Sara. His voice seemed to come from far away. "Everything will be fine," he said, as one might soothe a child. "Just you see." She saw James join them. He, too, said soothing words, but his sad eyes betrayed his true feelings. Con did not want to see them.

Rick reached out and gently grasped her hand. "Thank you," he said softly. "Thank you for saving my life."

Con stared at the hand holding hers. It looked strong despite its long, almost delicate, fingers—a hand used to work, already a little worn by living. It pulled her from the void of unfeeling.

"I guess I did," she said, as a glimmer of animation returned to her face. *But not for long*, she thought darkly.

"I've never met anyone so brave," he said, squeezing her hand a little tighter.

"I just did it without thinking. I'd hardly call it brave."

"I would," said Rick.

Con met Rick's eyes. He gazed at her as if she were the entirety of his world, as if nothing else mattered. No one had ever looked at her that way and despite their approaching doom—or perhaps because of it—Rick's gaze met a desperate need within her. She saw in his eyes the adoring look

she had always dreamed of and longed for. It filled her with
joy mingled with almost unbearable sorrow. *Why only now?*
she lamented.

"I can't believe this is happening," she said.

"I wish I was wrong, but I can't see how," said Rick.
"Everything fits together so neatly. Now, it all makes sense."

"This makes sense?" said Con bitterly.

"I should've figured it out earlier," said Rick. "In all
Earth's history, this is the most spectacular event. The only
one you could pinpoint precisely. Of course they'd build an
observatory here. How could I be so stupid!"

"Don't blame yourself; everyone lied to us."

"That's true. Joe had me going up to the last minute," said
Rick.

"He talked Green out of shooting us."

"Only to save his own skin."

"I don't want to talk about Joe," said Con, "or Daddy or
anyone else. Let's go to where we had our picnic."

They walked to the beach, then slowly strolled along the
shore, as the wind and the surf roared in their ears. Con
paused to pick up a shell. She held it for Rick to see. "The
pink ones are my favorites," she said.

"It's beautiful."

"I want to see as many lovely things as I can." Tears were
glistening in her eyes. "I want every moment to count." Still
holding the shell, she wrapped her arms around Rick and
kissed him on the lips. For a moment, his expression was
one of surprise. Con murmured to him, "Aren't you going to
kiss me back?"

"Con," said Rick, his voice filled with wonder and tenderness. He lovingly brushed a tear from her cheek, then
embraced her as their lips touched, and the wind called their
names.

The wind had Joe's voice. "Rick! Con!" They turned and
were startled to see Joe running down the beach. "Thank
God, I found you! We've got to go."

Rick stared at Joe in disbelief. "Why the change of heart?
Green kick you out?"

"Of course," Joe replied. "But I had to convince him that
I thought I was going. Otherwise, he never would have got
into the probe."

"Where's Daddy?" asked Con.

"Left with Green," replied Joe. "He's who Green wanted. Soon as I entered the coordinates, I was surplus."

"Did Daddy get Sara?"

"Nope."

"So he left her," Con said with sad finality.

Rick held Con tight as he looked suspiciously at Joe. "You've told us so many lies, why should we believe you now?"

"I only lied for your own good," answered Joe.

"And look where we are," said Rick.

"We don't have time for this!" said Joe. "You said we had a chance to survive."

Rick stared at Joe, the distrust clear on his face.

"Look," said Joe, "I want to live. Don't you? Tell me where we need to go, and I'll get you there."

"Rick," said Con. "We can't give up, not if we have a chance. We have to go with him!"

"All right," said Rick. "We'll go."

The three of them raced down the beach. As they ran, Rick asked, "Are the others ready?"

"They're staying here."

"What?"

"They have their reasons."

They ran as hard as they could, too hard to continue talking. When they reached the staff tent, they were out of breath.

"Rick," said Joe between gasps, "this is your plan. Tell us what we should take."

"As much clothing as you can," said Rick. "We should get cooking pots and utensils. Flashlights. Water containers. Blankets. Food. Con, grab your clothes from your room, then meet us back here."

Con ran off toward her quarters.

"Pandit and James said to help ourselves to their stuff," said Joe as they pushed clothes into their duffel bags.

"Are you sure they won't come?"

"I tried my best to convince them. They won't budge."

"And Sara knows that 'returning in seconds' is just bull?"

"I explained it," said Joe, "but she wouldn't listen."

"You told her the opposite just before Greighton left."

"God help me, I did," said Joe. "Yet if I hadn't, Greighton might have balked. Then you and Con would have surely been shot."

"You're right," admitted Rick. "It's Sara's decision. I just wish it was different."

"Me too," said Joe. "Me too."

Rick began to go through James's things, pulling out shirts, pants, a sweater—anything that would provide warmth. He felt like a thief rifling the dead. *He won't be needing them*, he told himself. Somehow, that made him feel worse.

Meanwhile, Con was rapidly sorting through her clothes, trying to imagine what she would need in the times ahead. She tossed aside a delicate pair of dress shoes, a lacy top, and her brassieres. She kept the dresses for the cloth. As she stuffed her things in her bag, she couldn't help but wonder what she would be wearing in a year or two. *Animal hides? Leaves? Will we become naked savages?* All the prospects depressed her.

As she headed for the staff tent, she saw Sara with Pandit. Sara stared anxiously at the door through which Con's father had departed, silent tears streaming down her face. It was impossible to remain angry with her. Con had never seen anyone so forlorn.

"Sara, please come with us."

Sara turned and noticed Con for the first time. "What would John think? Coming here to find me gone?"

"He can't come back," said Con. "Didn't Joe explain?"

"What does Joe know about love? About devotion?"

"This isn't about devotion, Sara."

"You don't understand. John needs to find me waiting for him. I won't let him down."

Con ached with pity for Sara. *I do understand*, she thought. *I loved Daddy too*. She remembered all the birthdays and holidays where she, too, had expectantly watched a door. Con also understood she could not help Sara, that trying to dissuade her would be an exercise of futile cruelty. She turned to Pandit, who had been silently watching the exchange.

"Pandit . . ."

"I will be staying with Miss Boyton."

"But . . ."

"I, too, understand something of devotion. She will not be alone, come what may."

Con had to stifle sobs to say, "Good-bye, Sara. When you see Daddy, tell him I love him."

"I will, Constance."

"Good-bye, Pandit. Take care of Sara."

"Good-bye, Miss Greighton."

Con spotted James sitting in the dining pavilion, sipping coffee. She ran to him, and as she approached, he said, "Lovely morning, reminds me of the Serengeti."

"Don't tell me you're waiting to be rescued, too," said Con.

"Me?" said James. "No, I'm rather like Pandit. There are things I won't leave behind."

"What are you talking about?"

"This morning," replied James. "Rick says it will be the last of its kind for a very long time."

"Knowing what will happen, how can you stay here?"

"Knowing what will happen, why do you want to live in a ruined world?" replied James. "Can you really conceive of what you're fleeing to?"

James's question hit a nerve. When he saw Con's distressed reaction, he immediately regretted asking it. "I'm just too old to start over again," he said gently.

"I won't leave Rick," said Con.

"You shouldn't," James said. "He's a good man. You two take care of each other."

"We will."

"Then you'd better run along."

"Are you sure you won't come?"

"And miss this morning? Not for the world."

"Good-bye, James."

"Good-bye."

James watched Con run through the glade until she was hidden by the trees. Then he refilled his cup and recalled the sight of lions in the morning.

19

JOHN GREIGHTON SHIFTED UNEASILY ON THE BENCH AS he watched the island dwindle below them. He had a fear of heights and the transparent craft around him offered no sense of security. The pulsating red symbols on the strange control panel made him nervous also. They reminded him of warning lights.

"Was it wise to leave Joe behind?" he asked Green. "Wouldn't it be safer with a pilot?"

"These probes run a predetermined course. Once Joe set the new destination, he was useless. Worse than useless, he was someone who could talk."

Greighton gripped the edge of the bench tightly. "Are you sure this is right?"

"A little late for that, isn't it?" said Green caustically. "What do you want? To be down there with your fiancée? With your daughter?"

"I was only asking if this was the right move. That kid might be fooling us."

"Oh, he was sincere, all right. Pistols do that to people. If he was lying, he would have cracked."

"How can you be sure?"

"I have some experience in these matters."

Green's words gave Greighton a chill. "So you weren't bluffing?"

"You're either with me or against me. He could have spoken to me first. Instead, he tried to work behind my back. I won't tolerate that. If your daughter hadn't interfered, he'd be gut-shot."

"She's always been willful, a real handful. My ex's fault."

"She'll be more docile after she's waited for you on that island."

"I'm not so sure," said Greighton.

"The sooner your research department solves our technical problems, the sooner you'll find out."

"Won't a rescue attempt be risky?" asked Greighton.

"Naturally."

"Then we should postpone any attempt until we're established in the eighteenth century."

Green looked at his companion with new respect. "I see your point."

"I got where I am by knowing my priorities. It won't matter to them when we set out to pick them up."

"That's true," said Green. *More true than you know.*

The probe continued to ascend until the island was but a dot in the wide expanse of sea. They were level with the mountaintops to the west when they stopped climbing. Unlike the other time machine, this craft did not halt in mid air. Instead, it began to travel south, following the coastline.

Green was disturbed by this development, yet he was certain Joe had not played him false. Hadn't he expected to be sitting beside him? *Another change in plans,* he thought. So far, the changes had not worked out badly. He still had a time machine and Greighton was firmly in his grasp. All the witnesses on the island were eliminated without any effort on his part. Only Ann Smythe and her assistant were left to be dealt with. To top it off, he doubted that Greighton would be overly upset when he discovered that a rescue of his daughter and fiancée was impossible. Perhaps he already knew. Green watched the coastline sliding beneath him and relaxed. *It's only a slight delay*, he reflected. *Fortune's been running in my favor.*

CON STRUGGLED UP the path to the plane, laden with a bag filled with bottles of mineral water. It was a heavy and cumbersome load. *When it's gone, we'll be drinking from puddles.* She had been having thoughts like that with each bundle she hurried to the plane. So many things would be the last of their kind, from pretty clothes to pastry. She was already beginning to miss them. All the while, James's question echoed in her mind—*Can you really conceive of what you're fleeing to?* Each regret was a bleak hint.

Rick was running down the path in the opposite direction. He slowed only momentarily to call, "Stay at the plane. I'm getting the last load."

Con turned to watch him speed away. "Okay," she said weakly. He was all hustle now, shouting orders and running frantically. She understood why, but she still felt abandoned. Her thoughts returned to that moment on the beach, when he had held her and kissed her. Though she knew it was absurd, the idea of embracing by the sea as the world ended seemed wondrously romantic. Standing alone on the path, Con feared Rick's adoring look might never return, that it would be worn from his face by the hardships ahead, and her only moment of love was already past.

Con moved slowly toward the plane. When she reached it, she heaved her burden atop the jumbled heap in the rear. A bag toppled from the pile and a cake, snatched half-baked from the oven, fell to the floor. Con picked up the cake pan. It was still warm. She set it back in the bag and looked at the wet batter spilled at her feet. Its sweet aroma filled the plane, and she felt the pangs of hunger. *How can I be hungry at a time like this?* Yet she was. She squatted and scooped the batter from the floor with her hands. *This is the last cake,* she thought, as she licked her fingers clean. When she was finished, she collapsed in a seat and began to weep, convinced her descent into savagery had already begun.

RICK AND JOE lugged the heavy camp stove up the path to the plane. Although the day was still cool, and a breeze blew in from the sea, they were both drenched in sweat. They moved as fast as their exhaustion would allow.

"Are you sure this is worth bringing?" asked Joe. "We're going to run out of propane."

"We'll find some use for it," said Rick.

"Yeah," said Joe. "Set it over a campfire and pretend we're still civilized."

"Look, Joe," said Rick crossly. "This is our only chance to supply ourselves. There's no coming back."

"That doesn't mean we should drag off everything we can lay our hands on. This extra weight will slow us down."

"So what?" countered Rick. "You said that plane could cruise forever."

"What about the dark?" answered Joe. "You said it will get dark."

"What does that have to do with it?"

"Those solar panels won't be much good then."

"Oh, great!" said Rick. He suddenly let go of the stove. As Rick's end fell, the stove wrenched free from Joe's grip and crashed on the ground, barely missing his feet.

"What the hell!" shouted Joe.

"Why didn't you mention the panels earlier?"

"I thought it was obvious," answered Joe. "Maybe if you stopped running around shouting orders and thought for a second . . ."

"We carried this thing halfway to the plane! You should've said something before."

"Well, I'm saying it now," said Joe. He shook his head. "You've got to get a grip, man."

Joe and Rick glared at each other over the stove. Joe was the first to make peace. "Neither of us is thinking clearly. Who can blame us? The world doesn't end every day."

"It's not going to end," said Rick irritably. "That's the whole point of leaving here."

"Then let's leave," said Joe. "Are we taking this stove, or not?"

"Leave it," said Rick.

"You sure?"

"Hell, Joe, I'm not sure of anything," said Rick. "Look, I'm sorry I blew up."

"Forget it," replied Joe.

Mindful that every minute counted, they broke into a tired, shambling jog to the plane. They arrived to find

Con in her seat rubbing her red eyes, trying to pretend she hadn't been crying.

"Are we going?" Con asked.

"Yeah," answered Rick.

Joe sat in the pilot's seat and started the engines. The seats grabbed their occupants as the plane began to rise in the air. Once they were aloft, Rick explained to Joe how to read the numerals on the countdown clock.

"Thirty-one minutes!" said Joe. "That's all we got?"

"You have to multiply that by 1.4 to turn it into our time," said Rick.

Joe did the math quickly in his head. "Oh, *forty-three* minutes. That's *loads* more time." He extended the wings of the plane, then took it into a steep climb. "Okay, Rick, where we going?"

"Eventually, we'll want to go to the southern hemisphere, but we can't head that direction now. That would take us toward the impact site. We need to be someplace safe when this thing hits."

"Could you be a little more specific?" asked Joe.

"We should be on the ground, for starters."

"I figured that much out," said Joe sarcastically.

"Head north and inland. When the tsunami comes we'll want to be away from the coast and on high ground," said Rick.

"Anything else?" asked Joe.

"There'll be an earthquake, so we should stay clear of steep terrain," said Rick. "Afterward, the heat and the falling meteors will start forest fires. I guess the ideal place would be upland, away from the forests, but not too close to the mountains. It should be near water, a small river would be best."

Joe activated the holographic map and studied it. "I wish Sam had shown me how to figure airtimes," he said. "Seat-of-the-pants was fine for touring, but now . . ." He stared at the map, trying to remember how long it took them to reach past destinations. He pressed another button, and a map appeared in front of Rick's seat. "I've indicated a possible landing site," he told Rick. "What do you think?"

Rick looked at the ethereal miniature landscape that
floated before him. A red dot flashed in one of the shallow valleys between the foothills of the mountain range.
A tiny squiggling blue line ran through it. "Nothing farther north?" he asked

"You can look for yourself," replied Joe. "That's one
place I'm sure we can reach."

Rick chose not to second-guess Joe's judgment. "How
far from the coast do you think it is?" he asked Joe.

"It's hard to say," Joe replied. "Seventy-five . . . maybe
a hundred miles."

"I guess there's no way to tell how wooded it is."

"Not until we get there."

Rick sighed deeply. It wasn't much information on
which to base such an important decision. "It looks okay.
Let's hope it is."

Joe locked the destination in, and the map disappeared
from in front of Rick. There was a slight sense of accel-
eration, but the sea below still seemed to slide beneath
them at a leisurely pace.

"Is this as fast as it goes?" asked Con.

"I'm afraid so," replied Joe.

Con had been sitting in withdrawn silence. When she
spoke up, Rick guiltily realized he had totally ignored
her. "You all right?" he asked.

"All right?" she said fiercely. "Why wouldn't I be all
right? Daddy's deserted me, the world's about to be
smashed, and I'm here like someone's forgotten laun-
dry!"

"Con . . ."

"Thanks for asking," she said caustically, then turned
away to stare at the landscape below.

Rick looked at the sulking girl next to him. It seemed
strange that so shortly ago they had been kissing on the
beach, preparing to die in one another's arms. That moment seemed easy and natural. Now, he was at a loss for
what to do or say. It was especially hard with Joe close
by, witnessing it all. He tentatively reached out to touch
Con's hand, but she moved it away.

With a deep sigh, Rick abandoned his attempt to mol-

lify Con. Instead, he turned his attention to the landscape
below. They had just reached the coast and were flying
over cypresses. Rick tried to memorize the sight of trees
bathed in sunlight. It might be the last time he saw either.

JOHN GREIGHTON'S DISCOMFORT from being in a transparent aircraft gradually lessened as his annoyance grew.
The flight had lasted far too long. The mountains and the
inland sea had been left miles behind as they sped south-
ward at breathtaking speed. They had traveled over water
in a straight line, but, from their high altitude, a coastline
was always visible to the west. Now the landform in the
distance was a broad peninsula, and Greighton could see
a sliver of ocean on the far side. Finally, after almost two
hours of travel, the time machine slowed to a stop and
hung suspended in the air. "It's about time!" he said.

Green did not answer. He had been strangely silent
through most of their journey. Greighton turned toward
his companion and noticed for the first time that Green
was staring almost straight up. He had a dumbstruck expression, and Greighton gazed upward to see what he was
watching.

There was a different moon in the blue sky. It was
pocked with craters like the old one, but it was not round.
Its irregular shape seemed to change as he watched.
Greighton realized that it was slowly tumbling in space.
That accounted for some of the object's changes, but not
all of them. It was steadily growing larger. Soon it was
bigger than the old moon and brighter, too.

"That kid was telling the truth," said Greighton. "You
had no idea about this, did you?"

Green didn't answer.

A chill passed through Greighton. It was physical as
well as emotional—the cabin was growing cold. His
breath condensed when he exhaled, and frost began to
form on the clear wall in front on him.

"Pete, can't you do something? We should go!"

Green remained dumb. Greighton grabbed him and

shook him violently. "Goddamn it, Pete! Listen to me!
We've got to go!"

Green looked at him with frightened eyes before glanc-
ing at the control panel. "Didn't you listen?" he said. "I
can't make it work." The despair in Green's voice terrified Greighton. Green returned his attention to the meteor
above, while Greighton examined the panel, trying to figure it out. He soon gave up. It was hopeless; nothing
written beneath the controls made the slightest sense. The
flashing red symbols seemed to taunt him in their urgency. They were the only things on the panel that were
remotely comprehensible. They looked like an almost
complete row of zeroes.

⦿⦿ : ⦿⦿⦿ : ⦿ : ⦿▢ : ⦿⦿

FOLLOWING THE RIVER upland, Joe was watching identical numbers. "We have about five minutes to find a
landing site." He scanned the mile-wide valley beneath
them. Nestled among rolling foothills, it was filled with
lushly green, but scrubby, vegetation. A shallow river,
scarcely larger than a broad creek, meandered across its
floor. The only sizable trees were clustered near the riverbank.

"I wish the ground was more open," said Rick.

"This is the best we've found so far," said Joe. "Besides, it all looks pretty green."

"It's going to dry out real fast," said Rick. "But I guess
we don't have much of a choice."

"No we don't," said Joe.

"Settle down close to the river in the most open spot
you can find."

Joe banked the plane and brought it to a hover over a
slight rise about thirty yards from the river's bank. The
plane's long silver wings withdrew into the tips of the
black stubby ones. Then the aircraft descended vertically
until it rested on the ground. Fern fronds swallowed the
lower half of the plane. Joe shut off the engines. Everything was peaceful. The only sounds were the soft rustle

of leaves, an occasional birdcall, and the music of water rippling over stones.

"What do we do now?" asked Con.

"Wait," said Rick. "Wait and pray."

JAMES NEVILLE FELT drawn to the sea. It reminded him of the plains of Africa. Although it was different from his boyhood home in every physical aspect, it felt the same. It made him aware of his insignificance. Practicing a profession where cold food or warm wine assumed the proportions of disaster, this perspective gave him comfort. In the end, nothing mattered. A man's dust was equally at home on the savanna or at the seashore.

PETER GREEN SCRAPED the frost from the cabin wall with his fingernails. It was so cold in the time machine, his fingers stung as if they had been struck by a hammer. It didn't matter. Despite his horror, he had to see. The meteor was so close that he could make out its rough and pocked surface. It seemed very bright and very near. Although it was no longer directly overhead, Green knew it would hit close by.

The surface of the meteor glowed red as it entered the atmosphere. The red intensified and became orange, then yellow, then white. While the transition took only seconds, Green's racing mind perceived it in slow motion. He had time to experience it all. He saw the ocean lit as if by a spotlight. He saw a glowing mountain of rock, taller than Mount Everest, fill the horizon. He saw a flash of brilliant light as meteor struck the earth and velocity and mass converted into the energy of millions of hydrogen bombs. He saw the frost on the time machine instantly vaporized as light of excruciating intensity flooded in. Then Peter Green saw nothing but darkness.

John Greighton saw the light though closed eyelids and the hands that covered his face. He could see the shadow of his finger bones while his hands blistered. He was still covering his face when the time machine jerked violently, as if struck by a giant sledgehammer, and was sent spinning through the air. He smashed his head against a wall and blacked out.

Greighton regained consciousness to the sound of whimpering. "I'm blind, I'm blind, I'm blind, I'm blind," said Green's voice. Greighton opened his eyes and discovered he was not.

"It looks exactly like Hell," said Greighton in an awed, frightened voice.

"Tell me what you see," begged Green.

"There's a hole, a big round hole where the ocean used to be."

"How big?"

"It's huge! I can't see the bottom or the other side. It's gotta be over a hundred miles across and it's red-hot. But that's not all—everything's on fire! The land . . . the whole damn sky. It's Hell. That's what it is—Hell."

"Goddamn Joe!" cursed Green. "I'll kill him! I'll kill him!"

"No need. He's dead," said Greighton. "They're all dead."

As Greighton spoke, the crater's sides collapsed inward, enlarging its diameter as the ocean, pushed aside by the impact's blast, flowed back to pour over the crater's lip. Huge jets of steam rose up, obscuring everything except the glow of flames. The cabin was hotter than a sauna, but something was working hard to cool it down. Greighton turned his blistered face toward a draft of cool air and saw movement. The strange, immaterial cylinder in the time machine's central column was beginning to change. Thin incorporeal tendrils shot beyond the column, altering everything they touched.

"Pete!" shouted Greighton. "The time machine! It's starting to work!"

"Thank God!" said Green.

"We made it!" shouted Greighton joyously. "We're saved!"

20

JAMES STOOD ON THE BEACH WATCHING WHAT SEEMED to be a second sunrise to the south. The illusion was spoiled when the rising "sun" began to flatten and spread. Racing across the sky, like a rapidly approaching storm, came a glowing wall of flame. Habit born from a lifetime of caring for others made James think of Sara and Pandit. Despite his intention to die alone, with that moment approaching, he found he could not forsake his guest and his staff.

Racing back to the guest quarters, he found Sara and Pandit in the dining pavilion, drinking champagne. As strange as it seemed, Sara had changed her outfit and was wearing a flimsy pleated dress. *Perhaps,* thought James sadly, *she dressed for Greighton's return.*

SARA DRANK CHAMPAGNE, trying to wash away her ever-growing despondency. She could not remember whether this was her second or third bottle, but it wasn't enough. The nagging, insistent voice within her would not be silenced, no matter how drunk she got. *John's not coming back*, it said. *You're not as desirable as you thought*. Even her favorite dress—John's favorite, too— did not give her the assurance she craved. That assurance had dwindled with each anxious moment, until little was left. She felt emotionally drained and helpless. Beauty had been her greatest power and, put to the test, it had failed her.

Pandit sat by attentively, but had long ago ceased to tell her "everything would be fine." She could see now he had never been sincere about that. Yet, as she realized

his words were false, she perceived his deeper sincerity.
He had not abandoned her. In his gaze she saw the devotion she had always hoped to see in John's. To him,
she was desirable. It was a comfort.

James raced to the table, then, in a voice that seemed
unnaturally calm, said, "I suggest we retire to the shelter
of the guest quarters. A storm is approaching."

Sara and Pandit walked from beneath the pavilion to
gaze at the sky. To the south, it glowed ominously in
swirling incandescent colors. The colors advanced toward them as they watched. Without further urging, they
hurried to Green's former quarters. There, they discovered that the hole Joe had kicked through the plaster was
sealed by a featureless silvery panel.

"A door!" said James. "Maybe there's refuge after all."
He approached and looked for a means to gain entrance.

"Perhaps," said Pandit, "it will respond to your commands."

"Open," said James. The doorway remained sealed.
"Let us in! Bloody Hell, open up!" James tried other
commands with rising urgency and eventually resorted to
pounding the metal door with his fists, but it did not
budge. "It was a false hope," he said at last.

The fiery clouds were nearly overhead, and the landscape outside assumed the color of blood. Sara ran into
the bathroom and cowered in the corner, as far from the
light as she could be.

"I can't stand it," she sobbed.

Pandit followed after her. He uttered the only true
words of comfort he could. "I am here, Sara." As he
spoke them, he realized it was the first time he had ever
called her by that name.

Even as Pandit spoke, a horrendous crash resounded
through the chamber like millions of exploding bombs.
It was more than a sound—it was a physical presence.
Even within the stone shelter, it hit them like a fist and
smashed them against the wall. The noise became a pain
that vibrated their very bones for agonizing seconds before it died away. Then there was silence, except for the
ringing in their ears. Pandit ventured from the bathroom

to find James sprawled insensate against the wall. "Sara, come quickly," he called, "James is hurt."

Sara ran out and gasped at the sight of James's crumpled body. "Is he dead?" she asked.

Pandit saw James's chest move. "He is breathing," he stated. "We should move him off the floor."

Sara and Pandit carefully lifted James to the bed and stretched him out. Sara went to the bathroom and wet a washcloth to place on James's brow. When she did, she saw it was starting to swell. She got a second washcloth and gently washed the blood from his upper lip and the corners of his mouth. Caring for another calmed her own terror and distracted her from the nightmarish scene outside the colonnade.

The force of the concussion had stripped the trees of their leaves. The few that still stood were silhouetted against a sea and sky that appeared merged into a restless inferno. Meteors slashed downward. Usually they burned out in a burst of brilliant light, but occasionally they crashed into the sea, sending up huge plumes of spray. In the unnatural light, the plumes looked like spurting wounds. It became searingly hot.

"Pandit," said Sara, "what will we do?"

"We will live," he replied, "for as long as we can."

CON, RICK, AND Joe watched the sky from inside the plane. The concussion had passed through the valley, briefly lifting the plane as it went. The aircraft now rested ten yards closer to the river, but still upright. The foothills that had partially sheltered them from the full force of the concussion also screened the sky to the south. An eerie glow presaged a change. Then, like burning oil spreading over the surface of a pond, fire spilled over the heavens. It rapidly advanced until it reached to both horizons. The sky painted the landscape with nightmare colors. Con was reminded of Hieronymus Bosch's ghastly paintings of Hell. *Only the demons are missing,* she thought. The Damned, she feared, might prove to be themselves.

"What happened?" asked Joe at last.

"Vaporized meteor and rock are falling back into the atmosphere and igniting," said Rick.

"I see shooting stars," said Con, with a combination of fascination and terror.

"I feel like I'm in an oven set on broil," said Joe.

The heat became oppressive. Con sat limp in her seat, her face flushed and her clothes wet with perspiration. "Maybe we should go to the river," she said.

"Not yet," said Rick.

As if to affirm Rick's reply, a grinding, rumbling sound filled the air. The mountains to the south moved as the Earth rippled. The rapid advance of the disturbance was plainly marked by the destruction caused by its passing. Whole mountainsides gave way to crash into the valleys below. The noise grew louder and louder, until suddenly the foothill to the south rose up. It no longer behaved like earth and stone, but moved like a swell on the ocean. Seconds later, the ground beneath the plane rose also in the first and greatest of a series of undulations. The formerly solid ground assumed a liquid nature, and the plane bobbed upon it like a cork.

Con heard herself screaming as a childhood nightmare came true and the Earth attempted to swallow her. The violent movement of the plane and the churning dirt and vegetation outside made it impossible to know if they were, indeed, being buried alive. Con fell to the sloping floor of the plane, then slid down upon the jumbled supplies in the rear. Rick tumbled beside her. She grasped him so tightly it would leave marks, pressed her face into his chest, and squeezed her eyes shut. She clung to him while the plane bucked and rolled. Eventually, the movement diminished. The Earth grew calm. Con opened her eyes.

The sky was still visible through the transparent part of the plane. Joe clung to his seat, a shocked expression frozen on his face.

"Is everyone all right?" asked Rick.

"I think so," said Joe.

"Just shaken up," said Con.

"How about the plane?" asked Rick.

Joe scrutinized the control panel. He noted, for the first time, that the flashing red symbols had disappeared. All the indicator lights were still lit, however. They told him that the aircraft's systems still functioned. "She looks okay from the inside," he said. "I'd better take a look outside."

Joe pressed a button, and an opening appeared in the rear of the plane. Scorching, dry, dusty air poured in. All three of them clambered out into the inferno to see what the earthquake had done. Their first concern was the plane. It sloped, frozen in the process of sinking into the Earth tail first. The two rear legs of the landing tripod were half-buried and only the two tips of the aircraft's V-shaped tail protruded from the ground. Joe started digging around the tail with his hands. He discovered that the ground, which had been so recently fluid, was solid again. In fact, it was hard.

"We're going to need tools to dig this out," said Joe. He disappeared into the plane and began rummaging about the supplies. While Joe searched the plane, Rick and Con surveyed the landscape about them. Rick had studied the effects of earthquakes, but no one had ever experienced one of this magnitude. There were numerous places where the Earth had behaved like a liquid and flowed. Some hillsides looked like brown glaciers. The river's course had changed. It flowed forty yards from the plane now. It was wider and brown with mud. The trees along its former bank slanted at crazy angles or had toppled over. One tree trunk appeared to have dropped straight into the ground.

Joe emerged from the plane carrying a large serving spoon and two soup spoons. With an apologetic smile he said, "These were all I could find."

SARA TENDED THE unconscious James by sponging his face and arms to cool him in the stifling heat. She had no idea if it did any good, but she liked to think it did. Meanwhile, Pandit kept a wary eye on the sea outside. A series of waves racing over its surface, warned him of the approaching earthquake. "Sara," he cried, "we must carry Mr. Neville to safety."

"Isn't it safe here?"

"Look at the sea."

Sara looked through the colonnade and saw the immense swells traveling toward the island like a range of watery hills. Pandit was already at her side, raising James from the bed. "We can take him to the bathroom."

They had just managed to carry James inside the small room and huddle with him in the corner, when the entire island groaned. They heard the sound of cracking stone, and the whole room began to shake and rise. The lights went out and a pipe burst, spraying them with water. From outside the colonnade came the rumble of falling rock and a cloud of dust filled the room.

Sara and Pandit were just getting their bearings when they heard a different sound. This time it was a deep roar. Water crashed through the open bathroom doorway, slammed into the wall, then quickly filled the room. Pandit had but a moment to gasp in air and grab hold of Sara before they were completely submerged. As he prepared to die, he remembered his mother cooking lentils and Sara asking for fruit.

The water began to flow out of the room, dragging Pandit and Sara with it. Sara held on to Pandit as tightly as he to her. The retreating wave dragged them as one across the outer room, slamming them into one of its stone columns. The blow knocked the breath out of Pandit, and he swallowed seawater. Then the water pulled them beyond the room onto a pile of boulders just outside. Pandit's lungs screamed for air as his mind began to grow dark.

Suddenly, he was coughing and sputtering on top of jagged stones. Sara, up to her knees in the ebbing water, was tugging at him, trying to get him to his feet. "Pandit!" she cried urgently. "Another wave is coming!"

Somehow, Pandit found the strength to rise, and with Sara's help he stumbled across the sodden, sand-strewn room back to the meager shelter of the bathroom. The second wave hit with almost the force of the first, but the water rose only to Pandit's and Sara's chests. When it began to flow out, they dived beneath its surface and grabbed hold of the toilet fixture. This time, they were not sucked from the room. Five more times, the waters reached for them, each time with weakened force. Several more waves broke against the mound of stones left by the avalanche outside the colonnade.

Finally, it was over. Sara and Pandit emerged from their shelter to discover the room filled with several feet of sand. A huge fish with wicked teeth flopped upon it. There was no trace of James. The grief Pandit felt for his friend and employer contrasted with his joy at saving Sara. She was covered with scrapes and welts, her hair was bedraggled, and her dress was a tattered rag, yet she never seemed so beautiful to him. Her eyes made all the difference. She gazed at him as if she saw him for the first time. Not as a servant or an adoring buffoon, but as a man. A man who had risked everything for her. Risked everything and won.

Pandit hugged Sara close to him. "Rick was wrong," he said. "The wave did not overcome us. We overcame it."

Sara returned his embrace, then searched for his mouth with her lips.

JOE GRABBED THE handle of the serving spoon with both hands and began digging into the earth to free the airplane. Rick and Con took the soup spoons and immediately joined in. No one had to say how important the plane was to them. Without it, they would be stranded on one of the most devastated parts of the planet. All their plans counted on them getting far away. That knowledge made them attack the earth with desperate intensity.

It was much harder work than they expected. The rocky soil had been compacted by the shaking and yielded grudgingly to their meager tools. They were emotionally and physically drained to begin with, so digging in the searing heat quickly pushed them to exhaustion. Joe became woozy. The spoon dropped from his nerveless hand, and he wavered a bit before slumping over. Con grabbed a water bottle and splashed his face.

"Wha . . . what?" said Joe in a slow, slurred voice.

"Heat exhaustion," said Rick to Con. "Let's get him inside the plane."

They helped Joe into the plane; then Rick made his way up the inclined floor to the control panel. Thanks to the tape labels, he was able to close the opening and turn on the environmental controls that cooled the cabin. Meanwhile, Con gave Joe water and wiped his forehead with a damp cloth. He slowly recovered.

"I'm really sorry, guys," said Joe weakly.

"We were stupid to work in that heat," said Rick. "It could have been any one of us. We've got to be more careful."

"But the plane," protested Joe.

"We can work when it's cooler," said Rick. "This heat won't last."

"Speaking of being careful," said Joe, "we should turn off the environmental controls. Our power supply isn't going to recharge anytime soon."

"I don't know," said Rick. "Maybe we should leave them on a bit longer."

"Well, I know," replied Joe. "We'll need that power. Look, I'm okay now." On unsteady feet, he made his way to the control panel and turned off the air-conditioning. Then he returned to the rear of the plane. "What do we do now?"

"Rest," said Rick.

"We could eat," said Con, trying not to sound too eager.

Joe cracked a genuine smile. "Leave it to Con to think of food."

"It's a good idea," said Rick. He searched though the pile of supplies and found three leftover breakfast rolls and handed them out.

"Best rolls in the world," said Joe, trying to sound lighthearted.

"Only rolls in the world," said Rick.

Con looked at the cinnamon roll in her hand and savored its aroma. She felt so hungry that it hurt, but she forced herself to eat slowly. The roll only whetted her appetite. When she was done, she noticed Joe was watching her.

"I'm not very hungry," he lied. "Would you like to finish mine?"

"I couldn't," said Con.

"Sure you could," said Joe, forcing his half-eaten roll into Con's hand. "It shouldn't go to waste."

"You should save it for later," she protested.

"And have it go stale?" said Joe. "What would Pandit say?"

Con gave in to Joe's coaxing and her hunger. She bit into the roll as tears welled in her eyes. She swallowed with difficulty. "Thanks, Joe."

PANDIT AND SARA searched for James. Roaming the island, they discovered that the earthquake and the waves had transformed it. The grove of trees was completely erased, replaced by an expanse of wet sand littered with dead and dying sea creatures. A battered mosasaur lay on the rock pile in front of the stone living quarters. It was huge and frightening even in death. The dining pavilion was gone without a trace, as was the staff compound. The shoreline had changed also. In some places, the beaches had disappeared; in others, they were larger. The protected beach had lost some of its sand and extended farther inland. Pandit wondered if the device that protected it still functioned. They found no sign of James. He had utterly vanished.

The mounds of sand and fallen rock altered the look of everything, so Pandit could not be sure if the structure of the island was different. Still, he thought it might be so. The stone rooms seemed more elevated than they were before. Strangely, they were the one feature of the island that had changed the least. Whether by pure luck or amazing engineering, they had survived virtually intact. In fact, they appeared to have repaired themselves.

When he and Sara returned to Green's former quarters, the burst pipe no longer sprayed water, and the plumbing and lights functioned as before.

That was their sole piece of good fortune, aside from their survival. All the supplies and the contents of all the rooms were gone. In their entire search, all they had found was a shattered dresser and a single shoe that had belonged to Con. The sea had washed away much of the plaster in the storerooms, revealing that all three quarters had doorways that led deeper into the cliff. Featureless silvery panels solidly sealed all the doorways. Whatever lay behind them was beyond their reach.

Throughout the search for James, Sara's apprehension grew as it became apparent their situation was desperate. There were few material resources to fall back on. She had gone from being the future wife of a billionaire to a woman whose sole possession was a tattered dress. It was a fall from fortune almost too drastic to comprehend. She struggled to get a grasp of her new reality.

The center of that reality was Pandit. When she had kissed him, it had been purely impulse. That morning, he had been a nobody. His attraction to her had been amusing and pathetic. He was plump, and his unfashionable face was not particularly handsome, even by natural standards. She had thought that his intense dark eyes—and his cooking—were his only good features.

Now, Pandit was the last man on the world. As they roamed the island, Sara considered her impulsive kiss. She still wondered about its consequences. *Will I regret it?* She imagined what it would be like if John, instead of Pandit, were stranded with her. Wealth and power had been John's essence. *What would he be like without them?* Pondering this question, Sara realized she would rather be with Pandit. John had shown his true nature when he abandoned her. Sara felt she could rely on Pandit. She knew she would have to. His formerly amusing and pathetic adoration was now her greatest and, perhaps her only, security. She would do her utmost to ensure he never lost it.

PANDIT WAS NOT a practicing Hindu, much less a devout one. Still, he understood the capriciousness of the gods. They had destroyed the world and got him the woman he adored. He received their largess with gratitude but wariness. He knew the appropriate response was to savor the moment. It came naturally to him, for his genius as a chef lay in his sensualism. He appreciated Sara's beauty in the same way he did the taste of a rich and exquisite sauce. He saw her perfection as something good in itself. She reminded him of the goddesses carved on the temples, holy in her carnality.

The fiery sky had extinguished. In its place were thick black clouds that glowed dimly in a dark shade of sullen red. Lightning and the burning forests on the mainland provided the brightest light. Although it was just past noon, the world was wrapped in dusk. When the glow left the clouds, it would be night.

In the still, heavy heat, Sara and Pandit were drawn to the coolness of the sea. The water was so calm that the violence it had wreaked earlier seemed almost impossible. Sara shed her tattered dress and waded out into the sea. There, she splashed water on her hot skin. Pandit watched her, knowing that she was doing this, in part, for his benefit. Her gesture filled him with joy and desire and gratitude. He pushed aside all the concerns that weighed upon him and lived only in the present.

Pandit first noticed the wave as a darker line on the dark Montana Sea. It puzzled him, for it seemed somehow distorted. He was about to warn Sara when he saw it was pointless. It was the tsunami's gigantic scale that made it look wrong. As it rolled toward them, Pandit could see fires miles inland wink out. Sara was, as yet, unaware of their approaching destruction, her eyes were solely on him.

"You are so beautiful, Sara," said Pandit. "I told Rick you were a goddess. Now I know it is true."

Sara smiled at his words.

"I need to hold you, Sara."

Sara emerged from the sea and walked toward him with
a conscious sultriness. As she left the water, it began to
flow away rapidly, first exposing the beach and, then, a
vast expanse of seabed. Sara turned and saw the tsunami.
It was the size of a dark mountain. She ran into Pandit's
open arms and he embraced her. "I cannot save you this
time," he said softly. "But I will be with you until the
end."

Sara pressed her perfect body against Pandit's chubby
one as he took one last glimpse at the oncoming wave. It
blotted out much of the sky. It was black, except for its
very top, where foam cascaded down in waterfalls. The
foam's whiteness reminded Pandit of the mourning
clothes at a Hindu funeral.

Pandit turned his mind from the advancing destroyer
and concentrated his entire being on Sara—her smooth
softness . . . her smell . . . her warm vitality. He caressed
her back, wishing to still her trembling. She stopped
shaking. The calmness of surrender came over them both.
Sara gazed into Pandit's eyes with a look he recognized
as the gods' parting gift.

21

THE INTERIOR OF THE PLANE SLOWLY GREW HOTTER AND
hotter, yet no one suggested turning the environmental controls back on. None dared to say their comfort was worth
any of the precious store of energy. They removed as much
clothing as modesty allowed, then suffered without complaining. Joe and Rick stripped to their shorts. Con briefly
thought of removing her shirt also, but did not. That she
would even consider it depressed her, and she resolved to
resist the erosion of civilization. They arranged the pile of

clothes and supplies in the rear of the plane to make it as comfortable as possible, then lay upon it. The space was cramped, but the inclined floor permitted them to lie nowhere else. Lying there, sweating and torpid, each felt the heat radiating from the others' bodies. In those conditions, it was impossible to truly rest. All the while, it grew darker outside. Only talk kept their minds from dwelling on their discomfort.

"Rick," said Joe, "you seemed to know what was going to happen, I mean the earthquake and all. How come?"

"Paleontologists have been studying the K-T event for almost a century."

"Why do you keep calling it that?" asked Con.

"K-T is an old geological name for the stratum that divides the Mesozoic Era from our own. The 'K' stands for '*Kreide*,' German for 'chalk,' and the 'T' stands for 'Tertiary.' "

"How enlightening," said Joe dryly.

"Even before Luis Alvarez proposed that the K-T boundary was evidence of a meteor impact, scientists knew it marked the end of an era," said Rick.

"So that meteor is what killed off the dinosaurs?" asked Con.

"Paleontologists have been debating that ever since Alvarez," said Rick. "Probably that observatory was built to finally settle the question."

"Then the people who built it must come back!" said Con with excitement.

"They won't," said Joe. "Sam wiped it out in the future."

"How can that be?" asked Con. "It still exists. We were there. And who's Sam?"

"Sam was the guy Green stole the time machine from," said Joe. "He's the one who changed history to eliminate the observatory."

"I still don't understand," said Con.

"Time flows in only one direction," said Joe. "Any change in the flow of time affects only events upwhen from that change. It's sort of like dumping dye into a river—only the water downstream gets colored. It doesn't matter where you come from, only where you dump the dye. Sam changed history sometime in his past, but our future."

"You don't know that for a fact," said Rick. "There are other possibilities."

"Returning to the island would waste our time and the plane's power," said Joe flatly.

"How can you be certain?" asked Con.

"I knew Sam. He wouldn't have left things to chance. He changed history, all right. I'm certain about another thing, too. I don't want to meet any more people from the future. Even if it *were* possible."

"Why?" asked Con.

"Judging from Sam, they'd treat us like dirt," said Joe.

"He was just one person," said Con. "Humanity's bound to improve."

"Is that so?" retorted Joe. "If you believe that, why don't you visit what's left of the Holy Land?"

"That's . . . that's a special case," said Con.

"Because it proves my point? I could come up with others," said Joe. "Rick said we'd go to someplace that's safe. That island's not on my list."

Rick silently watched the exchange and wondered why Joe was so against returning to the island. *Ultimately*, he realized, it *doesn't matter why. Joe's opinion carries the most weight. Only he can fly the plane.* While Rick was not convinced that history had been altered, he was also disinclined to return to the island. Passively waiting to be rescued ran against his temperament. It also seemed like a foolhardy gamble. *Joe might be right,* he thought, *or time travelers might take weeks or even years to return.*

"We're better off relying on ourselves," said Rick, "than counting on a miraculous rescue."

"Yeah," said Joe.

"Then what chance do we have?" said Con. "We're only three people, and this meteor just killed all the dinosaurs."

"It didn't kill them all," said Rick, "at least not yet. Some people think the impact and the extinctions were just coincidences. That's what everyone's been debating since 1980."

"Now that you're the foremost authority in the world," said Joe, "maybe you'd give us your opinion on the matter."

"I think the effects of the impact precipitated the mass extinction," said Rick.

"So we're in for a wild ride," said Joe.

"I'm afraid so," replied Rick.

"May I ask how wild?" said Joe.

"First, the debris from the impact and the soot from the fires will blot out the sun. Photosynthesis will stop."

"For how long?" asked Con.

"Estimates vary," replied Rick. "Several months, at least."

"Several months?" said Con in despair.

"Why do I think that's not all the bad news?" said Joe. "You said something about cold."

"Without sunlight, the Earth's surface temperature will slowly drop below freezing."

"Winter in the middle of summer," said Con bleakly.

"That's one reason why we should head for the southern hemisphere. It's fall there, and the change won't be as drastic to the ecosystem."

"So things should be okay there," said Joe, "once the sky clears."

"There's also the problem of acid rain," said Rick. "The nitrogen-oxygen compounds formed in the impact will be converted to nitric acid. The ocean's chemistry gets thrown off for a millennium. There's also a period of global warming caused by greenhouse gases."

"In short, all hell breaks loose," said Joe.

"Why did we ever leave the island?" said Con, the discouragement heavy in her voice.

"The dinosaurs perished," said Rick, "not because they were primitive or inferior, but because their world changed too rapidly. Their adaptations worked against them, and they died out. Human beings are flexible and smart. We'll find a way to survive."

Rick began talking about changes in vegetation, the "fern spike," and the proliferation of wind-pollinated plants over insect-pollinated ones. *He sounds like he's lecturing a class*, thought Con irritably. *He's talking about my future, not some science experiment.* Now that the excitement and the terror of their escape had subsided, thoughts of that future weighed heavily upon her.

Con saw that her choice to flee with Rick was not the result of any deliberation. At the time, her only thought was

that they were escaping death. Fear had caused her to flee—
fear and Rick. Now she faced a life as the only woman
among two men. She could see so many potential problems
and conflicts, it made her head spin. *Will I have children?*
The idea of childbirth under such conditions was frightening.
A more frightening question arose. *Will I even have a choice
in the matter?* Con realized that the norms of society would
no long apply. *The three of us* **are** *society.* She contemplated
the two men lying so close to her in the enervating heat. *Rick
had set out to kill a man. Joe had helped Green escape.* She
wondered what they would be capable of when civilization
wore off. It worried her that she didn't know.

"Rick," said Con, "let's talk about something besides this
damned K-T thing. Tell us about your brother."

"Tom?" said Rick. His hand automatically caressed the
worn knife sheath that hung on his belt. "He was mother and
father to me after my folks were killed. I guess he's the
reason I love fossils. Every kid is crazy about dinosaurs, but
who has a paleontologist to tuck him in at night?"

"So you never grew out of it," said Joe.

"No, never. You know, despite everything, he would love
being here. The K-T fauna were Tom's specialty. A lot of
people assume the mammals all made it through, but Tom
was able to show . . ."

"God, Rick!" said Con peevishly. "Do you have a one-
track mind?" She turned to Joe and, hoping to steer the conversation back toward civilization, asked, "Do you have a
family?"

"I'm divorced," he said. "My daughter lives with her
mother."

"What's your daughter's name?" asked Con.

"Nicole, Nicole Corretta Burns," said Joe in a soft, melancholy voice. "She'll be fifteen this August seventh."

"You must have married young," said Con.

"While I was in graduate school. Nicole was born a year
later." In the dim light, Con could see Joe shaking his head.
"I wanted to give my girl everything."

"What children really want is love," said Con.

"She had that, but she didn't have my time," said Joe ruefully. "Frank, my college roommate, and I started a small

R&D company, and we put everything, our whole lives, into it. We developed a neural interface that we were sure would make our fortunes."

"You sound bitter about it," said Con.

"Yeah," said Rick. "What happened?"

"We needed capital, and Frank brought in Peter Green."

"*Green* was your investor?" said Rick.

"No," replied Joe, "Green hooked us up with a bunch of Russians. I should've figured they were mobsters, but Frank assured me they were legitimate. Guess I wanted to believe him. I kept fooling myself until the drug raid."

"Drug raid!" said Con. "What did drugs have to do with it?"

"Frank had agreed to work on stimuplants in exchange for the financing," said Joe.

"Electronic drugs?" asked Rick.

"Hooked up with the right chip, the neural interface made the perfect stimuplant. It was the state-of-the-art high. They were making them right under my nose."

"And you didn't know?" asked Con.

"No, but tell that to a prosecutor, especially after Frank turned up dead. They said it was suicide, but I'm not so sure. Anyway, I lost my family, the business, and my reputation. The only person who helped me was Green."

"Green?"

"Yeah. He said he didn't know about the Russians and felt bad about what had happened. He paid for my lawyer and hired me when I got out of prison."

"That sounds out of character," said Con.

"He was just getting his hooks into me. I did little jobs at first. Gray stuff. Reverse engineering. Security overrides came later. The deeper I was in, the dirtier the jobs got."

"Why did you put up with it?" asked Con.

"I was going to leave, and Green guessed I was. One day he picked up Nicole's picture from my desk. 'Cute kid,' he said, 'but it's an old picture.' Then he gave me a new picture, taken with a telephoto lens. Oh God!" cried out Joe, in remembered anguish and rage. "My little girl! All the while, Green had on this big grin, pretending he was giving me a gift instead of threatening my baby."

"And you helped him and Daddy escape?" said Con.

"I did what I had to do," said Joe.

"But . . ."

"That's the one thing I won't talk about," said Joe. "I have my reasons."

"Joe . . ."

"You and Rick are my family now," said Joe, "and I'll do anything for you. Except talk about this morning. Please respect me on this."

An awkward silence followed. Finally, Rick broke it by saying, "We should try to sleep. It'll cool off, and we'll want to be rested when we dig out the plane." The suggestion excused everyone from further conversation. Con lay still in her sweat-soaked clothes and tried to get some sleep, but it was impossible. It was too hot, she was having hunger cramps, and her mind raced from one fearful scenario to another. Perhaps it was too early to sleep. She had no idea what time it was. It might be only afternoon, although it was darker outside than any night she could remember. The red glow had left the clouds, and there were no stars or moon in the uniformly black sky.

22

AFTER WHAT SEEMED LIKE HOURS OF TROUBLED THOUGHT, Con drifted into an uneasy sleep. She dreamed of Sara and Pandit. In the dream, Sara wore the dress Con had felt was so shamelessly revealing. She no longer wept. Instead, she was placing strawberries between her teeth and feeding them to Pandit. She turned to smile at Con, red juice running down her chin and on to her breasts. "I told you," said Sara smugly. "You should've stayed on the island."

Con woke up thinking her breasts, too, were stained with

berry juice. A sweat-soaked tee shirt clung to them instead. As she sat up, she felt the need to relieve herself. Rick and Joe were both snoring, and she tried not to disturb them as she rose and groped for the door.

The darkness was almost absolute. The only light came from a faint orange flickering in the clouds. She stepped on Joe, but he only grunted. She could not see him, but she heard him move as he changed positions. Even more cautiously than before, she felt for the door. After several minutes, her hand touched a raised button. She pressed it, and an opening formed in the plane's fuselage.

The smell of smoke immediately assaulted Con's nose. It was strong and acrid and caused her eyes to sting. Fortunately, Joe had programmed the door to recognize her, so it would close when she left the plane. Con quickly stepped outside. The ground beneath her bare feet felt hot and baked. *Rick said it would cool off*, she thought. She wondered when that would be. The smoke explained the flickering glow in the clouds; it was the reflection of distant fires. The air was as hot as before, perhaps even hotter, but, at least, it was dry. In the privacy of darkness, Con pulled off her shirt. She felt some momentary relief as the perspiration evaporated from her torso. She spread her damp shirt over a fern bush to dry before walking into the brush. The foliage that had been so green and lush when they landed, felt withered and dry now. It crackled beneath her feet. Touch and sound were the dominant senses in this shadowed world. Con glanced back toward the plane and was alarmed that she could barely make it out. A few more steps and she would have lost sight of it entirely.

When she woke up inside the plane, she thought about going to the river to bathe. Now she realized how dangerous that would be. She could hear the river in the distance and smell its muddy wetness, but it was totally invisible. Bathing risked getting lost. She thought of her first morning on the island and of floating among the ammonites. That blissful, sunlit moment seemed ages ago. *It was another world*, she reminded herself. That a shallow, mud-choked stream seemed inviting was almost too ironic to bear.

Con squatted among the ferns, feeling like a savage. *I bet-*

ter get used to this, she told herself. She knew it was but the
first, and probably the least, of many indignities. When she
stood up, the hunger cramps that had kept her awake so long
returned with redoubled force. Thinking of food, she recalled
that people ate fern shoots. *Fiddleheads, that's what they're
called.* She remembered seeing them listed once on a restaurant menu. There, they were served with Hollandaise sauce.
Con groped among the fronds, feeling for coiled shapes. Her
fingers touched something that felt right, and she tugged it
from the plant. It was stiff and dry and had a woolly skin,
but she stuffed it in her mouth. It reminded her of a dried-
out asparagus. Eagerly, she sought more. She moved from
one fern to another, seeking to sate the gnawing emptiness
inside. Most of the few fiddleheads she found were too bitter
to eat, but she continued foraging. Every once in a while,
she glanced anxiously toward the plane to make sure she
could still see it.

Her search took her farther and farther afield, for most of
the fiddleheads had already uncoiled into fronds. Yet, the
plane was still visible because the orange reflection on the
clouds had grown brighter. The smoke was thicker also.
Con's eyes watered from it. She looked upwind and could
see the foothills for the first time. Their tops were silhouetted
against a hazy orange glow. A hot, smoky wind began to
blow, rustling the dry leaves. The fires were no longer distant.

Con stumbled through the brush to the plane and put on
her shirt. It was already dry, but it felt oily against her skin.
The opening appeared in the plane as programmed. Con
called into it. "Rick! Joe! Fire's headed our way!"

Two bleary, sweat-soaked faces were illuminated in the
plane's opening by the orange glow. "Oh crap!" said Joe
wearily.

"We'd best start digging," said Rick. His tired voice
sounded dispirited. Rick vanished, then emerged from the
plane with the three spoons. "Remember what happened to
Joe. Let's not push ourselves too hard," he said.

Rick's admonition was thwarted by the glow beyond the
foothills. As they worked, it grew brighter, driving them to
attack the earth with increasing desperation. The baked

CRETACEOUS SEA   191

ground seemed harder than before, and their progress was
measured in inches. The handle of Rick's spoon kept bending. When he straightened it for the seventh time, it snapped,
forcing him to dig with the bowl. Con bloodied her fingertips
trying to claw out a rock while she wept in frustration. Joe
worked steadily and stoically, but without hope.

The glow grew brighter and began to waver. Occasionally,
a stronger blast of wind would choke them with smoke. By
the time Joe had to lie on the ground to reach to bottom of
his hole, the first tongues of flames appeared at the crest of
the hills. From those tongues, fire dribbled down the hillsides.

"Joe," said Rick, "what will fire do to the plane?"

"I have no idea, but I don't think we should stay to find
out."

The fire advanced rapidly through the dry scrub. The
flames rose high into the sky, filling it with false stars that
burned out or fell to the ground and ignited it. Even though
it was still distant, they could feel the blaze's heat.

Joe entered the plane and turned on its interior lights. The
white light seemed overly bright to their eyes. "We'd better
pack up and make for the river while we still can," he said.

"We should take our clothes, blankets, the guns, flashlights, and as much water as we can carry," said Rick, "and
hope the rest of our stuff makes it through with the plane."

They quickly stuffed three duffel bags with clothes, water,
and the flashlights, then grabbed the two guns. Joe shut off
the lights and, for a few moments, they found it hard to see.
When their eyes became reaccustomed to the dim light, they
headed for the river. They had to climb over the fallen trees
that marked the river's old bank, then scramble down the
dry, stony hill that had been its former bed before reaching
water. The tepid, shallow stream was laden with dirt and
flowed through a tangle of partially uprooted plants.

Rick felt the leaves of a plant standing in the water. "This
stuff will burn," he said.

"I see a spot downstream that looks clearer," said Joe.

They headed in its direction. Although the water was only
ankle deep, the earth beneath it had turned into a deep layer
of mud, and the going was slow. Once, the muck pulled off

Con's sneaker. She groped in the mud until she found it. Then she washed it off as best she could before putting it in her duffel bag. She removed her other shoe and did the same. By the time she caught up with Joe and Rick, they were uprooting dried plants and tossing them downstream. They were already covered with mud. Their duffel bags and the guns hung on the gnarled branches of a small overturned tree.

"We need a fireproof spot," said Rick.

Con placed her duffel bag with Rick's and Joe's, then joined them in pulling up plants. Most of them came up easily from the soft mud. The deeply rooted ones that didn't were stomped down into the muck. Gradually, the clear spot was widened from five to ultimately fifteen feet. While they worked, the flames advanced.

Driven by the fire, panicked animals arrived long before the flames did. Con could hear them splashing through the water. Sometimes she could also make out a shadowy form in the ever-thickening smoke. A lone Triceratops lumbered by so close she could hear its ragged gasping. The appearance of the animals did not frighten Con. Instead, it gave her hope, for it was evidence there still were other living beings in the world. Joe's reaction was different. He walked over to the upturned tree, grabbed a gun, and turned it on. "Fresh meat," was all he said. The words made Con's stomach rumble.

Joe stood vigilantly at the perimeter of their clearing and strained to see through the smoke. Twice he fired at vague fleeing shadows, but missed both times as the haze defeated the gun's targeting scope. Con and Rick watched him as they crouched down close to the surface of the water, where the smoke was less dense. The smoke thickened into choking clouds that drove Joe, coughing and wheezing, to abandon the hunt. He hung the gun on the overturned tree, then flopped down on his back in the water next to Con.

"You know," said Joe as he settled in the ooze, "this isn't half-bad. Like some fancy spa."

Con followed suit and lay down full length also. By placing her hands behind her head, she was able to keep her face above the water. The water in her ears shut out the roar of the oncoming fire, and the air was less acrid. The mud and the lukewarm water were not entirely refreshing, but they provided some relief from the heat. Exhausted and emotionally drained, she was past caring about anything else. She was no longer hot, and that was sufficient for the moment. Con closed her eyes. A feeling of numbness came over her, the closest thing to peace she had experienced since the previous morning.

Rick remained sitting upright, breathing through his wet shirt, as he watched anxiously for the onrush of flames. Reason told him they had done everything they could and now they must sit tight. Still, he wanted to be on guard. The fleeing animals were all gone. *That's the difference between intelligence and instinct*, thought Rick. *The river's the only safe place to be and they ran right through it.* The dark land on the other bank only looked like a refuge. The river, choked with tinder-dry plants, would prove no barrier to the fire. It would pass over this puny obstacle and continue its pursuit. The animals would be overcome in the end.

Yet Rick's intellect could not calm the fear he felt as flames became visible through the smoke. They rose much higher than he had imagined they would. The terror of yesterday's events lacked the immediacy of these flames. The burning sky had remoteness and even grandeur. This had the visceral impact of a blowtorch pointed at his face. Rick was about to lie prone in the water when he remembered that the guns and the duffel bags were still in the tree branches. They might burn when the fire passed over the river. He was about to retrieve them when he heard the sound of a very large animal approaching. He froze to listen. It came from upstream, and it seemed that the creature was not crossing the river but walking down its middle. *So much for my theory about blind instinct*, he thought. He wondered what creature had the sense to remain in the water. From the rhythm of its footsteps, they sounded like those of a biped.

Rick shook Con and Joe, while he strained to see what was making the noise. Con sat up, her hair and back dripping with mud. She rubbed her eyes and looked around stupidly. When she saw the flames, her eyes widened in fear.

"What's up?" asked Joe. "Shouldn't we be lying down?"

"Something's coming!" said Rick.

A towering shape materialized from the smoke. It was a huge Tyrannosaur, taller than either of the two they had spotted on their excursion. The flames had reached the river, and the foliage above its surface was beginning to ignite. Flames licked at the creature's flanks, and it roared in pain and rage. Then it spied the patch of cleared water and headed for it. Rick was rising to dash for the guns when the dinosaur bounded into the clearing and blocked his path. He made a startled jump backward, lost his footing, and fell. As he went down, a yard-long foot splashed in the water just inches from Con's leg. The foot rose again, and Rick saw sharp, eight-inch claws dripping with mud.

Joe seized Con by the waist, pulled her toward him, then rolled over. The maneuver bought them two feet of safety. Afraid to stand up, Rick, Joe, and Con scrambled on their hands and knees away from the oversize talons. The mud fought their every movement. They struggled in frantic haste, aware the *Tyrannosaur* might maim or crush them without even noticing it.

The entire river was on fire by then, yet the safest place was close to the flames, for the giant creature would not stay still. No matter where it stood, it was too large to avoid the fire entirely. It moved constantly and erratically, churning the slow-moving water into a muddy pudding. Several times its heavy tail missed bludgeoning them by inches. Sometimes, when it bent forward to lift its tail up as high as it could, they could stare into its tormented yellow-green eyes. They appeared not to stare back, as if they were blinded by pain. Then the creature would jerk its head away, seeking respite in another position. None came and it roared hoarsely as parts of its hide began to blacken, and to bubble with huge blisters.

Con huddled with Rick and Joe near the burning perimeter of the clearing. She dared not take her eyes off the frantic monster in their midst, even though watching it exposed her to the searing heat. The Tyrannosaur held her in thrall, as might a gun pointed at her head. Every detail of the massive legs was impressed into her brain—the rippling muscles, its pebbly, mud-caked hide, the dewclaw above the rear of its foot and, most of all, the three, wicked claws at the ends of its huge, birdlike feet. The animal seemed less of a living creature than a force of nature, a smaller but equally deadly cousin to the meteor, the earthquake, and the burning sky. It could kill her with equal indifference. Her mangled body would register to its tortured mind as only a difference in the texture of the mud—if it registered at all.

Wet mud offered the only protection from the flames, aside from the shallow water. Rick, Joe, and Con scooped it up and helped each other to coat the exposed parts of their bodies to keep them from blistering. The mud quickly grew hot and had to be refreshed with new coats. While they did that, they kept a wary eye on the Tyrannosaur. Rick slathered mud on Con's neck and shoulders saying, "Everything will be fine." His words reminded her of Pandit and Sara.

When the vegetation in the river burned to the waterline, the flames extinguished. Gradually, dark spots appeared in the riverbed. They enlarged until the river was a corridor of darkness between two burning walls. The Tyrannosaur was released from its flaming corral. It wandered downstream on unsteady feet.

"It won't live much longer," said Rick.

"It's strange," said Con, "but I feel sorry for it."

"So do I," said Joe, "but if I had my gun, I would have shot it in a heartbeat."

"The guns!" cried Rick in panic.

The tree where they had hung the guns and their duffel bags had been trampled, and only a few of its branches were visible above the mud. Con, Rick and Joe ran over to the spot and began to search for their belongings. The bags had floated downstream only a short distance before getting snagged. They were soaked and muddy, but only slightly singed. The guns were nowhere to be seen. Carefully, but anxiously, they groped in the churned-up river bottom for them. After several minutes, Joe let out a triumphant yell. It died in this throat when the gun emerged from the water bent into the shape of a "V." Joe removed the cylinder filled with the silvery ammunition, then angrily flung the ruined gun into the river.

Rick found the second gun close to where Joe found the first. He rinsed the mud off as best he could. The weapon appeared intact. Rick turned it on and rows of red, yellow, and blue lights glowed on its side. "Don't try to fire it," said Joe, "until we can clean it."

"Can we move upstream and get out of this mud?" said Con.

Without another word, they began to walk upstream, carrying their sodden duffel bags. The plants had burned down to the waterline and, although their charred remains blackened the stream, it looked more like a normal river. They came to a spot where the water was almost a foot deep. The current had cleared the vegetation and even some of the mud. With an exhausted sigh, Con sat down. Rick followed suit.

The water reached up to Con's waist. It was marginally cleaner, and she used it to wash the mud from her face and hair. An updraft carried the smoke away, and the fire, now contained by the river, no longer seemed threatening. After the terror of the Tyrannosaur and the burning river, this felt safe. It was even relatively cool. Tired as she was, Con felt a little of the exultation she had felt when she successfully descended the cliff.

Joe remained standing. He opened his duffel bag and pulled out the driest shirt he could find. He asked Con to hold his bag and proceeded to clean the gun with the shirt. When he was satisfied, he returned the shirt to his bag.

"Con, would you watch my stuff for me?" asked Joe. "I'm going to get you dinner."

Con nodded, and Joe started to head upstream.

Rick called after him. "Won't you get me some, too?"

"You can have Con's leftovers," Joe called back. "Providing she leaves any."

Rick smiled at Joe's crack about Con's appetite, yet it reminded him of a serious concern. Her souped metabolism was an advantage in a world of plenty, but they were no longer living in that world. He worried how she would fare in the time of want that lay ahead. Rick gazed at her in the firelight. She was slumped forward on the two duffel bags, watching the fire's reflection on the river. Her face was drawn and dirty, yet bore a hint of a smile. Rick found that smile utterly endearing. He reached out and tenderly rubbed her wet, muddy back. Con's only reaction was that her smile became slightly more pronounced. Rick spoke to her, more from hope than conviction. "Everything will be fine."

23

CON WAS ASLEEP WHEN RICK HEARD THE CRACK OF JOE'S gun from far up the river. Although Rick would have liked to see Joe's kill, he knew he should stay with Con. The valley's scrubby vegetation had not provided the fuel for a sustained blaze, and it was getting dark again. The trees at the former riverbank still burned, as did shattered patches throughout the valley, but the main fires had moved to the far foothills. The flames that were so recently menacing, now seemed like homey campfires. Rick would miss them when they burned out.

Before Joe returned, Rick found it necessary to take out a flashlight to guide him. He set the output on low to conserve the battery and listened for footsteps. It seemed like a long time, before he heard any. Eventually, he heard Joe coming. He shined the beam upstream and caught sight of Joe. He had a broad smile and was carrying a five-foot-long object on his shoulder. It was the severed limb of a bipedal dinosaur. It looked to Rick like it came from a Hypsilophodontid.

"Got one of those little guys," said Joe. "It was like shooting a fish in a barrel."

"That's great, Joe!" said Rick. "But how did you butcher it?"

"Sliced it with the gun."

Rick pointed to the still-burning trees. "We can cook it over there."

Joe looked at Con slumped over the duffel bags. "How long has she been asleep?"

"She nodded off right after you left. She's exhausted."

Joe shook his head. "This is because she's souped, isn't it?"

"Most likely," said Rick.

"All she's had was a muffin and a half," said Joe. "That was stupid on our part. We've got to keep her fed."

"Well, let's get this cooked," said Rick. He walked over to Con and gently shook her. "Joe's brought some dinner."

Con looked sleepy at first, but the idea of food soon had her wide-awake. She and Joe waded to the shore. There Con put her shoes back on to protect her feet from smoldering embers. Meanwhile, Rick searched the river for a branch to use as a poker. When he found one, he joined Joe and Con by a still-burning tree. Joe used the gun to cut the tree into logs that Rick then pushed together. Soon they had a healthy blaze going. Rick took out his knife and cut the leg at the knee joint, then skinned the two pieces.

"Garçon," said Con, "may I see ze menu?"

"Ah, Mademoiselle," replied Rick, "perhaps you would care to hear ze specials first."

"But of course," replied Con.

"Tonight we feature ze Hypsilophodontid àla carbonization."

"Stop there. That's my favorite."

"And how do you prefer your Hypsilophodontid? Medium, rare, or well-done?"

Con looked at the two bloody chunks of flesh, and quickly said, "Well-done. Very well done."

Joe dug a flashlight out of his duffel bag. "While you two yack, I'm going to check on the plane." He switched on the light and headed into the darkness.

As soon as Joe mentioned the plane, a pall came over Con and Rick's banter. Escaping the fire and finding food would mean little without the plane. It seemed impossible it could have survived the fire. They feared Joe's investigation was merely a formality, and he would soon be back to confirm the worst.

Rick tried to concentrate on cooking. He poked the fire until he had a pile of glowing embers, then placed the meat upon them. It hissed, and the smell of burnt flesh rose into the air. *This will be well-done, all right.* Using his poker, he turned the meat to try to cook it evenly. Soon both joints were thoroughly black. Though this kept him busy, his main attention was always on Joe.

The movements of Joe's flashlight marked his search for the plane. Rick and Con watched them silently, neither wishing to give voice to their dread. Apparently Joe was lost, for the light zigzagged over the landscape. Then it went out, leaving Con and Rick staring into darkness. A light, brilliant to their eyes, appeared. The transparent portion of the plane glowed, and they could see Joe in its interior, sitting in the pilot's seat. The light disappeared, and shortly after, they heard a shout of joy. Joe's light came straight toward them, bobbing as Joe ran.

Joe rushed into the light of the fire shouting, "The plane's fine! The plane's fine!" He gave Rick a bear hug, then lifted Con up and whirled her around. Every aspect of his grimy face was a picture of absolute bliss. "It's more than fine. It looks untouched, like it's brand-new! Thank God for such a plane!"

Rick tested the roasting meat and declared it ready for a celebration. Joe and Rick found a large, flat stone in the dry riverbed to serve both as dining table and serving plate. They carried it over to the fire; then Rick placed the two pieces of blackened limb upon it. Rick passed his knife around and each cut away strips of meat. The meal that followed was more festive than any served at the dining pavilion. The charred dinosaur meat, tough and unseasoned, seemed like a feast to all. The warm bottled water was appreciated more than Peter Green's chilled champagne.

Joe grinned as he watched Con eat ravenously. "Take your time, Con, no one's going to steal it from you."

Con smiled back as she chewed.

"This reminds me of camping with Tom," said Rick.

Joe chuckled. "Must have been a hell of a childhood."

"I know it sounds crazy," replied Rick, "but right now, I feel good. We've been through a lot, and now it's going to start getting better."

"I certainly hope so," said Joe

"There are parts of the world untouched by the impact. Sure, it'll get dark and cold there, too, and the acid rain will fall there also, but it won't be like here. There will be unburnt wood for fuel, tools, and shelter."

"How about food?" asked Con.

"There'll be food, too."

"And how do we get to this paradise?" asked Joe.

"The route will depend on the plane," replied Rick. "How far can we get on its batteries before it needs to recharge?"

"The energy storage system is different from batteries as we understand them," said Joe. "The panels always kept it near maximum. I don't know how far we'll get without the panels working."

"Could we fly over open ocean?" asked Rick.

"I wouldn't try it while it's dark."

"Then we should head north, skirting the shore of the seaway until we can fly above land to the east coast of North America. If we travel north along the coast, we should reach some less damaged areas."

"Why head north?" asked Joe. "Won't we be heading into the cold?"

"It's the darkness that will make things cold, not the latitude. We can wait there until the sunlight returns, then fly to southern Africa."

"If we want to end up in the southern hemisphere, why not fly to South America now?" asked Con.

"That would only work if we could make it all the way in one trip," said Rick. "We'd be flying right over the impact site, and there's open ocean between North and South American in this period."

"So we go to Africa in two hops," said Joe.

"That's safest," said Rick. "If we run out of power in the darkness, we'll be over someplace we can land. Someplace better than here."

"It should work," said Joe.

"As long as you can fly in the dark," said Rick. "You can do that, can't you?"

"Yes . . . in principle," said Joe. "That holographic map also works as a night guidance system, though I can't say I've ever tried it."

"Do you think it's safe?" asked Con.

"With vertical takeoffs and landings, it won't be too risky," said Joe.

"Before you know it," said Rick, "we'll be sitting out the darkness in our snug little cabin."

Con imagined a cozy log cabin in the woods with a fire in the fireplace. Her full stomach gave her such a sense of well-being that the vision did not seem implausible. She yawned contentedly.

"We should bring back the rest of the meat," said Rick.

"Yeah," said Joe wearily. "You're right. It's sitting in the river."

Con got up. "Let's get it over with."

"You need to stay here and keep the fire going," said Joe. "It's getting dark again, and we'll need it to guide us back."

"I can pull my weight," said Con. "You don't have to coddle me."

"I'm not," said Joe. "This is a job that needs to be done."

Con looked like she didn't quite believe him, but she agreed to Joe's plan. He left the gun for her to cut more wood, then headed to the river with Rick. Although they carried flashlights, they did not turn them on in order to conserve the batteries. The fire on the far hills still provided enough dim light for them to make their way. They walked along the riverbank, which had been cleared by the fire.

"It's a ways up," said Joe. "We won't need to turn on a flashlight until we reach the bend."

"Let's hurry. I don't like leaving Con alone."

"She's got the gun," said Joe, "but I feel the same way."

"Maybe she'd better come along," said Rick. "That fire should burn on its own."

"I wanted her to stay behind because we have to talk . . . about her . . . and come to an understanding"

"An understanding?" said Rick. "What do you mean by that?"

"There are only three people in the world," said Joe. "Two men and one woman. We need to set things straight."

Rick looked at Joe. In the dim light it was impossible to read his expression. "What things?" he asked warily.

"I'm her papa now."

"Her what?"

"Her papa—her father—but not like that poor excuse Greighton."

"Her papa? You said she was a rich bitch."

"She's not rich anymore."

"So now she's only a bitch," said Rick.

"Don't use my words against me," said Joe angrily. "Things change. I owe her."

"Owe her what?"

"My protection," said Joe, "and I *will* protect her."

"What's gotten into you?"

"I don't owe you an explanation. All you have to know is this—You may be the only young man in the world, but that doesn't mean you're entitled to her."

"I never said I was."

"Good," said Joe. "She has to choose you by her own free will. That means she's free to refuse you, too."

Rick looked suspiciously at Joe's shadowed face, wishing he could see his eyes. "And choose you instead, I suppose."

"I wasn't thinking like that at all," said Joe, sounding insulted. "That's why we need to talk. She's probably worried we're going to fight to see who drags her off into the bushes."

"Come on, Joe, she knows we wouldn't do that."

"Does she? You don't sound convinced yourself," said Joe. "Women need to worry about such things. They have a lot at stake—they're the one's who get pregnant. Con's no fool. She's worried. We've got to let her know where things stand."

"And where do they stand?" said Rick.

"I'm her papa. You want to marry her, you gotta ask me."

"Who said anything about marrying?"

"I did," said Joe. "And I'm a strict father. I won't see her hurt. Do I make myself clear?"

Rick was taken aback by Joe's intensity. "Look, Joe, I haven't really thought about it."

"You need to," said Joe.

Rick didn't know how to respond. The depths of Joe's feelings and the unusual form they took surprised him. They would be more understandable if Joe had declared his rivalry for Con. Yet, as bizarre as Joe's behavior seemed, it appeared benign. *Maybe he feels bad about misjudging her,* he thought. *Or, perhaps, this has something to do with Nicole.*

When Joe broke the silence, his voice was friendly and calm again. "I'm on your side, Rick, I really am. It's just that I'm on Con's side more. It's the least I can do."

"I'd never, never do anything to hurt Con," said Rick.

"She needs to know that," said Joe.

"I can't just say 'I'd never hurt you.' It'd sound phony."

"I'm not saying you should," said Joe. "Actions speak louder than words. Don't take her for granted. Pay attention to her needs and not just the ones she talks about. Sometimes, those are the least important."

Rick sighed. "You make it sound complicated."

"It is complicated," said Joe. "Only a fool thinks it isn't."

"And how did you learn how to do things right?"

"By doing everything wrong," answered Joe.

CON POKED THE fire with the branch, pushing the logs together so they burned more vigorously. The fire was comforting despite the heat it gave off. It was still too hot to enjoy that, but the light was welcome. Only a few small fires still burned in the vicinity of the river. Darkness was reclaiming the land. She wondered if it was day or night above the thick clouds, not that it made the slightest difference. She wanted to put another log in the blaze and turned on the gun to cut one. The rows of indicator lights appeared on the gun's side. She noted that two of the red lights, which indicated the charge, were no longer lit. She reconsidered the need for another log, then turned off the gun.

The partly eaten dinosaur limbs still lay on the flat rock. Con sat down and pulled off a piece, eating from appetite rather than hunger. *With a little salt, this would be good*, she concluded. *It tastes better than the one Rick shot.* She hoped their journey would end close to the sea, where they could make salt. With even the vestige of her appetite sated and the fire burning high, Con thought of other comforts. She looked at her filthy body. Those parts not caked with mud were coated with soot. A bath was certainly in order.

Not wishing to rummage through her duffel bag with greasy hands, she decided to find clean clothes after she bathed. There was just enough light from distant fires to make a flashlight unnecessary. After ensuring the fire had enough wood, she headed for the river. Once she reached its shores, she searched for a spot where the water was more than a few inches deep. She had to walk a ways before she found a suitable spot. Even there, only eight inches of brown water flowed over the muddy bottom. Con took off her shoes and her clothes and tried to clean them as best she could. In the darkness, it was impossible to tell if she had done any good. She folded her "clean" clothes and placed them on her shoes and attempted to wash herself.

The water felt good, but gritty with ash and dirt. Con recalled her remark to Sara about "smelling like myself." The concept had taken on more pungent meaning. She reeked. *Pretty soon*, she mused, *I won't even notice*. She thought of how Sara might react in her situation. The idea of Sara bathing in a muddy river was simultaneously amusing and saddening. Con bathed standing up because of the ooze on the riverbed. After a while, she assumed she was a clean as she could get. She left the river to stand on its bank and try to wash the mud from her feet. Then she put on her shoes and carried her wet clothes back to the fire.

RICK AND JOE found the Hypsilophodontid and butchered it as best they could. It was small for a dinosaur, but it was still a heavy animal. Both of them had to strain to flip it over so they could remove its other hind limb. Rick tried to cut off its tail, but it was sheathed in bony tendons. He settled on the forearms and shoulders, the remaining haunch, and strips of muscle from the back and upper tail. The meat made a heavy and bloody load.

As they headed back, Rick said, "We should cook all of this tonight, it'll keep longer."

"I suppose you're right," said Joe with a sigh, "but I'm pooped."

"So I am I, but we can sleep in before we dig out."

"Remind me to phone room service and cancel the wake-up call."

They struggled along the riverbank and were glad when their fire appeared in the distance. Soon they could see Con standing before it, holding the gun. As they approached nearer, Rick saw she had changed her clothes. Once they were in the circle of firelight, he could plainly see she was wide-eyed with fear. He also noticed that the gun was turned on and the safety was off.

"Con!" said Rick with concern. "What happened?"

"I went bathing in the river," she said in a frightened voice. "When I came back, the meat was gone!"

24

RICK EXAMINED THE GROUND FOR FOOTPRINTS, BUT THE baked earth offered no clues about the creature or creatures that had raided the camp. "I wasn't thinking," he said. "I just assumed that the fire had driven off the wildlife."

"What do you think it was?" asked Con.

"I'd guess it was a small carnivore," said Rick, "like the one I shot."

"A nightstalker?" said Joe.

"I prefer *Noctecorreptus greightonae*," said Rick.

"Well, Con's namesake just stole her breakfast," said Joe. "You'd better cook some more."

Cooking all the meat was the most sensible thing to do, yet Rick wanted with all his being to put it off. He fought the impulse, knowing they couldn't afford to let their precious food spoil. Even cooked, it wouldn't last long. Every step of preparing the meat required all Rick's effort, for he felt completely drained. He imagined that the others felt the same way. He removed the thick hide, then sliced the muscle beneath into strips for Con to cook on the embers. The end product of all this labor was black and stiff and looked barely edible. Rick wished they could smoke and dry the meat into jerky, but there was nothing at hand from which to construct a drying rack. The fire had stripped the land of its resources.

While Con and Rick worked, Joe stood guard. Once, he thought he saw a pair of eyes reflecting the fire's glow, but they disappeared by the time he grabbed a flashlight. If it was the thief, it was its only appearance.

By the time all the meat was cooked, it was so dark they had difficulty finding the plane. Not daring to leave the food untended, they carried it all as they blundered about. When Joe's flashlight finally shone on the plane, Con's clean new shirt was covered with charred grease. She was beyond caring. They secured the food inside the plane, then, leaving its lights on as a beacon, headed back to the fire for the rest of their belongings.

Following in the rear, Joe found himself stumbling in the darkness. "Damn!" he cursed, as he tripped over something. "We should've brought a second flashlight."

"We'll get the drill down eventually," said Rick.

"Yeah, about the time the batteries go dead," said Joe.

"By the time that happens," said Rick, "some of the dust will have settled and we'll be able to tell day from night."

"What I want to know is how that damned dinosaur of yours finds its way in the dark," said Joe. "I swear it was watching us."

"I only assumed it was a nightstalker," said Rick. "I don't know for sure."

"With a name like that," said Joe, "isn't it likely?"

"If it's a *Noctecorreptus*, the answer's simple," replied Rick. "It hunts mammals, and the mammals of this period are nocturnal. It has huge eyes and well-developed olfactory lobes."

"So what it can't see, it can smell?" asked Con.

"That's about it," said Rick.

"Oh God!" Con said in a shaky voice. She imagined the nightstalker watching her as she bathed, trying to decide if she was edible.

Rick sensed her concern. "They eat rat-sized prey. That's what I found in the stomach of the one I shot. They're probably scavengers, too. Most small carnivores are. That explains why one might have stolen our meat."

Con was calmed by Rick's answer, but not completely. *Who knows what an animal will do when driven by hunger?* She reflected that, on this matter, she might be more expert than Rick. She was very aware of how powerful hunger could be.

When they reached the fire, they retrieved a second flashlight from a duffel bag. With it, the return trip was quick. They entered the plane and spread the damp contents of their bags on the floor to serve as bedding. It was still hot and close in the plane, but it was safe. Very soon, everyone fell into the dreamless sleep of the exhausted.

AN EMPTY STOMACH woke Con. It was dark, but day and night were meaningless distinctions. Mingled with the odor of mud and sweaty bodies was the smell of charred meat. Her mouth watered at the thought of it, but she would not permit herself a single bite before Rick and Joe ate, too. Instead, she groped for a water bottle and had a drink. The bottle was nearly empty. Before long, they would have to refill it at the river. Hopefully, they would need to do it only once.

Lying in the dark, Con imagined what their new home would be like. She assumed they would be able to reach the eastern seaboard in the dark. Rick had told her the Appalachian Mountains would be as tall as the Rockies. She pictured a seaside forest with towering mountains in the background. The dinosaurs would be gone, but along with fish, reptiles, and birds there would be small mammals to eat. Perhaps she could catch some to raise as livestock.

Facing the fire and its aftermath with Rick and Joe had made it possible for her to envision a life with them. Their bonds had strengthened and, with them, her hope that things would work out among them. She wasn't exactly sure what form their arrangement would take, but she was less worried about it. Con sensed that both Joe and Rick cared for her, but in different ways. She cared for them, too, enough even to deny her hunger.

RICK WOKE NEXT. Feeling for the water bottle, he touched an arm, and heard Con whisper, "Is that Rick or Joe?"

"Rick," he whispered back. "Have you been awake long?"

"It's hard to tell, I can't see a thing."

"The next few days will be the worst of it. Everything's up there—debris from the impact, soot from the fire, and rain clouds, too."

"Rain," said Con wistfully. "What a lovely idea."

"It'll pour soon as it cools a bit. A lot of water was evaporated during the impact and afterward by the heat."

"I'll take it all. I could use a shower." Con sniffed. "You could too."

Rick gasped in mock indignation. "What a personal remark!"

"More a scientific observation."

"You hungry?"

Con snorted at the question. "What do you think?"

"No point in waiting for sunrise to eat."

"Shouldn't we wait for Joe?"

"That meat will probably spoil before we can eat it all. We should eat as much of it as possible before it does."

"You don't need to ask me twice. My only problem is finding the food in the dark."

"Why don't you use a flashlight?" said Joe.

"Did we wake you?" asked Con: "I'm sorry if we did."

"That's okay," Joe replied. "The walls in these rooms are paper thin. Think about that before you try any hanky-panky."

"Rick mentioned breakfast . . ." said Con.

Joe laughed. "Back on your favorite subject. Breakfast sounds good to me." He felt around until he located a flashlight, then turned it on. The light made everyone squint. He found the meat and handed a strip to Rick and two strips to Con before taking one for himself.

"That's not fair," said Con.

"I know," said Joe. "You can have more when you finish that."

"You know what I mean," said Con.

"It seems to me," said Joe, "that 'fair' means everyone gets what they need. Would it be fair to give the same portions to an adult and a child?"

"I'm not a child," said Con.

"You're missing my point," replied Joe. "In terms of our food requirements, Rick and I are children, and you're an adult. I know I kid you about your appetite, but I'm serious now. In the lean times to come, you'll need to get more if we're all to suffer equally." He saw Con's eyes were beginning to tear up and turned off the flashlight. "We should save the batteries."

"Joe . . ."

"We need to take care of each other," said Joe. "To do that, we have to understand each other."

Con swallowed with difficulty. "Thanks, Joe."

"Don't think about it. I only hope someone would do the same for Nicole."

Rick, Con, and Joe ate in silence for a while, each absorbed in private thoughts. Rick eventually broke the quiet by asking Joe for the flashlight. "I need to step outside for a moment." Con quickly wiped her wet face before the light went on. Rick pressed the button on the wall, and the opening appeared. The air that came into the plane was slightly cooler than earlier, but now it was humid. Rick walked out of view, then returned in a minute to shine the light into the holes around the plane. One of the holes around a landing leg was filled with a rock.

"Is this the rock you were talking about, Con?"

"Yeah, I couldn't get it up."

"No wonder. It looks like most of it is still buried."

From inside the plane Rick could hear Joe moan, "Oh God, I hate digging."

"Then let's get it over with," said Con.

Joe turned on another flashlight and searched for their digging implements. He supplemented them with a table knife and a fork. "I thought we'd get high-tech," he said, showing them to Rick and Con.

When they went outside to resume digging, their flash-lights illuminated a landscape of gray ash enveloped in darkness. All the fires were gone, and no orange glow relieved the perfect blackness of the sky. For all they could see, they could have been lost in a cave. The effect of the burnt landscape was equally oppressive. Joe attacked the ground with his spoon. "I want out of here."

They dug methodically, aware of the danger of pushing their bodies in humidity that had more than made up for the drop in temperature. Con made her hole wider and wider, trying to find the edges of the rock. Rick, lying on his stomach, finally scraped the foot at the end of the landing leg. Only the front part of the leg was uncovered; the rest was still encased in dirt. Joe's hole was the largest, but he had the largest area to uncover.

Under an unchanging sky, they found it impossible to gauge how long they worked. Only the soreness in their bodies provided a vague measure. Otherwise, each moment blended with the last into timeless drudgery. Progress was slow. They worked until hunger and fatigue forced them to rest and eat. Despite their efforts, they were still far from done.

Only marginally rested, they resumed digging, and the work proceeded even more slowly than before. Con was beginning to feel it would never end when something hit her bare foot. The sensation was repeated on her leg. She shined her flashlight on her leg and saw a spot made by a drop of water, a raindrop. She assumed the spot was black because of the soot and ash that covered her. However, as more drops began to hit her, she saw the rain itself was black. The others noticed it, too.

"Is this goop rain?" said Joe.

" 'Fraid so," said Rick.

"I suppose it's black from smoke and dust," said Joe.

"With a little acid thrown in," replied Rick.

"Should we be out in it?" asked Joe.

"Well, I'm going to keep digging," said Con. "I hate this place."

The few scattered drops increased in number until there was a steady rain. The water was warm, but it was gritty and it stung the eyes. Con dug with her eyes closed, opening them only occasionally. When she did, the black rain made for an eerie sight. The rain's inky curtain swallowed the flashlight's beam. It transformed Joe and Rick into watery chimney sweeps, bathed in liquid soot. The ashy ground soon became a sticky puddle of black muck. *So this is the shower I yearned for*, thought Con.

The rain made the digging easier as it softened the baked earth. Con found that she could widen her hole more quickly. At last, the earth came up in large spoonfuls, and she wished they had thought of bringing water from the river. That would be unnecessary now, for the rain came down in torrents. Con was able to uncover the stone. It was water-smoothed and over two feet in diameter. It rested against the plane's leg, covering part of the foot. Con began to dig around the stone's edges, hoping to find a surface to grab. As she dug, it became apparent the rock was nearly spherical. Lifting it was beyond her strength and would probably require all three of them.

The water that had aided Con's digging turned against her as the stone disappeared beneath its rising surface. Further digging only brought up thin, watery, black mud. Water, mud, and ash began to fill the hole. Con looked around and saw Rick and Joe were in the same predicament. Joe's hole resembled a large puddle. He attacked it furiously, using both hands to fling water and mud. The rain filled it faster than he could scoop. When the side he was working on began to collapse into the hole, Joe flew into impotent rage. He slammed his fists into the sodden earth, splattering himself with muck. As if to mock him, the rain fell even harder.

"We've got to stop," said Con, shouting over the rain.

"We're so damn close!" Joe shouted back.

"Digging's only making it worse," said Con.

"Con's right, Joe. We're going to have to wait out the storm."

"We waited out the heat, and look where that got us," retorted Joe.

The rain came down with such fury the holes vanished under a sheet of black water. Joe's head slumped in resignation. "Okay," he said, "it's got us beat for now."

They stood in the rain and tried to rinse the ash and mud off themselves. The effort reminded Con of her bath in the muddy river. Then, they entered the plane and searched for dry clothes among the jumbled supplies before turning off the flashlights and changing in the privacy afforded by total darkness.

This was the third time circumstances had forced them to abandon digging out the airplane. They sat listlessly in the darkness as the rain pelted their shelter with increased fury. Con turned on her flashlight and shined it on the clear portion of the plane. The soot-darkened rain made it almost opaque. She turned off the light, feeling depressed and defeated.

Rick felt in the dark until he touched Con's hand. "Everything will be fine," he said.

"Stop saying that!" said Con more harshly than she intended. "I'm not Sara, so don't act like Pandit! You don't know how things will turn out! So far . . . so far . . ." She halted on the verge of crying. ". . . nothing's gone right."

Joe's calm voice came out of the darkness. "He does know how things will turn out."

"How?"

"Out there in that hell, without the benefit of shelter or understanding, are little creatures—our ancestors. He knows they made it. That means we can, too."

"Those were rats," said Con.

Rick piped in, "Rodents hadn't . . ."

"Don't get scientific on us," said Joe. "Con, the important thing is to have hope. If you give up, you're doomed. If you believe everything will be fine, it's self-fulfilling."

"I was unaware those were such magic words," replied Con with a sarcastic edge.

Joe didn't rise to the provocation. His voice remained

calm. "It's not the words that count. You count." When
Con didn't reply, Joe turned on his flashlight and began
to rummage through the disordered supplies. "Let's see
if we have anything that goes with dinosaur meat."

Joe looked through their hastily collected foodstuffs.
He reflected that if Pandit had been a worse cook, their
supplies would have been more ample. Pandit, who believed in fresh ingredients, eschewed plastic food
pouches. The only one they had contained peaches. He
put it aside along with another item and brought out a
box of crackers. "This should cheer us up," he said without irony.

The crackers, accompanied by the charred dinosaur
and the last of the bottled water, served for their meal.
Joe kept his light on so they could see as they ate, though
it lacked the festive quality of a campfire. The crackers
were limp, and the meat already smelled faintly of decay.
Despite that, Con ate heartily.

As Joe had hoped, the food lifted Con's spirits somewhat. Still, she found her surroundings dismal. The
sloped floor of the plane required them to use their
clothes and other supplies to make a level surface to sit
or lie upon. As a result, their trampled "floor" was assuming the character of a rat's nest. The last cloth garments they would ever own were damp and stained with
mud and soot. Con's companions were even more dirty
and disheveled. Judging from the way Rick and Joe
looked, Con was glad she didn't have a mirror. She resolved that if clean rain ever fell, she would take a
shower in it.

Joe turned off the flashlight when they finished eating.
No conversation followed in the dark as the rain continued to fall steadily and heavily. They were all tired, and
the oblivion of sleep seemed particularly inviting. One
by one, Rick, Joe, and Con found its refuge.

CON AWOKE IN the timeless dark. It was still raining
hard. She had no idea how long she had slept, but she
felt rested. Her spirits were improved also. *Joe's right,*

she thought, *I need to maintain a positive attitude*. She grabbed a flashlight, then tiptoed to the front of the plane. The meat was stored there. The sweet odor she had detected at the last meal was stronger now. Nevertheless, her stomach grumbled. *I won't eat until the others do, regardless of what Joe said*. Ignoring her hunger, she placed her flashlight close to the transparent fuselage and turned it on. Its beam illuminated the rain running down the plane's skin. It was clear. She turned out the light and sat down in a seat.

Joe whispered in the dark, "What's up, Con?"

"I was checking the rain. It's clean now. I thought I might take a shower in it."

"That sounds like a good idea," said Rick.

"Let Con go first," said Joe. "The showers are definitely not coed."

"I wasn't suggesting . . ." began Rick sheepishly.

"Glad to hear it," said Joe.

The darkness gave Con privacy to undress before she left the plane. She exited into the downpour. Her first impression was how strange it was to be unable to see. She remained within touching distance of the plane, for touch was her only guide in the perfect darkness. It told her that she was standing in water over her ankles and the hard-baked ground had dissolved into mud. The rain felt pleasantly cool against her skin. It fell with stimulating force. She lifted her head back and let the heavy drops massage her face. Opening her mouth, she drank. The rain had a slightly sour taste.

Con used her hands to try to scrub herself clean. *What I wouldn't give for a bar of soap and some shampoo*. When she was grabbing things for their escape from the island, it never occurred to her to take some. *I just always took them for granted*. Objecting to their perfume seemed idiotic to her now. *Perhaps I can figure out how to make some at our new home*.

Someone turned on a flashlight inside the plane and light spilled into the darkness. Con whirled quickly to see if anyone was watching her. No one was. Once she determined that, she turned her attention to the newly illuminated landscape. As far as she could see, there was water. It gave the impression she was standing in a shallow lake, except that a lake had no current. All the debris that floated upon the water was moving slowly in one direction. Con realized she was standing in the river.

The light went out, returning Con to the dark. As she tried to wash her back, she thought of Rick. His strong, rough hands would make quick work of the task. She found the idea of him touching her like that pleasantly exciting. *Joe would object*, she thought. It occurred to her that her own father would object only because Rick was the help. He'd have no qualms about someone like Peter Green doing it. Con shuddered; the mere idea was repulsive.

Con finished washing, entered the dark plane, and dressed. Joe and Rick took their turns getting clean. She thought briefly of shining her flashlight on Rick as a joke, but when she imagined Joe's reaction, she decided it was a bad idea. After Rick and Joe returned and dressed, Con turned on a flashlight. Everyone's clean faces and bodies marked an encouraging resurgence of civilization.

Con's hunger reasserted itself. "We should probably eat that meat before it spoils more," she said.

"I don't think so," said Joe gravely. He went to the rearmost part of the plane and retrieved a flat object wrapped in a fairly clean shirt. "Not on your birthday!"

Joe whisked off the shirt to reveal the half-baked cake, covered with peaches, as he and Rick sang "Happy Birthday." Con looked stunned for moment, then hugged both Joe and Rick.

"Rick told me that today's your birthday, assuming it *is* day."

Con didn't know whether she was going to laugh or cry. She felt like doing both. "I . . . I don't know what to say."

"Say," said Joe, "that it's the happiest day of your life."

25

FOR A BRIEF, SHINING TIME, CON'S WORLD WAS COM-
prised only of love and the sweet taste of peaches. As a chef,
Pandit would have been appalled by the ruinous state of his
cake. Half-baked and moldy, only the peaches had rescued
it. As a man, however, he would have been delighted by its
effect. None of his creations ever produced more happiness.

"When we get to our new home," said Con, "we'll grow
our own wheat, and I'll learn how to bake."

Rick was starting to explain how grass, and therefore
grain, had not yet evolved when Joe cut him short with a
sharp look. "I'll make you an oven," said Joe. "We'll have
cakes sweetened with honey."

"I'll bake you and Rick cakes for every birthday," said
Con.

"That's going to be a lot of cakes," replied Joe.

Encouraged by Joe, Con's happy talk of their future home
continued. Rick abandoned his scientific objectivity to join
in creating this bucolic vision. They would raise birds for
their eggs and catch fish in the ocean. There would be fruits
and vegetables. The world would be safe, purged of the fearsome dinosaurs, to be inherited by the meek.

Yet while Rick participated in Joe's kindly conspiracy, his
thoughts were drawn to the river outside. By the time he and
Joe had finished washing, the water level had risen to just
below their calves. The current had increased also. Rick sur-
reptitiously looked outside and confirmed that the river had
continued to rise. Eventually, the sound of water rushing
against the plane became something he could no longer pretend to ignore.

"We should place all our stuff on the seats in the front part of the plane," said Rick.

"Why?" asked Con.

"I want to look outside, and it might get wet when I open the door."

The grim present replaced the idyllic future as they moved their gear and clothes to safety. Rick took a flashlight and stood in front of the door. "Someone better close the door as soon as I'm outside."

Con rose and positioned herself next to the door button. Rick hit the button and jumped as soon as the opening appeared. Water poured into the gap in the fuselage and Con struck the button immediately after Rick cleared the plane. The wall became whole again, leaving a foot of dark water in the rear of the airplane.

Rick slipped when he landed and fell with a splash. He stood up quickly and signaled that he was okay. The slanted plane resembled a sinking boat, with Joe and Con peering out as its passengers. The dreamy look was gone from Con's face, replaced by concern. *So much for cheering her up*, thought Rick despondently.

He turned his attention to the most pressing matter at hand—the state of the plane. Ducking beneath the surface of the water, Rick felt for the holes they had dug. They had completely filled in with mud. He experienced the helpless frustration humanity always felt whenever nature destroyed the fruits of toil. Anger and despair seized him, and he had to fight from their grip. *I must assess our situation*, he told himself. He forced his thoughts into an objectivity that counterfeited calmness. Giving a reassuring wave to his audience in the plane, he waded out into the rainy darkness.

The airplane rested on a small rise, and Rick took care to stay on its crest as he headed uphill. Upon the crest, the water reached only to his knees. If he veered either left or right, the water quickly reached his waist. Staying on course was not easy. The muddy bottom was slippery, the way was crooked, and the current applied a steady pressure against him. The drowned uphill path was a gradual one, and Rick was forty hard-won yards from the plane before he was free of the river's grasp. He shined his light, trying to gauge the extent to which the formerly sluggish and shallow stream had grown, but the driving rain defeated his efforts. The flashlight's beam petered out without ever revealing an end to the water. *It's probably filling the valley*, he surmised. Rick tried to remember where they were in relation to the valley. He recalled flying over its broad green expanse. If his recollection was right, the river had grown mighty indeed. With the rain unabating, it would grow mightier still.

There were only two possibilities: They could wade to high ground to sit out the rain or they could attempt to fly free from the river's grip. The latter seemed like a hopeful course. The hard-baked earth had become soft mud. *Perhaps the current has even scoured away some of the dirt*, thought Rick. *We might break free. It would be worth a try.*

The prospects of escape filled Rick with anxious excitement as he returned to the plane. He hurried back as fast as he could. As he fought against the current, it felt stronger, and the water seemed higher. When he was a few yards from the plane, the opening automatically appeared and Rick cursed as he saw water pour into the fuselage. He entered the plane as fast as possible and closed the door. Standing ankle deep in water, he peered at Con and Joe perched in the front of the plane. They said no words to him. It was unnecessary—their agitated looks expressed it all.

"Joe," said Rick, "we might be able to fly free from this place."

"I don't see how," said Joe. "We're still buried."

"The river's softened the ground, maybe even washed some of it away. I think we should try to blast loose."

Joe shook his head. "This craft is built for endurance, not power and speed." He looked at the water that submerged the rear part of the cabin. "All that ballast won't help either."

"We've got to try," said Rick urgently. "The river's rising fast. If we can't fly out, we'll have to abandon the plane for high ground."

"Leave the plane?" said Con in dismay.

"Either that or drown," said Rick grimly.

"Okay," said Joe, "I'll give it a shot." He walked to the pilot's seat and dumped the gear upon it on the floor. Some of it slid down into the water. When Con started to fetch it, he said, "Leave it. It won't matter, whatever happens."

Con and Rick stuffed the clothes remaining on the other seats into duffel bags before sitting down. Joe flipped a switch, and the seats grasped their sides and shifted position to compensate for the tilt of the aircraft.

"Here goes nothing," said Joe, as he pushed a button.

The river beneath the wings boiled, and muddy water splashed against the underside of the plane. Rick felt a vibration and, for a glorious instant, he thought they were breaking free. The vibration stopped as Joe turned off the engines.

"Can't you try again?" asked Con is a disheartened voice.

"I'm sure I felt something," said Rick.

"What the hell," said Joe in a dead voice. He pushed the button and the river boiled again. He left the engines on until all hope was extinguished. They were stuck.

Joe turned off the plane, and the seats relaxed their grip. Rick rose with a sigh. "I'll make the first trip," he said. "I'll take a load of stuff and an extra flashlight to high ground and leave a flashlight there as a beacon."

"I'll go, Rick," said Joe.

"No," replied Rick, "you're the pilot."

"A pilot without a plane," said Joe.

"It'll still be here when the rain stops," said Rick.

"Of course," said Joe for Con's benefit. "This old girl's been through fire, what's a little water."

"It seems to me that I'm the one who should go," said Con.

Rick and Joe both shouted "no" simultaneously with such vehemence that she did not argue.

"Look, Con," said Rick, "I just made the trip. It'll be safest for me."

Once they resolved to leave the plane, they worked hastily to do so. Each packed their clothes in their duffel bag. Then they distributed the remaining supplies among the three duffel bags and a fourth bag to make four equal loads. Rick grabbed a bag, opened the door, and departed on the first trip. Water poured in the opening, but Con and Joe did not close it. They left it open to watch Rick's progress.

The water was up to Rick's thighs, and he moved slowly.

Gradually, his light became a misty apparition in the driving rain. It moved unsteadily as it diminished in the distance. The wandering light stopped, then separated into two—one light that stayed put and another that slowly approached Joe and Con. The anxious time until Rick returned was measured by the rise of the water level within the plane. It had reached Con's calves by the time Rick stood before the opening. Outside, the water was waist-deep.

"Toss me another bag," he said, "then sling your bags over your backs so we can hold hands. The current's getting strong."

They formed a human chain with Joe at the lead carrying the flashlight, Rick in the middle, and Con at the rear. As Con entered the river, she felt it tug at her legs, and she gripped Rick's hand tightly. The pelting rain was no longer refreshing, and her breath smoked in the chill, dank air. The slippery mud sucked at her feet.

About halfway to safety, Con called out. "Hold up a minute, my sneaker's come off in the mud." Aware of what a disaster losing a shoe would be, Con released Rick's hand to search for it. Leaning over to grope for her shoe, Con exposed her torso to the force of the current. It pushed her over. She struggled to regain her footing as the river forced her off the crest of the ridge. The river bottom was farther down each time her feet sought it. As more of her body submerged, the current had more to push. It took only a few seconds before she was completely in the river's power.

"Con!" screamed Rick, as he fought to get loose from Joe's grip.

"Use your head!" yelled Joe as he struggled to keep Rick from diving into the current. As he fought Rick, he found Con with his light. "We've got to guide her to the shore. Two people in the river will only make things worse."

Keeping the light beam on Con's terrified face, Joe rushed with Rick to the bank. Twice, Rick slipped and was saved by Joe's strong hand. Once on shore, they raced to catch up with Con.

"Con," yelled Joe, "swim toward the light, but don't fight the current. Come in at an angle."

Soon they were jogging parallel with Con, following her

slow progress to safety and shouting encouragement. They could see that the duffel bag was both help and a hindrance to her. The air trapped inside helped to keep her afloat, but the bag interfered with her movements. Foot by foot, she came closer to the shore, and Rick prepared himself to rush in and help her the moment it seemed feasible. Then, when Con was only ten yards from Joe and Rick, a tributary barred their way. They watched helplessly as the side stream pushed Con farther from shore. They kept their light on her as she dwindled into the distance, finally to be swallowed by darkness.

AS CON STRUGGLED to keep afloat and reach the shore, the light had been her star of hope. She knew Joe was directing it, but she could see only the light. It had grown brighter and brighter before it had begun to fade. Now it was gone, and hope was gone with it.

The duffel bag slowly filled with water and lost its buoyancy. Con thought of its precious contents as it turned into a deadweight—warm clothes, a flashlight, two blankets, a water bottle, a pan—so many useful things, all irreplaceable. Now the possessions that were supposed to sustain her were dragging her toward death, tempting her with the peace of oblivion.

The memory of Rick and Joe and the peaches made her choose life. Con freed herself from the bag and it sank into the depths. Still, the river sought to claim her. In total darkness, she had no sense of where to go. All she could do was try to keep her head above water. Con was a strong swimmer, and she was smart enough to conserve her energy. As long as she did not fight the current, it was relatively easy to stay afloat. The river was strong, but not particularly turbulent. She also realized that death was patient. She would eventually tire, as swimming in the chilly water sapped her energy.

Con was beginning to feel the onset of fatigue when something bumped into her. She could not tell what it was, but she instinctively grabbed hold of it. The object was very large, and it bobbed slightly under her weight.

She had difficulty maintaining a hold on its wet knobby
surface, which seemed inflated like a huge rubbery balloon. After a few puzzled moments, she realized that the
object must be the bloated corpse of a dinosaur. *I'm probably hanging on to its belly.* Con groped around for a
limb to grab hold of and soon found one. From its size,
she imagined it was a forelimb. Rigor mortis had made
it as stiff as a tree branch. She grasped it, and the corpse
shifted with her weight. Her macabre raft would not permit her to get out of the water, it rolled when she tried
to pull herself up, but it did allow her to rest. The rest
would buy her a little more time. *Maybe an hour or two*,
she thought, wondering if it was worth the effort to hold
on. Yet, she did hold on. Con and the dinosaur floated
together, beyond hope—two lost souls in the inky Styx.

26

AS THE WATER SLOWLY NUMBED HER BODY, CON WON-
dered if she were already dead. *This is surely not Heaven*,
she thought. Yet neither did it seem quite like Hell. It reminded her more of the Hades of the ancient Greeks—sun-
less, chill, and dreary, a place without any passion except
regret.

The corpse she clung to abruptly stopped, jarring her
loose. It began to deflate, venting a putrescent stench. The
odor acted as smelling salts, reviving Con's senses. She realized her feet were touching mud. As her mind cleared, Con
decided she was either stranded on a shoal midstream or
washed close to a bank. Her eyes gave her no clues as to
which. She moved to her left, and the water became deeper.
She retreated to the right, then moved farther in that direction. The water became shallower. Slowly, she felt her way,

measuring her progress by the depth of the water. When she could no longer touch the dinosaur, the river reached her waist. Its current was strong.

The prospect of safety made the threat of being swept away all the more terrifying. The river bottom was as slippery and treacherous as when she had first slipped and, this time, there was no light to guide her. Worse, she was near the end of her strength. If the river overpowered her again, she knew she would quickly drown.

For a while, Con's fear paralyzed her, and she stood trembling as the current clawed at her legs. Then, with difficulty, she composed herself and started inching her way in the dark. Sometimes, she took a wrong path, and the water became deeper. When that happened, she retreated to strike out in a new direction. In this blind, blundering manner, she found where the water was shallower until, at last, her feet sank into only muck.

Con fell to her knees, then collapsed on the mud. Rain pelted her and, as she rested, the river swelled until it washed over her legs. With effort, Con crawled a few yards up the embankment, then collapsed again. In her exhaustion, the only emotion she felt was a dull form of relief. Only gradually did some strength return to her. She sat up and removed her remaining shoe. Tying its laces together, she hung it around her neck. Con's sole resources consisted of that single shoe, a tee shirt, a pair of shorts, and a pair of panties. The pockets in the shorts were empty except for a few seashells.

Con stood up and let the driving rain wash the mud from her. Then she began to falter uphill. Her only orientations in the dark were up and down; otherwise, she had no idea where she was headed. "Up" promised escape from the river and, perhaps, relief from the muddy cascades that flowed over her feet. Using her bare feet as groping hands, she climbed with little steps. Moving felt good, despite the effort it required. It brought a bit of warmth, and it gave her a sense she was doing something.

Slowly and cautiously, Con made her way in the dark. Occasionally, she stumbled into the remains of a small scrubby tree or bush. Every time she felt the wood, it crumbled in her hands. *It's only charcoal*, she surmised. Once her foot touched a rock. She bent over and picked it up. Flat and rounded like a cobblestone, it fit well in her hand. *A tool*, she thought, *and a weapon, too*. Recalling the nightstalker, she took comfort from the stone, as would her ape ancestors. It offered a defense against claws and teeth, however meager.

Con did not step on the dinosaur—she bumped into it with her chest. For a terrified instant she thought it was still alive, but her free hand soon told her differently. The creature was stiff and lifeless. She explored the body that barred her way. It was very large. She encountered a leg and traced her hand along its length until she reached a huge foot ending in large clawed toes. Such a foot was burned into her memory. It belonged to a Tyrannosaurus. She felt her way toward the head and as she did so, her feet detected that the dinosaur's corpse blocked the flow of water down the hillside. She squatted down and discovered that there was a cavity formed between the corpse and the ground. The Tyrannosaurus had collapsed on its side with its back turned uphill. Its lower abdomen, stiffened by projecting bones that formed the front of its pelvis, made a shelter from the rain. Con dug in the rain-softened earth with her hands to enlarge the cavity. Eventually, she excavated a space in which to wedge her body. She crawled out of the rain, curled up, and fell into the merciful arms of sleep.

CON STOOD BEFORE an immense pink cake decorated with white confectionery roses. There were nine lit candles on top. The smell of burning wax blended with the aroma of vanilla and sugar. "Make a wish! Make a wish!" called voices around her. Con made her wish, the same one she had made for the last three years. She blew out the candles. "Cut the cake! Cut the cake!" called the voices. Con was very hungry, and though the cake smelled wonderful, she hesitated. As she held the knife poised over the cake, her eyes were on the door. She was waiting for it to open and make her wish come true.

Con's dream dissolved, leaving only hunger and memories of vanilla and disappointment. The memories faded as the hunger grew. She awoke. Her feet were cold. She looked at them and was surprised that she could see them. They were black with mud.

Rain still fell from an almost, but not completely, black sky. It had the eerie, unnatural look of overcast night reflecting a city's lights, except this dull sky was without color. Its feeble light was strongest overhead, suggesting that, despite a predawn level of illumination, the light of a noontime sun filtered through the thick clouds. Meager as it was, this was the first daylight she had seen since the sky had burned. She crawled out from her shelter to look around.

The rain was not as heavy as before, yet in the dim light, it obscured most of the landscape. Con could see the near shore of the river, but not the distant one. She could vaguely discern the silhouettes of hilltops nearby. She was standing close to the crest of a hill. It was a bleak and barren place. Whatever had grown there had burned, and even the ashes had washed away. The dead Tyrannosaurus was the only landmark. Con climbed to the top of the hill to get a better view. There was nothing new to see, the barrenness was complete.

Con peered into the gloom, hoping to spot a light. There was none. She reasoned that Rick and Joe must be conserving the batteries. Drawing in a deep breath, she shouted as loud as she could, "Rick! Joe! I'm here!" She listened intently for a reply. The only sound was rain. She called out again. "Can you hear me?" Silence was her answer. She screamed, hoping the shrill sound would carry farther. Silence. She screamed again, then over and over. Her cries voiced her despair, her fear, and her loneliness long after she abandoned hope for a reply. They turned into sobs that racked her as she stood alone in the empty, shadowy landscape. Only hoarseness and the cold caused her to stop crying.

Con held her head back and tried to drink the rain and ease her raw throat. I did not work; too few raindrops hit her open mouth. She was forced to drink from a puddle. She sucked in the muddy water through clenched teeth in an attempt to filter some of the dirt.

"Where should I go?" she asked herself aloud in a

hoarse voice. Speaking eased her loneliness. She knew little about surviving in the wilderness, but she did know purposeless wandering would only hamper rescue. It seemed foolhardy to leave the hilltop without a destination. Furthermore, she was poorly dressed to be out in the weather. The rain had already chilled her. She would need shelter to live. Her gaze returned to the dead dinosaur on the hillside. "Is that the best I can do?" Scanning the barren land around her, she concluded it was.

Con returned to the Tyrannosaurus. The clean air of the hilltop had cleansed her sense of smell, so, as she approached the carcass, she recognized the onset of decay. Still, she knew she had little choice but to stay. "I ignored the smell before, I guess I can do so again." With resignation, Con set about improving her shelter. First, she piled earth against the dinosaur's uphill side to seal the drafts and scooped out a little trench to divert the flow of water around it. Next, she dug in the earth to enlarge the cavity that was her den. She scoured the hillside for rocks to build a crude wall between the front of the dinosaur's abdomen and the ground. A gap in the wall served as a doorway. Just outside the doorway, she excavated a hole to collect rainwater to drink. "If only I had something to cover the doorway," she said, "it would be almost cozy."

Her exertions warmed her, but sapped her energy. The hunger pangs transformed into stomach cramps. She knew her body was running out of fuel, fuel she would need to fight the cold. Con crawled into her cramped, muddy den and removed her shirt to wring it out before putting it back on. The mud-caked garment was only slightly less wet.

Speaking to herself, she said, "God! I'm hungry!" Yet the problem was not a lack of food, but rather its nature. Her situation was ironic. "You're lying under tons of meat." Only it was raw flesh, rotting on a hillside. In comparison, the charred dinosaur meat was dainty fare. Here, nothing would obscure the fact she would be devouring a dead animal. The idea made her squeamish.

The only other option was to starve. "I'm not hungry

enough yet!" By her very declaration, she admitted she
would be. *When will "hungry enough" be?* she asked
herself. *When I'm sick? When I'm so weak I can barely
move? When I'm freezing to death?* The sensible thing
would be to eat while the meat was less spoiled and she
still had some strength. She resolved to eat some and
quickly encountered a problem. "How can I take a bite?'
Con felt the thick hide above her. She'd need a knife to
penetrate it. The idea of her gnawing through the tough,
bumpy skin was ludicrous. "I could chew for hours without making a hole." Thoughts of her puny teeth made Con
think of the Tyrannosaur's knife-like ones. An idea came
to her. "They can be my teeth, too." She emerged from
her den, rock in hand.

Even in death, the Tyrannosaur's head was fearsome.
Its nightmarish mouth seemed too large for a natural
creature. Only a wheelbarrow of flesh would fill it. Above
the mouth, a large yellow-green eye stared blindly sky-
ward. Con looked into it, but only saw her mud-stained
face peering back. She returned her attention to the
mouth and its teeth. Con felt a pointed, six-inch tooth. It
was sturdy and curved, with edges that had razor-sharp
serrations like those on a steak knife. She struck it with
her rock at the gum line. The blow sent the tooth flying
into the partly open mouth and Con had to stick her
whole arm between the jaws to retrieve it.

Tooth in hand, Con surveyed her forty-six-foot-long
meal. "I wonder what's the best part to eat?" She chose
an arm, purely for convenience. Compared to the massive
body it looked tiny, yet it was the size of a man's and
more heavily muscled. Con discovered the serrations on
the tooth sliced easily through the thick skin. Dark, sticky
blood oozed slowly from the incision. She sawed through
muscle, tendons, and cartilage until she held the severed
limb in her bloody hands. Despite the cold, she butchered
it in the rain rather than where she would rest. She separated the upper arm at the elbow and sliced through the
skin and peeled it away. "Brunch is served." Con placed
her stone, her Tyrannosaur tooth, and the lower arm next

to her shoe within her den, then crawled inside with her food.

The rain had soaked and thoroughly chilled her, but she did not want to wring out her shirt with bloody hands. Instead, she formed her body into a tight ball to try to get warm. In that position, she bit into the raw meat. It was tough and stringy. Tearing off a piece with her teeth was difficult. The flavor was not pleasant. The flesh was strongly gamy, with the odor and metallic aftertaste of stale blood. Con chewed thoroughly before swallowing. Despite her hunger, she felt like gagging. "I need to eat this. It may be a while before Rick and Joe find me." Con used the tooth to slice though the muscle, making it easier to chew. Methodically and stoically, she devoured a pound of the meat. Afterward, like a wild carnivore, she lay in a semistupor as her heavy meal digested.

Con's thoughts drifted from question to question. *How long have I been here? How far did I travel down the river? When will Rick and Joe reach me?* She had no idea. Often, her thoughts took frightening directions. *What if they think I'm dead? What if they can't reach me? What if they were here while I slept? What if they've left?* As quickly as these questions arose, she tried to banish them. The answer was terrible to contemplate, and it was always the same. *I'll die alone.* Then, only one question remained. *How soon?*

She forced her thoughts to happy outcomes. "They'll come for me. I know they will." She imagined running to hug Joe and Rick. "They'll say, 'We thought you were dead.' And I'll answer, 'Takes more than a little water to kill me!' And Joe will say something smart. And Rick will gaze into my eyes like he did on the beach." She envisioned telling them all about her narrow escape as they walked back to the plane. They'd arrive to find that the water-softened earth was easy to dig. "No . . . they'll have already dug it out. I'll step in and we'll fly away."

In an effort to realize this happy vision, Con climbed again to the rainy hilltop. The sky was darker than before, and the view was even more limited. The rain muffled her hoarse cries. She returned to her shelter more chilled and more discouraged.

Before an utterly black night enveloped the world, Con made three more fruitless and disheartening trips to the hilltop. By the last visit, her voice was barely audible. She forced herself to eat more meat before settling in for the dark hours ahead. Con stuffed mud into the cracks in the stone wall and decided her damp shirt would keep her warmer if it sealed the doorway. She set it in place by feel since it had become too dark to see. Then, curling into a tight ball, she tried to sleep. Eventually, she succeeded and dreamed of kissing Rick on a warm sunny beach as the world ended.

WATER FOUND ITS way into Con's den and woke her. It was absolutely dark outside, but her ears told her the rain was falling heavily again. She stuck her hand out into the night and found it was colder than before. She had no idea where the rain had penetrated her defenses. In the dark, there was no point in venturing into the downpour to investigate. "Best to wait for light." Until then, she was resigned to endure the puddle that was forming beneath her.

She ate some and drank a little from the puddle outside her doorway. Awake, she pondered a new dilemma—she was losing her voice. Every time she spoke to herself, it was evident. "How will I call for help?" She recalled that hikers were advised to carry whistles because their unnatural pitch attracted attention in the wild. "That's useless information." She wished she had learned how to whistle. She pursed her lips and blew, but the skill that had eluded her for eighteen years still did so. Con pondered if there was some other way she could signal Joe and Rick. She recalled a lecture about aboriginal art that discussed musical instruments. She remembered flutes made from wood . . . clay . . . reeds . . . and bone. "Bone!" The lecturer had shown a picture of a man piping a tune on his enemy's arm bone. "I could make a flute!"

Groping in the dark, Con found the Tyrannosaur's

forearm and the tooth. She worked by feel to strip away
the skin and muscle around the two bones of the arm.
Deciding that the smaller of the two bones would make
a likely flute, she set to work using the serrated tooth to
saw off the bone's ends. The hard tooth enamel cut
through the softer bone, but only slowly. Not being able
to see hampered her. She did not finish the job until dim
light returned to the sky. By then, both ends of the bone
were scored all the way around. Placing the bone on the
ground, she set the tooth edge in the scored groove and
struck it like a chisel with her stone. The tooth broke
through the bone into the marrow. Con turned the bone
and repeated the process until the end of the bone fell
off. She did the same to the other end. The result of her
labors was a seven-inch-long marrow-filled cylinder
about an inch and a half in diameter.

Con gouged some of the marrow out with her fingernail
and ate it. The fat it contained produced a pleasing sensation in her mouth. She got out as much as she could
with her finger, eating it all greedily. Then she splintered
the other bone, using two rocks from her wall. She ate
the marrow in that bone also, but what she really wanted
was the splinters. She used one to clean the remaining
marrow from the cylinder and to scrape its interior walls.
She looked through the hollow cylinder and judged its
walls were still too rough.

Con removed the lace from her shoe and threaded it
through the hollow bone. Then she pushed mud into the
bone to serve as an abrasive and, clamping the bone with
her teeth, pulled the lace back and forth with her hands.
She polished her bone flute in this manner until the lace
frayed and snapped so many times she could no longer
tie together a usable length. She washed the bone clean
in the puddle and inspected the inside. It looked smooth.

"Now I'll see if it was all worth it." Con put her lips
to the bone and blew across the open end like the man
pictured in the lecture. The sound of wind came out,
nothing more. Con tried different ways of blowing, and
sometimes the windy sound would rise in pitch. She continued to experiment until, for a fraction of a second, she

produced a tone. It took many tries before she made the tone again. "At least I know it works." She practiced until she found just the right lip shape and position to consistently produce a note. Then she worked on volume. After a while, she could blow the note loudly whenever she picked up the flute.

Con emerged from her shelter into a torrential rain. If it hadn't been cold, she would have appreciated how the rain washed the mud from her body. She took her wet tee shirt and put it on before trying to waterproof her shelter. The trench she had dug to divert the rain had clogged, and a puddle had formed against the back of the Tyrannosaur. She redug the trench, draining the puddle. Only when that task was finished, did she set about signaling with her flute.

The rain had turned the view from the hilltop into one of unbroken gray. Even the river below was invisible. Con pressed the top of the flute against her lower lip, formed her upper lip into the correct shape, and blew. She moved the flute slightly until a clear tone issued forth. *I should blow in a distinctive pattern*, she thought. She settled on three short notes followed by a pause and then one long note. She played it over and over until her frigid hands shook too violently to make a steady tone.

I've got to get out of the rain. Con sensed that getting this chilled was life-threatening. It would be hard to get even marginally warm in her meager shelter. Signaling from the hilltop would be a delicate balance between the hope of rescue and the threat of exposure. A miscalculation would be fatal. Con envisioned herself dying from cold while signaling to no one. Then she imagined Rick and Joe walking by as she hunkered beneath the carcass. Each scenario was as frightening as it was probable.

At the moment, the cold heavy rain made up her mind for her. It seemed to be doing its utmost to defeat her efforts. Con doubted if her notes carried far or that Rick or Joe would even be out in such weather. *I should eat something and try again when the rain lessens.* She stumbled downhill, cold and defeated, to get the tooth and cut some more meat. When she approached the Tyrannosaur, she noticed that some of its rib cage was exposed. *It wasn't like that before!* She was positive that part of the carcass had been untouched when she climbed the hill. *Something else is eating it, too.* She looked about warily into the gray rain. *Nothing.* Nevertheless, she was not reassured.

Con quickly cut some meat from another part of the carcass, then retreated to her shelter. She bailed out the puddle on its floor with her hands, assured herself that the rock wall was intact, and removed her shirt before entering. Inside, she carefully stretched the tee shirt across the doorway. Then, she placed her rock and the Tyrannosaur tooth where they were readily at hand. Only then, did she eat. As she curled up half-naked in the mud, a bit of warmth returned to her. The racing metabolism that kept her constantly hungry also allowed her to warm up. Within half an hour, only her bare feet felt frigid. Now, she shivered only when she thought of what might be outside.

RICK AND JOE slogged by the riverbank in the gloomy half-light of noon. Despite wearing ponchos, they were wet and miserable. The rainfall had increased all morning until it fell in a near-blinding torrent. Everything more than twenty yards ahead was obscured. Still, they continued, keeping tense eyes out for whatever the river had washed up. Both pretended they were looking for food. They were really looking for Con's body.

"I should have been the one to hold on to her," said Joe in a low, sad voice.

Rick reacted as if Joe had struck him. "I didn't let go, goddamn it!"

"I was going to protect her . . ."

"And I screwed up," said Rick. "Why don't you come out and say it."

"She's gone, isn't she?"

"She let go of my hand to grab her shoe."

"So that makes it okay," said Joe bitterly. "As long as it isn't your fault . . ."

"Is that what you think, Joe?" shouted Rick with anger and anguish. "I loved her!"

"Love?" scoffed Joe. "You only knew her a few days. You had the hots for her. That's not love."

"How the hell would you know?" answered Rick.

"I'll tell you what love is," said Joe. "It's holding your baby girl for the first time and knowing the woman you adore is her mother."

"Too bad you abandoned them to make drugs."

Joe's face tensed with rage. He turned on the gun and flicked off the safety. "I could kill you for that."

"Go ahead," said Rick. "You think I care?" He struggled to keep from sobbing. "Come on. Do it. Then I'll be with Con."

As Joe watched Rick, the anger left his face to be replaced by profound sorrow. He switched off the gun. "I'm sorry, Rick. I'm so down, I'm talking shit."

"I never met anyone like her, Joe. She was so damned brave and funny and smart and pretty. She was wonderful."

Joe sighed deeply. "She was something, all right."

"I know she went down fighting."

"No question about it," said Joe. "We'll find her and put her to rest."

They walked for a while in the gloom before Rick spoke again. "Joe, I didn't mean it about . . ."

"I know your didn't," said Joe. "What made me mad was, in a way, you were right. I was so wrapped up in my company, I forgot to take care of them." He shook his head dolefully. "Yeah, I abandoned them."

The shape of a mangled duckbilled dinosaur, washed up by the river, loomed out of the rain. A nightstalker was feeding off the carcass. Joe raised the gun and fired. The little carnivore tumbled into the river. Rick ran to fetch it before the current swept it away. When he returned, Joe looked at the dead animal with undisguised disgust.

"Filthy creature," said Joe.

"It's better than eating carrion," said Rick. He began to butcher it on the spot.

"It tastes like carrion," replied Joe. "We *are* eating carrion, only secondhand."

"I was hoping for a change, too," said Rick. He cut off the lower leg at the knee, then sliced off the meaty upper leg close to the pelvis. It looked like a huge turkey drumstick. Rick did the same to the other leg, then threw both on his shoulder as he and Joe resumed walking. The rest of the nightstalker lay in the mud to rot.

"I don't understand why there are so damned many of those things," said Joe. "They're the only living animals we've seen since the fire."

"I don't know why either," said Rick. "Maybe they lived in burrows and were protected. Maybe they're just tough."

"They're tough, all right," said Joe. "Even Pandit couldn't make one edible."

"Chewing gives us something to do at night."

"At least Pandit cooked it," said Joe.

"We will, too," said Rick. "When the rain stops."

"I'm not holding my breath."

The rain fell unabated as Rick and Joe continued their melancholy search. They walked another a mile before encountering a swollen stream that barred their way. For the third time since they abandoned the plane, they had to make a lengthy detour into the foothills to find a place to cross. By the time they approached the river again, it was getting dark.

"Better find some high ground," said Rick.

"Yeah," said Joe tiredly.

They climbed to the crest of a small hill overlooking the river and dug a circular drainage trench. Rick placed his poncho over the muddy ground inside the circle; then, Joe stepped on it as Rick slipped under Joe's poncho. Rick and Joe sat down and used the shared poncho as a tent. Taking out his knife, Rick peeled away part of the hide on the nightstalker's drumstick. He cut a piece of the muscle and handed it to Joe.

"Thanks," said Joe as he made a wry face and began to chew. After he swallowed, Joe pulled out a water bot-

tle. "Care for some Chateau de Floodwater? I recommend
it with nightstalker."

"What vintage?"

"I believe it's 65 million B.C."

Rick sniffed. "A disappointing year."

"You can say that again."

Eating together under the poncho, Rick and Joe shared
body heat. The warmth they obtained was the closest
thing to comfort they had the entire day. As Rick ate his
foul dinner, he felt a deep bond to the man so close to
him. Despite their differences, theirs was the special
comradeship that soldiers had experienced since the beginning of time. It was a kind of love, though Rick would
not have used that word. *Now, it's only the two of us
against the whole world*. Their adversary, Rick had little
doubt, would win eventually. *But not before we bury
Con*, Rick resolved. *After that, I don't care what happens*.

27

AFTER DARKNESS FELL, THE PATTER OF THE RAIN LESS-
ened. Huddled in her den, Con could hear soft, squishy footsteps and occasional hisses from beyond her thin cloth doorway. There seemed to be more than one animal outside. *How
can they know what they're doing?* she wondered. Somehow,
they did. Her hearing, made acute by fear, picked up the
sounds of teeth scraping bone and of sniffing. *Perhaps one
is sniffing outside my doorway, tired of rotting meat*. The
image terrified her, and she clutched her rock and the tooth
harder. *How can I fight something I can't see?* The answer
was she couldn't.

Sometime during the long stretch of night, Con's exhaustion substituted the terror of dreams for the terror of what roamed outside. She awoke, tired and stiff, to dim light, rain, and fear. She had not dared to drink from the puddle all night, and she was very thirsty. *I can't hide here forever*, she told herself. Cautiously, she pulled the shirt aside and peered out. The nocturnal visitors were gone. Emboldened, she drank deeply from the puddle, despite the water's unpleasant taste. When her thirst was quenched, she withdrew into her den to eat. The raw flesh that lay on the muddy floor smelled. Con questioned the wisdom of eating it, but decided she had little choice. She swallowed only a few bites before she vomited.

Con crawled from her den and let the rain wash the foulness from her body. It was a gentle rain, though raw. Con was thoroughly chilled before she felt clean enough to put on her shirt. She drank again from a puddle, attempting to cleanse the taste in her mouth with dirty water.

The Tyrannosaur's night visitors had accelerated its ruination. Most of its ribs were exposed, and much its viscera lay half-eaten on the ground. The odor of putrescence filled the dank air. One look, and Con knew the carcass could no longer serve as food or shelter. *I won't last long in this rain*, she thought drearily. As she stared at her former refuge, Con realized the creature's hide had held back the assault of decay. Because that defense had been so thoroughly breached, rot had set in rapidly.

Con saw that the waterproof skin might be a resource for her survival. She surveyed the hide for a large area that was still unmarred; then, using the tooth, she began to flay it. The thick hide did not peel away easily. Con found she had to carefully run the tooth between the skin and the body to get it loose. It was hard work that left her covered with blood and rancid grease. Her most trying moment came when she slipped and her leg entered the Tyrannosaur's abdomen up to the knee. The smell that issued forth was almost overpowering.

After much hard work, Con was able to drag a heavy patch of hide from the carcass. Its irregular shape was approximately five feet square. She carried it to the crest of the hill, then stretched it out with the raw side to the ground. With that accomplished, she walked down the hill to the river. She bathed the smell of the carcass from her body and thoroughly washed her clothes. The process chilled her even more, but she dared not smell like the carrion eaters' food. When she thought all the taint was gone, she returned to her den for the tooth, her stone, and the flute.

The nightstalker appeared as she was retrieving her things. It stepped quietly from behind the Tyrannosaur, then froze when it saw Con. *I'm supposed to be invisible*, she thought. Clearly, she was not. The carnivore stared at her intently with its large yellow-brown eyes. Although it was slimly built and stood less than four feet high, its sharp teeth and wicked claws made it fearsome. The animal appeared to be in its element, with feathers as unruffled by the rain as a duck's. The tragedies that had unfolded upon the world appeared not to have harmed it in the slightest. Rather, they seemed to have provided the nightstalker with abundant opportunities. Con sensed it was trying to determine if she were one of them.

Tucking her flute and the tooth into a pocket, Con surveyed her shelter wall for a likely rock. She slowly bent over and picked one up. As she did so, she saw the nightstalker's two slashing toe claws rise. Con threw the rock with the quick fluid motion she had acquired pitching varsity baseball. The projectile grazed the dinosaur's chest. It gave a cry and retreated ten yards before turning to stare again at Con. She picked up another rock and threw it. This time was a near miss. The nightstalker did not retreat, but it did not advance either. Con sensed a delicate truce. With a wary eye on the nightstalker, she quickly removed her shirt to use for carrying stones. She spread it on the ground and piled all the rocks that were suitable for throwing upon it. When she was done, she gathered up her bundle and retreated slowly, never taking her eye from the creature that stared back. As Con retreated, the nightstalker advanced until it reached the Tyrannosaur. It stopped there and began to feed.

Con circled around to the hilltop. She rolled up the hide, slung it over her shoulder, then picked up her bundle of stones with her spare hand. Spying another hill about a mile down the river, she headed for it. Between the hills was a small stream that was not too swollen to cross. She unrolled the hide and began to scrape it with the tooth and scour it with mud. Every once in a while, she rinsed it off in the running water and sniffed it. She repeated the process several times before she was satisfied its scent was unlikely to attract nightstalkers. She bathed one last time before heading to the next hill.

By the time Con climbed to the hilltop, she was thoroughly cold and exhausted. Cutting, cleaning, and carrying the heavy hide and the repeated bathing had cost her dearly in terms of warmth and energy. Her stomach cramps had returned, and there was nothing to sate them. "Perhaps it was all for nothing," she said tiredly. She emptied her shirt of rocks and put it on. Then she dug a small circular trench to drain off the rain and a basin to catch it. She arranged her possessions within the circle—the pile of rocks, the cobblestone, the tooth, and the flute—then sat down among them and wrapped herself in the hide. She suddenly thought of the shoe she had left behind. "I won't need it." She lifted the flute to her lips and blew three short notes, paused and blew one long one. This would be her song. She intended to stay upon the hill and play it until dark. If she survived the night, she would play it the next day. Con knew she was capable of nothing more. Those four notes would be her last cries for help and, perhaps, her dirge.

RICK AND JOE began to walk the riverbank as soon as there was light to see. Although it was springtime in the northern hemisphere, the darkened "days" were short because the sun's light could penetrate the atmosphere only when it was high in the sky. They walked in a nether world where everything was a dimly seen shadow. Each rock, each corpse by the river revealed its true nature only when they approached closely. This dreary world did not lend itself to conversation, and they seldom spoke.

They spied a pale shape in the water and waded out to investigate. It was a small Hypsilophodontid. Its hide had been abraded, leaving only bloodless flesh. When they returned to the shore, Joe said, "Oh God, that was horrible. For a moment I thought . . ."

"Me too," said Rick, not wanting to hear the end of Joe's sentence.

"How far do you think we should search?"

"I haven't a clue," said Rick. "I've no experience in such matters. It's hard to tell how far we've gone."

"Hell," said Joe, "I've even lost track of the days, if you can call . . ."

"Shhhh!" said Rick urgently. "I hear something."

Joe listened. "I hear it, too. Just barely. Is it a bird?"

"I don't think so," said Rick. "It's too regular, and there's only one note."

"Three short . . . one long . . . three short . . . one long . . . three . . . Con's signaling us!" cried Joe. "It's got be her!"

"CON!" yelled Rick at the top of his lungs.

He and Joe listened for a response, but the faint signal continued unchanged.

"Doesn't she hear us?" asked Rick. He shouted again and, this time, Joe joined in. They called Con's name until their throats were raw. Each time they paused, the distant tones showed no reaction.

"It's no use," said Joe. "The wind and the rain are muffling us. We've got to get closer."

"Yeah, but where's that?"

They both listened intently to the faint sound. It seemed to come from no place in particular and it was a while before they could even agree that it was originating downstream. Once they made that determination, they headed in that direction. They ran along the slippery, rain-drenched riverbank, pausing only to catch their breath, to listen for the signal and call out in hoarse voices. Each time, their cries had no effect—the signal continued unaltered. They proceeded in this manner, with growing frustration, until a side stream barred their way.

The torrent of brown water was impossible to cross. "Another goddamned detour!" said Joe in frustration.

They began moving upstream, looking for a place to ford. They were too tired to run anymore, but they scrambled along the muddy slopes as fast as they could. As they went, the signal grew fainter and fainter. After a while, they could not hear it at all. The only sounds were rushing water and the steady fall of cold rain.

THE TYRANNOSAUR HIDE kept most of the rain off of Con, but it did not provide any warmth. Con drew her body into as compact a shape as possible and still blew upon her flute. Sitting tightly cross-legged, she hunched over and held her arms close to her chest. One hand grasped the hide around her while the other held the flute. The hide formed a crude hood, but rain still soaked into her hair.

Con could not get warm. The longer she sat playing the flute, the colder she got. Her hands and feet became so frigid they hurt. She had to stop signaling for a period when she shivered so violently she could not make a note. After the shivering stopped, she felt exhausted. Every muscle was stiff, and her hands and feet were numb. Con found it increasingly difficult to concentrate on making the simple pattern of notes. Her mind clouded over, and lethargy set in. The dark world became darker still, and she slumped over. The flute fell from her icy hand.

JOE AND RICK returned to the river as the light in the sky began to wane. The sound that had beckoned them was gone. Its absence pushed Rick to the verge of panic. That Con was alive at all was a miracle, but miracles have their limits. He knew that exposure to cold rain could quickly lead to hypothermia.

Joe sensed his agitation. "Maybe she has shelter and has gone in for the night."

"Are you willing to bet her life on that?" said Rick.

"No," replied Joe. "When it gets dark, we'll use the flashlights. Screw saving the batteries."

"Let's think about this," said Rick. "She's probably on this stretch of river, but where?"

"We hole up on high ground at night," said Joe. "I bet she does, too."

"I agree," said Rick. "Maybe she's found a cave, but the hilltops should be the first place we look."

They headed for the first hill overlooking the river. When they climbed it, they found nothing. The light was dwindling rapidly, and they hurried to the next hill as fast as their exhausted bodies permitted. The reward was another desolate view. The next hill was but a distant black shape against a nearly black sky. They were about to descend when Joe spotted three nightstalkers feeding on the slopes below. He turned on the gun and said without enthusiasm, "Dinner."

Two of the nightstalkers quickly looked up as the gun cracked and the third nightstalker fell. After a brief pause, they resumed eating. "Uncaring bastards," said Joe. He marched down the hill to retrieve his kill. The nightstalkers were feeding on a Tyrannosaur's carcass, and the smell of their meal did not make Joe look forward to his. The two remaining animals stood their ground as Joe approached. Their yellow-brown eyes stared at him in an unnerving way. "Shoo," he said. They stayed put. "Not afraid of me? You should be." Joe adjusted the gun's power level and fired. The two carnivores exploded into a bloody mist, leaving only their lower legs to topple in the mud. Joe turned off the gun. It was a waste of power, but a satisfying one. He was bending over to pick up his and Rick's dinner when he spotted Con's shoe.

"Rick, come down here quick!"

By the time Rick arrived, Joe had his flashlight out and was peering into the remnants of Con's den. "She must have stayed here," he said. "See, here's her shoe."

"God, it stinks!" said Rick. "She stayed under this?"

"Looks like it. See where it's dug out? There's a drainage trench in back."

Disregarding the stench of the rotting Tyrannosaur, Rick leaned into the den and pulled out two bone fragments. "Look at these, Joe. They've been sawn."

Joe shook his head in amazement. "How the hell did she do that?"

"Beats me," said Rick. "I'd bet these have something to do with the sound we heard. Probably a bone whistle or something."

"She's one hell of a girl."

"But she abandoned her shelter," said Rick, the concern clear in his voice.

"It's easy to tell why."

"She may not have found another," said Rick. "We've got to find her tonight!" He took out his flashlight and began to scan the rain-washed slopes for footprints. He found numerous prints made by bare feet that seemed fresh, but they went in several different directions. He studied them carefully, knowing that his conclusions could be life-and-death ones. "She went down to the river, but she came back," he said, talking mostly to himself. "She went to the hilltop several times, but there's one set of prints going around the hill. Let's follow those." Rick and Joe traced Con's journey around the hillside, but stopped when they encountered a set of prints leading down toward the next hill. They followed the trail until it disappeared halfway down the slope, washed away by runoff.

By the time they located where Con had scraped and washed the hide, it was absolutely black. The flashlights' beams were beginning to fail and Joe turned his off to save its battery. Rick's feeble yellow light illuminated the raindrops more brightly than the ground. "I don't see any trail!" Rick said in frustration.

"Then let's head for the high ground," Joe said.

They headed up the next hill, using the slope of the ground as much as the flashlight to guide them. When they reached its crest, Rick scanned about, "Nothing," he said, spitting out the word like a curse. "Nothing but that rock."

Joe turned on his light. It was brighter than Rick's. "Since when does a rock have a foot?"

CON WAS WANDERING in a cold, dark place when she heard the sound of waves washing upon a beach. Their sound was as regular as a heartbeat. She dropped to her hands and knees and began to crawl toward the sound. The cold mud she was crawling through turned to warm sand. She looked around, and the darkness was gone. She could see snowcapped mountains towering over a bright green forest. Near the forest's edge was a wooden cabin, and Joe and Rick stepped out of it. Con waved to them, but she did not want to rise from the sand—it was too pleasantly warm to leave. Instead, she lay down and waited for them to come to her. Instantly, Rick was lying beside her. He was crying and whispering at the same time. Over and over he repeated the same word.

Con opened her eyes, but there was nothing to see. The warm sand became skin pressed against her bare back, her bare legs, and her bare chest. Arms wrapped around her and legs pressed against hers. Fabric was piled over her. Her head rested on something soft, and a stubbly cheek touched hers. Someone was breathing in her ear and softly whispering her name.

"Rick? Joe?"

Con heard Rick's quiet voice next to her ear. "We're here. We found you."

"What . . . what are you doing?"

"Sharing body heat," he said. "You're suffering from hypothermia."

"I feel warmer now. I thought it was a dream."

"It's no dream, thank God," said Joe.

"So I'm not dead?"

"No . . . no you're not," said Rick.

Rick's voice sounded far away. Con felt warm wetness on her cheeks. She wondered, *Whose tears are those?* She was too groggy to decide. The sound of waves returned, and soon they lulled her to sleep.

28

WHEN CON AWOKE IN THE MEAGER LIGHT OF DAY, SHE was confused. She was wearing clothes, and they were dry. There were socks on her feet, a sweatshirt warmed her torso, and long pants covered her legs. She lay beneath blankets and was covered by a poncho. She could also feel someone nestled against her back. She looked at the arm around her waist.

"Rick?"

"Yes."

"I'm clothed. I thought I was . . ."

"That was only to warm you up," said Rick quickly and awkwardly.

"Where did you get dry clothes? Where's Joe? How's the plane? Is there anything to eat?"

Rick laughed. "You sure wake up fast!"

"Will you answer my questions!"

"All right. The clothes were dried the hard way—body heat under a poncho. Joe's out hunting. We've got some leftovers from last night."

"And the plane! Tell me about the plane!"

Rick hesitated before saying, "Gone without a trace."

The news hit Con like a blow. "Are you sure?"

"We're sure."

"Oh," said Con softly, and she began to cry.

Rick held her until she stifled her sobs. "When I was alone," said Con, "thinking about our cabin kept me going. I wanted to be there so much."

"Don't give up hope. We'll get through this yet."

"How?" asked Con. The doubt in her voice was plain.

"You want to eat something? We can discuss my plan when Joe returns."

A hint of a smile crept onto her face. "You know me too well," she said. "Want to shut me up? Put food in my mouth."

"I wasn't trying to do that."

"Why not? It works."

Con turned to look at Rick's face in the dim light that filtered through the poncho. It was dirty, unshaven, and haggard, but his loving expression made it beautiful to her. She was reminded of the gaze he had on the beach, when he believed they were doomed. Although his look brought her joy, it also gave birth to a disturbing thought—*Maybe he still thinks we're doomed.*

EVER SINCE CON had been found, Rick had turned his thoughts to their dire situation. Until her rescue, his plans for the future had not extended beyond putting her to rest. If that sad duty was not to be merely postponed, he knew he must come up with a strategy for survival. He had spent much of the night weighing unpromising alternatives, before choosing one he had previously rejected. It was a desperate plan, if it could be called a plan at all. It was more of a gamble, and a long shot at that.

I'm truly the guide now, Rick thought. *Joe and Con will expect me to show the way.* He realized that, despite their precarious circumstances, he must exude confidence. That knowledge burdened him, for as a scientist he dealt in probabilities, not certainties. The course he would propose was a calculated risk at best. Yet, as the guide, he would have to keep his doubts to himself. He was aware that a positive attitude enhanced the chances for survival. In facing the times ahead, a sense of hope would be crucial. Rick resolved to instill one in Con and Joe as he struggled to foster one in himself.

As Con ate leftover nightstalker, Rick mentally rehearsed what he would say. His thoughts were interrupted by the sound of footsteps from outside the poncho, followed by a thud. A cheerful voice called out. "Joe's Bed and Breakfast. I hope my guests are decent."

Con threw off the poncho. "Joe!" she said joyfully.

Joe was standing, wrapped in the Tyrannosaur hide, with a dead nightstalker at his feet. "You get under that poncho, young lady. You weren't easy to warm up."

Con complied, and Joe crawled beneath the poncho to join her and Rick. She immediately threw her arms around him and hugged him tightly. "You're all damp!" she said.

"That dinosaur skin is a better fashion statement than it is a raincoat," said Joe with a grin. He looked at the bone Con had been gnawing. "You're not going to spoil your breakfast, are you? I've prepared something special."

"What?"

"Nightstalker à la Joe. It's served very rare."

"You shouldn't."

"I know," said Joe, "but since the bastard ate you out of house and home, it seemed only fitting."

Con laughed, and her laughter brought happiness to Joe's face. "Rick's going to tell me all about your plans," she said.

"Plans?" said Joe, giving Rick a puzzled look. "Plans are good. Let's hear them, Rick."

"First, we need to set up a temporary camp. Someplace out of the rain."

"That sound's fine," said Joe. "But why temporary?"

"I see it as a base to hunt and build up our food supplies and our strength. As long as there's carrion, there'll be nightstalkers for food."

"Oh goody," said Joe.

"Don't complain," said Con. "You should try what I had."

"I've seen that carcass," said Joe. "I can't believe you ate that thing."

"Remember, I was sleeping under it," replied Con. "I got used to the smell."

"We could do a lot worse than eat nightstalker," said Rick.

"You still haven't answered my question," said Joe. "Why a temporary camp?"

"Soon as the weather clears, we'll head out," said Rick.

"To where?" asked Con.

"We'll follow the river to the sea," said Rick. "To the sea and back to Montana Isle."

"You call that a plan?" said Joe. "What's the point of going there?"

"I think there's a chance people will return to the observatory now that the impact's over."

"You're kidding yourself," said Joe. "No one's coming back there."

"You don't know that for sure," retorted Rick. "This time-altering thing is only a theory. It's just as likely they vacated the observatory for safety reasons."

"You agreed it was pointless to return," said Joe.

"That was when we still had the plane."

"So now, when we have to slog through cold rain, it's suddenly a good idea?"

"With the dust layer blocking the sun," said Rick, "the water cycle will shut down. Things will dry up and stay dry until sunlight returns."

"I'm for staying here," said Joe. "We can settle down and a make a place for ourselves."

"Look, Joe," said Rick, "let's not argue about this in front of Con."

"Don't go off," said Con. "I'm part of this, too. You can't decide without me."

"She's right," said Joe. "It's her life you're risking, too."

"Okay," said Rick with a sigh. "I was hoping it wouldn't come to this." He sighed again. "We have to go because the ecosystem has collapsed. We're subsisting on scavengers that are living off carrion. It's an inadequate diet to begin with, especially in cold weather. It'll be snowing next and . . ."

"Snowing?" said Con.

"Yeah," said Rick. "And soon, even the nightstalkers will run out. If it were just you and me, Joe, I wouldn't care. But Con, I can't . . . I can't watch you starve. If we

stay here . . ." Rick stopped speaking, unable to utter the
words that weighed so heavily on his mind. *So much for
exuding confidence*, he thought.

Rick, Joe, and Con were but inches apart beneath the
poncho. Con peered into Joe's dark eyes, saw his hesitation and sadness, and realized that the decision was hers
alone. She was quiet for a while before she spoke. "I want
to try to go to back to the island."

"All right," said Joe. "We'll spend this 'summer' by
the shore." His lips formed a smile, but the sadness never
left his eyes.

JOE, RICK, AND Con breakfasted on raw nightstalker.
When she wasn't chewing the tough meat, Con recounted
her adventures while Rick and Joe listened in amazement.
Rick was relieved that the talk centered on Con and that
he was not pressed for the particulars of his plan. For the
moment, it was enough that it had been accepted. There
would be plenty of time for details later.

After breakfast, Rick and Joe went through their duffel
bags to provide Con a wardrobe. Rick was closer to
Con's size, but Joe insisted in contributing equally. The
result was ill fitting and almost comical, but warm. Re-
placing Con's missing shoe was the biggest problem. The
best they could do was one of Rick's sandals, worn with
three pairs of socks. Joe made Con take his poncho. "I'll
use the hide, it's bound to soften up in time."

"We could soften the skin by chewing it," said Rick.
"That's what Eskimos did."

"Well, aren't you a font of wisdom," said Joe.

"We could all help chew," said Con.

"I don't trust you, Con," said Joe with a grin. "You
might swallow."

Rick plucked the nightstalker and stuffed its down into
the pouch on his poncho before he finished butchering it.
Once that task was done, they headed out to find a shelter.
The dim light made it difficult to survey the countryside.
Most of what they saw was silhouetted or wrapped in
shadow. Nevertheless, they stayed close to the river. That

was where carrion was found and, with it, their food—
the nightstalkers that fed upon it. They followed the river
for miles, and though they encountered a few corpses,
they saw no scavengers. Then, after they turned a bend,
Con said excitedly, "There's something wading in the
river." She pointed to a small bipedal dinosaur struggling
to reach the shore.

"That's not a nightstalker," said Joe.

"I'd say it's a hypsilophodontid," said Rick.

"Good eating," said Joe, turning on his gun.

"Wait till it gets to shore," said Rick. "We don't want
to lose it to the river."

Whether it was injured or suffering from the cold, the
dinosaur moved sluggishly and unsteadily to the bank.
When it reached shallow water, three nightstalkers suddenly appeared. Whether they had been hiding by the
bank or had crept up without anyone seeing them was
impossible to tell. Although the carnivores were two feet
shorter than the plant eater in the river and considerably
lighter in build, they approached it boldly. Two circled
around their prey to cut off its escape into deeper water,
while the third barred its way to shore. The hypsilophodontid froze as the nightstalkers slowly advanced. Their
attack was sudden and frantic. Using their enlarged toe
claws, they slashed at their victim, which seemed inca-
pable of defending itself. The wounds they inflicted initially appeared minor, unlike the deep gashes of the
Dromaeosauruses. Instead, the nightstalkers bloodied
their prey in a rain of lesser blows until it was disem-
boweled and collapsed into the water.

Joe turned to Rick. "You said they ate only little
things."

"Obviously, I was wrong," Rick replied.

Con said nothing, but she shook as she relived the
memory of her last night under the Tyrannosaur.

Joe methodically shot the three nightstalkers. "That's
our food, you little bastards."

Rick and Joe waded out into the river to butcher the
hypsilophodontid while Con stood guard with the gun.
Rick and Joe decided to cache most of the meat in the

river by wedging it under stones. Finding enough stones took time, as did finding a suitable site for the cache.

"I hope this is worth all the effort," said Rick.

"I'm so sick of nightstalker," said Joe, "it'd be worth it if it took all day!"

Con had borrowed Rick's knife to slice some leg muscle into strips while Joe and Rick piled the last rocks on the cache. "Come and get your hypsilo-whatever," she called. "It's rude to make a lady wait for lunch."

"Start without us," Joe called back. "We're almost done." Then he said to Rick in a low voice, "I agreed on your crazy journey because of Con, but won't you reconsider? I don't want her to suffer needlessly."

"Joe, she's *souped*," Rick whispered back. "She's already thinner. She looks like she hasn't eaten for a week."

Joe glanced at Con and shook his head. "She does."

"Joe, I'm not fooling myself. I know our chances aren't good, but I can't think of anything better."

"I just want to take care of her. There are worse deaths than starving."

"Dying without hope is one of them," replied Rick.

Joe looked at Con sadly. "Yeah, I guess you're right."

The subject of Rick and Joe's conversation was voraciously devouring her second strip of raw meat when they came to eat.

"Better than nightstalker?" asked Joe.

Con, her mouth full, nodded vigorously.

After their meal, they headed out again. As they walked, Rick pondered the behavior of the nightstalkers. He did not think the attack in the river was characteristic. They didn't seem evolved to hunt large prey. *Under normal circumstances, I suspect they don't*, he thought. *They appear to be adapting their behavior to the new environment.* As a scientist, he found that hypothesis interesting, worthy of further study. As a guide, he found it disturbing. They would have to be more wary in the future.

Several miles farther down the river, they spied a pale line in the hills close to the riverbank. As they approached the hills, they could see that line was a stretch of low limestone cliffs. The cliffs were about a hundred yards from the swollen river, and they were cut by a series of gullies and small canyons. A stream flowed from one of the latter, and they followed it into the cliff.

Within the narrow canyon, they found both trees and shelter. The small trees formed a tangled grove of conifers and small hardwoods that crowded the stream and extended to the canyon walls. They all appeared dead, but they were unburnt. Rick discovered shelter farther into the canyon. It consisted of a five-foot ledge. It was halfway up the cliff wall and protected by an overhang. With some difficulty, Rick was able to scale the twelve-foot wall leading to it. Standing on the ledge, Rick surveyed his surroundings. Before the impact, he would have considered the canyon a dismal place. Its walls screened out much of the feeble light from the dark sky. The dank vegetation that choked its floor was as brown and lifeless as the trees. Yet compared with the burnt and barren valley, the canyon was a place of bounty. The stream that flowed through it ran clear, and there was ample wood. He called down to the others watching below. "This is perfect! It's dry and protected enough for a fire."

"A fire?" said Joe. "How will you manage that?"

"Your guide has a trick up his sleeve."

"The real trick," said Joe, "will be climbing up to that ledge in the dark."

"We'll enlarge the holds," said Rick. "The limestone's pretty soft."

"Before you do that," said Joe, "let's go back for that meat."

"Yeah," said Con. "We'll feast tonight in our new home."

For the first time since they had abandoned the plane, they did not have to carry all their possessions. These were tossed up to Rick, who stowed them safe and dry on the ledge. Taking only the gun, they made a quick journey to the meat cache. Although they were burdened with as much meat as they could carry, they hurried back quickly. All were eager to return and set up camp.

The first order of business was to store the meat out of
the reach of nightstalkers. They considered hanging it
from a tree, but ended up sinking it in a deep pool in the
stream and covering it with rocks. That would serve until
they could construct a more convenient cache. Rick
found a pointed rock and began enlarging the handholds
and footholds leading to the ledge. As Rick worked at
his task, Joe and Con gathered firewood. By the time it
grew dark, Joe and Con were able to climb to the ledge
easily. They deposited a pile of wood there and also a
layer of conifer boughs to serve as bedding. A few feet
from the bedding and close to the back wall of the ledge,
they had placed a semicircle of stones to serve as a fireplace. The woodpile lay close by. On either side of the
fireplace, piles of stones held two forked branches upright. These were to support the cooking spit.

Joe and Con watched with expectant excitement as
Rick knelt before the fireplace. He pulled out his knife,
then unsnapped a pouch on its sheath. From it he removed a light gray, rectangular stone. "It's an Arkansas
stone," he explained, "for whetting the blade. But there's
something else you can do with it." Rick struck the stone
sharply with the back of the blade and a spark flew. Then,
he bent over the fireplace, stone and knife in hand. A
small mound of nightstalker down rested against a pile
of dry shavings from a tree limb. Above those were
twigs, then branches. Rick repeatedly struck the stone
with his knife blade until a spark flew into the down. He
blew gently. The down smoked and glowed red; then, a
tiny yellow flame appeared. The flame spread to the shavings and, from there, to the twigs and branches.

Con felt a primal joy at the sight of the flames. They
seemed to promise everything good—warmth, light,
safety, and food. She hugged Joe, then grabbed Rick and
kissed him.

Joe grinned. "You sure have a way with the ladies,
Rick."

Con held on to Rick's arm. "He does. Of course, the
true way to a girl's heart is through her stomach."

Joe laughed. "Better feed her, Rick." He handed Rick the meat spit to position over the fire.

As dinner cooked, the warmth and light of the fire reflected off the light-colored walls of the ledge and made it bright and cozy. The meat roasted slowly. Its aroma filled the air, and Con's mouth watered in anticipation. The stream water in the bottles was crystal clear. Some boiled in a pot to make meat broth. Joe leaned against the wall and gazed into the fire with a contented look. Everything about the evening filled Con with a sense of well-being. Cuddling up to Rick with a happy sigh, Con forgot the dark and wet world just a few feet away.

29

CON AWOKE SANDWICHED BETWEEN JOE AND RICK. ALthough two blankets and a poncho covered them, a damp draft told her that it had grown colder. The blankets were thin ones, made for mild spring nights, and it was the two men who kept her warm. She doubted either Rick or Joe was as comfortable as she, despite the fact Joe had dubbed her "Miss Central Heat." There was some truth in the nickname, for when she was well fed, she found it easy to stay warm. Staying well fed was quite another matter. Hunger had become her constant companion.

In the stillness broken only by the quiet sounds of rain and Rick and Joe's breathing, Con felt at peace. The terrible night in the river and the almost unbearable loneliness that followed it were behind her. She might be dirty, ragged, and homeless in a ruined world, yet, for the moment, she was content. She was alive and warm, and soon she would eat. Best of all, enveloped by Rick and Joe, she felt safe. Con did not reflect on how little it took to make her happy. Instead, she was thankful for receiving so much.

Con's thoughts turned to the leftover meat, and she began to stroke Rick's face to wake him. He made a pleasant, sleepy sound in his throat. Con's touch became more tender as she explored the contours of his face with her fingers. Rick placed his hand gently on the back of hers, then turned his head to lightly kiss her inner wrist. Con forgot her hunger as a yearning of a different sort took hold. Rick turned, and their faces were but inches apart. His fingers mirrored hers as they softly brushed her cheeks . . . her lips . . . her throat. Con moved closer so their lips lightly touched. There was an exquisite delicacy in the way their mouths met in a subtle caress. Then, in a rush of passion, they pressed their lips together and kissed. Con moved so Rick could embrace her more completely.

"Anybody hungry?" asked Joe loudly. Without waiting for an answer, he said, "I know you are, Con. Rick, I bet you're peckish, too. Long day ahead of us, a very long day."

Rick sat up so abruptly that he pulled the poncho off them. Joe acted as if nothing had happened at all. He sat up and calmly put on the hide parka. "I'm going to gather some more wood. Rick, could you work your trick with the fire? Con, some hot broth would be nice."

As soon as Joe left, Con giggled at Rick's discomforted look. She quickly kissed him, and said, "I see we have a chaperon."

"He said he was going to be your papa," said Rick. "Now I know what he meant."

"Joe's sweet," said Con, "but Daddy never cared what I did."

Rick soon had the fire going. Con cut up the scraps from last night's dinner, which were as cold as if they had been refrigerated, and put them in the pot to boil. Joe returned with an armload of wood. "Rick," he said, "could you give me a hand? I've got more piled up in the grove."

"Sure."

Once they were away from the ledge, Joe turned to Rick. "I know you love Con, just don't love her to death."

"What?"

"Don't do anything that will compromise her health.

Sometimes, when things look bleak, men and women behave recklessly. For her sake, promise me you won't. Do you know what I mean, or do I have to spell it out?"

Rick blushed. "I get it."

Joe looked at him with sympathy and understanding. "If you truly love her, you'll wait."

"I'll wait."

LIFE IN THE canyon quickly fell into a routine of preparing for the trip to the sea. Joe, with his antipathy for nightstalkers, spent most of each day hunting them, while Rick and Con dedicated their time to preserving his catches. The damp air made smoking the meat the only means to accomplish that. They cut all the meat they didn't need for their immediate use into thin strips and hung them from a rack above a fire. Keeping the fire going proved to be the most time-consuming task for Rick and Con. Once all the fallen wood was gathered, branches had to be broken or hacked from the trees. It was grueling work in the frigid rain. The gun would have made the work easy, but they dared not use it. Its solar recharger was ineffective in the dim light, and the gun's depleting charge was too vital to be wasted on jobs that could be accomplished by brute force.

Besides these daily chores, each took on other tasks. Con scraped the Tyrannosaur skin and stretched it out near the fire to dry. Afterward, she and Rick chewed the stiff hide until it was soft and flexible; then Con tailored it using sinew and a bone awl. Rick cut down three stout hardwood saplings and fashioned them into spears, hardening their whittled points in the fire. He constructed a sturdy stone meat cache on the back of the ledge for their growing store of dried meat. Joe built a low stone wall around the sleeping area to serve as a windbreak.

Initially, Con felt almost like a newlywed setting up house. That romantic notion quickly passed, worn down by the grind of survival under hard conditions. At night, there was no privacy at all. The daytime, when she and Rick were alone together, was filled with toil in harsh

weather. Fatigue, hunger, and cold marked her days. She
was often irritable and withdrawn. While Rick remained
affectionate, Con questioned her desirability. Bathing
was a frigid ordeal she avoided. She was dirty and
smelled of wood smoke and clothes that were never
changed. She had sores and rashes. Her hands were raw
and calloused. All the twenty-first-century ideals of
beauty and hygiene—white teeth, smooth legs, clear skin,
glossy hair—were unattainable. Feeling worn and un-
lovely quenched her ardor. Romance became a distant
dream, like a full belly and warm feet.

Con's domestic feelings found other outlets. In anticipation of their journey, she began to fashion jackets by
stuffing a layer of nightstalker down between two shirts
and sewing them together. She obtained thread by pains-
takingly unraveling a scrap of cloth. She carved an eye-
less needle from bone and patiently pushed the thread
through the cloth for each stitch. The resulting garments
were warm, but greasy feeling, and the shafts of the
feathers made them prickly. Nevertheless, they quickly
became indispensable clothing as the weather changed.

It was changing for the worse. The rain diminished and
became a frigid drizzle. It's dank chill penetrated their
clothes. Only fire kept it at bay, yet wood was too difficult to cut to maintain more than a meager blaze. Con
rationed the wood and built a decent fire only when Joe
returned, chilled and wet, from the day's hunt. It was the
one time of the day when she was truly warm. The cold
made Con reflect that her life had become even harder
than her legendary ancestor's. *At least she had her log
cabin*, she thought.

The food situation changed also. Every day, Joe would
go out to hunt for nightstalkers. At first, he would return
after only a few hours with two or sometimes three. Then,
it began to take him longer and longer to make a single
kill.

"I had to walk miles downriver for this one," he said
to Rick after a daylong hunt.

"Just as I feared," said Rick. "Game's getting scarce."

"It's more than that," said Joe. "They're still around.

Sometimes I even see them, but I can't get within range of the targeting scope. I don't get it—I used to walk right up to them."

"These animals seem capable of adapting their behavior."

"I thought dinosaurs were stupid," said Joe.

"They're as smart as birds," said Rick, "and some birds are pretty smart. Crows understand about guns."

"So I'm walking farther and farther to plug the ignorant ones who haven't figured it out."

"That sounds like the case."

"Well that's great!" said Joe. "Those sneaky bastards are still around, and we can't even eat them."

"Did someone say 'eat'?" asked Con, as she brought some wood up to the ledge.

Joe smiled. "I was saying the nightstalkers are getting scarce."

"Scarce?" said Con incredulously. "I had to scare off three from the canyon this morning."

"What!" said Rick.

"Yeah, right after Joe left," said Con. "I was cutting firewood, and they walked right in, bold as anything. Threw rocks at them, and they ran off. Hit one."

"I don't like the sound of that," said Rick. "Not at all."

THE NEXT DAY, sleet fell. The three of them hunkered on the ledge, leaving it only to get wood for the fire. Joe did not hunt, and they dipped into the store of smoked meat for the first time. The fire was a meager one, and they retreated to the sleeping area while it was still light. There, they huddled together for warmth and tried to sleep and forget the cold.

They awoke to find snow on the ground. There was only an inch, but they knew it would not melt. The pall of ash over the sky stopped the sun's warmth. Every snowfall would remain to form an ever-deepening blanket.

"Now that it's stopped raining," said Rick, "we should think about heading to the island."

"Yeah," said Joe without enthusiasm. "I'd feel better if we had more rations to take with us."

"So would I," said Rick. "We can put off leaving a day or two."

As soon as he finished eating, Joe left to hunt. He did not return until it was almost pitch-black. He was empty-handed and discouraged. Con built up the fire while Rick got some dried meat to make broth.

"I found tracks," said Joe after he warmed up a bit, "but I didn't see a damned one."

"Couldn't you follow their trail?" asked Con.

"I tried that without luck. They avoid me now." Joe shook his head. "I never thought I'd want to see a nightstalker."

"They seem to be particularly adaptable animals," said Rick. "I can't think of a paleontologist that would have predicted it."

"Rick, why don't you go out tomorrow?" said Joe. "You're the guide, I'm only an engineer. Maybe you'll have better luck."

Rick agreed to Joe's suggestion and went hunting early the next day. New snow had fallen, and he was surprised to find his first evidence of nightstalkers right below the ledge. The tracks of three animals were plain in the snow. They were obviously fresh, for a light snow was still falling. *They probably smell our smoked meat*, he surmised. Rick followed the trail for several miles without getting a glimpse of the animals that had made it.

Rick abandoned his pursuit and headed for the river. The flood was over, and the river was returning to its original size. To reach it, Rick had to travel over the muddy ruin of the valley. It was not yet cold enough for the mud to freeze, and he sank up to his ankles in cold muck while walking to the shrunken river's bank. He was looking for carrion, nightstalker food. All that he found had been picked clean. The snow hid the tracks of the scavengers, but he assumed they were nightstalkers. Rick followed the river for miles, but the only living thing he saw was a single bird, pecking at some bones on a mud bar in the middle of the river. The desolate landscape looked caught in the midst of winter, not late spring. The brown water provided the only color; everything else was black, gray, or white.

When the light began to wane, Rick headed back toward camp. He avoided the muddy floodplain, to make better time and investigate new territory. He was still over a mile from camp when he spied blood on the snow. He hurried to the site and found the remains of nightstalkers. It was impossible to tell how many, because they had been so thoroughly torn apart. Blood, feathers, and scattered bits of gnawed bone were all that was left. Tracks made it clear they had been slaughtered by their own kind. Rick knew that cannibalism among adult predators was high-risk behavior, an indicator of desperate times. *They're definitely running out of food,* he thought. The memory of the tracks by the ledge became more ominous.

There was no sun to set, so only the darkening of an already dark sky marked the onset of night. Rick began to jog toward the canyon, knowing once night fell, it was impossible to see anything. He thought of the warm fire and of Con waiting for him. The little shelter, meager as it was, had acquired some of the feelings of home. He looked forward to returning to it.

Con scampered down from the ledge as soon as Rick entered the canyon. Joe began to build up the fire. A brief look of disappointment came to her face when she saw he was empty-handed, but she quickly covered it up. "Joe and I spent the whole day getting wood," she said. "We can have a nice big fire tonight."

Rick smiled and gave her a kiss. "That sounds wonderful."

"Any luck?" called Joe.

"Nope," said Rick.

"So it's not just me," said Joe.

"These are cagey animals," said Rick. "Did you see the tracks beneath the ledge?"

"Yeah," said Joe. "I don't like it."

"Neither do I," said Rick.

"What can we do?" asked Con.

"They adapt, we adapt," said Rick. "Joe, could you dig out the flashlights and see if they have any juice?"

Joe disappeared into the sleeping area. Two pale beams shone briefly. "There's some life in them yet."

"Good," said Rick. "Tonight we'll stay home and hunt."

Rick warmed himself by the fire as he explained his plan. "Joe and I will stay up with the flashlights and the gun to wait for our visitors."

"How's that going to work?" asked Joe. "They only come around when it's pitch-black."

"We'll rig the pot like a bell and attach a piece of dried meat to it. If we hear the bell ring, we'll turn on the flashlight and zap whatever we see."

Joe grinned and rubbed his hands together. "Sounds like fun!"

Two sticks were crossed and lashed over the opening of the pot, and pebbles were tied to threads suspended from them. When the pot was moved, the pebbles clinked against its interior. They tied a piece of meat beneath the pot and hung it from a tree. Once the alarm was set up, Joe and Rick returned to the ledge to wait.

Con found it was too cold to sleep alone, so all three of them stayed up and silently ensured no one dozed off. The night wore on without a sound, not even wind. Many hours passed before they heard a soft clinking sound. Three short rows of tiny colored lights glowed as Rick turned on the gun and placed his eye to the targeting scope. Joe switched on the flashlight and a nightstalker was caught in its pale beam. Rick pulled the targeting trigger, then the firing trigger, as the gun tracked the fleeing animal. A single crack downed the beast.

Con screamed as a pair of large yellow-brown eyes rose and peered over the ledge. Sharp claws grasped the stone just inches from where she sat. Joe swung the flashlight at the feathered head, striking its toothy snout. The light went out. Rick fired blindly into the darkness while Con groped for the second flashlight. When she turned it on, its beam revealed a single nightstalker lying dead in the snow and two sets of tracks heading from the canyon into the night.

THE NIGHTSTALKER RAN with her child from the place of strange smells. She ran with surety, for her eyes could distinguish the black trees from the slightly less black ground. She saw the dawn behind the clouds and used it to her advantage. It was easier to hunt when the prey was blind.

As she ran, she did not grieve for the child left behind. Grief was something she could not understand. Pain, she understood—hunger, too. Hunger governed her life and directed her thoughts. When the pain left, she would remember the place of strange smells. One of those smells was food. Maybe more than one.

30

NO ONE CONSIDERED SLEEPING, DESPITE HAVING BEEN UP all night. Rick lit a fire on the ledge so they could have warmth and light as they waited for the sky to brighten. While Joe stood guard with the gun, Rick climbed down to retrieve the pot and to pluck and butcher the nightstalker. By the time that task was done, light had returned to the sky.

Joe took some pieces of the nightstalker and dropped them into the pot in which water boiled. "It's only proper to serve our visitor," he said cheerfully.

"That raid was a sign we need to head out," said Rick.

Joe's cheerfulness left him. "I wish we got all those sneaking bastards," he said. "I don't fancy camping out with them. Maybe they were after us last night."

"They were after our store of meat, not us," said Rick.

"Besides, predators are territorial. We'll leave them behind when we go. The nightstalkers we encounter on our journey will be naive about guns and humans."

"That's good to hear," said Joe, not sounding convinced.

"Are we leaving today?" asked Con.

"There are still some last-minute preparations to make," said Rick. "We'll go when we're ready. We're not being chased out."

"No," said Con in a distant voice, remembering the yellow-brown eyes. "Of course, we aren't."

"Joe," said Rick, "do you know what a travois is?"

"Isn't that what the Indians used to drag their stuff?"

"Yeah, two long, trailing poles with a platform in between. Do you think you could make some for us?"

"Sounds easy enough."

"Great," said Rick. "Con, could you turn the two ponchos into a tent?"

"I'd have to cut them up," she said. "Won't we need them later?"

"We'll need a tent more in the snow," said Rick. "It won't rain again until it gets warm. By then, we'll be gone."

"I'll start unraveling some thread," she said.

"Good," said Rick. "I'm going to smoke what's left of the nightstalker."

Despite their exhaustion, they worked most of the day preparing for the journey to the sea, napping only briefly. As darkness came upon them, it was clear they were spending their last night on the ledge. They made the evening fire extravagantly warm, for they intended to burn all the wood they couldn't take with them on the travoises. The comfort and festiveness of the blaze made the prospect of leaving the ledge even more melancholy. As crude as it was, it had become home. The fact that it no longer felt safe did not diminish their sense of loss. At times, Rick thought Con was on the verge of crying, and she clung to him after dinner, almost like a child seeking reassurance. He was aware that he could not fathom the nightmare she had endured alone in the cold, dark world. Yet tomorrow, he would lead her back into it.

There was enough wood to have a small blaze throughout

the night. They had agreed to keep guard during the dark hours, in case the nightstalkers returned. Rick theorized that the nightstalkers' sensitive eyes could see in the early night and early morning, when humans were still blind. Those were the most dangerous times, and he volunteered for those watches.

RICK STARED AT the semicircle of snowy ground that was dimly illuminated by the fire. The only movement was the lightly falling snow. Occasionally, he heard Con moan in the throes of a nightmare. Otherwise, it was silent. He imagined their upcoming journey and pondered their chances of being rescued. They seemed very small. *Joe doesn't believe there are any*, he thought. *Yet, what other choices are there?* Rick could think of none. He had an additional worry. It was in the form of a nagging question. *Is Joe hiding something? Does he know more about the island than he's letting on?* He had come to trust Joe, and it bothered him that he would even have such questions. Nevertheless, they would not go away.

Although Rick had assured Joe and Con that the nightstalkers had only been after the meat supply, they worried him also. He knew mammals were their natural prey. *We're safe because there were no mammals like humans in the Cretaceous*, he told himself. *They won't think of us as prey.* Yet, as a scientist, he knew such reasoning was unsound. *How can I know what those animals think?* It was a question, like so many others, for which he had no answer.

LIGHT RETURNED AS Rick finished the last watch. The light snow that had fallen throughout the night continued to fall. The loaded travoises below the ledge were covered with an inch of flakes. Rick built up the fire and placed a pot of water upon it. When it boiled, he threw in the last of the fresh meat. It was frozen and took a while to cook. When breakfast was ready, he woke Con and Joe.

They ate silently until Joe spoke. "Con," he said, "I've been watching you. You're not eating enough."

"I'm not hungry," said Con.

"Don't give me that," retorted Joe. "I know you better than that. Rick, talk some sense to this girl."

"You won't be helping us by not eating," said Rick. "We all need to be at our peak for this journey."

"I'm eating," replied Con. "I eat as much you and Joe combined."

"And you're losing weight," said Rick. "I can see it in your face. No short rations on this trip. Promise me. You'll need food to keep warm."

"I promise," said Con.

"Good," said Joe. He went to the bag of smoked meat and pulled out two pieces. "I'll believe you when you eat these."

Con nibbled at the meat at first, but soon she abandoned the pretense that she wasn't hungry and wolfed the rest down.

When Con finished eating, she, Joe, and Rick made their last-minute preparations for the journey. Con slipped on a sock she had made from a scrap of poncho over the socks on her sandaled foot. They placed their extra clothing in a single duffel bag. The load was small because they were wearing most of their clothes already. They packed the meat spit and its holder along with the pot. Rick secured the meat supply to a travois, then covered it with conifer bough bedding. The rest of the supplies had been previously loaded. They wrapped rag scarves around their heads, and Con handed out mittens she had made from socks stuffed with feathers. Joe slung the gun over his back. Everyone grabbed a spear. It was time to leave. As they left the canyon, each made their good-bye in their own way. Con made hers with quiet tears.

The dim light and the falling snow made it hard to see very far, not that there was much to look at. The fire and the flood that followed it had scoured the land of all but a few blackened stumps. Even those were disappearing beneath snow. The view had the bleak sterility of the arctic. The brown river marking the way to the sea was the most prominent landmark in this austere, trackless country. Following it was not difficult. The snow was not yet deep, and it aided them in dragging the travoises over the hardening ground.

They walked for several hours before stopping to eat and rest. Afterward, they continued their journey. They left the valley behind them as they crossed an open plain. There, fire had also cleared the land. The few trees they encountered had been reduced to blackened trunks, standing like lonely monoliths in an abandoned graveyard. Several hours passed before they saw another brown line in the distance to their left.

"Damn," said Rick, "a tributary! We're trapped in the fork."

"Looks like a detour," said Joe.

"Maybe not," said Rick. "Let's take a look."

Within fifteen minutes, they were standing by the other river. It was only sixty feet across and flowed sluggishly. Rick paced along its bank, studying the river carefully. "It doesn't look too deep," he said finally.

"It looks deep enough," replied Joe.

"Only one way to find out," said Rick. "Con, could you look the other way?" He removed his shoes and placed them on a travois.

"Why? What are you doing?" asked Con.

"I'm going to find out if the river's fordable, and I can't risk getting my clothes wet."

"Con," said Joe, "don't look at this crazy man. Rick, have you gone nuts?"

"It might take us two days to get back to this spot if we make a detour," said Rick. "I'd rather walk twenty yards through the water."

Rick grabbed a spear and waded into the water naked. When he was midstream, the water reached halfway up his chest. It got shallower as he approached the far bank. When it was clear that there were no deep sections near the bank, he turned around and headed toward Con and Joe. Rick was shivering violently by the time he reached the shore. He quickly dried himself with a shirt he had set aside for the purpose then, just as quickly, dressed.

"We can do this," Rick said.

"Do what?" said Joe. "Get buck-ass and wade in the river? I don't think so."

"Listen to my plan first," said Rick. "We can rig two travoises like a stretcher so you and I can carry everything high and dry in one load. We'll build a fire on the far shore before Con crosses."

"She's supposed to cross naked, too?" said Joe. "No way!"

"If the nightstalkers are tracking us, the river will stop them," said Rick.

"Seems like your theories on nightstalkers are very flexible," said Joe. "Yesterday, you said we were leaving them behind."

"I'll cross," said Con. "If you promise not to look."

"Con . . ." said Joe.

"Rick's right. We'll save a lot of time, and I'll feel safer on the other side."

"You're not going to do this," said Joe firmly.

"You're not my father," replied Con.

"Not that you listened to him, either," said Joe. "Okay, I know when I'm beat. Let's get this over with. Only this time, Con, no peeking at Rick." He laughed at Rick's reaction.

Joe and Rick unloaded two of the travoises and combined them to make a litter. Then they piled all the supplies upon the litter to form a single load. It was heavy, but manageable. They undressed, placed their clothes on the litter, and made a hurried crossing. Joe swore the entire time until the fire was lit. When the fire was blazing, Rick called out, "Con, we're ready for you to come over."

"Then turn around," she called back. "I'll yell if I need help."

When Rick and Joe's backs were turned, Con quickly undressed and stuffed her clothes into a duffel bag. She was already cold when she entered the water, holding the bag over her head and dragging the empty remaining travois. The freezing river felt like knives. When it reached her breasts, Con thought that she would be paralyzed by the cold, but terror forced her stiffening legs to keep moving. By the time she reached the shore, she was shivering so violently she had difficulty drying herself and dressing. Without the fire, she was sure she would not have been able to dress unassisted. It was more than modesty that prevented her from asking for help. Con did not want Rick or Joe to see how prominent her ribs had become.

AS THE PAIN in the nightstalker's snout faded, the demands of hunger grew stronger. Still, she waited until darkness to visit the canyon and the place of strange smells. Even before she reached the ledge, she sensed a change. The big things with the terrible black stick were gone. She could neither hear them nor see them, and their strange scent was old. Drawn by the odor of food, she approached the ledge while her offspring prowled the snowy grove behind her.

There was the aroma of blood on the ground. It did not make any difference to her that it was her child's blood. The important thing, the only thing that mattered, was there were no scraps left to eat. She tested the air and detected another scent of food. It was the same smell as the meat left after the brightness and hotness had passed. She had grown familiar with that scent. The black flesh was good to eat, although it tasted strange. Everything was strange now. Things looked different, smelled different, the very air was different. Despite that, she had always been able to sate her hunger . . . until now. Food had grown scarce, then disappeared altogether. If she did not find some soon, she would be driven to eat her remaining child. That would be her last resort, for the child aided in hunts and would fight if attacked.

The black flesh smell came from the ledge. The nightstalker climbed up to investigate. The smell was strong, but it was also old—one lightness old. She leapt off the ledge. Her child hissed when she landed and prepared to defend itself, but its mother did not attack. Instead, she sniffed the cold whiteness. The black flesh smell was there too, mingled with the odor of the big things. The cold whiteness made the scents faint, but not too faint for her to follow. They led out of the canyon and guided nightstalkers in the dark. When the scent led beyond the nightstalkers' territory, they did not halt. The world was different. Only the strongest of the old instincts still governed—the need to eat.

31

CON, JOE, AND RICK HUDDLED CLOSE TO THE DYING FIRE on the riverbank, trying to extract the last of its warmth. They rose from the muddy circle of melted snow only when the fire's final embers died out. "We can probably make a few more miles before it gets dark," said Rick. Without discussion, Joe and Con loaded up their travoises and headed out.

As they marched, Rick tried to determine if crossing the river had been a wise choice. He was beginning to see their situation in terms of the harsh arithmetic of biology and physics. As mammals, they had to maintain a body core temperature of 98.6°F. A six-degree drop in that temperature meant death. As it got colder, more energy was required to maintain body heat. Ultimately, everything boiled down to a matter of calories, calories from fuel and calories from food. Fire warmed them externally and food warmed them internally. When the wood ran out, only food would warm them. If the food ran out, their bodies would consume themselves in an effort to stay warm. The insulating fat would go first, worsening the problem of keeping warm and hastening the decline toward death. Every decision Rick made was a calculation based on that knowledge. The river crossing had cost them energy he hoped to recoup by shortening their journey.

As they tramped by the river, Rick looked at Con's pale, thin face and wondered if his calculation was correct.

Light faded from the sky, forcing them to halt before total darkness fell. "We're going to need a place to store our food," said Rick. "Someplace safe from animals."

"We haven't seen a living thing all day," said Joe.

"We can't risk losing our food to raiders," replied Rick. "We'd best play it safe."

"Why don't we keep it in the tent?" asked Con.

"And have visitors?" replied Rick.

Con grew wide-eyed at the thought of a nightstalker in the tent.

"I'm with Rick on this," said Joe. "Better safe than sorry."

"The ground's too frozen to dig, and there are no trees to hang our food from," said Rick, "so a stone cache seems our only choice."

"We'd better build one quick," said Joe. "It's getting hard to see."

While Con set up the tent, Rick and Joe searched the river's shore for stones to construct a food cache. They discovered a rocky stretch of riverbank not too far from camp that was covered with stones of various sizes. They carried the largest ones they could lift to higher ground and fitted them tightly together to form a circle. Working together, they carried two flat rocks to serve as a cover. Rick returned to the campsite and extracted the night's rations from the food bag before bringing it to the cache. He placed it within the circle of stones, then he and Joe lifted the two flat rocks to cover it. As an extra measure, they piled more stones on top and pushed snow around the cache.

"That looks safe enough," said Joe. "How much did you leave out for our dinner?"

Rick sighed. "Probably not as much as we need. It's so damned hard to figure out how to do this. If I could be sure how long we'd be walking, that would help."

"My guess is we're seventy-five to a hundred miles from the sea," said Joe.

"I figured a hundred," said Rick. "If we make twenty miles a day, we'll get there in four more days."

"Do you think we covered twenty miles today?" asked Joe.

"It's hard to say," admitted Rick. "I decided to be pessimistic and divide our rations for six more days of travel."

"You think like an engineer," said Joe. "It's good to have a safety factor."

"It'll make for skimpy meals, unless we find some game."

"Let's split everything four ways," said Joe. "Con gets half and you and I get a quarter each."

"That sounds like a good plan," said Rick. "I hope Con goes along with it."

"We'll make her," said Joe.

"She can be real hard headed."

"She'll eat," said Joe. "She has to."

Joe and Rick returned to find the tent set up. Con had brushed the snow from its interior and spread the conifer boughs for bedding. She was in the process of packing snow around the outside edges of the tent as they arrived.

Rick made one of his calculations and decided to make a fire. That way, they could have warm broth with dinner, and there would be a lighter load to carry the next day. He rationed out the wood, which was almost as precious as the food, to start a blaze. He cleared the snow from a patch of ground close to the tent and set nightstalker down next to some tinder. By the time he had a fire going, it was pitch-dark. While the small fire was cheerful, it also emphasized the totality of the blackness surrounding them. The flames quickly died down to embers, and they barely had enough time to cook their broth. As Rick expected, Con protested the division of the rations, but, in the end, he and Joe prevailed. They finished their meal in near-total darkness, with the dull red embers providing more of an impression of light than its actuality. Afterward, they huddled together in the tent and went to sleep.

CON AWOKE TO cold and hunger. Both had become constants in her life, waxing and waning in intensity, but never leaving entirely. Usually, the hunger manifested itself as a dull ache and the cold as a wearing discomfort. She had learned to ignore both, and they did not wake her. The sound did. A soft, distant scratching noise disturbed the black quiet of the world. Con instantly thought of the meat cache.

"Rick! Joe!" she cried. "Something's stealing our food."

Instantly, the feeble yellow light of a flashlight broke the darkness inside the tent. It was enough light for Joe to find the gun. He switched it on, and he and Rick burst from the tent. Cold air flowed in as Con stared into the dark. The flashlight's pale beam stabbed into the night, but petered out before reaching the stone cache. Con could not tell if the scratching had stopped or was drowned out by Rick and Joe's noise. She watched the yellow light advance into the darkness until it illuminated a pile of snow-covered stones. When the light stopped moving, Con heard Joe curse and confirm her fears. "God damn thieving bastards!"

Guided by the light, Con walked over to the food cache. The circle of stones and the heavy stone lid were intact. They had been too heavy for the nightstalkers to move. Instead, they had tunneled beneath them in two places. The tracks in the snow told the story of the raid.

"There were two of them," said Rick after a moment's study. "They're traveling together."

"Our friends from back at the ledge?" asked Joe.

"Maybe," said Rick. "Who can tell?"

"I bet it was them," said Joe. "They were smart enough to stay out of sight all day, then go straight to the meat."

Rick said nothing, but began to pull away the stones that lay atop the cache's lid. "Let's see how much they got."

The batteries in the flashlight were almost dead, making it maddeningly difficult to determine the extent of the damage. Like anxious misers, they counted their remaining food. The skills the nightstalkers used to invade mammal's burrows had served them well in this case also. The tunnels were small, but obviously sufficient. Half the food was gone.

Con had a sick feeling in her stomach. She felt assaulted in a fundamental way. She needed that food to live, and these creatures had taken it. Rage and despair fought within her.

"We'll get them!" said Joe with murderous intensity. "Tonight, we'll wait for them like we did before. They'll repay us for what they stole. They'll pay with their own damned flesh!"

They left the plundered cache and returned with the food sack to the tent. They did not need the flashlight to guide them, for a hint of light had returned to the sky, and they could discern the tent against the snow.

"They're able to see in dimmer light than we can," said Rick, "and they've taken advantage of it, but I suspect they're as blind as we are in the middle of these black nights."

"So far," said Joe, "most of your theories about night-stalkers have not panned out."

"You're right," said Rick, "but we should be extra careful right after dusk and just before dawn."

"I'm going to be careful every damn minute until those two are dead!" said Joe.

Rick built a tiny fire to boil some dried meat in an attempt to extend it by making broth. By the time the pot boiled, the fire had reduced to embers. Rick, Joe, and Con huddled around them, passing the pot to drink. Afterward, they shared the gray, soggy meat. It was a meager breakfast and a melancholy one.

Rick was starting to pack up when he heard Con say "Oh, great!" and saw her head for the bag of clothes. She began to rummage through it with a frustrated and upset look on her face.

"What's wrong, Con?" he asked.

Con did not answer. Instead she muttered to herself. "Of all times, why now?" She pulled a faded tee shirt from the bag. It had a dinosaur skull printed on it, along with the words "Hell Creek Dig—2056." She turned to Rick, and asked, "Can I have this?"

Rick looked at his favorite shirt, one that evoked memories of a special summer with Tom. Nevertheless, he said, "Sure."

"You won't get it back," said Con.

"That's okay."

Con read the puzzled look on Rick's face. She reddened a bit, and said, "It's that time of the month. Can I borrow your knife? I'll need to cut this up."

Rick handed Con his knife, and she retreated to the tent. She emerged after fifteen minutes, looking grumpy and uncomfortable.

"Will you be all right today?" he asked.

Con sighed. "I'll be fine, but this is going to be a real pain. I'll have to stop every once in a while, and I'll have to wash these damned things out each night. God knows how I'll dry them."

Con looked so miserable, Rick gave her a kiss, and said, "I'm sorry."

"Just be glad you're not a woman."

They finished breaking camp and followed the river through the cold, desolate landscape. Rick assumed they were traveling over an upland plain like the one where they had found the ceratopsid herds. Only a trace of carbonized vegetation hinted he was correct. He had seen the aftermath of a wildfire once, but it was nothing compared to this. He imagined a hurricane of fire passing over the plain, incinerating everything to ash. The land it left behind appeared devoid of life, sterilized by flame and scoured by flood. If there were any creatures about, they were hidden.

Joe, for one, was absolutely sure there were at least two creatures about. He stared into the gloom, hoping to spot the two nightstalkers. The gun was slung in front of him, ready at an instant's notice. Yet Joe was almost certain his adversaries would not reveal themselves. They would wait until dark.

The three slowly trudged mile after mile. Twice, they had to ford streams. Both were shallow, merely requiring that they remove their shoes and roll up their pants. Despite that, the brief crossings were torture. The streams' edges were lined with ice, and the near-freezing water left their feet stinging long after they had crossed. Later, they encountered a thirty-foot meteor crater, filled with floodwater. A scum of slushy ice covered the water's surface. They halted there for lunch.

Rick handed out extra rations, for in his careful arithmetic of calories, he had decided to gamble on catching the two nightstalkers. He looked at the extra food they ate at the meal as an investment that could be recouped, even multiplied, through a successful hunt. Success would require they be alert and rested. They would stop early today, build a fire, and eat well. He made these decisions without consulting Joe or Con. The burden of leadership had become his alone. When he rationed out extra meat, they accepted it without questioning. Likewise, they accepted his other decisions—even those that risked their lives.

Rick had not grown comfortable with risk, as much as he had grown numb to its danger. Everything they did was potentially life-threatening. In the twenty-first century, none of them would have drunk from a river. Here, they often had no choice, even though a waterborne illness could easily be fatal. So could a simple scratch. Luck, as much as good judgment, had kept them alive so far. Although Rick tried to weigh each move, in the end, each move was a bet where lives were wagered. Tonight he was betting that they could kill the nightstalkers.

Long before it grew dark, Rick began looking for a campsite that would favor them in the night's hunt. When they encountered a broad, level area, he decided to stop. "We should camp away from the riverbank," he said, "so they'll have to approach us in the open. We'll make a tripod from the travois poles and hang the food bag below it. After dinner, we'll set the pot there and rig it as an alarm."

"I can hardly wait," said Joe, grinning in anticipation. "I want the last watch."

"Con," said Rick, "you take the middle shift. You and Joe should sack out early. I'm going to start dinner now." Rick went to the food bag and took out a generous ration of food. *Tomorrow*, he thought, *this should be heavy with frozen meat.*

Joe and Rick began to erect the tripod while Con set

up the tent. After the tent was up, Con retreated inside for a few minutes. When she emerged, she carried a small bundle to the river. It was a while before she returned. When she did, besides carrying her wet bundle, she dragged a large branch. "I brought you guys a present," she said.

"Driftwood!" said Rick as happily as if she had brought them a cake. "Is there more?"

"This was all I saw."

Rick brushed dried mud from the branch. Four inches in diameter and dry, it promised warmth when they needed it most. Working together, Rick, Joe, and Con were able to break it into three pieces. As Rick began to build the fire, Con used some firewood to construct a makeshift drying rack close to it. "I'll need to dry my rags," she said, with a mixture of annoyance and embarrassment.

The fire was the biggest they had made since the last night on the ledge. The meal they cooked upon it seemed ample to their shrunken stomachs. The hunger that gnawed at Con's insides, diminished to mere discomfort.

"I hope it's warmer by the sea," said Joe. "Being cold all the time is tiring."

"It sure is," said Con. "I'll sleep well tonight." Her mood had improved with the food and once she was able to remove her dried rags from sight.

"You should go to bed soon," said Rick. "I'll set up the alarm."

"I will when the fire dies down," said Con. "I haven't been this warm in two days."

After the fire, the tent felt frigid to Con, and huddling with one person was not as warm as sleeping with two. Nevertheless, she and Joe quickly fell asleep. Rick sat at the entrance of the tent with the gun and the flashlight in his lap. Only his head protruded into the cold night. He clutched the two sides of the tent flap beneath his chin, like a buttonless overcoat. The flap provided no warmth, but it did keep out the drafts. As Rick sat, the cold entered and stiffened him. There was nothing to see. He probed the darkness with his ears, listening for the crunch of taloned feet in the snow and the soft clink of stones against the pot. Like Joe, Rick assumed the nightstalkers would come just before dawn. That assumption did not ease his vigilance. Fear kept him alert. He was not afraid of the animals as adversaries, but he feared the consequences of another successful raid. By stealing food, the nightstalkers would kill them as surely as if they tore out their throats.

There was no way to measure the passage of time. Uncounted hours of blindness passed, and still Rick did not wake Con. He wanted her to rest as long as possible. Sleep was one of the few gifts he could give her. The thought of her sleeping, oblivious to worry and suffering, filled him with tender satisfaction. Only when fatigue began to overwhelm him did Rick reluctantly shake Con and whisper, "Your watch."

Con grunted and sat up. She could see nothing and groped about until she touched Rick. They did everything by feel. Rick guided her to the tent flap, then handed her the flashlight and the gun. Before Rick settled next to Joe, he whispered, "Don't keep too long a watch; Joe really wants his chance."

"I'll be sure to wake him in time."

Con felt Joe's warmth leave her back as Rick's breathing became slow and regular. Her grogginess left her. Outside were things that threatened her and those she loved. She feared them in a more primal and instinctive way than Rick. They were not mere thieves to her. She had sensed their lurking presence too long to think of them in impersonal terms. She felt that nightstalkers had watched her from the beginning and had drawn ever closer. Tonight, Con prepared for a confrontation that had been building for weeks. Her fingers felt the gun until they rested on the safety. She was ready for them.

Like Rick, Con had no way to tell how long she stood watch. The approach of dawn was not heralded by the coming of light, but rather by the quiet sound of feet in the snow. A rush of adrenaline brought her cold-numbed body to a state of tense readiness. Con turned on the gun and switched off the safety. Her right finger gripped the firing trigger. With her left hand, she aimed the flashlight toward where she thought the tripod stood, ready to turn it on when she heard the pot clink.

The footsteps stopped and, for a moment, Con thought that she might have imagined them. Then she heard them again. They proceeded more slowly, as if the animals were suddenly aware of her presence. Con waited for the clink of the pot. It seemed forever before she heard it. She pressed the flashlight's switch.

Nothing happened. The darkness was still unbroken. The pot chinked more loudly, then she heard it fall to the ground. There was a tearing sound. Con imagined a head in the meat bag. She became aware of a second set of footsteps off to the left. An image came to her, one of the nightstalkers approaching the Hypsilophodon from different directions. A terrible insight came to her. *The food bag isn't all they're after.*

How can I shoot them in the dark? Con had mere seconds to answer her question. Suddenly, she knew. She felt along the barrel for the control switches and moved one until the yellow lights indicated the power was at maximum level. Next, she adjusted the firing spread to its widest setting. To her fear-sensitized ears, the dark was alive with noises—the crunch of feet in snow, the tearing of cloth, and the click of teeth. Con pointed at the sounds and fired. A loud "crack" resounded. Con moved the gun to the left and fired again. She pointed to the right and fired once more.

Joe called out in the dark, "What's happening?"

Rick's groping hand touched her shoulder. "You're shaking," he said.

"They were here," said Con.

"Did you get them?" asked Joe.

"I don't know. The flashlight's dead. I had to fire in the dark."

Rick and Joe hushed and strained their ears for any indication of the nightstalkers. The dark was absolutely silent. Con looked down at the gun. Its indicator lights were dark. She pressed the gun's switch to make sure she hadn't turned it off unaware. She hadn't. The gun had expended the last of its charge. "Better grab the spears," she said in a shaken voice. "The gun's useless now."

Huddled together for warmth, they sat in the tent and waited for the light. Both flashlights were dead, and only dawn could reveal what had happened. Rick held his unsheathed knife while Con and Joe gripped spears that were next to useless in the confined tent.

"You got 'em, Con," said Joe, "I know you did."

"But I used up the gun," said Con in despair.

"You did the most sensible thing," said Rick. "Joe or I would have done the same."

"Yeah," said Joe, "if we were smart enough."

"With those bastards gone, we won't need the gun," added Joe.

Con was cheered until light returned and revealed the story of the night's events. Outside the tent were three large ellipses where the gun's blasts had scoured the ground of snow. Beyond the ellipses, the snow was tinted by pulverized debris. The snow behind the central ellipse was pink. That bloody stain was the only remains of the nightstalker vaporized by the gun's discharge. The tripod was gone also, as was the food and even the pot. Con began to weep uncontrollably.

Rick held Con in an effort to comfort her. "Everything Joe and I said was true," he said. "We would have done the same thing."

"I've ruined everything," sobbed Con.

Joe also wrapped his arms around Con. "Con . . . Con . . . Con . . ." he murmured. "We'll be all right. Don't blame yourself."

"Why not?" she said bitterly.

"We still have each other," said Joe softly. "You're what really matters."

Con looked into the eyes of the two men, and saw Joe was telling to truth. She mattered more to them than the food. Con realized her grief distressed them, so she bottled it up. Through an effort of will, she stopped crying and forced a wan smile upon her face. "I'll be okay," she said.

Rick left Con and Joe to investigate the scene more

closely. Blood drops on the snow soon caught his eye.
They lay on the outer margin of the left ellipse. Rick
scrutinized the blood drops and the tracks associated with
them. He wandered away from the campsite twice before
he read their entire story and returned to tell it Joe and
Con.

"One of them was wounded," said Rick. "But it got
away."

32

AS RICK PREPARED TO RESUME THE MARCH TO THE SEA,
he knew all their hopes rode on the slim chance that people
had returned to the island. Yet, even that desperate gamble
required them to reach the shore with enough strength to
make a signal. His mind focused on strategies for achieving
that goal.

The arithmetic of calories had been dismally simplified.
There was no food. Their only nourishment was the previous
evening's meal. *Thank goodness we ate well*, he thought.
That was the only plus in his calculations. His thoughts
dwelled on reducing the minuses. *We must conserve our energy!* With that objective in mind, he forbade Joe to track
the wounded nightstalker. It was a decision Joe challenged,
but he conceded in the end. "You're the guide," was all he
said. Rick also drastically reduced the loads they were to
carry. Everything that wasn't absolutely essential was abandoned—the flashlights, the cooking and eating utensils, the
conifer bough bedding, and their summer clothes. The cooking pot was already gone. The hardest thing to leave was the
bulk of the firewood, but the loss of the travoises made it
necessary. That they burned with the bedding to warm themselves before they started out.

As they stood before the blaze, Joe picked up the gun and threw it in. Rick attempted to pull it out. "When sunlight returns, the gun will recharge," he said.

"So?" replied Joe. "By then, our fates will have been sealed, one way or another."

Joe's right, Rick thought, *the gun's only deadweight now*.

Rick stepped back and watched the gun burn. The three stared into the flames, lost in their private thoughts. When the fire died down, Rick went over to the remaining travois, grabbed its poles, and started off. Without a word, Con and Joe followed.

FOR A TIME, the nightstalker was governed only by fright and pain. She hid in a gully and licked the stump that had been her left hand until the blood flow was stanched. Then, in the stoicism of wild things, she turned her attention away from her injury and back to the needs of survival. She must eat to live. That fundamental imperative overwhelmed her fright and her pain. The animal left the gully and warily returned to the place of the big things.

When she arrived, the big things were gone. A wide expanse of cold whiteness was stained pink and held the aroma of food. Frantic with hunger, she licked the pinkness that promised nourishment, yet yielded none. Her tongue went numb with cold before she stopped. Eventually, she left the pinkness and approached the spot where the big things had slept. She sniffed it. There was the scent of food there also. It was not the burnt flesh smell, but, rather, an old familiar one—the blood smell of mammals. The nightstalker had sensed it for the first time yesterday. About the sleeping place, the aroma was strong and tantalizing. It also hung about the trail the big things made when they had departed.

Logic was alien to the nightstalker's brain. It made no reasoned arguments. The big things looked strange and smelled strange, but they had the blood smell of food. Hence, they were prey.

The creature knew instinctively that it must follow the

trail. The empty expanse of cold whiteness held no other opportunities. The prey was large, and it carried the terrible black stick, but the nightstalker was desperate. At the end of the trail were warm meat and a chance to live.

THE WORLD WAS eerily quiet. As Rick, Con, and Joe silently trudged through the falling snow, the only sound was their muffled footsteps.

As Rick walked, he considered the many unknowns in his calculations—the weather, the distance to the sea, the wounded nightstalker, and, foremost, the human spirit. He had read tales of hardship where seemingly healthy persons surrendered and died while others, suffering more grievously, endured. That intangible, the will to live, had made the difference. Their wills would soon be put to the test. There was no way to tell how each would fare in the hard times ahead. Rick wondered, *When I'm starving and freezing, will I give up?* He looked at Con and hoped, for her sake, he would not.

Rick turned toward Joe and was reassured by what he saw. Joe was the picture of fortitude and purpose. Wearing the Tyrannosaur hide poncho over his jacket and carrying his spear, he looked fierce and savage. His expression matched his dress. Vengeance smoldered in his eyes.

"It's out there," he said grimly. "I know it's coming."

"Better that it wear itself out tracking us than the other way around," said Rick, repeating his earlier argument.

Joe did not reply. Instead, he paused and stared back into the distance, looking for his enemy. The falling snow drew a gray curtain over the landscape. He saw nothing. Joe turned and caught up with Rick and Con.

Throughout the day, Joe and Rick took turns pulling the travois. It was laden with kindling and firewood, all covered by the tent. Con carried the remaining supplies in a bag rigged as a pack. It was a light load, and she realized it. *They gave it to me because I'm the weakest one.* That idea chagrined her, yet she knew it was true. All her life, she had been strong and energetic, an athlete proud of her toughness. Yet her spendthrift metabolism had turned upon her, wasting her strength. Though her body was diminished, her spirit remained strong. She knew their journey through fire, flood, darkness, and cold was drawing to a climax. She was resolved to see it through to the end.

Growing hunger and exhaustion silenced the three. Talking required too much effort. Their dreary, monotonous march was no longer interrupted by meals, but Rick insisted they rest frequently. He was concerned that they might push themselves beyond the point of recovery. Accordingly, he called a halt for the day as soon as the slate gray sky began to grow darker.

They set about the routine of making camp. Con set up the tent and swept the snow from its interior with her sock-covered hands. There was no bedding to lay upon the frozen ground, so she maneuvered the travois platform inside the tent and covered it with the few items of clothing they were not wearing. With that task accomplished, she grabbed her spear and her soiled rags and headed for the river. Joe and Rick had already left camp to search the riverbank for driftwood.

THE NIGHTSTALKER HAD smelled the nearness of the big things long before a pause in the snowfall made them visible. She was about to retreat when she noticed the herd had broken up. Instinct told her this was an opportunity. The smallest of the big things, the one fragrant with blood, was alone by the river. The terrible black stick was nowhere to be seen. She looked for the other big things and saw they were far away. The desperate need of hunger overcame her remaining wariness.

Ingrained skill, inherited from thousands of generations of successful hunters, guided the animal. Surely and stealthily, she approached the prey. The closer she came, the more its aroma excited her. Soon . . . soon . . . soon she would eat.

CON SAW A flicker of movement from the corner of her eye. She grabbed her spear and whirled in that direction. Her forgotten rags drifted away. The nightstalker froze. It was only twelve feet from her. Con stared into its large yellow-brown eyes and tried to read its intentions. They were inscrutable, but the sickle-shaped toe claws rose.

The spear seemed to puzzle the carnivore. Con feigned lunges, hoping to scare it off. The nightstalker held its ground while its head tracked the spearpoint with rapid, precise movements, the way a bird might. *It's quick,* thought Con. *It's looking for an opening.* With a few quick steps, the creature advanced to just beyond the spear's reach. Con pulled her spear back and assumed a defensive posture.

"Rick! Joe!" she cried. "Help! The nightstalker! It's here!"

Con heard the sound of distant running feet, but she dared not take her eyes from her foe. Only a slight tensing in its haunches foretold its spring. With dazzling speed, the nightstalker launched itself into the air. Con swung her spear to meet it and felt the spear's point rack along her attacker's rib cage. The point lodged momentarily between ribs as the nightstalker's weight and the momentum of its leap pushed the spear downward. A foot slashed out so fast that Con did not see it, and a claw tore her jacket sleeve, spilling down into the wintry air.

The nightstalker hit the ground with the spear still in its ribs. Con tried to push the spear home, but the creature leapt back. As it did so, Con felt the tip of the spearhead snap.

"I've got a sting!" she yelled at her enemy.

The nightstalker stared back, ignoring its latest wound. It seemed to study the spear. Then it began to move like a prizefighter, dancing and feinting. Con jerked the spear one way then another, trying to keep pace with the nightstalker's movements. It advanced and retreated, waiting for her to make a mistake.

Joe appeared running along the top of the riverbank. Intent on Con's spear, the nightstalker turned too late. Joe's spear entered its feathered abdomen, then pushed the nightstalker down into the mud. Joe bellowed in triumph over his writhing enemy. Putting all his weight on the spear shaft, Joe drove the point through the nightstalker's body and deep into the mud.

Like an undead monster, the impaled nightstalker pushed its body up the spear's shaft. Before Joe could jump back, it struck like a snake and buried its teeth into his forearm. Joe cried out in surprise and pain. Con stabbed at the creature with her broken spearhead, ruining a yellow-brown eye. Still, the creature held on as it thrashed about in its death throes.

Rick came running. He dropped his spear and pulled out his knife to saw at the creature's throat. Blood sprayed them all before the nightstalker went limp. Rick pried open the dead animal's jaws and released Joe's arm from their vise-like grip.

For a moment, Joe stood shaken and dazed; then, a grin crept over his face. The grin broadened and a gleam entered his eyes. "Damn!" he said. "That was one tough bastard. But I got it. I sure as hell got it!"

Con looked at Joe's bloody jacket, unable to tell what blood was his and what was the nightstalker's. "We'd better look at that bite," she said.

"It's only a scratch," replied Joe.

"We should still clean it," said Rick.

"With what?" asked Joe. "River water?"

"It's the best we have," said Con.

Joe dragged the nightstalker back to camp while Rick retrieved the driftwood he had dropped, and Con found the wood Joe had left behind. Only when Rick got the fire going did Joe remove his jacket. On both sides of his upper right forearm were a series of punctures surrounded by a darkening bruise. Some of the punctures were deep, and the serrations on the rear of the nightstalker's teeth had made the wounds' edges ragged. The deeper ones still bled. Using a wetted rag torn from the cleanest shirt she could find, Con washed the blood away. She felt the loss of the pot most keenly now, for there was nothing to boil the water in. After the wound was cleaned, she bandaged it with the remains of the shirt.

Con tended Joe with concerned tenderness and occasionally her face quivered with repressed sobs.

Joe put on his jacket, regarding its bloodstains as military decorations. He did not permit his wound to cloud his jubilation. His mood was infectious. Soon Rick and Con felt encouraged and relieved. The pile of driftwood made a respectable blaze and its light and warmth cheered them further. Soon they would be cooking dinner on it. The promise of warm food danced in the flames.

"Con," said Joe, "you did great! You killed that bastard as much as I did."

Con grinned, feeling that she had partly redeemed herself from last night's disaster.

Rick began to butcher the nightstalker. They would use every part they could. He plucked the down and saved the skin. He had read that it was possible to boil water in a skin bag and thought they could try to do so in order to clean Joe's wound better. He threw away most of the viscera, even the liver since, in some carnivores it could be poisonous. He kept only the heart. That he would cook specially for Joe. He sliced all the meat into strips and laid it on the snow to freeze. Since there were no large stones from which to construct a cache, he planned to put the food in the tent. If necessary, they would defend it with their lives.

While Rick finished the butchering, Con set about boiling water. She dragged some glowing embers from the fire and circled them with rocks. Then she took a section of nightstalker hide to the river and, gripping it to form a pouch, brought water in it. When she placed the hide over the embers, the water transferred the heat from the skin, preventing it from burning. Eventually, the water boiled. Though Joe protested it was unnecessary, Con cleaned his wound again with the boiled water. Pinkish brown and flecked with wood ash, it did not look as clean as the river water. Joe patiently let her minister to him once again and thanked her when she was done.

They roasted strips of nightstalker on the coals and boiled broth in the skin. Drinking the broth without spoons or a pot to pass proved awkward. After some experimentation, they settled on crouching like a dog drinking from its dish. As Rick sipped the broth, he keenly regretted leaving the utensils behind. He feared that the others felt the same way, but neither Joe nor Con said anything. It was an evening for looking to the future, not regretting the past. The sea could not be that far away. Most likely, only a few days of travel remained.

Joe held aloft the stick that skewered his foe's roasted heart. "To the last of the nightstalkers!" he said. He bit into the warm meat with relish.

"To friends," said Rick, sipping from the water bottle.

"And future friends," added Con, "may we meet them soon."

They lingered around the fire until it dwindled to ruby embers gleaming against the velvet night. Now that they had food again, some of the urgency they had felt throughout the day's march had lifted. Before they retired to the tent, Rick gathered the meat to bring inside with them. It was already frozen.

RICK AWOKE AFTER a poor night's sleep. Without the conifer bough bedding to insulate the ground, it was too cold to sleep in a prone position. They had slept back-to-back in a tight circle upon the travois platform, with their knees drawn close to their chests, sharing the two meager blankets. It was an uncomfortable way to sleep, and, despite his fatigue, Rick had kept waking throughout the night. Joe looked like he had not slept at all.

"How's your arm?" asked Con, who also looked more tired than usual.

"It's fine," he said. "Just a little stiff."

"We should look at it," said Rick.

"Don't bother," replied Joe. "I *said* it was fine."

Rick was too tired to argue. Instead, he brushed the snow off the cold campfire, piled the last few pieces of driftwood on the charcoal, and made a fire. He roasted some meat for breakfast and some more for lunch while Con boiled up some broth. As they ate, Rick noticed Joe used only his left hand and held his right arm stiff and straight.

"I'll pull the travois today," said Rick. "You should give that arm a rest."

"I'm fine," snapped Joe. "I can pull my weight."

"Then bend your arm," said Rick.

Joe started to bend his arm, then winced. "All right," he said with resignation. "You take the travois today, and I'll take it tomorrow."

"I should tend your arm again," said Con.

"Why bother?" replied Joe. "You've washed it and bandaged it. There's nothing more you can do, and it's tender right now. I'd rather you didn't touch it."

Con gave Joe a dubious look. "Are you sure?"

"I'm certain."

Con and Rick made Joe stay by the dying fire while they packed up camp. When everything was ready, they headed out. With food in their bellies and little or nothing to carry, they set a good pace initially, despite their fatigue. The sea beckoned them with the hope of rescue. They left the upland plain and entered the burnt remains of the forest. Ruined tree trunks spread to the horizon, standing like black obelisks in the snow. Trees littered the ground also. Fortunately, the fire had pruned them to crumbling, charred cylinders. Rick was able to drag the travois, which was loaded with little more than kindling, a few sticks of firewood, the frozen meat, and the tent, over the fallen trees without assistance.

Still, the obstacles slowed them down. The sleepless night also began to take its toll. Their pace slackened to a slow trudge. The line of march stretched out, with Rick at the lead, Con in the middle, and Joe at the rear. They walked mechanically as their minds hazed over with fatigue.

The landscape they passed through continued to change. They encountered mounds of flood debris, caked with frozen mud. The clearest path was close to the river, which flowed broader here, but sluggishly. The flood was long over, and the world was drying out and freezing. The snowfall was sporadic and light. The few streams they encountered were shallow and had mostly frozen over.

Toward late morning, they came to a river bend and saw what they thought was a huge stack of driftwood. When they approached more closely, they realized the pile consisted of corpses weathered to bare bones. Thousands of animals had been washed up on the riverbank. Under other circumstances, Rick would have spent happy hours examining the skeletons. Instead, he looked at them with tired indifference. The only thing that caught his attention was a lone, thin nightstalker. It hopped feebly about the bones, scavenging for the last scraps of frozen flesh. The scrawny creature looked like a pale brown wraith and, like a ghost, it was indifferent to the living. Rick, Con, and Joe marched by without the scavenger's notice. They had become invisible again.

If Joe saw the nightstalker, he gave no sign of it. He walked silently, his face a dull mask to hide his pain. Though Joe tersely rebuffed Rick and Con's expressions of concern, they grew more and more worried about him as the morning passed. At lunch, Joe barely ate. Afterward, his slow pace slackened to a shamble. After a few, painfully slow miles, Rick halted. Snow had begun to fall more heavily, and Joe was so far behind he was only a shadowy gray shape. Rick cursed himself for his lack of attention. Con caught up with Rick and slumped down on a log, her face drawn. Together they waited for Joe.

He approached with an unsteady shuffle. Each step seemed to require painful effort. His face was flushed. Despite the cold, he was perspiring.

"We're making camp now," said Rick.

"No, no," said Joe in a weak voice. "It's too early. I'm . . . I'm fine."

Con took off her sock mitten and felt Joe's brow. "You're burning with fever!" She looked into his eyes and saw pain and growing confusion.

"I'm . . . I'm sorry," said Joe in a slow, tiny voice. "I let you down." His eyes welled with tears of frustration as snowflakes melted on his hot, sad face.

33

"SEPSIS," RICK SAID TO CON IN A HUSHED VOICE, AS THEY
looked for a site to pitch the tent. Joe sat on a burnt log
nearby, staring blankly at the snow.

"What?"

"Blood poisoning," said Rick. "Who knows what germs
that thing had in its mouth."

"What can we do?"

"Keep him comfortable and let his body fight the infection.
That's about all."

"Will he be all right?"

"I don't know," said Rick. When he saw Con's reaction,
he quickly added, "Joe's tough. If anyone can beat this, he
can."

Rick spotted the black hulk of a huge toppled tree in the
distance and suggested that they erect the tent there. "We can
build our campfire by the tree trunk and use it to reflect heat
into the tent opening. It will serve as a windbreak, too."

As Rick dragged the travois to the tree, Con led Joe to the
site. He no longer pretended that he was not ill, but passively
let her support him as he shuffled through the snow. His mind
was succumbing to the fever, and he scarcely knew what was
happening. Rick and Con quickly erected the tent and made
it as comfortable as possible, though they had little to work
with. The travois's small platform of woven sticks was covered with the hide poncho to serve as a bed. Con cradled
Joe's head on her lap and patted the perspiration from his
brow with her sleeve. Rick used the remaining wood to build
a fire just a few feet from the tent opening. Only the kindling
was left.

"I've got to find some driftwood," he said, handing Joe's

spear to Con before grabbing his own. "I'll be back as soon
as possible."

"Okay," said Con distantly.

Rick did not reflect on the irony of looking for driftwood
in the middle of a forest. The only unburnt fuel was wood
that had been in the river before the fire struck. Every dirt-
caked branch he found on the riverbank was a rare find. He
walked half a mile before he accumulated a small armload.
He returned, added wood to the blaze, then cradled Joe while
Con went to the river and tended to her needs.

After Con left, Rick gently shook Joe until he opened his
eyes. "Joe, I need to ask you something."

"What?" asked Joe faintly.

"Is there something about the island I should know? Something you haven't told me?"

"The island?"

"Why didn't you want to go there?"

"Don't," whispered Joe.

"Don't what?"

"Don't let Con . . ." Joe furrowed his brow in puzzlement
and confusion.

"What about Con?"

Joe stared at Rick without comprehension. "You're not
Con." After a minute, he closed his eyes and returned to a
fitful sleep.

Con returned with washed rags and a few sticks of driftwood. "There's not much wood out there," she said. "How
are we going to keep him warm?"

"Look for driftwood farther downriver and hope we get
lucky," replied Rick. "I was stupid to leave the bedding. He
would have been much warmer with it."

"That bedding filled an entire travois!" said Con. "I'll tell
you the same thing you told me—stop blaming yourself. You
made the best decision for the situation. You didn't know
Joe would get hurt."

"I'm the guide," said Rick.

"That doesn't make you omniscient," retorted Con. "So,
are you going to look for more wood, or am I?"

"I'll go."

Rick hurried to gather as much driftwood as he could before it grew dark. While he searched, he racked his brain trying to think of ways to improve the bedding. The stark reality was that the fire had consumed everything that was soft and insulating. *It'll take a miracle for me to find something*, he thought. On his third trip for wood, he walked several miles downriver and barely found the campsite in the gloom. No miracle had occurred—they would sleep on the small, lumpy platform.

"Joe woke up while you were gone," said Con in a hurt voice. "He thought we were on the island."

"What did you tell him?"

"That I was taking care of him, but . . . but . . ." Con burst into tears and finished her sentence haltingly. ". . . he said . . . he said I was a rich bitch . . . and didn't know anything."

Rick entered the tent and gently embraced Con. She convulsed with sobs as she tenderly cradled Joe's feverish head. "You know he didn't mean it," Rick said softly. "He's delirious, and you're exhausted." He held her for a long time while she cried herself out. When she calmed, he asked, "Are you hungry?"

A ghost of a smile came to her face. "That's a silly question."

Rick was too tired to make broth and simply cooked the frozen meat on the coals. They ate, then tried to sleep. The night was mercifully calm, and the tree trunk radiated the tiny fire's warmth into the tent. Joe was unable to sleep sitting up, so Con and Rick lay on either side to keep him warm. The lumpy travois platform kept their torsos off the frozen ground, but not their legs. Despite the cold and discomfort, they fell into an exhausted sleep.

They were awakened by Joe, who suddenly sat bolt upright. He turned around to face the glowing embers and the darkness surrounding them, accidentally kicking Rick in the process. Joe was oblivious that he had done so. His attention was fixed on some unseen vision.

Joe laughed loudly, and his sweat-bathed face broke out into a grin. "Well, well, well, if it isn't Peter!"

Con shook Joe's shoulder and called his name.

He turned briefly in her direction. "Shh! Mr. Green has something to say."

Joe listened to the darkness. "You didn't want me to come," he answered. His grin grew broader.

"Now why would I want to do that?"

Joe heard the night's reply. "No . . . No," he said. "You see, I know where that probe goes. I always knew. Sam told me."

The grin left Joe's face, and it hardened. "It's too late."

After a few moments of silence, he grew angry. "You can't scare me!" he shouted. "You can't hurt anyone now! You're in Hell!"

The anger left Joe's face and was replaced by a look of consternation. "No . . . No!"

"You," he said in a small voice. Frantically, he turned toward Con and tried to shield her from his vision. "Don't look!" he cried in anguish.

Con could feel Joe's hot, moist hand tremble as it covered her eyes. After what seemed like a minute, he sighed deeply, and his hand left her face. Joe's vision had departed. He gently folded his good arm around Con and pressed her head to his burning cheek. "I wish you hadn't seen that," he whispered.

"Seen what?"

"You were never supposed to know." Joe began to cry with deep wrenching sobs that jerked his body like blows. His words came out like gasps. "I'm . . . sorry . . . Con. I'm . . . so . . . sorry." The animation drained from Joe's face as he was overwhelmed by exhaustion. He stopped crying. Rick and Con gently lowered him down to rest. As he fell asleep, he murmured over and over again, "I'm sorry. I'm so sorry."

Con lay down quickly and feigned sleep to avoid discussing Joe's hallucination with Rick. She felt she had to sort things out herself. Con pondered what had just occurred, trying to decide if it was a meaningless delusion or the revelation of a terrible secret.

Am I lying next to the man who caused my father's death? she wondered. It seemed possible, even probable. *It would explain a lot.* Yet the explanations led to deeper confusion. She had grown to love Joe. *If my suspicions are true, what does he deserve? My hate? My forgiveness? My pity? My love?* Sometimes, she felt he deserved them all.

And Daddy? What about him? She could remember him promising Sara to return. *Did he make me the same promise?* Con couldn't remember. She was unsure if it even mattered, her father kept so few promises. *What does Daddy deserve?* She didn't know. She felt empty. Her emptiness made her feel guilty.

The night dragged on as the turmoil in Con's mind fought with her body's exhaustion. Sometimes she slept, and the turmoil invaded her dreams. She saw the shade of her father standing outside the tent. "Don't call me Daddy," it said. "Call me sir." In another dream, Joe stood in the dark, holding a cake covered with peaches. "I'm sorry," he said. "I'm so sorry." When a dream woke her, the wearing round of questions renewed until, tired and answerless, she fell to dreaming again.

Other things also conspired to keep Con from resting. The fire would die down, and the cold would wake her. Rick would feed the fire, and that would wake her also. Joe cried out in pain whenever something touched his wounded arm. Twice, he shivered so violently that he woke her. When light returned, Con felt she had scarcely slept.

Rick woke with the light and used the last of the driftwood to build the fire up. He set up the skin to make broth. Once again, it would be necessary to stretch their rations. The nightstalker had been starving and had yielded little meat. He looked at Con as she stared bleary-eyed from the tent. Dark circles surrounded her eyes. He hoped their sunken appearance was an illusion caused by the circles, but her cheekbones seemed sharper also. She dully watched him cook without saying anything.

Joe still burned with fever, and his flesh, too, seemed to be melting away. Rick could tell they were not going anywhere that day. His best strategy would be to gather driftwood. He thought that he could rig something with the travois poles and strips of cloth to carry bigger loads of wood.

The warm broth seemed to perk Con up a little. She woke Joe and patiently fed him broth from the cupped palm of her hand. Joe was dazed and confused throughout his meal and went to sleep soon afterward.

"Sleep's the best thing for him," said Rick. "You look like you could use more, too."

"I kept thinking about what he said last night," said Con.

"He was out of his head," said Rick. "It was meaningless babble."

"He thought Green was here," said Con. "Daddy, too, I think."

"So?"

"Don't play dumb with me," said Con irritably. "Surely it's crossed your mind, too. Joe tricked Green and Daddy into that probe, knowing it wouldn't take them home."

"You don't know that."

"Well, he lied to somebody," replied Con. "Either to Green and Daddy or to you and me. He told us the probe wouldn't take us back."

"It's a side of Joe I don't want to think about," said Rick.

"But I have to," said Con. "It's eating me up."

"There are so many possibilities," said Rick. "Joe helped Green . . . Joe tricked Green . . . Green tricked Joe. It's pointless to think about it. All I know is that Joe helped us."

"It's not your father we're talking about," retorted Con.

"You're right," admitted Rick. "It's not." He pondered the situation for a minute before he spoke again. "I'm going to have to get more wood. I plan to make a quick trip to get enough to keep the fire going while I make a long one to really stock up. I'll be gone most of the day. Considering what you suspect, how do you feel about staying with him?"

"I'll manage," said Con.

Rick removed the two travois poles from the platform and tore strips of cloth from the scraps of a shirt to use in tying driftwood to the poles. When that was done, he bade Con good-bye and headed for the riverbank. The fire was almost completely out before he returned.

"How's Joe?" he asked.

"Still sleeping, but he doesn't look good. Even without taking off his jacket, I can tell his arm's all swollen. It smells bad, too, and he's still really hot."

"Maybe we should look at his arm," said Rick.

The "jacket" consisted of two shirts stuffed with night-stalker down. Joe's arm had swollen until it was jammed in

the sleeve like a sausage in a casing. The only way to remove
the jacket was to cut it off. Yet, Rick and Con knew, once
they had done that, they couldn't really treat the arm. They
had only water and rags to fight the infection. All they would
accomplish would be to deprive Joe of the jacket's warmth.
In the end, they decided to leave it alone.

The most effective thing they could do was to maintain a
fire to keep Joe warm. Con tended the fire and Joe, while
Rick searched for more wood. He had been gone for almost
an hour when Joe began to stir. Con lifted him partly upright
and held a water bottle to his hot, dry lips. Joe drank, then
slowly opened his eyes. "Con," he said in a hoarse voice.

"How do you feel?"

"Been better."

"Joe?"

"Yeah?"

"Do you remember last night?"

"It's all fuzzy."

"You said something about the probe Green and Daddy
left in."

A stricken look came to Joe's face. "I did?"

"Joe, you must tell me the truth. I need to know where
that probe went."

"No you don't."

"I know you're afraid to tell me. You think that . . . that
I'll hate you if you do."

A look of profound sadness crept over Joe's face, and he
turned his head to hide his tears.

"I won't hate you," said Con. "I just need to know."

"I'm sorry, Con," whispered Joe.

"Where did it go?"

"Nowhere."

"Nowhere?"

"Only data returns to the future. The probe self-destructs."

"Oh," said Con quietly.

Joe began to cry softly. "I'm sorry, Con," he said between
sobs. "I'm so sorry. Green would have never gone without
him. I tried to make it up to you. I'm sorry."

Con looked at Joe and knew she could never hate him.

She was still confused, but one thing was clear to her—she must soothe Joe's anguish.

"I forgive you."

His look of sorrow faded. "You do?" he asked like a hopeful child.

"He left me, Joe. He left by his own free will. But you stayed. You took care of me."

Joe's face grew peaceful. "Yeah," he said faintly. "I took care of you." He slowly sank down and slept.

RICK WALKED ALONG the riverbank, collecting driftwood as rapidly as he could. When he accumulated a small armload, he set it in a prominent place for pickup later, then headed off, carrying only the travois poles. By that means, he hoped to accumulate enough wood to make a large load. It was important to collect as much fuel as possible, for there was food for only one more meal. The only thing that stymied Rick's efficient plan was a scarcity of wood. He had already picked the riverbank clean for several miles from the camp. When he reached virgin territory, driftwood was still scarce.

Since he would carry a load only on the return trip, Rick's gathering technique allowed him to cover distance more quickly. Before too long, he was miles downstream and approaching a bluff that towered over the river. It was the highest landmark in the flat landscape. *If I climb it*, he thought, *maybe I can see where we are.* Rick left the poles by the river and began to ascend the bluff. He climbed despite his concern that the delay might cause him to get caught by the dark as he returned to camp. The risk seemed justified, for it was his first chance to study the trail ahead. Viewing conditions were ideal. No snow was falling and the dark gray of the sky had not yet begun to deepen.

Rick ascended the bluff and was rewarded for his effort beyond his wildest hopes. The river flowed through the snowy landscape until it crossed a dark, wavy line toward the horizon. The line had the appearance of debris left on a seashore at high tide. Even from this distance, it was

plain that the line was the high-water mark of the tsunami. Beyond the line lay the sea.

For the first time since Joe had become ill, hope returned to Rick's heart. The sea was no longer a distant
goal. He could see it. From where he stood, he could
make out the spire of Montana Isle near the horizon.
Upon it, he envisioned scientists like himself—people
with medicine for Joe, food for Con, and the means to
return them all home. Enough wood for a hundred signal
fires lay in the mounds deposited by the tsunami. It
seemed to him to be a sign that this harsh world was
relenting and loosening its grip on them.

With energy born from hope, Rick headed down the
bluff to collect his wood. Even when the poles bent under
the heavy load, his light heart sped him along. There was
still light when he returned to camp. As he approached
the campsite, Rick was puzzled to see that the fire had
gone out despite the fact that there was still wood. He
dropped his load and rushed to the tent. When he peered
in inside, Con was cradling Joe's head as she slowly
rocked back and forth. Joe appeared to be peacefully
sleeping.

"Con?"

She looked up at Rick. Tears had made pink trails on
her grimy face. Con blinked to clear her eyes. "Joe's
dead," she said.

34

THERE WAS NO DOUBT THAT JOE WAS DEAD. RICK HAD
felt his cooling wrist for a pulse and found none. His bearded
face had assumed the rigidity and stillness of sculpture. His
voice, so full of humor, was silent. Everything told Rick

that Joe was dead, yet Rick's mind could not form a vision of the world without him. For a while, Rick lived in two worlds: the familiar one, with Con and Joe, and the alien one, where Joe lay still in the tent.

Carefully and methodically, Rick built up the fire. He placed a bit of down, a handful of tinder, and a few sticks of kindling beneath some driftwood. He struck a spark with his knife and whetstone and blew softly until the down glowed orange, then burst into flame. When the fire spread to the driftwood, Rick thought, *That will make Joe more comfortable*. Then he remembered cold no longer bothered Joe, and his eyes filled with tears.

Rick heard a faraway voice. "It happened so fast," said Con. "He opened his eyes and looked right at me, but he didn't see me. He said, 'Nicole, Nicole, it's dark.' He felt about until he touched my face, then he smiled, and said 'Nicole' again. And I said 'Daddy.' And he said 'I love you, Nicole. I never wanted to leave you.' And I said, 'I know. I love you, too, Daddy.' You should have seen his face, Rick. He looked happy. He looked so happy that I said it again 'I love you, Daddy. I love you.'" Con began to sob. "He was so happy. You should have seen him. And then . . . and then his hand dropped from my cheek. At first I thought he was sleeping, but his eyes were open. Then I knew . . ." Con dissolved into tears and was unable to continue talking.

Rick entered the tent and wrapped his arms around Con. They wept for Joe together. Entwined in grief, they also clung to one another for reassurance. Rick and Con were the last two people in the world, and they had just been shown how fragile a vessel is a person's body. Joe's death made the prospect of unbearable loneliness frighteningly real. Each felt they would rather die themselves than have the other leave them.

For a while, they were paralyzed by their sorrow. Yet, as they embraced in the tent, the cold eventually forced them to mind the necessities for living. Rick added wood to the fire and recalled the wood he had left behind when he had run to the tent. That reminded him of the news that he had thought would bring so much joy.

"When I was getting driftwood, I climbed a bluff and spied the sea."

"The sea?" said Con.

"It's only a day's hike."

"He got so close," she said sadly.

"There's piles of stuff left by the tsunami. There must be tons of driftwood."

"For a signal fire?"

"Yeah," said Rick, "a huge one. They can't possibly miss it."

"If there's anyone to see it," said Con listlessly.

Rick looked at Con with concern. "You're not giving up? Joe would have never wanted you to do that."

"I'm just tired," said Con. "I'm tired all the time."

"I'm going to get the wood," said Rick. "It'll only take a minute. Get warm, and things will look better."

The sky had turned gloomy. Soon it would be utterly black. *How I miss the moon and the stars*, Rick thought, as he headed for his abandoned load. *Tonight will be long . . .* He envisioned trying to sleep as Joe's body slowly froze outside the tent. . . . *very long.*

When Rick returned, he found that Con had dressed Joe's body in the Tyrannosaur hide.

"Won't we need that for our bed tonight?" asked Rick.

"I made it for him!" said Con vehemently. "We won't be able to get it on him after he . . . after he . . ."

"You're right," said Rick quickly. "Oh course, you're right."

"He's coming with us Rick."

"What?" asked Rick, wondering if Con's mind had snapped.

"I thought it out," continued Con. "We can take him with us on the travois."

"Why?"

"The signal fire will be his funeral pyre, too. That way, no matter what happens, he'll leave this world with us."

"Con, that's . . ."

"Crazy? Is that what you're thinking? We can't bury him, the ground's frozen. And I'll never leave him for the night-stalkers to find. Never!"

Rick looked at Con, searching for signs of a shattered mind. The gleam in her eyes could be read either as resolution or madness.

"We can do this," said Con in a firm voice. "We owe it to him."

Seen in the cold arithmetic of calories, it was an absurd idea. A dispassionate person would have abandoned Joe's body. A more dispassionate one would have used it. Yet Rick had come to respect the importance of things that were not easily calculated. He saw that having a goal was vital to Con. Her wasting frame already seemed sustained more by her will than by their meager rations. He knew she would do her utmost to put Joe to rest. Taking him to the sea would help ensure that Con reached it also.

"We'll get him there," said Rick. "His fire will light up the world."

A look of relief came to Con's face. She hugged Rick. "I was worried you'd say 'no,' and I didn't think I could do it myself."

Rick looked at Con with respect. "You would've tried though, wouldn't you?"

"Of course."

Though it was a painful job to do so soon after Joe's death, Rick and Con bound the poles to his body so they could take him to the sea. They realized that by morning he would be frozen stiff, and the task might be impossible. They arranged his hands in a position of repose and placed his bloody spear within them. Con stood and addressed him. "Good night, Joe. We're taking you to the sea. I don't need to forgive you, because you did what you thought was right, and you always took care of me. I know Nicole loves you and would be proud of you. I love you, too."

"Amen," said Rick.

They left Joe in the tomb-dark night and returned to the fire. There were three strips of meat left, each no larger than a strip of bacon. Rick pleaded with Con to eat them all, but the most she would take was two. They ate their last meal slowly, trying to stretch it out. Throughout their pitiful dinner and long afterward, they talked about Joe. As they shared their stories, it seemed like they had known him for years, rather than weeks. Rick added wood to the fire, and they crawled into the tent and tried to sleep. Con lay on her side, curled up tightly. Rick lay behind her—his chest to her back, one arm thrown around her and his face in her hair. Never had Con seemed so precious to him. Or so fragile.

RICK WOKE WITH a sense of urgency. They were in the final stretch. The goal of all their hardship and sacrifice lay within reach, but just barely. That thought both excited and frightened him. *Tonight we'll find out if it was all in vain.* He realized that Con was approaching the limit of her endurance. So was he. To further lighten her load, they would leave the tent behind, wagering everything on being rescued. Speed would be of the essence, for in the relentless mathematics of survival, each minute in the cold cost calories.

Joe, stiff as a wooden statue and strapped to the poles, made a macabre travois. It was a manageable load, but just barely. Con, who, like Rick, wore one of the thin blankets as a cloak, carried everything else—down and kindling to start the signal fire, a spear and a water bottle.

When they reached the riverbank, Con asked. "How far do you think it is?"

"See that bluff near the river?"

Con gazed into the distance. Snow was falling again and the bluff looked faint and far away, a gray hump near the horizon. "I think so," she said.

"I saw the shore from the top of that bluff."

"So the sea's behind the bluff?"

"Well . . . no," said Rick, "but I could see it from there."

"Oh," said Con with disappointment.

Soon after they started out, it became clear that their progress would be slower than Rick had planned. He had underestimated the difficulty of dragging Joe's body. Despite having lost many pounds, Joe was a heavy and awkward burden. Rick's muscles had shrunken and the weight of the poles on his now bony shoulders chaffed and bruised them. When the pain became unbearable, he

had to halt and rest. As the journey wore on, the halts
became more and more frequent.

They reached the riverbank below the bluff after hard
hours of travel. The view from there was unchanged, offering no hint of the tsunami debris mounds that Rick
had spied from above. Instead, the bleak, burnt forest
spread out as before. The cold land looked empty of life,
a place where even the nightstalkers had departed.

With the bluff behind them, there was no visible goal
for them to reach. Their pace lagged and, after a while,
even Rick was beyond caring. In his exhaustion, it took
all his effort to keep moving. He set little goals for himself. First, they were to reach the next bend in the river.
Then, they were to reach a blackened tree trunk a few
dozen yards ahead. By the time it started to grow dark,
his goals had been reduced to taking the next step.

"We have to stop," said Rick. "I can't go on."

Con wordlessly dropped her pack. Despite her tiny
load, she looked every bit as exhausted as Rick felt. Rick
realized that his urgency to finish their journey had
clouded his judgment. He had pushed himself and Con
too hard and still failed to reach their goal. Now, they
were at the end of their strength and would spend the
night in the open. If his miscalculation was not to be
fatal, he would have to think more clearly.

"I'm going to look for driftwood," said Rick. "Will you
be all right?"

"I'll help you," replied Con in a tired voice.

They walked along the riverbank looking for wood. It
proved just as scarce as at the last camp. Though they
moved as quickly as their exhaustion allowed, racing the
gathering darkness, it was soon clear they wouldn't find
enough wood to burn all night.

"We'll have to dig a snow cave," said Rick.

"A snow cave? I thought we wanted to be warm."

"It's better than being out in the open. We'll snuggle
close to keep each other warm."

"From a log cabin to a snow cave," said Con. "You
sure know how to lower a woman's expectations! But I
like the snuggling part."

Rick smiled and felt encouraged that Con still had her sense of humor.

As they walked along the bank, Rick spotted a charred trunk of a large fallen tree. On one side, the snow had drifted to the height of the four-foot log. "There's a likely spot," he said.

"You'd better get Joe and our stuff, then," said Con. "It's really getting dark. If you tell me how to make the cave, I'll dig it."

"It's not hard," said Rick. "Dig a small entrance tunnel at the base of the drift and enlarge the interior cavity to fit the two of us. Just don't collapse the roof while you're digging it."

"The snow feels pretty firm," said Con. "I don't think that'll be a problem."

Rick dumped the wood near the drift and hurried off to retrieve Joe. By the time he returned, it was getting difficult to see. Rick started a small fire with some of the driftwood, setting aside the rest for the next morning. While Con warmed her frigid hands, he finished the snow cave. Afterward, they crouched over the tiny blaze until it was only embers, then retreated to the cave.

It was so dark by then, as Rick huddled with Con beneath the snow, he could not see her face inches from his. "Con," he whispered, "I love you. I loved you even back on the island."

"You're not saying that because you think we're not going to make it?"

"No," he said. "I just want you to know how I feel."

"I already know," whispered Con. "This sounds like a cliché, but I think we were destined for each other. I've the strangest feeling—like I've always known you. Rick, we're going to spend the rest of our lives together."

Rick softly kissed Con and prayed that the rest of their lives would be longer than one night.

A FAINT, GRAY light filtered through the snow. Rick woke, stiff and frigid. The first thing he did was to see

if Con was breathing. "Con, wake up. It's our last day."
Con opened her eyes.

"How do you feel?" he asked.

"Cold," Con replied groggily.

"I'm going to get the fire started," said Rick as he
pushed his way through the outer wall of the snow cave.
The morning air was colder than the inside of the cave,
but no snow fell from the dark sky. He brushed the
night's snow off the driftwood and grabbed some down
and tinder from Con's pack. By the time Con stretched
and hobbled over to Rick, flames were spreading from
the tinder.

"What a night," said Con. "My left foot tingled and
hurt after you went to sleep and kept me up. Do you know
you snore?"

"I do now."

"Well, my foot's fine this morning. It's not even cold."

Rick anxiously glanced at Con's sandaled foot. The
outer sock on it looked icy. "Can you wiggle your toes?"
he asked.

Con looked upset. "No."

Rick gently felt her foot. It felt hard and cold beneath
the frozen socks. "You have frostbite."

"What should I do?" asked Con in a frightened voice.
"Rub snow on it? Thaw it by the fire?"

"Just leave it alone. As long as it's frozen, you can
walk on it. When we're rescued, it can be treated. It'll
be fine."

"And if we're not rescued?" Con looked at Rick and
caught him wiping his eye. "Well . . ." she said in a very
quiet voice, "then it won't really matter."

They lingered by the fire, trying to get warm and to
steel themselves for their last day of travel. Finally, Con
said, "Let's go."

Rick walked over to Joe, who was covered with a thin
shroud of snow. He hefted up the two poles. As soon as
they touched his shoulders, he felt as if they had been
there for hours. The slow march to the sea had begun.

The air was clear of snow, and it wasn't long before
they spotted what looked like a series of low hills ahead.

"The mounds left by the tsunami!" cried Rick. Their spirits lifted, and their pace quickened. Still, it took hours to reach the mounds, for the trail was rough, and it challenged their limited stamina. When they finally approached them, they could see they were made of boulders, black mats of seaweed, entire trees, and other debris piled high by the giant wave. In many places, the undulating piles towered several stories high.

The flood had cleared a pathway through the debris, and Rick and Con stayed close to the riverbank. A harsh, cold wind arose and blew at their backs as if to inflict one last measure of suffering before they ended their journey.

Finally, they reached the outermost mound. The wave had uprooted miles of forest and deposited a bounty of wood. Some of it was burnt, but much was intact. Rick and Con looked at it in awe, trying to envision what force could do such a thing. Some of the boulders were the size of automobiles. Immense trees were shattered into splinters, while others seemed delicately plucked like flowers and left to wither with all their leaves intact. Jumbled among the remains of the forests were those of the sea. The bones of a mosasaur ornamented a pine. A broken ammonite shell, over six feet in diameter, lay like a discarded beach toy.

When they rounded the mound, the sea lay before them less than a mile away. The sloping landscape leading to the shore had been reshaped by the tsunami and left barren and rippled. Only a few mounds of debris, smaller than the ones they had just passed, broke its emptiness. One was a huge pile that consisted mostly of unburnt wood. Rick pointed it out to Con.

"That could be our signal fire," he said.

"And Joe's funeral pyre," said Con, her eyes filling with tears. "What a light it'll make."

They dragged Joe's body to the mound and Rick laid down his burden. Joe had aided him one last time—he had helped get Con to the sea.

"I want a closer look at the island," said Con

"So do I," said Rick.

The persistent wind had swept the ground of snow. At first, it was easy walking. Then, they encountered sandy patches that were as tiring to cross as snow. Farther on, the sandy patches grew into undulating dunes. Each seemed taller than the preceding one, and each was more exhausting to climb. Finally, they ascended a twenty-foot-high dune and had an unobstructed view. The shore was only forty yards away. Gentle waves broke on the dark sand, their foam resembling lace on velvet. Beyond the surf lay the sea. It was a dull pewter under a dark slate sky. Close to the horizon, the black spire of Montana Isle bridged the two.

They strained their eyes for some sign that the island was occupied, but detected none.

"Do you think anyone's there?" asked Con.

"It's too far away to tell," replied Rick. "We'll find out tonight when we light our signal fire. In the darkness, no one could possibly miss it."

The wind momentarily shifted, and the cold air turned heavy with the stench of putrescence. The foulness made Con nauseous, yet Rick's curiosity drove him to approach the shoreline and investigate. The darkness in the sand was the stain left by a soup of decay. The waves were oily with it. Before him was stark evidence that acid rain, darkness, and rot had done their worst to the shallow sea. It was dead.

35

CON AND RICK SLOWLY TRUDGED BACK TO THE DEBRIS pile, knowing it would be their last journey. The wind was in their faces on the return trip, and, though it was stingingly cold, it cleared the stench of the sea from their noses. As they walked, the calmness of resignation came over them both. They had done everything they could. Once they lit the signal fire, their fates were beyond their control.

They reached the mound where they had left Joe and took shelter behind it from the wind. Rick pulled wood from the pile and stacked it a few feet from a large tree trunk at the mound's base to make a fire. He lit it and soon had a huge blaze going. He and Con sat on the ground, leaned against the tree trunk, and warmed themselves. Rick put his arm around Con's shoulder as they watched the flames.

"I'm going to need help getting Joe on top of this mound," he said. "But rest as long as you want. There's no hurry."

"I'll rest better once it's done," said Con. "I need to do this soon, while I still can."

Rick looked at Con, so pale and thin, and feared she was already preparing for death. "Tonight we'll really light up this place," he said. "They'll come running."

Con simply nodded.

After they had rested a bit and were warm, they looked for a means to get Joe atop the mound of wood. On one side, a tree trunk formed a ramp leading to the top of the fifteen-foot-high pile. It was the only reason they succeeded in raising Joe to the top. When they finished, Con collapsed from the effort and lay staring blankly at the fire. Rick warmed some water in a seashell and held it to her lips. She drank, smiled wanly, then went to sleep.

Rick had heard of something called the "white death" that afflicted soldiers on Napoleon's Russian campaign. Malnourished men quietly fell asleep and froze. For a dreadful time, Rick thought the same was happening to Con. It grieved him to see her lying there, yet he could not bring himself to wake her. Instead, he fed the fire to keep her warm. He also prepared Joe's pyre so, when the time came, the fire would spread quickly. As he worked, he prayed that when the pyre lit the night, there would be only one body atop it. When he had done this last thing and fed the fire one more time, Rick lay next to Con and fell into an exhausted sleep.

It was dark when Con woke him a kiss. The fire was burning brightly, and Rick was warm. He stared about groggily.

"It's time to say good-bye to Joe," said Con.

Rick still felt exhausted. "How long has it been dark?"

"Not long. I see you got everything ready. Thanks."

Rick rose and, after stretching his stiff muscles, took a flaming brand from the bonfire. "This tribute was your idea," he said. "You should light the pyre."

"We should do it together."

Each holding the brand, they advanced to the kindling and wood Rick had placed at the base of the mound on the windward side. Flames danced and spread, fanned by the wind. They rose ever higher into the black sky and illuminated the landscape with reds and oranges. The fire grew so hot, it drove Con and Rick back. They sat on the ground, which now seemed pleasantly cool, and watched the spectacle of light. Somewhere within it, Joe was ascending to the sky.

Rick felt an anxious excitement as he scanned the night sky where he thought the island lay. Any moment he hoped to see the lights of a plane.

Con did not share his optimism. "It's as if my cabin's burning," she said sadly.

"Your cabin?"

"The cabin I dreamed of while I was alone. The place where I was going to make you and Joe honey cakes. I guess I don't need it anymore."

"You won't need it because we're going to be rescued."

Con nodded, but otherwise seemed lost in her own thoughts. "Will you make me a promise?" she asked.

"Anything."

"Will you make me a pyre, too? It doesn't have to be as big as Joe's, just something bright and warm."

"Con, we don't need to talk about that . . ."

"Yes we do." Con lifted her jacket to reveal a rib cage where every bone was sharply defined. Beneath it, her abdomen formed a deep cavity. "I don't want to leave you, but I'm souped." She smiled ruefully. "My parents wanted me to have every advantage."

Time passed, and the sky above the sea remained dark. Rick's hopes faded. As the future lost its promise, the present became paramount. It seemed to him that, as Con's body dwindled, her spirit was more apparent. *It wants to break free,* he thought, *and leave her body behind.* He craved for that spirit to linger as long as possible. Rick held Con in his arms and tried to savor each heartbeat.

Intent on one another, Rick and Con did not see the pinpoint of light that rose from the sea. Blue-white, it mingled with the swirling red sparks ascending into the black sky, but unlike the sparks, it moved purposefully and grew ever brighter. Even when the light became an airplane, Rick and Con remained unaware of it. The plane descended and disappeared behind the pyre.

The two figures that approached from the beach were still far away when Rick spotted them. They appeared to be children. Their clothing shimmered, reflecting the flames. He squeezed his eyes shut to clear them of tears, then stared to make sure they weren't an illusion.

"Con!" he cried joyously. "We're saved!"

Con rose to her feet, her expression one of disbelief and wonder. Rick rose with her. He wrapped one arm around Con and waved the other, calling out. "Over here! We're over here!"

One of the figures reacted to Rick's shouts by pointing an object in his direction. The end of it briefly glowed blue. Con gave a startled cry, jerked violently, and fell to the ground. Rick turned to call her name, but a jolt of pain froze the word in his mouth, as the world dissolved into blackness.

36

RICK BECAME AWARE THAT HIS EYES WERE OPEN. HE HAD no idea how long they had been that way. When he blinked, they felt dry and scratchy. He tried to move and found that he could not. For a terrified instant, he thought he was paralyzed. Then he realized this could not be the case, for he

was still aware of every sensation in his body. There was a
presence in his mind that blocked his efforts to control that
body. What it was, he had no idea, but he thought he knew
its source. *That thing that glowed blue did this to me.*

Rick stared into a flat surface that shone softly. It looked
vaguely familiar. He was laying on something flat and soft,
yet gritty. The air was warm. He was naked.

There was the noise of people entering the room. He heard
voices. The sounds they made were utterly alien. He had
never heard a language, if it was a language, that remotely
resembled it. It seemed to be a string of vowels that were
sung as tones, interrupted by lip noises that vaguely sounded
like the letter "B." The effect was that of a recording played
too fast and backward.

A childlike face appeared over his. She had a metallic-
colored dot in the middle of her forehead. Rick wished he
could say something, even make some small movement to
communicate, but he lay powerless. *My eyes are playing
tricks, or that child's gigantic*, he thought. The face disappeared, and hands touched his body. The touch was not like
that of a physician. There was rough indifference in the way
he was prodded and examined. It was as if he were a corpse
or a specimen, something that could not feel pain or indig-
nity.

The hands left him, but the voices were still nearby. Rick
found that, through an act of intense concentration, he could
regain some control over his body. Slowly, he turned his
head in the direction of the voices. He was lying on a sandy
bed. Next to him lay Con, emaciated and naked. What
seemed to be three huge children, two boys and the girl, were
standing near her. The boys had the same metallic dot on
their heads as the girl. Their clothing was of a strange pattern,
with surfaces that were sculpted into elaborate organic designs. It was made from a material that shimmered and
changed shade as they moved.

The girl bent over Con and began to examine her in a
manner that outraged Rick. Somehow, he had to make her
stop. He concentrated on forming a word. Before he could,
one of the boys saw that Rick was staring at them and

pointed an object in his direction. Rick felt a jolt of pain and became unconscious.

FOR DAYS, CON existed in a netherworld, only dimly aware of the passage of time. Things were being done to her, but she did not know what. Something was fogging her mind, and whenever it began to clear, a jolt of pain sent her plummeting into darkness. At last, she was left alone and gradually became aware of her surroundings. The vague, confused memories of her ordeal made little sense and, once again, she wondered if she were dead. If that were true, then she was spending the afterlife in one of the stone rooms on the island.

The room was not as she remembered it. There was a thick layer of sand and beach debris on the floor. The bed she lay upon was also sandy. The most radical change in the room appeared between the stone pillars in the colonnade. An immaterial, translucent plane bridged all the openings. It had the opalescent look of an oil slick on a puddle. Like an oil slick, its colors swirled and changed. Beyond the colored plane, the world outside was only faintly visible.

Con examined her nude body and saw it had also changed. It was no longer bony. The washboard pattern of her ribs was obscured by soft skin. Her breasts were no longer shriveled. The muscles on her legs and arms had returned to their former sizes. Her frostbitten foot appeared normal. As she examined her restored body, she discovered a recent needle mark near a vein of her inner elbow. Strangely, none of her other ailments had been healed. Her sores and rashes remained. She was still dirty. Some of her clothing was laid next to her on the bed. It was dirty also, but had an acrid smell, as if it had been fumigated. She dressed, although the clothes felt greasy and scratchy next to her skin, and their fumes stung her eyes.

"Rick!" she called out in an uneasy voice. The eerie opalescent plane seemed to absorb her words. Con approached it. The colors reacted to her presence, the hues becoming more vibrant the closer she came. As she reached out to touch them, her fingers began to tingle. When they were a few inches away, the tingling turned to pain. Con jerked her hand back, and the pain slowly disappeared.

She became truly frightened. Someone had tended to her, but only minimally. *This scarcely seems like a rescue!* she thought. Rather, she sensed that she had been kept alive for some purpose other than her own benefit. Looking for evidence of her keepers, Con spied footprints on the sandy floor. Most led to the empty former storage room. Little of the plaster on the far wall remained, and the doorway it covered was now revealed. It was sealed by a featureless silvery panel. The trail of footprints ended there. Con dreaded what might happen when the panel opened.

"Calm down," she told herself. "First things, first. I've got to take care of myself."

Con checked out the bathroom, which was also choked with sand. Despite this, it still responded to her commands. Con craved a hot bath, and immediately began to scoop the sand from the tub. Someone had already cleared out the toilet.

The hot water helped ease Con's apprehension, but only slightly. The tub was gritty. There was no soap or shampoo, and neither were there towels, yet after what she had been through, a bath of any sort was the height of luxury. After Con had cleaned herself as best she could, she washed her filthy clothes. It took several water changes and much hand scrubbing before she had a marginally clean tee shirt along with a pair of panties and trousers. The socks were beyond saving, and the shoe and sandal were unnecessary. Con decided to remove the nightstalker down from her jacket before attempting to clean it.

Con was wringing out her clothes when she heard voices in the room. It sounded like people rapidly singing a tuneless song while popping their lips. Con quickly began to dress in her wet clothes. She had her panties and her tee shirt on when two people entered the bathroom.

One of them pointed something at Con. The other spoke in perfect English. "Understand there is a weapon pointed at you. If you move suddenly, it will stop your mind."

Con slowly raised her hands. "I understand."

"You will come into the outer room and sit down on the bed."

Con obeyed. There was a third person waiting in the room. He held the charred remains of the gun. Con looked at him and the two other persons. Her first impression was that they were prepubescent children enlarged to the size of six-and-a-half-foot-tall adults. They had the bodies of young gymnasts and perfectly symmetrical faces. Their dark hair and eyes and their olive complexions, accentuated by the metallic dot on their foreheads, gave them an East Indian look. In their imposing presence, Con felt like a toddler among the "big kids" at elementary school. Despite their youthful appearance, these people carried themselves with the gravity of adults. Their large, stern faces were devoid of childhood innocence.

"Who are you?" asked Con. "Where's Rick?"

"Are you referring to the male?" asked the person who looked like a gigantic fourth-grade girl.

"Yes, is he all right?"

"We will ask the questions," stated the boyish man with the weapon. "You will answer them."

"Please," begged Con. "I have to know about Rick."

"We will inform you about his status when we are satisfied by your responses," said the woman. "Truth is essential. Do you understand?"

"Yes," said Con meekly.

"Where did you get this?" asked one of the men, holding out the remains of the gun.

"It was on the plane."

"Where did you get the plane?"

"It was here on the island."

"Who constructed this facility?"

"It was already here when we arrived," said Con. "I thought you built it."

Her three interrogators began conversing among themselves in their strange, rapid language. *I don't think they expected that answer,* Con thought. She decided their question, and the reaction her response provoked, proved Joe's assertion that history had been changed. *Yet, if that's the case, why are they here?* The rapid conversation ceased, and the second man produced what appeared to be a small rock from the folds of his clothing. He spoke to it and a gray, rectangular plane materialized in the air a few feet in front of Con.

"This is data from an unknown probe," said the woman. "Identify what you see."

An image appeared in the rectangle. It was so clear, Con felt she was peering through a window. On the other side of the window were her father and Peter Green. Green was moaning and covering his eyes. They were inside the cabin of the probe. Beyond the probe's clear walls there appeared to be fog or smoke, brightly illuminated by the glow of flame.

"Daddy!" she cried out.

Con's father turned and seemed to look straight at her. His face was red and blistered, except for two hand-shaped areas around his eyes. "Pete!" shouted her father. "The time machine! It's starting to work!" Green replied, "Thank . . ." The screen went blank. The man spoke, and it disappeared. Then the man put the rock away.

"Who were those two individuals?" asked the woman.

Con covered her face with her hands and began to weep. "That's my father, my father." When she looked up, one of the men had the weapon pointed at her. "What happened to him?" she asked between sobs.

"No questions," barked the man with the weapon.

"He was destroyed with the probe," said the woman. The woman's reply sparked an angry discussion among the interrogators. Con continued to weep as they argued.

"Cease crying," said the man with the weapon, when the argument ended. "If you persist in being uselessly emotional, I will fire."

Con stifled her sobs and told them about Peter Green and how he had acquired the time machine. Each statement she made elicited a rapid barrage of additional questions. The interrogation continued for over an hour, and though Con answered every question directly and truthfully, her interrogators became increasingly impatient and irritated. The men, in particular, seemed very annoyed.

The woman said something in their language, and the questioning stopped. "It is tiring to deal with an inaccessible mind," she stated. The three moved to go. The man with the weapon raised it in Con's direction, but a rapid remark from the woman caused him to lower it. All three of them headed for the silvery panel, which opened as they approached.

"You said you'd tell me about Rick" called Con, as they departed. They did not answer her. The panel sealed itself as soon as they were gone.

Con was shaken and confused. The three individuals had told her nothing directly, except that her father and Green were dead, and she had already known that. Con was left to surmise what she could from her observations and from the nature of the questions she had been asked. Her first conjecture was that the people were from the future and their strange appearance was normal for their kind. They certainly were not children. Their somewhat androgynous bodies seemed strong and fully developed, though the woman's shape only hinted at feminine curves.

Con found their manner extremely upsetting. It went beyond condescension or even contempt. *They acted like I wasn't human,* she decided. The men took no more effort to conceal their repugnance toward her than would a person before an animal. The woman was only marginally better. Her curiosity seemed stronger than her aversion. Only the woman had looked Con in the eye.

The more Con thought about her interrogators, the more distraught she became. She was very worried about Rick. *Is he alive? Why wouldn't they tell me that?* A sickening thought came to her. *Maybe they've disposed of him!* "Disposed" seemed the appropriate word. Con felt they treated her like a stray animal, to be locked up in an empty shed. *How else could they have left me here, naked and dirty? Perhaps,* she reasoned, *they thought I wouldn't mind.* It seemed hard to believe that people had grown so insensitive. *Maybe I'm being punished for stealing the time machine.*

The time machine was clearly their major concern. Most of their questions were either about it or its associated technology. They primarily wanted to know about the time travelers' contacts with others. It seemed to Con like they were trying to track the path of a contagion. It was also clear from the interrogation that these people had been unaware of the observatory's existence. Apparently, only the data from the probe tipped them off that it existed. Con guessed that the rock-like object contained the information that had been sent to the future. *Did it reach our time to sit around for centuries, perhaps millennia?* It was the least of the mysteries that bedeviled her.

Con was too agitated to sit still. She had her former body back and, with it, her restless energy. While she appreciated her renewed vigor, she suspected the motives of the strangers who had restored it. *I'm not rescued*, she thought as she paced across the sand-covered floor, *I'm captured. Captured and caged.*

In need of something constructive to do, Con grabbed the jacket and began to brush the sand off the bed. Once the bed was clear, she decided to tackle the floor. She scooped a handful of sand and threw it at the shimmering barrier between the columns. The sand passed through the barrier as if it weren't there. "At least I can clean my pen," said Con. "I don't have to live like an animal, even if I'm treated like one."

Con had cleared sand from only a small portion of the floor when the silvery panel opened. The woman entered, carrying the weapon in one hand and a large grayish pink cube in the other. Con rose slowly and raised her hands above her head. The woman advanced into the room and placed the cube on the corner of the bed. All the while, she kept the weapon trained on Con.

"You may lower your hands and feed yourself," the woman said.

"You don't need to point that at me," said Con. "I'm not a savage."

The woman did not lower the weapon. "A savage, I presume, is something that is dangerous?"

"You speak English so well, how can you not know what a savage is?"

"The data for your language came from this facility's verbal control system. It is incomplete and fails to define many of your words."

Con, encouraged that the woman had answered a question, pressed her for more information. "You said you would tell me about Rick."

"When we are satisfied with your responses."

"I've answered all your questions. Why won't you tell me anything?"

"We are doing what is necessary."

"Can't you tell me if he's all right? At least do that."

"What is the reason for your persistence in this matter?" asked the woman. "Are you mating?"

Con was insulted. "How is that your concern?"

"I study *Homo sapiens*."

"*Homo sapiens?* Why not say 'people'?" retorted Con.

"As a paleontologist, I prefer precise terms."

"Then you should say you're an 'anthropologist.' That's the correct word."

"No," said the woman evenly, "I used the proper term. I study extinct species. We are *Homo perfectus*."

The woman's matter-of-fact comment belittled Con more than any insult. Con grasped the gulf between them as the word "subhuman," with all its implications, sprang to her mind. Con's assertiveness transformed to unease and, for a moment, she was speechless. When she spoke again, it was in a less confident tone. "Please tell me about Rick."

"You still have not explained the reason for your interest."

"It's because . . ."

"Because what?"

"Because we're in love."

"That is another term for which I have no definition."

"It's an emotion," said Con. "I guess you could say it has something to do . . . to do with mating."

The woman looked intrigued, but said, "After more satisfactory sessions, we may allow you contact with him."

"Then he's alive?"

"Yes," said the woman. "I will tell you that."

"Thank you," said Con joyfully. "Thank you!"

The woman watched Con's reaction with apparent interest, but she did not respond to it. Instead, she pointed to the cube lying on the bed. "There is sufficient nutrition for your accelerated physiology." After saying that, she left the room. Although she did not turn her back on Con, she no longer pointed the weapon at her. Con thought, *I guess that's progress.*

As soon as the woman departed, Con bubbled over with excitement. "Rick's alive!" she shouted. "He's alive!" She happily danced about the sandy room, then whirled until she dropped dizzily on the bed. She felt hungry and pulled a corner off the cube the woman had left. It had a texture that was a cross between gelatin and cheese and tasted like unsweetened fruit punch. It was not unpleasant, and it was very filling. Con ate only a small portion of the cube before her hunger was satisfied.

She returned to cleaning the room, trying to expend some of her energy. As she worked, she pondered how she could hasten the time when she could see Rick. *The woman said I'd see Rick after "more satisfactory sessions."* The ambiguity of that phrase worried her. *Did she mean more sessions as satisfactory as the last one?* If that were the case, Con wondered how many more interrogations she must endure. *Or did she mean the last session was unsatisfactory?* That also seemed plausible. *They looked annoyed by the end of the questioning.* Con tried to think how she might have provoked them, but she had no idea. It disturbed her that she didn't know. It disturbed her even more how she had lost control of her life and how her happiness was dependent on satisfying her captors.

37

THE FAINT WORLD BEYOND THE SWIRLING COLORS DARK-
ened to black, indicating it was night. Con slept and awoke
to a routine of confinement that dragged on for days. Her
life became one of profound loneliness, marked by bouts of
anxiety and long stretches of depressed boredom. There was
nothing to do once she cleaned the room and took care of
the jacket. Meals consisted of eating from a grayish pink
cube that was wordlessly delivered each morning. Filling the
empty hours became a trial. She slept as much as possible.
She took long baths. She paced for hours, tracing complex
patterns through the three rooms that imprisoned her. What
made Con's situation particularly hard was her ignorance.
She worried about what was happening to Rick. She worried
about what would happen to her. The woman provided no
further information. She had ceased to come alone, and she
was coldly formal in the presence of her companions.

The days passed so slowly that Con came to look forward
to her daily interrogations, for, although they were demean-
ing, they at least broke the monotony. Also, each session held
the promise that she might learn something about Rick. In
that hope, she was always disappointed. She was not even
given an indication whether the sessions were satisfactory to
her captors. They ignored all her inquiries. Indeed, they became so irritated when she made them, Con soon thought it
was prudent to stop.

While Con's interrogators provided her no direct information, she was able to learn things about them through observation. During one of the early sessions, Con observed
that the metallic dots on her captors' foreheads were more

than adornments. They were apparently involved in transmitting information. One of the men arrived in the middle of the interrogation and both of the others touched their dots to his. Afterward, the man's questions reflected an awareness of all that had proceeded in his absence. *That's what the woman meant when she said I had an inaccessible mind*, thought Con. *No wonder they get impatient asking questions*. Once Con was aware of the dot's function, she noticed its use on other occasions. Several times, she witnessed her captors touching various devices to their dots. That led her to speculate they were capable of directly inputting data. Con recalled the woman's statement that her English came from the facility's verbal control system and envisioned her downloading it through her dot.

Each session caused Con to conjecture on other matters as well. She came to believe that her captors were also concerned with business that did not involve her, since they visited infrequently. After they used holographic images and maps to question her about the last location of the airplane and the time machine, she thought they were sent to retrieve them. Later, when they grilled her about the observatory, she decided they were investigating that also. The most puzzling interrogation also proved to be the last. It was concerned with Con's plans after the vacation and the repercussions of her father's demise. Most of their questions involved public records. Con found herself explaining about such things as wills and diplomas and also about the different forms of media coverage. It was the first time they showed any interest in twenty-first-century sôciety. As always, they did not explain why.

When Con awoke the following day, the food cube was already on her bed. She did not see her captors the entire day, nor did they appear the following one. As disconcerting as the interrogations had been, their cessation was even more so. She still knew nothing about what had happened to Rick. As the slow hours passed, her concern for him became an obsession.

"Only that colored thing keeps me from him," she said to herself. "Only a little pain." She approached the colonnade and saw the colors turn angrily intense. She halted a half a foot away. "I can do this." Her skin tingled unpleasantly as she gathered up her resolve. Thinking of Rick, she gritted her teeth and stepped forward.

The flash of pain was excruciating and overwhelming. Con screamed and fell writhing to the floor. Only a portion of her foot passed through the colored plane, but agony rapidly boiled throughout her body. The torment was exquisite and all-encompassing. It became her only reality as she moaned and shook spasmodically on the floor. Gradually, the pain subsided until she recovered the presence of mind to examine her foot. It hurt so intensely she expected to find only a charred stump. Despite the searing pain, it appeared unscathed. She crawled away from the colonnade and curled up into a ball, too drained to climb onto the bed. As the pain faded to a dull ache, someone entered the room.

"I do not understand your behavior," said the woman. She stood over Con, gazing at her with a puzzled expression. "You understand the nature of the barrier. Why did you attempt to cross it? It was not a rational act."

Con smiled ruefully. "No, I guess it wasn't."

"You have not answered my question."

"I wanted to see Rick."

"I said contact would come after satisfactory sessions."

"I answered all your questions, and then you stopped coming," protested Con.

"My colleagues have the information they require," the woman stated, "but I still need information for my own studies."

Con sighed. "What do you want to know?"

"It concerns the male."

"Rick?" said Con eagerly. "Will you let me see him?"

The woman ignored Con's question. "Was your irrational behavior associated with the condition you called 'love'?"

"Isn't that evident?" asked Con.

"No," stated the woman. "Tell me more about this condition."

"Don't you people have the same emotion?"

"I cannot discuss ourselves with you."

"Why not?"

"I cannot discuss that either. You must answer my question."

"But surely you know about love from our literature and art. Your museums must be full of information."

"There are discontinuities in the record," the woman stated.

"This is a basic human emotion!"

The woman looked annoyed. "Why do you persist in evading my question?"

Although the implications of the woman's statements disturbed Con, she knew it was unwise to ask more questions. Instead, she tried to frame a satisfactory reply. "Love is so central to our culture, I thought you'd know about it."

"You wanted to be with the male nineteen days ago," stated the woman. "Why are you still interested?"

"Why am I still interested?!" said Con, perplexed by the question. "I love him, that's why."

"I do not understand your response," said the woman. "You said earlier that love is an emotion involved with mating."

"I said it had something to do with it," replied Con, feeling flustered.

The woman started to lean forward as if she were going to touch her forehead to Con's, but then halted.

"You forget," said Con. "I have an inaccessible mind." The woman smiled slightly. It was the first time Con had ever seen that expression on her face. "Love is a complicated feeling," she continued, "and while it has something to do with mating, it involves much more. When two people are in love, they want to be together. They *need* to be together. It makes them feel complete and happy. Love can last a lifetime."

"So it is not periodic?" asked the woman.

"Periodic?"

"Is it not determined by your ovulation cycle?"

"Are you asking me if I go into heat?" said Con with disgust. "Only animals do that."

The woman's face colored, and Con immediately sensed she had said something wrong. "Then, I am to understand," said the woman, more coldly than before, "that you are continuously in a state of 'heat' as you call it?"

Con tried to sound calm. "We *Homo sapiens* don't think of mating in that way."

"Yet you said love is central to your culture."

"It is," replied Con, "but some of it's private, too. It's hard to explain."

"You must try," said the woman.

Why must I? thought Con. Then, she answered her own question. *So I can see Rick.* "We separate our lives into private and public parts. When people fall in love, they usually tell their friends. If they get married, it becomes part of the public record. How they express that love is often private. Mating is a private part." Con looked at the woman, trying to determine if she was satisfied with her explanation. She could see growing impatience in her interrogator's face.

The woman stepped away abruptly. "You may see the male, this 'Rick,' as you call him."

The woman said something in her language, and the barrier vanished from between the columns. Con peered at the dark world beyond without truly seeing it. All she could think about was Rick.

"I will show you the way," said the woman.

Con followed, barefoot in the snow, to the room that used to be her father's and Sara's. The multicolored plane between the columns vanished at the woman's command to reveal Rick seated on the bed, staring despondently at the floor. With a shriek of joy, Con ran to him. Rick rose to meet her and they embraced.

"Rick! Rick! Rick!" sobbed Con. "I missed you so much."

"I missed you, too," said Rick. He softly touched Con's face and rejoiced in her nearness. They kissed and, for a long while, they spoke only the silent language of love. When Con eventually glanced toward the woman, she discovered that the colored barrier was back between the columns. They were alone.

"You look great!" Rick said. "You're not starving."

"Only for you."

"I had no idea what had happened to you," said Rick.

"They wouldn't tell me anything. I was afraid you were dead."

"I feared the same for you," said Con. "It's been horrible. I'm so lonely without you. For the first time in my life, it feels strange to sleep alone."

"How have they treated you?" asked Rick.

"They've left me alone, except to ask all sorts of questions about the time machine and stuff. The two guys act like I disgust them, but sometimes the woman's not so bad. I think she's studying me."

"Yeah, Jane's the curious one."

"Jane?"

"I gave them names," said Rick. "The two guys are Hitler and Stalin and the woman's Jane, after Jane Goodall."

"Never heard of her."

"She was a twentieth-century scientist who studied chimpanzees."

Con smiled wryly. "That's appropriate, they treat me like one. Did you know they call themselves *Homo perfectus*?"

"Perfected Man," mused Rick. "That sounds about right."

"Perfected?" said Con disdainfully. "They look like big kids."

"And we probably look like pinheads to them. They look like kids because of neoteny."

"What?"

"It's the retarding of development so juvenile traits are retained in adulthood. It's why humans have large heads. It's why baby apes look more like humans than the adults. Our friends just took it one step further."

"And those dots?" said Con. "They can transmit information through them."

"I think they're implants. A computer with a neural interface. I've seen them downloading to one another."

"I have, too," said Con. "Jane complained that my 'inaccessible mind' tired them."

"Yeah," said Rick, "talking to us drives them nuts. We must sound like the world's slowest stutterers."

"I noticed," said Con. "So you think they have computers for brains?"

"More like a computer in their head that their brain can access," said Rick.

"It'd sure make school easy," said Con.

"Toddlers could get educated in seconds," said Rick. "It'd change the whole concept of intelligence."

"But how could that happen?"

"It had to be genetic engineering. A change like that wouldn't happen naturally. Natural selection stopped working on humans long ago."

"Creating a new species of people?" said Con. "That seems impossible."

"It's not that far-fetched," said Rick. "You're souped. Joe worked on neural interfaces. Eventually, someone took it to the next level."

"But why would people want to change?"

"I doubt most did," said Rick. "New species usually start out as small, isolated populations."

"But that means there would be two kinds of people in the world and . . ." Con paused in alarm. "Rick! Jane said *Homo sapiens* are extinct!"

Rick sighed. "That's the pattern for our genus. When was the last time you encountered a *Homo neanderthalensis* or a *Homo erectus?* They used to share the world with us."

"Jane talked about a discontinuity in the record, but I think it's more than that. She doesn't seem to understand us at all."

"People wouldn't have volunteered to become extinct."

"So you think they destroyed everything?" said Con, appalled by the very idea.

"When the Spanish encountered the Indian civilizations," said Rick, "they not only destroyed them, they burned all their books as well."

Con shivered. "What's going to happen to us?"

"I don't know," he said, "but I have one hopeful theory. They asked me a lot of questions about my plans after our trip. Did they do the same to you?"

"Yes. What do you think that means?"

"Joe said they've discovered that actions downwhen alter the future. That's why they banned time travel—they're afraid of changing their own present. I think they're in a touchy situation. They know what they do to us will affect them."

"How?"

"History will be different if we don't return to our own time," said Rick.

"So they have to take us back. Then why haven't they?"

"Because history will be different if we *do* return to our own time."

"Now you're not making sense."

"Their problem is figuring out which course of action their present is based on."

"I get it!" said Con. "That's why they asked all those questions about public records."

"I think Hitler and Stalin are off doing research, and Jane's minding the cages."

"And she let the animals out," said Con with bitter humor.

"Jane Goodall came to care for the chimps she studied," said Rick. "She became their advocate."

Con sighed. "I doubt this Jane will ever care for us."

38

CON AND RICK CUDDLED AND TALKED FOR A BLISSFUL hour before the barrier between the columns vanished. Jane was standing outside in the snow. She carried the weapon in her hand, but she did not aim it. Looking at Con, she said, "It is time for you to return to your room."

Con pointed to the weapon. "That's not necessary," she said. "I'll go."

Con gave Rick a parting kiss, then rose with a heavy heart. Attempting to play the model prisoner, she walked quickly back to her quarters. Once she passed between the stone columns, she turned to face Jane. "Thank you," she said. "It meant a lot to me to see him." Jane said something in her own language, and the barrier formed between them.

Con was left staring at the opalescent colors that separated her from Rick. Seeing Rick made his absence all the more painful. Her recent joy only deepened her current sorrow. She threw herself down on the bed and sobbed.

When she had cried herself out, she began to brood about the future. There seemed to be two possibilities. One was blissful—she and Rick would return to their own time to continue their lives together. The other was bleak. *They'll dispose of us.* When Con tried to decide which was most likely, her heart sank. *They must do what they've done before.* It was very confusing, but the worst part was that she couldn't imagine that these people had ever sent them back. *Still,* she reasoned, *there was one version of time where they built this observatory. Perhaps, there are infinite variations of the future.* That idea was little help. *Which variation am I in?* Her prospects did not look good. *I'm in the one where our captors are nicknamed Hitler and Stalin.*

Con told the room lights to dim and went to bed. Sleep did not come easily. She lay awake envisioning Hitler and Stalin entering the room with weapons drawn to put her down like a stray dog in a pound. When she eventually dozed off, her fears brought forth vivid nightmares.

Con awoke in a sweat, thinking she held Rick's bloody corpse. The dim light of day filtered through the swirling colors. A new food cube lay at the foot of the bed. The fact that Jane had simply left the cube seemed ominous to Con. The troubled night had fed her sense of dread, and, as the day wore on, Con became increasingly apprehensive. She began to see her visit with Rick as a sign that the end was near, the equivalent of a condemned prisoner's last meal. Jane's statement that her coworkers had "the information we require" took on sinister implications. *They're done with me,* Con realized. *Now it's all a matter of waiting.*

Yet passively submitting to her fate went against the core of Con's being. As she paced her prison in restless agitation, she formed a desperate plan. She resolved to breach the colored barrier. She reasoned that if she ran and jumped, her momentum would carry her through the field regardless of how her body responded to the pain. *I endured it once,* she told herself. *When I recover this time, I'll be on the other side, free to find a way to Rick.* Still, the memory of her previous agony held her back. It took another anxious and lonely hour before her desperation overcame her apprehension. Finally, as the light outside faded, Con screwed up her courage. After several false starts, she made a running leap and curled into a ball as her body passed through the livid colors.

Con transformed into a creature whose only sensation was unbearable agony. She felt that her skin had been ignited, her bones crushed, and her muscles and entrails torn and mangled. She fell convulsing upon the snow, without the breath to scream or even moan. Pain washed her mind clear of thought and pushed it toward madness. She became less than an animal—a mindless, frenzied thing writhing on the ground in her own befoulment.

Existing only in a crimson universe of pain, Con was unaware of Jane's approach. She did not feel Jane lift her like a child. Only when Jane pressed a device to the back of her neck and her torment diminished, did Con become dimly aware she was lying on her bed in the stone room. As a cooling sensation spread through her burning body, the world slowly came into focus. When Con saw the swirling colors between the colonnades, she burst into bitter tears.

Jane disappeared, then returned to find Con shaking on the bed as if in the grip of a fever. She lifted Con up and held a vessel to her trembling lips. "Drink this," she said.

Con sipped the sweet, aromatic liquid. Warmth filled her mouth and throat. The shaking slowed, then stopped, and the last of the throbbing pain faded.

"No one has ever passed through the barrier," said Jane. "How could you do such a thing?" There was pity in her voice, but also a hint of wonder.

"I had to see Rick again," said Con quietly.

Jane placed a translucent ovoid in Con's hand. "You will want this," she said. "It is similar to soap." Then she left the room.

The liquid Con drank had the effect of restoring her energy as well as eliminating the vestiges of pain. Con entered the

bathroom, washed her reeking clothes, then bathed herself.
The soap was a luxury she relished. Moreover, it seemed to
be a token of a change in Jane's attitude toward her. When
Con left the bath, she was surprised to see the black of night
between the columns. The barrier was gone.

Is it a malfunction? An oversight? A trap? Con suspected
it was none of those. *Perhaps it's a gift*, she thought. Whatever else it was, Con knew it was an opportunity. She gazed
into the night for only a moment before she quickly dressed
in her damp clothes, dimmed her room's lights, and stepped
into the darkness.

As soon as she crossed beyond the columns, it was bitterly
cold. The glow from her ceiling provided the only light, and
it was barely enough for her to find her way. When she
reached Rick's room, it was too dark to tell if the colors
barred her way. With trepidation, she stretched out her hand.
She encountered no tingling, no pain. She shuffled into the
warm, pitch-black room and heard the reassuring sound of
Rick's breathing. She inched her way until she encountered
the bed. Then, she quietly undressed and crawled next to
Rick.

"Con?" said Rick sleepily after her groping hands found
his face and she kissed him.

When his hands found her, Con felt a delicious excitement
as he became aware she was nude. She giggled, and said, "I
wish I could see your face." Then she began to undress him.

"Do you think this is safe?" asked Rick.

"I don't care if it's safe," replied Con. "This may be our
only chance. I want you, Rick. It's right. I know it's right."

Con's hands discovered that Rick wanted her, too. They
made love in an awkward frenzy. Embracing afterward in the
dark, their passion returned, and they made love again. This
time, they went slowly. Exploring each other with tenderness
and love, they forgot where they were and lived in the eternal
now. When they were spent, a serene drowsiness came over
them, and they slept entwined.

Con dreamed she stood before the immense pink cake,
poised with a knife to cut it. As always, she hesitated and
looked toward the door, hoping for her wish to come true.
This time the door opened. Joe stood there, smiling and

healed. Con ran past the cake, and Joe hugged her, saying, *"Constance, I have a gift for you. It's from your father."*

"What is it?"

"A message."

Con woke to the warmth of Rick's body next to hers. She wanted to make love again, but light was returning to the sky, and she felt exposed before the open colonnade without sheets or covers. With regret, she kissed Rick awake. "I'd better go," she said as she looked for her clothes. She dressed quickly, then hurried back to her room.

Jane entered only a few minutes later, bearing a food cube. Con was wondering whether she should thank her for removing the barrier when Jane asked a question. "What is a chimpanzee?"

"It's an ape," replied Con. "They used to live in . . . Where did you hear that word? Have you been listening to us?"

"Respond to my question."

"So that's why you let me loose—so you could play Peeping Tom!"

"I do not understand your term."

Con stared at Jane as her emotions wavered between humiliation and anger. "You watched us last night!"

"I am a scientist. I conducted research."

"Are we nothing but specimens to you?" Con rose angrily to leave. Jane made no move to stop Con as she strode into the snow. When Con was halfway to Rick's quarters, she turned and shouted, "I SAID IT WAS PRIVATE!"

Rick's smile at Con's approach transformed to concern when he saw her furious expression. "What's the matter?" he asked.

"Jane's been watching us like bugs in a jar," Con said. "She probably recorded us last night for some damned lecture—'The Mating Habits of *Homo sapiens.*'"

Rick put his arms around Con. "Don't let her spoil last night," he said.

"Nothing can spoil that," said Con. "I'm just mad and embarrassed at once. What's worse, I should have guessed what she was up to. I feel so stupid."

"You're supposed to do stupid things," said Rick. "You're in love."

"Be serious," said Con. "This really bothers me."

"I'm sorry. It bothers me, too."

"We could be dead soon," said Con. "This is our last chance to be together and . . . and . . ." She dissolved into tears.

Rick gently held her. "Don't give up hope," he said quietly.

"I have a feeling we're not going back. I think that's what my dream was about."

"What dream?"

"I dreamed Joe brought a message from my father."

"That you were going to die?"

"No, I woke up before I heard the message."

"It's nothing," said Rick, "just your subconscious imagining things."

"I can't get it out of my head," mused Con. "Joe called me 'Constance,' and he never did that."

"It was a *dream*," said Rick. "Dreams don't make sense."

"For some reason, I feel this one should."

Rick shrugged. "What should we do about Jane?"

"I don't know," said Con. "I feel weird, knowing she's watching us."

"Last night was wonderful," said Rick, "but just being with you is wonderful, too. We don't need to make love."

Con was turning to kiss Rick when she saw the silver panel open. Jane entered the room, carrying a food cube. She put it down on the bed, while avoiding Con's glare. She looked at Rick with an expression that betrayed a hint of guilt. "What is an ape?" she asked.

"An animal closely related to humans," said Rick. "They're extinct in the wild."

"I see," said Jane. "Who are Hitler and Stalin?"

"Famous leaders," said Con quickly.

"Renowned for their compassion, no doubt," said Jane.

Jane stood silently and looked as if she were gripped by indecision. When she spoke again, her voice was softer. "I am not supposed to say anything to you, but . . . you should understand . . . this was a unique opportunity."

"An opportunity?" said Con in a resentful tone.

"My field of study is held in low esteem. Our ancestry is

considered distasteful and irrelevant. Time travel is banned, including the use of probes. Only the emergency brought us here."

"So you came along as the specialist on *Homo sapiens*," said Rick.

"Yes," said Jane. "I was only supposed to conduct the interrogations. Yet, when Con crossed the barrier . . ."

Rick stared at Con in amazement. "You crossed the pain field?"

"No human could have done that," stated Jane. "I was intrigued."

"You just called me by my name, and you still don't think I'm human?" said Con.

"It's a scientific fact," said Jane. "I am merely objective."

"And when you look at me with revulsion," said Con, "is that being objective, too?"

"It is sometimes hard to ignore ingrained attitudes," said Jane. "Your bodies are so . . . so exaggerated." As she spoke, her eyes focused on Con's breasts.

"What attitudes are you speaking of?" asked Rick.

"Ancient ones," said Jane, "dating back to the Purification."

"The Purification?" said Con.

"I cannot discuss it," said Jane. "What I have already said and done will get me in enough trouble."

"So letting me loose was not authorized," said Con.

"No, but I wanted to understand why you crossed the barrier," said Jane. "Such a thing is considered impossible."

"Perhaps it shows what you lost pursuing perfection," said Con.

Jane looked at Con thoughtfully. "Perhaps."

"Would her deed make any difference to your colleagues?" asked Rick.

"It is unlikely. I am an uncommon person with uncommon attitudes. Few people believe the past is important."

"This observatory doesn't reflect a disinterest in the past," said Rick.

"We did not build it," said Jane. "It is an artifact from a future that no longer exists."

"And you're here to ensure that doesn't happen to the current future," said Rick.

"That is our task."

"So when you discovered the probe's data," said Rick, "you came to stop us from playing with your fate. We're the apes in the control room, so to speak."

"You are very perceptive," said Jane.

"All we did was go on a vacation," said Con. "We're not playing with anyone's fate."

"Everything that occurs in the past affects the future," said Jane. "We are in an extremely delicate situation."

"Let us go," pleaded Con. "We won't change anything."

"We must take whatever action that results in our current reality," said Jane. "That is what my colleagues are researching."

"If our fate is already sealed," said Con, "can't we be left alone while we await it?"

Jane said something in her own language before she spoke again in English. "If you desire privacy, you need only to command it. I have instructed the room to comply with your wishes. You will not be seen or heard."

"Thank you," said Con.

"You will be left in peace," said Jane. "At least until my colleagues return today." She started to go, but stopped. "Good-bye, Con. Good-bye, Rick." Then she quickly departed.

As soon as Jane left, Rick said, "Give us privacy" and the openings in the colonnade filled with a softly shimmering silvery-blue.

"She changed," said Con.

"Yeah," said Rick. "It gives me hope for humanity."

"Too bad she said she was uncommon," replied Con. "I don't hold much hope for Hitler or Stalin. We don't have much time left." When Rick didn't respond, she feared he agreed.

They made love, knowing it might be for the last time, and their passion was bittersweet. Afterward, Con found her thoughts turning melancholy. She thought of Joe and then of the dream. *"Constance, I have a gift . . ."* he said. *"A message."*

They dressed and made the silvery curtain vanish so they could gaze upon the world. The sky was still dark gray, but not as dark as they remembered. They stepped beyond the stone pillars to feel the cold breeze from the sea.

"The smell's gone," said Con.

"The world's already beginning to forget," said Rick. "And, somewhere, our ancestors are poking their heads out from their holes and thinking, 'Whew! No nightstalkers!' "

Rick got a gleam in his eye. "Let's go to the beach."

"I don't have any shoes!"

"I'll carry you." Rick swung Con up in his arms and ran toward the beach. She laughed and screamed the whole distance. Rick halted at the water's edge. "We had our first kiss here," he said.

"I'm getting cold."

"A kiss will warm you up."

"Only one? Some guide. I'm colder than that."

Rick laughed and was bending to kiss Con when she cried, "Look!"

Rick followed her gaze into the sky. The silver disk of the descending time machine stood out against the dark clouds. The laughter departed from Rick's face. He carried Con back to his stone room. Watching from the room, they saw Hitler and Stalin returning after the time machine had landed. As they marched through the snow, they were trailed by a large, intricately textured cube that levitated a few feet off the ground. They entered the room to the left and disappeared with the cube. A minute later, the multicolored barrier appeared between the columns of Rick and Con's room. Rick grasped Con's hand as they watched the silver panel and waited to hear their fate.

The panel opened, and Jane and Hitler entered the room. Both were carrying weapons. Hitler pointed his at Rick and Con.

Pale and shaken, Jane began to speak. "My colleagues have returned with the archive . . ."

Hitler silenced her with a burst of harsh-sounding tones. Then he addressed Con and Rick. "Tell me the exact date you departed in the time machine."

"February 17, 2059," said Rick.

Without a word, Hitler left the room, followed by Jane.

Con was trembling. "I thought that was it," she said, "and there's still something I need to remember."

"What?"

Con's expression became one of desperate concentration. "I don't know, but it's important."

Only a few minutes had passed when the panel opened again. Hitler returned with Jane. Jane's face betrayed the bad news. "Con," she said, "you need to come with us." She spoke some words and the colored barrier vanished. Hitler gestured with his weapon, indicating Con should step outside.

Con turned pale and gently kissed Rick. "Good-bye," she whispered. "I love you."

Con stepped into the snow, then, with a wild look in her eye, turned to Jane. "I'm Constance!" she shouted. "I'm Consta . . ." Her words were cut off as the barrier reappeared.

Rick stared at the swirling colors as his vision blurred with tears. *It's so ironic*, he thought, *that in her last moments, she wanted to be known by the name her father called her*. The idea of Con, so brave and strong, reverting back to her childhood name seemed especially sad. Rick stood, waiting to die any moment, yet the minutes mounted. "Come on!" he said angrily. "Get it over with!"

An hour passed before the silver panel opened and Hitler entered with Stalin. Their childlike faces bore hard, cold expressions. Hitler pointed his weapon at Rick. "Take off your shoes," he ordered. Rick silently complied. When he was barefoot, he was told to lie down on the bed.

Rick lay down and stared at the weapon pointed at him, determined not to betray his fear. *Soon I'll be with Con*, he thought. The weapon glowed blue and the world dissolved into darkness.

39

EVERYTHING WAS A SOFT AND UNBROKEN BLUE. CON'S
face appeared, then Rick felt her lips upon his. "It's about
time you woke up!" she said.

Rick found it hard to move, and he spoke with difficulty.
"Where . . . where am I?"

"You're in Montana," replied Con, "It's June 29, 1878."

Rick's head cleared, and he found he could sit up. There
was tall grass all around him. Con squatted next to him,
dressed in rags and grinning broadly. "I remembered just in
time," she said. "I'm Constance, the family legend."

"You do realize you're making no sense at all," replied
Rick. "Are you sure I'm not dead?"

Con got a mischievous grin and gave him a playfully in-
timate caress. "You don't feel dead to me."

"Con!"

"It's all right. We're married. Maybe not officially yet, but
we are. I'm Constance Clements."

Rick looked perplexed. "I don't understand. Would you
please calm down and tell me what's happened?"

"We're here because I figured it out. It was the last name
that threw me. I thought I was Con Greighton."

"So did I," said Rick. "Who's Constance Clements? Other
than yourself, of course."

"She's the Greighton family legend, Daddy's only bedtime
tale. He was so serious about it. It always began, 'Never
forget about Constance Clements.' My mother thought he
was loony to tell it over and over again. I never understood
what the big deal was—until now. It was my message to
myself!"

"You still haven't answered my question," said Rick. "Who is she?"

"The woman who founded the family fortune. She and her husband came out of nowhere and were found in the prairie by a wagon train. They struck gold soon afterward, three mines in all—The Second Chance, The Paradox, and The Full Circle. Talk about hints! Once I figured it out for myself, I was able to prove to Jane, Hitler, and Stalin that I was that woman. That meant they had to take us here if they didn't want to change their own present."

"How could you prove that?"

"I knew the dates. I knew the names of the mines. I had all kinds of proof, and it all fit. But, most important, it's true—*I'm the legendary Constance Clements!*"

"I can't believe this, it's too fantastic."

"Spoken by a man who just visited the Cretaceous and survived the K-T impact."

"So the current version of time depends on our traveling from the twenty-first century to live in the nineteenth?"

"Yep," said Con, "and that thing Jane called 'the archive' bore me out. Hitler and Stalin looked really put out."

"The whole thing's mind-boggling."

"Isn't it?" said Con with a grin. "When you think about it, this must have happened before. Otherwise . . ." Con looked confused.

"It's a paradox, an infinite loop," said Rick. "Don't even try to figure it out."

"Maybe it started in another version of reality," said Con. "One many times removed from our own."

"Maybe. What I'm curious about is how could you have known about this woman? We're talking over a century between you and her."

"Never underestimate a strong-willed woman with money. Our children will name their daughters Constance and they'll pass on the story."

"That you traveled through time?"

"Not that story," said Con. "The story about you and me being found and the mines and the family curse."

"Curse?"

"That if the oldest daughter isn't named Constance or

doesn't learn her story, the family will be ruined."

"Who'd buy that?"

"Daddy did. Rich people can be very traditional; all my girl cousins are named Constance. Besides, there are lawyers involved."

Rick grinned and shook his head in amazement. "Constance Clements was quite a woman."

"She sure was," agreed Con. "Now that I know she's me, I'm even more impressed."

"What about her husband?"

"The geologist? He helped discover the mines. Then he retired to collect fossils." Con kissed Rick. "They were very happy."

Rick looked dazed. "So what now?"

"We won't be found for three days."

"Three days!" said Rick, in alarm. "You'll be eating grass!"

"Jane left us a supply of cubes for our honeymoon."

Rick lay back in the grass to enjoy the warmth of the sunshine. Con cuddled next to him. "First we'll build a cabin, then we'll look for gold. Of course, we won't find much until after Joe is born."

"Joe?"

"He was my final proof that I'm Constance Clements, the one that clinched it. They tested me."

"What are you talking about?"

"Joseph Burns Clements, silly. Your son. I'm pregnant."

"Pregnant?" exclaimed Rick. He looked at Con with an awed, silly grin.

"Yeah. We'll discover The Second Chance two months after he's born. In a year we'll be rich!"

"Con! You're going to drive me nuts if you keep telling me my future. Save a few surprises."

Con giggled. "That's no problem. I'm probably the most surprising woman in history."

Epilogue

TOM CLEMENTS GAZED UPON THE CROWD AT THE SYM-
posium, smiling and nodding to whomever he knew. Many
of his colleagues were there, along with his students and
former students. There were also numerous new faces. One
of those belonged to a slender, blonde-haired woman who
stared at him in a puzzled way. Thinking perhaps he should
recognize her, Tom acknowledged her gaze with a nod. The
woman hesitantly approached him. As she advanced across
the room, Tom looked at her more closely. She had the sun-
darkened face of someone who had spent a lot of time in the
field. Her tanned skin set off her light blue eyes. She was
clutching a bound manuscript. *A new doctorate*, he surmised,
networking for a position. When she was a few feet away,
he glanced at her name tag. It read DR. C. BROWN.

Dr. Brown also glanced at Tom's name tag and her reaction was one of surprise. It took a moment before she regained her composure. When she did, she blurted out, "Are
you related to Richard Clements?"

A look of sorrow passed over Tom's features. "I had a
brother by that name."

"No, I mean Richard Clements, the ammonite collector."

"I'm afraid not."

"He's not famous, but he was a pioneer in the field. A
contemporary of Marsh and Cope."

"Nineteenth century?" said Tom. "I fear my history's
weak. Besides, I'm mostly interested in Late Cretaceous and
Early Tertiary mammals."

"Richard Clements was way ahead of his time," said Dr.
Brown, waxing enthusiastic. "His collection is extensive."

"I've never heard of it," said Tom.

"It's still in private hands, my aunt's actually. It was in-
valuable in my research."

Tom tried to hurry Dr. Brown's banter to the point by asking the question he assumed she was hoping for. "Is that your paper?"

Dr. Brown nodded and handed it to him. He read the title aloud. "The Cladogenesis of Ammonites in the Pierre Seaway."

"I'm presenting it tomorrow," said Dr. Brown proudly.

Tom smiled, remembering his first presentation. *Definitely a new doctorate*, he thought. "So you spotted my name tag and thought I was related to your Richard Clements."

"No and that's the strange thing," said Dr. Brown. "You look a lot like him."

"Look like him?"

"See for yourself." She opened her manuscript to a page with a photograph. It showed a man in antique clothing standing behind a fossil ammonite that almost reached his waist. Tom stared at the picture in amazement, for the man had his brother's face. The caption beneath the photograph read, "R. Clements and *Splendidodiscus tomatis*." Tom translated the Latin in a soft voice. "Tom's splendid disk."

"The resemblance is remarkable," said Dr. Brown. "Did I say something wrong? You look upset."

Tom wiped his eyes. "Where did you get that photograph?"

"It's a family heirloom," said Dr. Brown. "Paleontology runs in our family."

"We've got to talk," said Tom urgently.

"About what?"

"Richard Clements. I think I own the first ammonite he ever collected."

Dr. Brown looked at Tom quizzically. "You just told me you had never heard of him."

"Please don't think me forward, but could we have dinner? We could eat at my place. There are things there I need to show you."

"What kind of things?" asked Dr. Brown.

"I have a hypothesis about your Richard Clements, a crazy, fantastic, wonderful hypothesis. Together we may be able to prove it. Bring your paper and whatever other material you have on him tonight."

"I haven't agreed to come," said Dr. Brown.

"Please say yes," pleaded Tom. "This is really important to me. If my theory's right, you'll be amazed."

"Can't you explain it now?"

"It's too complicated and too fantastic even to consider without some hard evidence. You'll need to see it for yourself."

Dr. Brown looked at Tom and tried to take his measure. There was a disarming sincerity about him that made her feel she could trust him. Adventurous by nature she had to satisfy her curiosity. "All right," she said, "I'll come."

"Thank you, Dr. Brown. You won't regret it. I'll make my famous chili."

"Call me Constance," she said. A smile crept on to her face. "It's only fair to warn you, I'm infamous for my appetite."

LUCASFILM'S
ALIEN
CHRONICLES™

A New Saga . A New Universe . A New Destiny .

Here is an epic set in a far distant universe—a saga of faraway planets and of races strange and more fantastic than any ever seen on our world.

Yet their struggles are universal: for justice, for freedom, for peace. Lucasfilm's Alien Chronicles is a sweeping trilogy that will transport you to another time, and another place where a legend is about to be born.

An Unforgettable Trilogy

__Book I: The Golden One   0-441-00561-6

__Book II: The Crimson Claw   0-441-00565-9

__Book III: The Crystal Eye   0-441-00635-3

Available wherever books are sold
or to order call 1-800-788-6262